STOLEN LIVES

D.P. JOHNSON

PINE CONE BOOKS

For Alison, Samuel and Isabelle

READERS CLUB

D.P. Johnson's Readers Club members get free books and unique items to accompany the books.

Members are always the first to hear about new books and publications.

See the back of the book for details on how to sign up.

LENA

LENA DEMYAN TOOK a clumsy sip of bitter champagne. It stuck in her dry throat and she swallowed hard, wincing at the discomfort. Was she the only human on the planet who hated the taste?

She set down her glass on the gold cocktail table and pressed herself into the wall, feeling the faint tickle of the music in her fingertips. It was a waltz, but nobody was dancing. The wall felt smooth and cool and comforting; it was her friend right now. Farther along, there were thick velvet, floor-to-ceiling drapes. If only she could slip behind them. Would anyone notice?

Lena surveyed the room, which was bathed in a red party-light glow. A cluster of girls caught her eye. One of them – ostrich-feather boa wrapped around her neck – threw back her head and drained her drink; another collapsed into a fit of laughter. Three men in tuxedoes, huddled to their right, were whispering conspiratorially and casting occasional glances at them. A blonde woman dressed in a Vixen of Versailles outfit circulated with an oversized bottle of champagne, topping up glasses.

In the far corner, Benja was standing, all Man-in-Black, with his arms crossed, guarding the fire exit. He was the only one not wearing an eye mask. He caught her gaze and unfolded his arms so that he could make a *'go mingle'* gesture with his index finger. She nodded in resignation and took a deep breath.

Despite the eye mask, she felt ridiculously exposed and self-conscious. The hem of her black corset dress rested at mid-thigh, and she tugged forlornly at the fabric, trying to stretch it over her bare legs.

In front of her, one of the men had taken the outstretched hand of the boa girl and pulled her, giggling, into their huddle. She linked arms with him and another of his companions, while the third man took out his phone and moved into position to take a photograph. The two men and the girl shuffled into a pose, their backs facing Lena. The sudden flash of the camera startled her, and for a moment she saw purple circles. The girl roared with laughter as another three flashes fired, then the men released her and she returned to her friends.

Lena blinked away the effects of the camera flashes, then looked again over at Benja. *'Go on, move,'* his expression implored.

Fearful of toppling over in her absurd stilettoes, Lena took a tentative step away from the wall. Who to speak to? What to say? She was embarrassed that her English wasn't up to scratch. The desire to improve it had been one of the many reasons why she had left Ukraine behind and come to England. She took another hesitant step, seeking Benja's encouragement, but he was now talking into his phone. Her eyes darted about the room, trying to settle on a friendly face. Another step forward.

One of the three men turned to look in Lena's direction and smiled. He peeled himself from the huddle and moved over to her, carrying a glass in his upturned palm: whisky, she guessed. Her fragile confidence crumbling like feta, Lena stepped back to prop herself once more against the wall.

'Hey,' the man said, 'I don't think I've seen you before. You new?'

He was a large man with a deep voice. His chin wobbled as he spoke. His eyes were dark and unreadable in the shadow of his black plastic eye mask. He reeked of sweet aftershave and neat alcohol. She guessed he was in his fifties.

'Yes,' she said, in a nervous whisper.

'What's your name, sweetheart?'

Panic rippled through her; Benja said that under no circumstances should names be exchanged. She paused for a moment, then decided to lie: 'Bella.'

The man smiled. 'That's a beautiful name for a beautiful lady. I'm John.'

He moved his bulky frame closer to Lena, blocking her view of Benja. She prayed he was watching out for her. He was there to keep her safe, make sure everyone played by the rules; she trusted him.

The man who said his name was John drained the remainder of his drink and – without removing his gaze from Lena – set the glass down on the cocktail table. His stomach was now pressing against hers. For several moments, he didn't speak or move. His nose emitted a strange whistle as he breathed – Lena would have laughed had she not been so frightened. The party noises merged into a distant, indistinct hum.

With a suddenness which made her jump, he planted his fat hands on her hips and leant in towards her. Instinctively she turned her head away, and in the next moment felt the disgusting sensation of him nibbling and licking her

3

neck. She squirmed and wriggled; in response, he tightened his grip.

Lena didn't know what to do with her hands, and found herself helplessly clenching and unclenching them. Her eyes flicked over the man's shoulder, towards Benja, hoping he could see their pleading. Benja caught her gaze, but instead of marching over to enforce the rules, he merely brought two fingers to his face and pushed up the corners of his mouth. *Smile, Lena. Just smile and talk to the idiots. No touching allowed. Pretend you're interested in their boring stories. That's all you have to do, darling; easy money.*

He'd lied.

She'd been duped.

It was all her own stupid fault for believing him. *Stupid, stupid Lena.*

As the man continued to lick and nuzzle and bite, Lena felt tears welling. She bit her lip and stifled the urge to scream. *Think of the money,* she counselled herself. But she didn't think of the money; she thought of home; she thought of her sisters; she thought of the shitty little apartment in Donetsk they shared, with its clanking pipes and peeling wallpaper; she thought of the sound of grumpy old Mrs. Petrenko above them, banging her walking stick each time Lena played her hip-hop at full blast, her nostrils twitching at the scent of rotten-egg fumes belching from the coke factory on the other side of the city.

The man's arousal pressed into her. He released a hand from her hip, then his clammy fingers were sliding up her bare thigh and under her dress. A sickening foreboding washed over her. He fumbled around her knicker elastic for a couple of moments, then his fingers were crawling over her. She inhaled a deep lungful of horror.

'Wait!' she cried, her voice breaking.

The man withdrew his hand and faced Lena. 'What is

it? Are you shy? I can take you somewhere private if you wish?'

Lena needed out. She forced a smile and said: 'I just need toilet, okay? Then I come back.'

'Okay, sweetheart,' he said, taking a step back and gesturing in the direction of the loos. 'No rush. I'll be waiting for you.'

She turned and hobbled away from him, wiping a tear from her cheek.

Benja intercepted her, grabbing her forearm. He brought his mouth to her ear and she felt his hot breath as he said, in her mother tongue: 'What the hell's happening?'

She feigned her best smile. 'I just need to take a pee. Okay?'

Benja released his grip. 'You'd better not mess this up. He's chosen you especially. He pays top money. Got it?'

'Of course!'

'I'm watching you,' Benja said, his voice laced with such menace that it squeezed Lena's heart.

She stepped through a curtained doorway, into a brightly-lit corridor; it took her a few beats for her eyes to adjust. She needed a plan. She needed to escape. Her heart was fluttering out of control and she willed it to calm. *Think.*

The corridor was windowless and there were two doors. The first door was locked. The second yielded to her push, and she walked into the room.

She gasped in horror. *Dear God.*

In front of her was a bare-buttocked man, grunting like a pig and thrusting like a maniac. The object of his attention was perched on the washbasin with her legs clamped around his: the girl with the feather boa, which she was now using like some kind of erotic lasso.

The pair were oblivious to Lena's presence, while she

scanned the room and determined there was no means of escape. The only window was tiny and, in any case, barred. Her heart sank.

Her only hope was that the other washroom was configured differently. She headed back to the corridor to wait for it to become free. God only knew what was happening inside; she shuddered at the thought.

Come on. It wouldn't be long before Benja or the man came looking for her. She paced the corridor.

And then she saw the answer.

A plain, grey box, high on the wall: a fuse box. Could it be her salvation? She had to give it a try.

Lena paused, to commit the layout of the building to memory and plot a mental escape route. Then she reached up to the fuse box on tiptoes, pulled down the flap and flicked the main switch.

The building was plunged into darkness. The music stopped and, for a moment there was complete silence, save for the sound of blood roaring through her body. Then the shouting and hollering started.

'Is this a game?'

'There's been a power cut!'

Lena crouched low, held out her palms in front of her and headed through the dividing curtain, into the party room. There were rectangles of blue light darting about: mobile phones. Blurred shapes moved around her. Where was Benja? She continued stealthily towards the fire exit, which she could just about make out in the residual, pale light. Her heels made no sound as they dug into the deep-pile carpet.

Nearly there.

Something brushed her arm and she held her breath.

'Lena!' a voice hollered above the cacophony. 'Where are you, bitch?' Benja – he was behind her, some distance.

It was now or never.

She got to the exit, pushed the bar and opened the door, just enough for her to squeeze through the narrow slit. As the door shut behind her, it made the slightest click.

Outside, the cold came as a relief from the stuffy, cloying air inside. It was mid-summer, but the dead of night; the sky was clear and starry.

She gripped the banister and click-clacked a fast beat, up the concrete steps to ground level: the car park. There was Benja's black Range Rover – her jeans, sweater and sensible pumps were in its boot. How she wished she had them now. No time to dwell.

Run!

Lena stole a glance behind her, cast off her heels and ran for her life.

She emerged gasping from a dark alleyway, into the sodium-orange light of the deserted high street, where she paused against a lamp post to catch her breath and discarded the stupid mask. Her bare feet throbbed and stung from the pain of running over gritty surfaces.

Lena caught a glimpse of her grotesque reflection in a plate-glass window, and shame pulsed through her body. Mascara tears; pasty legs; crimson nails… *Disgusting hooker.*

There was a distant rumble behind, and it took several beats to realize it was the sound of a car engine. She leapt back into the alleyway, pressing herself into the wall, and waited for it to pass. Her heart knocked against her ribcage. When she saw that it was Benja's Range Rover, she brought a hand to her mouth then, quickly gathering her wits, turned on her heel and ran back down the alleyway.

Lena zigzagged her way through silent residential streets, searching for signs of life, for someone to help her. She had no phone, no money and no friends – nothing.

She considered for a moment rapping on random doors. But, who would answer? And how could she possibly explain her plight? No, she needed to find a police station or a hospital. Then she'd be safe.

Lena had left the town behind an age ago and was now on a country road, lined with thick hedges, occasional trees and intermittent streetlights. The smell of morning dew triggered an awful thirst.

What time was it? She guessed somewhere around four a.m.; it would soon be light. Too exhausted and aching to run, she'd long settled into a gait which was part walk, part hobble. The cold pressed down and she rubbed her arms for warmth.

A nearby sign read *'St. Albans, 3.'* She had never heard of the place before. She prayed that it was a big town – or, better, a city.

The sound of a car engine loomed behind her, and she snapped her head around, fearing that it might be Benja. What would he do to her if he caught her? But the head-lights were a different shape and set closer to the ground; it wasn't him.

She contemplated sticking out a thumb, but then she thought about all those movies with the dumb, blonde hitchhikers; they never ended well. She sank her body into the hedgerow and waited for the car to pass. It sped by in a rattly blur, leaving behind a cloud of diesel fumes and a small pang of regret in Lena's stomach.

Perhaps fifteen minutes or so later, she emerged from a bend in the road, and saw ahead, under the glow of a streetlamp, two amber lights blinking. Intrigued, she edged forward, until she was able to see that it was the car which had earlier passed her, now seemingly broken down. A person was crouched at the rear, driver-side wheel.

She approached tentatively. 'Hey,' she croaked.

There was no response. She edged closer and saw that it was a man: tall and fair-haired. His left arm was in a sling, and he was cursing as he worked a wrench with his free hand.

'Hey,' she said again, her voice strengthened by a new confidence. She drew to within perhaps five metres of him – enough space to turn and flee if necessary.

The man turned to face her, then got to his feet ponderously, wincing in pain. The wrench clattered to the ground, making Lena jump. He regarded her with a look of shock, which turned to confusion, then pity.

She crossed her arms over her chest. 'I need police. Or hospital.'

'I-I-I see,' the man said. 'Well, as it happens, I'm heading to the hospital myself.' He chuckled nervously. 'It's my mother; they say she doesn't have long to live. But I've only gone and blown a bloody tyre!'

He looked down at his arm. 'Not been having much luck recently. Ha ha; guess you and me have something in common.' His voice was soft and kind.

'Can you help me?' Lena begged. She felt her eyes filling with tears.

'Well, it's going to take me a while to fix this wheel. Say, why don't you take my phone – call someone? The police, maybe. Let them know your situation, eh? I don't want you to think I'm some kind of pervert, looking to take advantage of a beautiful young lady.'

Lena smiled. He was a gentleman. An English gentleman. They did exist, after all!

'Thank you,' she said, blinking away the tears. 'Very kind.'

The man fumbled in his trouser pocket, then held out his phone to Lena. She stepped forward and took it.

As she tapped 999, the man said: 'Hey, where are my manners? You must be freezing. My jacket's in the car. Let me get it for you.'

Lena smiled, then put the phone to her ear. She waited for a few moments for the call to connect, but it didn't. As she looked at the screen to check the reception, the man emerged from the car with the jacket. He came over to Lena and tenderly wrapped it around her shoulders.

'No service,' Lena said.

The man tutted and rolled his eyes. 'Typical! That's the countryside for you. Why don't you take a seat inside? Wait in the warm, while I fix this damn wheel, then I can take you to the hospital. If that's okay?'

Lena nodded.

The man's thin lips split into a broad smile. 'I'm Troy, by the way. And, you?'

'Lena.'

'Lena,' he repeated, in a slow whisper. 'Just beautiful.'

She walked over to the passenger door and grabbed the handle.

She paused for a brief moment, weighing up the risks. Then she shrugged off a niggling doubt as paranoia, smiled and got into the car.

It was the last terrible decision that Lena Demyan ever made.

ONE

THE LIFT DOORS finally juddered open and a waft of stale urine greeted James Quinn, making him gag. He covered his nose and mouth with his hand, as he quickly scanned the filthy interior.

'Stairs.'

'It's the eighth floor, guv!'

'Be thankful it's not the fourteenth.'

Mel rolled her eyes and followed him into the stairwell.

Despite being a good fifteen years her senior, he was much fitter and had soon left her for dust. James enjoyed such petty torments.

Hot but relieved, he emerged from the dank stairwell into an external walkway, bathed in dazzling sunshine. While he waited for Mel, he made his way to the parapet, shielded his brow and gazed out across a panorama of urban decay. Below, a gang of shifty-looking youths huddled in a shady corner. In boredom lurked menace. He thought of his Audi parked metres away, and instantly regretted not taking Mel's Fiesta instead.

A pained gasp heralded Mel's arrival. He turned to see

her bent over, palming her thighs and panting like a spent marathon runner. He smiled. At least the exertion had brought a few moments of blessed respite from her incessant jabber. Everybody had at least one shortcoming and Mel's was verbal diarrhoea. His own faults were legion.

'So,' Mel said, between laboured breaths, 'what would you do in my position?' She looked up at him. Her face was beetroot and strands of sweaty hair clung to her forehead.

'About what?'

'You've not listened,' she wheezed, 'to a pissing word I've been saying, have you?'

'Not true,' he said. And he wasn't lying: the odd word of her latest monologue had breached his aural defence shield – not enough, however, that he could stitch them into anything resembling coherent sentences. He plucked a handkerchief from his pocket and dabbed his brow. 'Let's walk – time and tide, and all that.'

The concrete walkway loomed ahead like a dystopian tunnel, littered with the detritus of the dispossessed: cider cans, chip paper, a half-eaten kebab; a used condom lay shrivelled in a parched drainage channel. James wrinkled his nose.

'So, what was I talking about, then?' Mel said, her low heels clacking against the pavement, as she struggled to keep up.

He drummed his lips and embraced the only option available to him: an educated guess. 'Boyfriend trouble. Daniel.'

'Declan!' she screeched. 'I sometimes wonder why I bother wasting my breath.'

'Indeed.'

She gave an exaggerated sigh. 'Look, if you could just stop being a complete arse for a couple of minutes, I'll tell you again…' Her words drifted away and settled into a distant, annoying drone, like a wasp at a window.

Another noise pricked the edge of his consciousness. He stopped abruptly.

Mel halted, too. 'So… it all came to a head… now, when was it? Tuesday? No, Wednesday – definitely Wednesday–'

'Is the precise day of the week pertinent, Mel?'

She shook her head and narrowed her eyes. The look suggested pity. He'd seen it before. 'How on Earth did your wife ever put up with you?' she said. 'The poor woman must've had the patience of a …'

He heard the noise again.

'Shh!' he hissed.

'Don't tell me to shush, you patronizing–'

James pressed his forefinger into her lips. She grabbed his wrist and pushed him away.

'That's another one for the charge sheet,' she said: 'assault.'

'Well, what about all the GBH to the ear'ole you've inflicted on me over the years?' He wiped the smudge of lipstick with his handkerchief. 'Quits?'

He pressed his ear to the sun-warmed door of number 43. 'Hear that?'

Mel cocked her head and drew closer. 'Hear what?'

'A baby, bawling its eyes out.'

'Er, yes, that's what babies do, guv: cry. Hadn't you noticed?'

'But, aren't there supposed to be different kinds of signal? You know, hunger, discomfort, wind?' He paused, before adding: 'Distress?'

'Why are you asking me, like I'm expected to know?' She pointed to her chest; 'Just because I've got a pair of these, doesn't make me expert in all things paediatric.'

James raised his palms to Mel, hopeful of warding off another tirade. He listened at the door again. 'It's stopped.'

'You're bloody paranoid.'

'Maybe I'm just constantly alert to the possibility of danger. You should try it sometime.'

'What's that supposed to mean? I'm a good detective. I won't have anyone tell me otherwise!'

James smiled. She was a good detective: hardworking and smart, with sound judgement and a healthy skepticism. A good nose for bullshit, balls of steel, heart of gold; one of the best. A glittering future awaited her – not that he'd ever tell her, of course. He gestured ahead; 'Shall we proceed?'

'Spare me the chivalry crap, guv – went out with the ark.'

'As you wish, m'lady.'

Mel grinned.

They continued along the corridor. 'Remind me of the fella's name again?' James said.

'My boyfriend?'

'No! The chap in the flat.'

She sighed. 'How many times must I tell you? Vadim Simonov.'

'Just checking. Number fifty-four, yeah?'

'Hallelujah! You've actually remembered something!'

'Well, I'll never forget the fact that you can be a right royal pain in the proverbial.'

'You always have to have the last word, don't you?'

'No I don't.'

'See? You've just proved my point.'

James ran a finger under his hot collar. 'I feel like Lawrence of Arabia. When's this sodding heatwave supposed to end?'

'Hopefully not for a while yet: I've got a tan to top up.

You could do with some sun yourself, guv; I've seen more colour in a Greek yoghurt.'

'That's because I'm a creature of the night.'

'Sounds about right.'

They stopped at the door to flat 54. James turned to look at Mel. 'Ready?'

Mel arched her brow. 'P-l-lease! You know I could have led this one with a DC, guv; I'm a big girl now, and this kind of job is way below your pay grade.'

James rapped on the door. 'It's good to get out of the office; mixing with you plebs keeps me grounded.'

'Cheeky bloody sod.'

'He'd better be in, after all this exertion,' James said, knocking harder.

He went over to the window, but the curtains were drawn. He hopped back to the door and hammered again. 'Mr. Vadminov,' he hollered. 'Police. Open up.'

He felt the sharp jab of Mel's elbow. '*Simonov!*'

'I'm sure he gets the gist.'

James dropped to a squat, lifted the letterbox plate and shoved two fingers through the stiff, black bristles of the draught excluder, to create a peephole. He recoiled and turned away. 'Jeez, Louise! It bloody stinks in there!'

He pinched his nose and peered back through the bristly fronds. He could only make out vague shapes through the small gap, but sensed movement deep inside. 'I can see you're in there, fella,' he shouted. 'Open up!'

Moments later the door creaked open, and an invisible cloud of foulness engulfed him.

Stay in control, James.

The stench was something akin to opening a Tupperware container of vegetables, left to stew in the sun. He raised the back of his hand to stifle the gag reflex, swallowed hard and composed himself.

In the doorway stood a grubby little man, hastily buckling his belt. Greasy, black hair. Olive complexion. Beady, black eyes, almost invisible under the shade of thick brows. Days-old stubble. Stained vest, dirty jeans and bare feet. Overgrown toenails a shade of yellow, which suggested a fungal infection. The stub of a hand-rolled cigarette was stuck to his bottom lip.

James thrust his ID towards the man. 'Mr. Simonov? DCI Quinn and DS Barraclough, Hertfordshire Constabulary. May we have a word inside, please?'

The man raised pleading palms and shook his head. 'No English.'

'No English?' James repeated. 'That's odd, because my colleague here was speaking to a nice young lady at Barclays Bank only this morning, who said you had quite the line in banter. Isn't that right, Mel?'

'Indeed,' Mel said. 'May we come in, sir?'

The man sighed in resignation, flicked the cigarette butt at James's feet and reluctantly beckoned them inside.

The door opened straight into a living room-cum-kitchen. The scene was grim: part student digs, part crack den. Bass notes of indistinct music rippled from the flat below, through the sticky laminate floor and up James's body. The air hung heavy and hot. He wasn't sure he'd be able to bear it.

'Mind if I let in some fresh air, Vadim?'

Without waiting for an answer, James moved over to the window and parted the thick drapes. Light flooded in, highlighting a galaxy of dancing dust motes. He swallowed an urge to sneeze. A fly which was pinging against the glass made a grateful escape the moment he flung open the casement. He took a gulp of fresh air and turned back to face Vadim. 'Nice place you've got here. Couldn't let me have the name of your interior designer, could you?'

Vadim was shielding his eyes from the sudden brightness. 'No understand.'

James gestured to an armchair, which was literally falling apart at the seams. 'Please, make yourself comfy.'

James dropped onto the arm of an equally dilapidated sofa; it replied with a rusty squeak of protest. Between them was a cheap plywood coffee table, strewn with spent fast-food containers, dirty mugs, plastic cutlery and an overflowing ashtray. James picked up a small tin and sniffed it: cannabis. He set the tin down and tilted his head at Vadim. 'Medicinal?'

The man grimaced. His eyes flitted to the front door. Mel sat down with a graceless plonk on the other sofa arm, positioning herself to block an escape attempt. She had a figure a man less gallant than James might call 'stout', or perhaps 'big-boned'.

His nostrils flared at a sudden putrid whiff. He flicked a brown paper bag from the table to reveal a wizened, half-eaten sandwich: egg. His stomach growled and churned, and his cheeks puffed. He patted his trousers, desperately feeling for his mints. They weren't there. Shit! Must be in his jacket, back in the car.

'Peppermint Trebor do the trick, guv?'

'Ah, you're a lifesaver, Mel.' What would he do without her?

She tossed him the packet and he popped a mint inside his cheek, savouring the instantaneous relief. He threw the packet back to Mel, flashing her a grateful smile.

Vadim fidgeted and his eyes darted about the room.

'If you don't mind me saying, Vadim, you seem a little nervous. Relax. We're just here to ask a few questions, okay?'

Vadim blinked, and James took this as his cue to proceed.

'Now, I'll come straight to the point: we have reason to believe you've been depositing large quantities of cash in a third-party bank account. I can think of a million and one legitimate reasons for this, but perhaps you could just put our minds at rest that it wasn't anything… naughty?'

Vadim cleared his throat, then said: 'Am pizza delivery man. Collect payment for boss. Pay into account.'

'Pizza, Vadim? Now, that *is* interesting.' He turned and asked Mel: 'What's your favourite?'

'Hawaiian, guv.'

'Pineapple, Mel?! On a pizza?' He turned back to Vadim. 'That's bloody sacrilege, don't you think? Give me a meat feast any day of the week. How much at your gaff for a meat feast, Vadim? Large, deep-pan; side of garlic bread?'

Vadim furrowed his brow and smiled, awkwardly.

'Cat got your tongue, Vadim? Never mind, we can guess. What do you reckon, Mel? Fifteen quid? Ten, on special offer?'

'Sounds about right, guv.'

'And how much cash was deposited this week, Mel?'

'Just over eleven thousand pounds.'

'Eleven grand?' James made an impressed whistling sound. 'Now, that's a lot of pizza, Vadim. You're quite the businessman, it seems. Perhaps you and I could become partners; let me have a slice of the action – if you'll excuse the pun? What do you reckon? Notebook ready, Mel?'

'Yes, guv.'

'Good. Now, Vadim, if you could just let us have the name and address of the owner of the pizza business, that would be greatly appreciated; we'll just need to check everything's in order on the paperwork front. There's a good chap.'

A sudden thud against the back wall diverted James's

attention. He caught Vadim looking towards the source of the noise, with sudden panic in his eyes.

'Got company, Vadim?'

The man shot to his feet and leapt over the table; a stray foot sent the detritus flying about the room. Vadim barrelled headlong into Mel's chest.

With cool efficiency she seized control, twisting him into a headlock. 'Not so fast, sunshine.'

Another thud came from the other side of the wall.

'You okay handling him while I check it out, Mel?'

'No sweat, guv.'

James went through a rear door into a dark, claustrophobic lobby. Off of it were three doors; one was ajar. He poked his head through to a small, dark bathroom, which reeked of black mould and unflushed human waste. He held the back of his hand to his nostrils. The second door opened to a squalid bedroom. Nobody there. He returned to the lobby and tried the third door. Locked.

Scuffling noises came from the living room. 'You okay, Mel?' he hollered.

'Yep, all in hand here,' she shouted back, gritted effort evident in her voice.

He pressed his ear to the locked door and heard muffled cries.

'Stand back in there!' he shouted. Then, James kicked at the lock. Three attempts and it gave way. He entered the room.

'Jesus fucking Christ!'

A girl – no older than her late teens – sat on a bare mattress, dressed only in a bra and knickers. Her limbs were covered in bruises, some old; others fresh. She had pasty, mottled skin; long, dark hair drenched with sweat, sticking to her skin. She was gagged and bound with nylon cable ties, so tight around the ankles and wrists they had drawn blood. The windowless room was hot and stifling, barely bigger than the mattress.

He edged towards the girl, holding out his palms, trying to project calm. 'It's okay, sweetheart. I'm a police officer. You're safe.'

The girl recoiled, turned her cheek to James and pushed herself into the corner, shaking with fear.

He knelt before her and brought his hands up slowly, to remove the gag. Once removed, she took frantic gulps of awful, sordid air. James inspected the cable tie around her wrists.

'Give me one moment; I'll have you out of this.'

He dashed back to the kitchenette, vaguely aware that Mel and Vadim were engaged in a scuffle on the floor, near the front door. 'The bastard's harbouring a girl, Mel!' he shouted, as he rummaged through the under-sink drawer. 'Don't let him escape!'

He found a sharp paring knife and rushed back to the girl. As he sawed at the tie around her wrist, desperately trying not to hurt her, garbled, whispered words fell from her lips – almost a chant; eastern European.

'We'll get you to a safe place,' he soothed. 'The nightmare's over now. I promise.'

The cable tie gave out and the girl drew her hands to her shoulders, crossing her arms tight against her chest. James switched attention to her ankles.

As he broke quickly through the tie, a cry came from the living room: 'Guv, I need you now!'

'Stay here, sweetheart; we'll get you out really soon. I won't let anyone hurt you again.'

'GUV!'

In the living room, Mel and Vadim were still on the floor. Vadim was on his hands and knees, dragging himself towards the front door, but Mel clung to an ankle. As

Vadim kicked out behind with his free leg and struck Mel in the head, she let out an agonized yowl.

James ran over and threw his weight onto Vadim. He shifted himself into a seated position, straddling the man's buttocks. Vadim groaned and writhed, his hands flailing, and James grabbed the man's wrists, bringing his arms up forcefully behind his back.

'Cuffs, Mel?' James shouted over Vadim's protests.

'I thought you had them!'

'Shit! They'll be in my jacket, in the bloody car! Call uniform for support – and an ambulance.'

Vadim continued to groan and struggle.

'Put a sock in it. Arsehole!'

James sensed Mel getting to her feet, and making her way to the back of the room to make the call. Staring at the back of the man's head, James summoned all the willpower he could muster not to knock the piece of scum clean out. Vadim finally gave up the struggle. As James listened to Mel's call, he drew breath.

There was another sound in the room: footsteps. Mel's? No, they were too light; the padding of bare feet. He glanced over his shoulder, as the blurred shape of the girl streaked past him.

'Mel,' he cried, 'get her!'

The girl opened the door and flew out onto the walk-way. Moments later, Mel was in pursuit. Vadim grunted.

'Hey!' Mel yelled from outside. Then, silence.

James wanted to be outside, helping Mel to calm the girl, to convince her that everything would be okay. He couldn't bear the feeling of helplessness. He looked around in the mess of the upturned table and saw the ashtray – releasing one hand from the grip of Vadim's wrists, he grabbed it. He gave it one, maybe two seconds contemplation, before raining it down on the man's head.

Vadim was clean out. Shouldn't cause any lasting damage, but right now James didn't care. He leapt to his feet and dashed through the door.

Mel turned to him, her face drained of all colour. She shook her head almost imperceptibly, and turned back to look over the parapet.

No.

Please…

Not that!

Tentative, unsteady, James edged towards the parapet. He gripped the handrail and peered over.

A wave of giddy nausea shot through him, when he saw the body far below. Tiny. Still. Limbs bent at unnatural angles. He could make out the pool of blood around her head, even from eight storeys up. A crowd was already gathering to gawp at the ghoulish sight.

His legs buckled under him, and he gripped the handrail tighter still. Mel dropped her clammy hand onto his and squeezed him gently. Instinctively, he withdrew it.

'I'm sorry, guv,' she said. 'I tried to stop her, but I was too late.'

TWO

James turned back to face the open doorway to the flat. 'Yes… I know… not your fault.' Every sight and sound were suddenly blurry and indistinct; distant. Mel's presence faded.

He shook his head and things became sharp once more. 'Right… er… get on to that ambulance. Give the poor girl some dignity in death.'

Mel peered into the flat and turned to James. 'What happened to him?'

'Banged his head in the struggle. He'll live – more's the pity.'

Mel looked into his eyes. Unable to bear the weight of her enquiry, he shifted his gaze to the floor. She put her hand lightly on his forearm.

'Must bring back horrible memories, guv? I don't know why you carry on putting yourself through all this.'

He flinched at her words, but more at her touch. He quickly stooped to break the contact again. He picked up Vadim's discarded cigarette butt and brandished it.

'Bloody litter lout.'

. . .

As soon as support arrived, James took the opportunity to disappear from the scene, knowing that it was safe in Mel's hands.

He hurtled down the concrete staircase, and breathed a sigh of relief when he found his Audi unscathed. He stole a backward glance at the spot where the girl had landed; it was surrounded now by a cordon, an ambulance and numerous squad cars.

Simonov had been taken to the station at Hertford. James's hand curled into a fist at the thought of the horrors he must have inflicted on that poor girl. Questions swirled in his head: how long had she been there? Where was she from? What was her name? How had she got into Simonov's hands? Purchased, no doubt, from a trafficking syndicate. A commodity – that's what she was. Bastards!

He was going to root them out.

Every last one of them.

He'd intended to drive straight back to HQ – there was a ton of work waiting for him, after all. But his head wasn't in the right place, so he took a diversion to Stevenage. Something to help take his mind off the suicide.

He parked the Audi in the usual spot: on the double yellows, near the junction with Victoria Avenue.

Troy Perkins's grimy house was at the other end of the north-side terrace, which stretched the full length of Charles Street. Just like many of the streets in this part of town, named after monarchs, there was nothing remotely regal about it.

Immediately in front of Perkins's house sat his battered, red Peugeot 308. The number plate was obscured by a black Nissan, but James had committed the registration to memory years ago.

With the engine off, the temperature in the Audi soon rocketed. James's brain was frying. Celtic blood ran through his veins; he was better suited to winter. He opened the window a crack, then dabbed his brow with a neatly folded handkerchief, which he returned to the passenger seat, next to the camera.

His gaze returned to the distance. How many hours must he have clocked staking Troy Perkins over the years? He daren't do the maths; the answer would depress him. Well, depress him more.

Come on, Perkins – one opportunity, that's all I need.

He waited.

And watched.

Before long, his eyelids grew so heavy he could no longer resist, and closed them.

Just a few minutes, then.

THREE

Ten minutes.

Molly Tindall's frustration had been brewing for days. Weeks. Years, if she were being completely honest with herself. Time to lay it on the line. What was the worst he could do? Sack her? Make her life a misery; force her to quit? She wouldn't put anything past the vindictive old prick. But still, she had to do something about the situation.

She checked her watch.

Nine minutes.

She wanted it over and done with. She couldn't concentrate on her article. Was there time for a quick fag break? She plonked her handbag on her lap and raked through the random items, searching for her Marlboros.

Her phone buzzed, startling her. Who was calling now? The detective again? This time, to report a juicy new murder? Fat chance!

Molly let out a small groan when she saw it was Lucy from Especially4U. Lovely girl; thick as two short planks, but remorselessly positive and cheery.

She recalled the disaster of her last date: Colin from Stevenage. Colin Montgomery (yes, seriously), a chartered accountant. The words 'Colin' and 'Stevenage' should have set off the alarm bells, but then Lucy recalled his suggestion of that nice Italian restaurant in Hitchin – a favourite of Molly's. One of the waiters was *such* a dish. Gay, of course – weren't they all, these days? Add that to the fact that Colin was tall, dark, rugged and square-jawed, and how could she say no? *Shallow? Moi?*

Well, the evening didn't get off to the greatest of starts when Colin turned out to be less Orlando Bloom from *Lord of the Rings* and more Augustus Gloop from *Charlie and the Chocolate Factory*. 'Oh, God,' Colin said, when Molly plucked the photo from her handbag, 'there must have been some kind of mix-up at the agency. You're not too disappointed, are you?'

'Oh no, no, not at all, Colin,' she said, looking down as she fussed with her cutlery.

'Shall we do starters?' Colin asked.

'Let's just go straight to mains, shall we?' Molly replied.

By the time Colin whipped out a pocket calculator, to work out his share of the bill plus tip, Molly was ready to run for the hills.

'Would you like to do this again?' he said, smiling nervously, a fragment of spinach clinging stubbornly to an incisor.

'I might need to think about that one, Colin.'

Her phone continued to buzz. She didn't have the time or energy to speak to Lucy right now, and went to kill the call.

But, what if Lucy had found her 'The One'? She was getting perilously close to that age where beggars couldn't be choosers. Molly took the call.

'Lucy, hi. Not got much time; you'll need to be quick. Who have you got for me?'

'Oh, hi, Molly. I've got a lovely selection… somewhere… Give me a moment…'

Molly rolled her eyes and thrummed her fingers, as she heard Lucy tapping away at her keyboard. She checked her watch.

'Right, sorry, you know me and computers,' Lucy snorted. 'Here we are: so, I've got a Dwayne from–'

'No.'

'O-kay… Michael from Milton Keynes?'

'No.'

'Says he's got a one-bed barge, permanently moored on the Grand Union Canal. That make any difference?'

'For God's sake, Lucy! No!'

'Right. Well, let me see…' There was a pause and Molly heard frenetic mouse clicks. 'Ah, what about this one: his name's Simon and he's a psychopath in Cambridge.'

'Do you mean a psychologist?'

'Oh, yes, that's right. Is there a difference?'

'Not necessarily. Does he have a full set of teeth and his own hair?'

'Hmm, I can't promise anything for the teeth; he's kind of smiling awkwardly and they're all covered up. But I can confirm he's all there in the hair department. I don't know how you'd describe it, though: a ginger perm…?'

'For God's sake, Lucy! Do you have anyone *normal* on your books?'

'How are you defining "normal", Molly?'

'Tell you what, email me all the matches and I'll take a look through. Gotta go.'

'Will do, Molly. Have a good day.'

Molly dropped the phone, slumped in her chair and

pinched the bridge of her nose. When was it ever going to be her turn for a bit of luck?

Shit! She sat bolt upright. What was the time? Just gone ten. *Bollocks!* He hated poor timekeeping.

She threw her handbag back onto the desk, got to her feet and tottered over to Brian's office, in her ludicrously inappropriate high heels.

At his door, she paused and took a deep sniff of Aromastick. Stomach in, tits out, best smile. She rapped on the glass and burst in.

Brian jumped in his chair. 'Jesus, Molly! What have I said about barging in when the blind's down?'

'Sorry, Bri. We've got a meeting – ten a.m.?'

'I thought it was eleven?'

'No. Ten.'

Molly swung around to close the door, then turned back to Brian. She opened her mouth to speak, when a woman's voice interjected.

'Ooh, yeah, baby…'

'Busy, Brian?'

He jabbed at his keyboard with one hand and clonked the mouse with the other. His face flushed red.

'Oh, yeah… that's good…'

'It's not what it seems, Molly,' he said, his voice laced with panic. 'Got one of those malicious emails; I clicked on a link. Stupid, I know. Thought it was a council planning application.'

'Course you did, Brian. We've all done it.'

'Yes, right there, baby…'

Brian shook the monitor, jabbed the keyboard and clicked away at the mouse, but the woman's ecstatic monologue continued. He got to his feet, stepped away from his desk and moved over to fumble at a wall socket. Finally, he pulled out the plug and killed the computer.

He turned to Molly, pushed his glasses up the bridge of his nose and ran a flustered hand through his thin, grey hair. His high forehead glistened with sweat. 'So,' he said, his breathing laboured, 'what did you want to talk about?'

Molly took a deep breath. 'I'm going to cut right to the chase.' She sensed he would want her to – in the circumstances. 'I'm not happy with the direction the paper's heading. Nor my career. I'm meant to be Chief Crime Reporter, but all the pieces I'm getting are just lame; nonsense. I could write them in my sleep.'

'And, what do you expect?' Brian said, his tone indignant and forthright, suggesting he had already got over his embarrassment. 'We're a local rag, for God's sake, in a prosperous area. We can't go about conjuring serious crimes from thin air, just to make an exciting headline. That's not what you're suggesting, is it?'

Molly brought a hand to her chest. 'Of course not; I'm almost offended that you think I would ever do that. I just think we need to move with the times; do more investigative reporting. Dig deeper; explore difficult topics; prompt debate; get people thinking.'

'Investigations?' Brian laughed, in that awful, condescending way of his. 'What kind of investigations would you do around here?'

'I don't know,' Molly said. 'How about something like human trafficking?'

'Human trafficking? Round here? Have you been on the wacky baccy? You journos with your media degrees and stupid dreams; it's all pie-in-the-sky stuff. We have to face facts. Our market's shrinking; the youth of today get their news online, on their mobiles, and our readership is old and conservative – people who want to put their feet up in front of the fire with a cup of cocoa, dozing off over the cryptic crossword. They don't want *investigative* journalism. That's for the nationals, Molly. Our job is to serve our readers, the local community – and manage our decline with dignity and good grace.'

'But, Brian…' Molly said, but paused, unable to think of any words. The wind had gone from her sails.

'But nothing, Molly.' Brian stepped in to fill the silence. He placed his hands on his hips and changed the subject: 'How's the Kimpton piece going?'

Residents up in arms about fly-tipping. Boring. 'Haven't even started it.'

He looked at his watch. 'I want it on my desk first thing in the morning, okay?'

Molly sighed. 'Of course you'll get it. When have I ever missed a deadline?'

'Is that everything, Molly? 'Cos I need to crack on.'

Course you do, Brian.

'Well, there is one more thing.'

He rolled his eyes and sighed: 'And, what's that?'

'It's coming up to the two-year anniversary of the Wain Wood murder. I think we should put out another appeal for information; someone out there must know something. We should offer a reward.'

Brian laughed, mirthlessly. 'A reward? Over my dead body.'

Molly flicked her gaze to the heavy carriage clock on his desk. *Don't tempt me.*

'You seriously think one of our readers would be in any way immersed in that sordid little world?' Brian continued. 'If you do, you must be out of your tiny mind.'

Molly's eyes narrowed. Anger gripped her stomach. *Don't let him see it.* 'We have to do *something*!' she pleaded. 'That psycho's still out there! What if he strikes again? How would we live with ourselves, knowing we could have done something to stop him? Imagine the headlines, Bri, if we did get him: the Dell Ripper behind bars, where he belongs. Justice for poor Lena, at last.'

'No one gives a shit about scrubbers like her.'

Molly had to turn away. She couldn't bear to look at the man's pathetic face any longer; she might have been unable to resist the urge to punch him square in the snout. She reached for the door handle.

'See you later, Molly.'

She arranged her mouth into a thin smile and spun on her heel. 'Brian, just one more thing.'

He sighed: 'Yes? What is it?'

'Your flies are undone – thought I'd better just mention it.'

Brian looked down, then desperately fumbled at the zip.

'Shall we call it five hundred?'

He looked up. 'Huh?'

'The reward for Lena.'

Brian stayed silent.

'Ah, Brian, that's so sweet of you. I'll get onto the article straight away.' She blew him a kiss and swept out of his office.

Molly scraped the last spoonful of brown stodge from the container – lasagne? Shepherd's pie? Cottage pie? Who knew? – and dropped the plastic, microwave-meal detritus onto the coffee table.

She snatched up the large glass of Chablis, tucked in her feet and settled in for a cosy evening on the sofa. *Coronation Street* was on the telly and Mr. Darcy lay curled in a ball, on his chair under the window, purring contentedly. Her laptop sat next to her, propped on a Laura Ashley cushion. She had the article to finish, but right now she needed to distract herself from work, after another depressing day in the office. And she needed to know what was happening in Ken Barlow's sex life.

The fact that Molly derived her excitement vicariously from an octogenarian soap character was not lost on her. All she needed now was to belt out a solo karaoke performance of Celine Dion's "All By Myself", and her clichéd life would be complete.

She held her hand in front of her and splayed her fingers, imagining a great rock of a diamond glinting in the evening sunlight. It occurred to her then that she could count her true friends on that hand – and one of them was Mr. Darcy: he was the thumb. The pinkie was Celia, her long-suffering therapist. The three remaining digits were Sarah, Belle and Tania – all married (twice, in the case of Tania), sprogged up and dispersed across the country; she hardly saw them at all now. Gossip was exchanged via a WhatsApp group and the occasional spa weekend, where conversation would inevitably turn to children, making Molly feel left out. Sad.

She desperately wanted to be a mother, but she'd never met the right man. She wanted a girl – a sweet, girlie girl; long, blonde hair plaited into neat pigtails, flamingo-print ra-ra dress and ivory lace shoes. Her name would be Harriet, and that was non-negotiable – unless of course she turned out to be a boy, in which case he'd be a Fitzwilliam and just as loved, obvs. Right, who was she trying to kid? Harriet was so vivid in Molly's imagination that she could almost squeeze her tiny, soft hand. She would be as good a mum to Harriet as Molly's own mother was terrible to her.

At this thought, Molly glanced at the urn on the mantlepiece and gulped a mouthful of Chablis, which now carried a bitter note. The bitch had written it in her will that her ashes were to be scattered over Lake Windermere. Molly was tempted on more than one occasion to put her out with the Thursday night recycling, but she was a better person than that – although, not so good that she was prepared to travel all the way to the Lake District, and sully the home of William Wordsworth and Beatrix Potter with the incinerated remains of that spiteful old hag.

Dead for four years now, Joyce Tindall's presence still loomed large in Molly's life. Driven by nothing more than a sense of obligation, she'd nursed her mother during those final months of illness, without the faintest squeak of reciprocated gratitude. *'Margaret! More morphine!'* she recalled her shouting. *'It's MOLLY, mother!'* Molly wasn't in the least surprised when she discovered that Joyce had bequeathed the entirety of her modest estate to the Cats' Protection League. The woman couldn't stand cats – or any animal, for that matter – but they were still farther up the hierarchy of affection than her own flesh and blood. *Good riddance, bitch!* Molly had the last laugh when she contested the will, successfully convincing the court that her mother hadn't been of sound mind.

The sound of the *Coronation Street* credits rolling slipped into Molly's consciousness, and she cursed herself for allowing her mind to wander; she'd paid no attention at all to Ken Barlow's latest sexploits.

Now, what was she supposed to be doing? Ah, yes, the article.

She picked up the computer and placed it on her lap, then sighed. The article wasn't going to write itself – more's the pity. She hadn't had time to write it at the office, because she'd had to finalize the Perkins piece.

She chewed her lip in concentration. What angle was she going to take? The raw facts weren't going to use up many words. A row had escalated between two neighbours on a new Brady Homes development, on the outskirts of Baldock, culminating in fisticuffs in the street. It had started when one side complained to the other that they could hear them urinating through the dividing wall. Molly was sent to do the interviews, after the police had taken statements. Looking at her notes now, she realized it was going to be difficult to include any direct quotes in a respectable publication like the *Hertfordshire Evening Herald* (*'Why does he have to do it so loud? He sounds like he's firing a fucking water cannon into the pan,'* said Doug Metcalf, 44. *'It comes to something when a man can't have a slash in his own fucking pisser without the Gestapo being despatched,'* said Ray Shawcross, 56). Molly decided she was going to turn it into an exposé on the shoddy practices in the house-building industry. Not a crime? Well, it bloody well should be! Now, only a thousand words to crank out. At least she had a headline sorted: *'PEE'D OFF!'*

It seemed a fitting headline for her life story, too.

FOUR

JAMES ARRIVED at Welwyn HQ shortly after six a.m. Sleep had evaded him again. This time it was the image of the poor girl from the flats which was seared on his brain. He would see to it that the scum responsible were brought to justice.

There was also another good reason to arrive early: Major Crime Unit was moving to a new floor, to accommodate the team coming across from the Stevenage offices, and he needed to grab the best spot before anyone could claim it. By moving a couple of filing cabinets to create a barrier, and pivoting the desk to face the wall, he annexed a corner – hopefully, that should discourage social interaction.

It would be another two weeks on the floor, the facilities guys told him, before his new office was repaired; problem with the toilets on the floor above: leaking effluent, apparently. Lovely. He was used to being shat on from a great height, but only in the metaphorical sense.

Settling into his chair, he emptied the cardboard box he'd carried up from the third floor.

Among the stationery was the photograph of Lena Demyan – he tacked it to the wall. Murdered two years ago, her killer was never brought to justice. He regarded her pretty face for a moment, then closed his eyes and let his mind wander to a future in which a judge was sending Troy Perkins down for life.

James was jolted from his thoughts by the sound of heavy footsteps and a metallic thunk. For God's sake, he'd hoped for at least two more hours of peace and quiet. He spun around and smiled stiffly, when he realized who it was: a wheezing Ian Murdoch, supporting himself against a filing cabinet. The Super wore a t-shirt which barely stretched over his belly. A sweat patch in the shape of Chile stretched from collar to navel. Or was it Peru? Geography had never been his strongest suit; he was more a science and nature man.

James continued his gaze down to Murdoch's shorts. He had never seen his fat and oddly hairless legs before. Nor, it seemed, had the sun, judging by their alabaster hue. *Stop staring at his bloody legs!* James looked up to meet Murdoch's eyes.

'Been for a run, sir?'

'Well… erm…' Murdoch spluttered, before catching his breath, 'told Mrs. M I'd park up by Sainsbury's and jog to the office from there.'

'And?'

Murdoch reached for the water bottle he'd plonked on the filing cabinet and took a greedy gulp, then sighed. 'Saw chocolate muffins were on a two-for-one when I paid for my petrol. Polished them off, then didn't feel much up to running after that. Came up the stairs, though: four bloody flights!'

James forced a *'Gosh, that's impressive'* look; 'Wow!'

'"She Who Must Be Obeyed" sent me to the quack's,

to get my cholesterol checked out.' Murdoch brought a fat hand to his belly and leant in. 'Do you know what my score was?' A wide smile broke out on his face.

James groaned inwardly; he knew where this tedious exchange was heading. 'No, sir. Enlighten me.'

'Nine.'

'Right…'

'Out of ten! Like *ninety* per cent. That's *bloody brilliant*, I said.'

'O-kay…' James uttered.

'And do you know what he told me?'

James sighed; 'There's still room for improvement?'

'*Still room for improvement!*' Murdoch repeated, laughing manically, as if James had just cracked the world's greatest joke.

The laughing policeman fell silent then and his smile dropped, as if someone had flicked the power switch. 'Said I'd be dead before sixty if I didn't change my ways.'

'Oh,' James said, unsure of what else he could say.

Murdoch reached for a small Tupperware container and thrust it towards James, peeling back the lid. 'Bloody woman's given me chicken salad for lunch. Chicken salad! *That's* what's gonna kill me!'

'Right, well, good luck, sir. I'd best get on.'

James spun back around and switched on his computer. God, he hated small talk – such a waste of time and energy.

While he was waiting for the computer to fire up, James gazed back at Lena Demyan.

'No point crying over spilt milk, James.'

For God's sake, was he *still* there?!

'Sir?' James glanced over his shoulder, to see Murdoch wagging his finger at the photograph.

'It's been two years now and we're pressured with resources, as you well know. I want you focused one-hundred per cent on Solent. That's how we're going to prevent the exploitation of… women like that.'

James's fist curled into a ball under the desk. *Women like that?* Outrageous.

He turned back to his desk, as Murdoch sauntered off to his office, muttering: 'Chicken bloody salad!'

Later that morning, the MCU floor was a noisy throng. Well, it would have been, had James not been wearing his wireless, noise-cancelling Bose QuietComfort headphones. Cost him the best part of £300, but they were cheap at half the price. And, yes, he knew full well that saying made no logical sense; it was one of his mother's favourites. Say no more. He may have looked like Princess Leia, with her bun hair, but the message was clear: 'Bugger off, I've work to do.'

Without warning, the battery charge suddenly ran out, and the sound of laughter and chatter from beyond the filing cabinet barrier jerked James from his work. He removed his headphones and stole an irritated look at a group of young officers, gathered around a desk which was covered in cakes, biscuits and sweets. An email had done the rounds the previous Friday, asking everyone to bring something in to welcome the new contingent. He'd forgotten all about it, and hoped they'd be grateful for the half pack of Polos he raked from the bottom of his drawer.

Top brass said that the amalgamation of the Stevenage and Welwyn teams was done to 'streamline the service', 'improve operational efficiency', 'enhance collaborative working practices' and other such bullshit. All meaningless management speak, as far as James was concerned, to disguise the real motive: cutting costs. Life would be so much simpler if people said what they meant. If anyone had asked James for his cost-cutting ideas – which they didn't – he would have told them straight: get rid of all those lazy bastards eking out their time, waiting for the day they can draw on their final salary pensions. The force was riddled with such individuals, even in the age of austerity, and it would be a much better place without them.

Agitated into a lather now, James couldn't concentrate on his work. He needed some peace and quiet; a walk in the fresh air would do the trick. Trouble was, the only exit route took him past the cake gathering, when he'd thus far managed to avoid introductions. Was there anything more painful? Childbirth, he imagined. Disembowelment, of course. But, not much else. Choosing his moment carefully – the punchline of a seemingly hilarious joke being delivered by a huge guy holding court in the centre – James sidled by, staring down at his phone, as if he'd just received a gravely important message. Was he going to get away with it?

'Sir!'

Damn. Mel's voice.

James spun around, putting his phone into his jacket pocket and fixing a smile.

'Aren't you going to say hello?' Mel said, a hint of mischief in her voice.

He scanned the gathering. All eyes focused on him. Painful.

'Oh, yes. Sorry, been busy this morning. Welcome, everyone. Hope you're settling in nicely. If you don't mind, I've got to–'

'DC Porter, sir. Luke.'

The tall guy (six-four? Broad shoulders, square jaw, early twenties; rugby player?) stepped forward, hand outstretched, with a smudge of strawberry jam on his fingertip. James shook his hand, forlornly hopeful of avoiding contact with the sticky conserve. The guy had the tightest grip, and it took willpower not to wince.

'Welcome,' James said, through a rictus grin, before becoming momentarily distracted by a smattering of white powder on the guy's upper lip. Cocaine? No, icing sugar – but it didn't hurt to stay alert to the possibility.

'I… er… well, lovely to meet you all. Can't stop and chat, unfortunately… there's something important… I've got to get to. My desk's round the corner, over there, if you need me.'

'He hates being interrupted,' Mel said.

The others – except the cocky giant – smiled nervously.

'Don't worry,' Mel said, 'his bark's worse than his bite.' She punched James playfully in the stomach. 'He's a great big pussycat once you get to know him. Isn't that right, guv?'

'Mixing your animal metaphors there, Mel.'

'See what I mean?' Mel said, addressing the rabble.

'Not sure they're metaphors,' the giant said.

James flashed him a disdainful look, then whisked himself off to the safety of the stairwell.

'Guv?'

He'd descended a couple of flights, when Mel's voice echoed around the bare concrete walls. 'What?' He waited for her to huff and puff herself down to his level.

'Sorry about just now. I know how painful you find it.'

'Water off a duck's back. Now, what did you really want to say to me?'

Mel gave a knowing smile, then paused for a few

awkward moments, like she was searching for the right words. She didn't normally find it difficult to locate them. 'How are you feeling?' she said, eventually. 'You know, after the girl yesterday.'

'How am *I* feeling? What kind of question is that? Why don't you ask how that poor girl's mother will be feeling when she's informed? Have we got an identification yet?'

'No, guv. Still working on it.'

'Well, hurry up. And, what about him – Simonov, or whatever the arsehole's name is; have you charged him?'

'Not yet. Just want to be one-hundred per cent certain he's spilt all the beans.' Mel narrowed her eyes and tilted her head. 'Tell me you're not going to join the brothel raid, guv?'

'Are you done with the questions now? I need some fresh air.'

She puffed her cheeks and shook her head, pitifully. 'Yes, guv.'

James turned and galloped down the remaining flights.

He returned to the MCU floor half an hour later, his head clearer, and was pleased to see people mostly dispersed and seated at their desks, seemingly working. The din had mercifully subsided.

The giant – what was his name, now? Four letters; began with an 'L': Leon? Liam? Levi? Luke! – was bent over, propped on his knuckles like a silverback gorilla, at Mel's desk. He whispered something into her ear and she giggled. He stood up, tipped his head to face the ceiling and dropped sweets from his fist into his open mouth. God, James admired her resilience.

He suddenly realized he was watching the scene as if he were David Attenborough, lurking in the fronds of a

Rwandan jungle. He shook his head and resumed the brisk walk to his corner sanctuary.

Murdoch burst out of his office. 'James, five minutes, please.'

He sighed inwardly. Was he *ever* going to get any work done today?

'Take a seat,' Murdoch said, as he dropped his own fat arse into the leather chair behind his desk.

'I'd rather stand.'

'As you will.'

Murdoch's chicken salad was to the side of his mouse mat, and James watched – simultaneously transfixed and disgusted – as the Super rummaged inside it with his fat forefinger and thumb. Moments later, he plucked out a piece of chicken and proceeded to shake it, as though he'd netted a live stickleback.

'I'm thinking of doing a little welcome speech to everyone this afternoon,' Murdoch said, as he gobbled his catch.

'Okay,' James said, not sure where he fitted into the equation.

'Thought I'd start with a bit of humour. You know, set the tone, break the ice and all that. What do you reckon?'

'You know, this isn't really my thing, sir. Besides,' James glanced out onto the floor, 'it seems like they've kinda made friends already.'

Murdoch's attention shifted to his computer.

'Is this going to take long, sir?' James said.

Murdoch smiled and let out a throaty chuckle, his eyes fixed on his screen. 'What's the difference between a magic wand and a police baton?'

'Have you been Googling police jokes, sir?'

'One's for cunning stunts and the other's for stunning c–'

James coughed.

'Bit off-colour?'

'Maybe a tad.'

'I'd like you to join me, James. I think it would send the right message to the floor, that the senior officers are interested in their welfare.'

'What time are you planning to do it, sir?'

'Three.'

'Ah… no… sorry. Got a meeting with Special Ops, to plan the Solent raid tomorrow.'

'I see, James.' Murdoch sighed plaintively, leant back and laced his fingers over his stomach. 'You know, if you want to make more headway in the force, you need to be a bit more…'

'Collegiate, sir?'

James had heard it before, a thousand times – not least in his annual appraisal. Each year it was the same: James would spend an excruciating hour trapped in the Super's office, enduring a litany of tediously self-aggrandising anecdotes. Then, the hour would nearly be up, and Murdoch would suddenly remember James was the subject matter and not him. *'Can't fault your results, James, but in this day and age it's about more than just results, isn't it.'* ('Is it, sir?') *'If you want to climb the greasy pole, James,'* his tone insincerely avuncular, *'you need to be open to… how can I put this… expanding your skillset.'*

'Talking of Solent,' Murdoch said, jerking James back to the present, 'I got talking to one of the young officers from Stevenage, over a lovely strawberry scone; said he was keen to get involved. Told him you'd take him under your wing.'

Murdoch reached for the salad box and rummaged inside again. Seemingly now chicken-free, he upturned the box and shook the leafy contents into his waste bin.

'Okay,' James said. He had a sinking feeling. 'Which one?'

'Tall fella. Built like a brick shithouse.' Murdoch clicked his fingers in rapid succession, as he tried to recall his name: 'DC Porter.'

Of course.

'Keen as bloody mustard, he is, which is a rarity these days. Would be a crying shame not to take advantage, don't you think?'

Despite the mountain of evidence to the contrary, Murdoch was no fool; James knew he was getting Luke for a reason. The Super knew James preferred to work solo, or at least with a small, hand-picked team, where James did the picking.

'Not sure we need anyone new on the team at this stage, sir,' James said, slightly desperately.

Murdoch smiled. 'That doesn't sound very collegiate to me.'

James remained silent. It was futile to put up resistance, and he preferred to fight battles he had a chance of winning.

Murdoch looked at his watch and stood up. 'Hey, why don't you use my office to bring him up to speed? I'll be gone for a couple of hours.'

'Networking, sir?' James said. That was one of the items in the 'expanded skillset' Murdoch wanted him to possess.

'Force politics, James,' Murdoch said. 'You don't know the half of it.'

James held the Super's keyboard upside down and shook it – he couldn't restrain himself. Crumbs rained down onto the desk and he swept them into the waste bin with a piece of paper. He straightened up the monitor, keyboard and mouse, so everything was nicely square. *How can people live in such chaos?* He'd hate anyone to interfere with his desk this way, but James figured that Murdoch would either be grateful or not notice – probably the latter.

As he patted the edges of a stack of papers, James was struck by a curious thought: why was there no portrait of Mrs. Murdoch on the Super's desk? If he could be forgiven for stereotyping, the Super was the sort of man – big-boned, proud, born in the 'sixties and trained in the 'eighties – to have such an item on display. It would be an old, yellowed photograph, professionally done in a studio, with a fancy camera and soft lighting to flatter the skin. Her hair would be neatly coiffed into a bob, possibly held back with a headband. James had never seen Mrs. M, yet he had a strangely well-formed image of the woman in his head: a frumpy version of Penelope Keith; a houseproud battle-axe, ruling her slice of mock-Tudor suburbia with an iron fist. She would be C-of-E, W.I., conservative with a capital and a small C. Clipped vowels would disguise the embarrassment of her working-class origins. Carnal relations transacted with a petticoat on and the lights off. James had never heard the Super refer to her by anything other than 'Mrs. M'; in his head she was a Marjorie.

'So, the Super tells me you're keen?' James said. He was now leafing through a Solent file he'd prepared for Luke.

'Said she's having problems with her boyfriend. Think I may be in there.'

'Huh?'

James looked up. Luke was peering out through a slat in the blinds, presumably towards Mel. He counted to three in his head and exhaled slowly. Give the lad a chance.

'Operation Solent, I mean. What do you know about it?'

'Not much, if I'm being honest with you, guv,' Luke said. 'The Super kind of caught me with my pants down, if you know what I mean. Had to say something that didn't make me look a right dick.'

Not sure you'd have to say anything to achieve that outcome, James thought.

'Sit down then and listen, while I bring you up to speed. You'd better listen hard; I don't like to repeat myself.'

'Pardon?'

For God's sake! How did this cretin get through recruitment?

'Kidding,' Luke said, beaming. 'Go on, shoot.' Luke simulated pistol-shooting with his hands, then slumped down into a chair at the circular meeting table.

'Hilarious,' James said, his tone as dry as paper. 'Remind me to laugh at your next joke.'

James proceeded to explain Solent. It was an operation which involved the co-operation of forces across three counties: Hertfordshire, Bedfordshire and Cambridgeshire. Solent targeted an organized criminal network of human traffickers, who brought vulnerable women, typically from eastern Europe, to the UK, and sold them into prostitution.

'It's an ongoing war, and we've barely scratched the surface in three years,' James said, solemnly.

He looked to Luke and sighed. Shoving a notepad and pen in his direction, James said: 'You might want to be making some notes.'

Luke pointed at his temple and smiled. 'Don't worry, guv, it's all up here.'

I doubt there's much up there at all, James thought.

'This ain't glamorous. This is hard, relentless, often tedious work; it's a conveyor belt of misery. You up to it?'

'You bet. What do you want me to start on, guv?'

'Special Ops are going to raid a suspected brothel tomorrow; we got a lead yesterday. Guess you heard about the suicide?'

Luke's face broke into a beam and he rubbed his hands together, as if warming frozen hands over a November campfire. 'A brothel? Cool.'

'I think you may have a certain image in your head. You can forget about what you might have seen on a lads' weekend in Amsterdam.'

'How did you know about that, guv?' Luke said, dropping his smile.

James ignored him. 'We're talking ruthless, organized gangs bringing in girls from eastern Europe and Russia, on the pretence of giving them a new life, good earnings and bright futures.'

Luke exhaled, his lips making the sound of a balloon rapidly deflating. 'We gonna join the raid, then?'

'Wouldn't normally,' James lied, 'but it's the best way for you to get a true insight; get rid of the rose tint from your spectacles.'

'Where is it?' Luke asked.

James was momentarily distracted by his thoughts. 'What?'

'The brothel.'

'Oh, Stevenage. Your home turf, right?'

James opened the buff folder and removed some black-and-white photographs, then pushed them towards Luke. They showed a three-storey row of buildings: commercial premises on the ground floor, maisonettes above. 'Recognize the place?'

Luke screwed his face up in concentration, before it

snapped to a look of recognition. 'Yes, I know the place. A right shithole. Mum uses the launderette.'

'There's a café there – meet me at nine tomorrow morning. Take the file and read it overnight; you need to know every last detail. Copy?'

FIVE

Isn't it strange that the males are the pretty ones?

Kathy Gibbs could easily watch the birds all day.

She stood at the kitchen sink, hands wrapped around a mug of milky tea, staring out across the dewy lawn. A handsome male blackbird was darting about, pecking, tugging and casting nervous glances. Occasionally it would pause and look in Kathy's direction, tilting its head, almost as if reading her thoughts.

Dawn. Her favourite part of the day, when the world seemed clean and fresh and pure, full of promise. It felt like the joy of dawn was a precious secret she'd discovered – a secret she shared only with the birds.

The blackbird darted under the Portuguese laurel, its jet-black body camouflaged in the shadows, its yellow beak and the circle framing its eye beautifully vivid. Kathy was transfixed by the tiny circle; it grew larger and sharper as everything else shrunk and faded to a blurred smudge, as if she were looking through a telephoto lens.

She was transported to her wedding day, to John slipping the golden band onto her skinny finger; she remembered being terrified the ring would fall off. In the months leading up to the big day, she'd begged John to take it back to the jewellers, to have it made smaller. 'No,' he'd said, laughing, 'what's the point? You'll start getting fat again from the moment we marry, and you'll soon be complaining it's too tight!' He was right, of course. He usually was.

Kathy poured the remainder of her now cold tea into the sink, rinsed out the mug and placed it in the dishwasher. She raised her hand to the light, flexing her swollen fingers, suddenly aware of an uncomfortable tightness around the wedding band. It had crossed her mind, over the years, that she ought to have it enlarged – maybe even replaced with a better one. They could certainly afford it now. But, then she'd always chastise herself for having such materialistic thoughts; it would never be the same. There were thirty years of wonderful memories in those nine carats.

Dropping her hand to rest on the cool, granite work surface, Kathy shifted focus back to the lawn. Her eyes darted about, trying to locate her friend; she couldn't see him anywhere. He must have flown off – probably had a busy day ahead of him. Just like her.

C'mon, Kathy! Snap to it!

She made her way over to the fridge to gather the ingredients.

Today was going to be perfect.

She just knew it.

Kathy was a dab hand with the chef's knife.

It was a fortieth birthday present, and she'd cared for it like it was her baby: honed the blade, kept it sharp with a whetstone and stored it correctly (in a block on the work surface, not loose in a drawer).

She was expertly dicing the onions when she heard a noise in the hallway. Turning to look over her shoulder, a searing pain flashed in her finger; stupidly, she'd carried on chopping, as if on autopilot. She checked the damage, as a bubble of blood welled at the tip of her middle finger. Instinctively, she brought it to her mouth and sucked, turning on the cold tap with the other hand.

'Hey, Mum.' Mark's voice.

'Hello, love. I didn't hear you come in,' Kathy said, putting her finger under the cold stream. 'I've only gone and cut my bloody finger.'

'Let me take a look,' Mark said, as he approached.

Kathy looked down and saw that the water was running pink. The wound must be deep. *Daft cow*.

'Looks nasty. I'll dress it for you.'

Kathy turned to look up into her son's green eyes. They could melt the coldest heart. Mark towered above her – thank God the boys had inherited their dad's genes in that respect.

'Aren't you going to give your old mum a kiss first?' she said, turning her cheek. She felt his stubble brush against her skin, as he bent down to peck her. Closing her eyes for a brief moment, she savoured the warmth and the familiar scent of his deodorant, the same one he used as a teenager.

'Hey, you're crying,' he said.

Kathy wiped the tears with the back of her hand. 'It's the sodding onions,' she said.

When her eyes cleared, she saw that Mark was opening various drawers and doors. 'The first-aid kit's in the cupboard above the microwave – your dad moved it there to make way for some of his home-brewing kit. Said he ran out of room in the garage.'

'Assume he's still in bed?' Mark's tone was short and dismissive.

'Yeah. He didn't come up 'til the early hours this morning. You know what he's like, love.'

'Hmm,' he muttered.

Mark found the first-aid kit and brought it over to Kathy. She withdrew her finger from the water and dried her hand with a tea towel. Unwrapping a sticking plaster, he said: 'Is Shit Dick still coming over?'

Kathy smiled, wistfully. 'Ben said he'd be here by twelve.'

'What about Carla?'

'Yes, Carla, too. I've haven't seen them for months. It'll be nice us all being together again as a family; it's been too long.'

Mark tenderly wrapped the plaster around Kathy's finger.

'How are things going? You know, with…' Kathy asked, realising she'd lowered her voice.

Mark sighed and looked down at the table. 'Yeah, fine. Still early days.'

'Well, I'm pleased for you, love. Your dad will come round eventually; just give him a bit of time.'

'I'd better get my stuff from the car.'

Mark marched off. As he opened the front door, he turned and said: 'Oh, happy anniversary, Mum.'

'Sorry if we woke you, love.'

'I heard the door slam,' John said, opening the fridge and grabbing a carton of milk. He was wearing nothing but his boxer shorts.

'It's Mark,' Kathy replied; 'he's getting his stuff from the car.'

'Staying long, is he?' John took a swig.

''Til Monday, I told you. Ben and Carla are just staying over for one night. They'll be here around lunchtime.'

John returned the milk to the fridge and faced Kathy. He must have noticed her glance at his chin, and he wiped away a dribble of milk with the back of his hand.

Mark walked into the kitchen. 'Dad,' he said, with the slightest nod in John's direction, their eyes never meeting.

'Mark,' John acknowledged. 'Alright?'

'Yeah, fine.'

'Well, I'm going back to bed.'

Mark stepped to one side, looking down at his feet as John walked past him into the hallway, heading to the stairs.

Kathy waited until she heard the sound of John closing the bedroom door, before turning to Mark: 'Why don't you give me a hand with the vegetables, love?'

'What are we having?'

'Rabbit stew. Your dad brought one of his catches out of the freezer in the garage. I'm doing one of my special soups for starters.'

She wasn't going to be serving it until eight that evening – eleven hours away – but Kathy was going to slow cook the rabbit. It tasted much better that way, John said. Personally, Kathy didn't much care for game; turned her stomach, if she were being truthful. But John loved his weekend shooting trips with his pals, and bringing home his kills for the family. Some kind of deep caveman instinct, she supposed. Anyway, starting the prep now meant that if she messed things up, she'd have time to start again.

Get it perfect.

Mark picked up where Kathy left off with the onions. He was slow and methodical; his long, elegant fingers reminded Kathy of his piano-playing days. John didn't much like it, so Mark tended to play after school, before John returned from work. Kathy would enjoy getting dinner ready, as the melodies floated down from his bedroom. He had quite the talent – unlike the rest of them. It was such a shame he'd given up.

Mark flicked his gaze over to Kathy and frowned. In that moment, she realized she'd been standing there, staring wistfully at her handsome son. Her favourite son, if truth be told. Was it a wicked thing to have a favourite? She rationalized it by telling herself that she loved the boys equally, just in different ways.

'Right,' she said, slightly flustered, 'I'll start on the rabbit. Should be defrosted by now.'

'Everything okay with you and Dad?' Mark asked.

Kathy wasn't entirely sure whether that was a loaded question, or an innocent enquiry. She paused for a moment before replying: 'Yeah, fine, love; we're in a good place right now. Everyone who's been married for thirty years will have their ups and downs. We're no different.'

'Okay,' Mark said, and left it at that.

It was gone eleven and John was still in bed, Mark was out on a long walk and the slow cooker was on. Kathy had been doing the housework, and was now perched on the edge of the lounge sofa, the wedding photo album open on the coffee table in front of her.

She was twenty-one when she married; John was twenty-eight. They'd got together when Kathy was fifteen. John was her first and only boyfriend – the only man she'd ever loved. *It'll never last*, her mother had said. Well, Kathy had proven her wrong about that.

Flicking through the pages which charted the wedding day, Kathy smiled at the increasing shoddiness of the photography. Tony – one of John's mates – fancied himself as the next David Bailey. He'd bought himself one of those expensive S.L.R. cameras and converted his shed into a darkroom. John didn't see the point in spending a fortune on the wedding, even though his business was beginning to really take off by then. The trouble with asking Tony to take the photos was that he was very fond of his drink. Fond, too, it turned out, of Kathy's sixteen-year-old brides-maid, Rachel. By the time the D.J. was calling the first dance (Frankie Valli's 'Can't Take My Eyes Off You'), Tony was tending to a broken nose administered by Rachel's enraged and equally inebriated father, Adam. After some gentle persuasion and a stiff sherry, Kathy's blushing aunt Pat had kindly taken charge of Tony's Nikon. 'She's taken some smashing photos with our Polaroid,' Uncle Pete had said, proudly. 'She won't let you down, love.'

The creak of floorboards above her brought Kathy back to the present, and she snapped shut the album. When John entered the room, she was polishing the gold carriage clock on the mantlepiece. She turned to see her husband dressed in his golfing gear, and struggled to smile through the disappointment. He had taken the day off work especially for their anniversary, so they could all be together as a family.

'What time are you doing this dinner for?' he asked.

'Eight. I told you, love,' she said, smiling sweetly. 'Can't you at least wait for Ben and Clara to get here? I'm sure they're looking forward to seeing you.'

John looked down at his watch. 'No, I told the lads I'd be there for twelve. I'll see them later.'

'Okay, love. Have a nice time. Say hello from me, won't you?'

Kathy sometimes wished they had a cleaner. She felt

guilty for thinking it, but it was the truth. For sure, she was grateful for the house, the cars, the holidays; it was all beyond the wildest dreams she'd ever had as a little girl. But it was a big house and it took *forever* to clean.

'Why pay for a cleaner when you've got time on your hands to do it?' That's what John had said when she broached the subject with him. She couldn't argue with his logic. That was the problem: John could only be persuaded by logic and, as he'd told her on many an occasion, she wasn't a very logical person.

Kathy heaved the vacuum cleaner up the stairs and into their bedroom. John had left the bed in a state and the smell of stale body odour made her feel faintly queasy. She opened the window and hot summer air spilled in, but it at least created a small breeze to alleviate the smell. Kathy straightened the bedsheets and patted down the pillows.

The clock radio on John's nightstand showed one-thirty. Mark was still out and there was no sign of Ben and Clara. Kathy wasn't remotely surprised they were late; timekeeping was never one of Ben's strengths.

She looked out of the window, down at the gravel driveway. Before they were married, John told her his dream was to have a house with a horseshoe driveway. That and a lawn big enough for a sit-on mower. Well, bless him, he'd achieved his dream. The Jag and the Porsche were on the drive – Mark's battered old Fiesta, too; John must have taken the Range Rover to the golf club. They had a triple garage, but John mainly kept the cars on the drive; he liked to flaunt his success, did John. Well, to be fair to him, he'd come from nothing, and Kathy was proud of him for all he'd achieved from his hard graft.

Her gaze switched back to the nightstand. Should she? She hovered for a second, lightly flicking a duster over the surface. Then, she opened the drawer. *Stop this, Kathy. You're being paranoid.*

But she couldn't help herself.

Inside the drawer, she found a couple of John's fancy watches, a smattering of loose change and scraps of paper. Some receipts caught her attention: expensive lunches at some of the posh restaurants in town, taxi fares, petrol… Her mind was working overtime. Surely not again? *No, don't be so bloody stupid! He's a businessman, for Christ's sake! He'll need these for his tax return.*

See, she could be logical when she put her mind to it.

Kathy straightened the contents, trying to leave everything how she had found it, and closed the drawer.

Moving over to the wardrobe, she looked inside, casually flicking through the hangers, to decide what she was going to wear for dinner. She pulled out a nice floral dress, still wrapped in the plastic cover. She racked her brain, trying to think of the last time she'd worn it. Ah, yes, it was John's mum's seventieth, way back when. What a beautiful meal that was; they'd gone to the lovely Italian restaurant out of town – John's favourite. 'That's a beautiful dress, Kathy,' his father had said.

'You haven't seen what's under it!' John responded, laughing as he filled his glass with the expensive Malbec.

Kathy's phone buzzed and, after draping the dress over the bed, she took out her phone, to see that it was a text message from Ben.

'Sorry Mum. Running late. Had an argument with Clara. Will just be me. See you soon, B. xxx'

Kathy returned the dress to its hanger.

She was going to wear something black.

.   .   .

Kathy was just finishing a cheese sandwich when Ben finally arrived. Mark had returned from his walk and was watching TV in the lounge.

Ben walked into the kitchen, carrying a box wrapped in silver paper, which he handed to Kathy. Judging by how delicately – for him – he did so, she assumed it must be something fragile. Some kind of ornamental bowl, she guessed, from the size and weight. Expensive, too, no doubt. 'Happy anniversary!' he beamed.

'Thank you, love,' Kathy said, placing the box down on the table. 'I'll open this later with your dad, when he's back from golf.'

'Carla chose it.'

Kathy smiled. 'How is she? You said you argued. Nothing serious, I hope?'

He swatted his hand, dismissively. 'It's nothing. You know those Italians,' he said, as if that explained everything. 'Where's Twat Face?'

'I wish you two wouldn't call each other such horrible names,' Kathy sighed. 'He's in the lounge. Can I get you a bite to eat, love? A sandwich, or something?'

'Tell you what, Mum, I'd kill for a cold beer.'

'Check your dad's fridge in the garage.'

'It's not that home-brewed shit of his, is it? Last time I tried that I had the trots for a week.'

Kathy giggled, but then stopped herself. 'Even he will admit that he hasn't perfected the process yet. You'll find some lager bottles in there: that pilsner stuff he likes. Ask your brother if he wants one.'

'Ask me if I want what?' Mark said. He was standing in the doorway.

Ben spun around. 'Twat Face! I'm getting a beer. Want one? You students love your free drinks, don't you?'

'Hilarious as ever, Shit Dick,' Mark replied. 'Go on then, I'll have one.'

Ben disappeared into the garage, via the utility room, and Kathy caught Mark's gaze shifting to the box on the table. 'Just a little something from Ben and Carla, love.'

'I'm sorry, I can't really afford–'

Kathy walked over to Mark and put her hand against his chest. 'I know, love, and I don't expect anything from you. We're all here as a family – that's the most important thing.'

Mark was wearing a casual checked shirt, the red faded almost to pink. The top two buttons were undone. Instinctively, she moved to the lower button, but Mark brought his hand in front of hers to stop her.

'Sorry, love,' she said, dropping her hands to her sides, and wiping them nervously on the back pockets of her denim skirt.

'I've got a card in my bag for you. I'll go and get it.'

'Ah, that's lovely, sweetheart. Thank you.'

As Mark was walking up the stairs, Ben came back into the kitchen, carrying two lager bottles. Kathy opened the cutlery drawer, found the bottle opener and handed it to Ben.

'How's the business?' she asked, as Ben opened both bottles.

He took a deep swig of beer before responding: 'Roaring, Mum. Absolutely roaring.'

'I'm so proud of you, love. So is your dad – not that he'd ever tell you.'

Ben smiled and took another gulp, virtually emptying the bottle.

Mark entered the kitchen and handed Kathy the card. The envelope wasn't sealed and nothing was written on the front. Mark had clearly learnt that hack from his dad: it meant the envelope could be reused. Kathy paused while she exaggeratedly admired the card and the message inside, then moved to place it temporarily on the windowsill.

'You've left the fucking price tag on, Twat Face,' Ben said, laughing.

Kathy quickly turned the card over and scraped the '99p' sticker off with her fingernail. 'I do that all the time,' she said. 'There's no need for them to put these stickers on like this.'

Ben held out a lager to Mark, arm fully stretched and head turned, as if returning a lost sock. Mark grabbed the bottle and a small amount of beer fell onto Kathy's parquet floor.

'Why don't you two go and have a catch-up in the lounge, while I make the soup?' she said.

She watched as the boys walked through the doorway, their frames virtually filling the space. How could they be so alike, yet so very different? That's what everyone asked. Kathy would find herself, just like now, recalling a time when that wasn't so.

It dawned on Kathy that she'd worked up her own thirst.

She was filling the kettle when she sensed a flicker of movement in her peripheral vision: shifting her focus to the lawn, she saw her blackbird friend. He appeared to be in a spot of bother with a male intruder. The pair were standing perhaps four or five metres apart, sizing each other like avian gladiators; Kathy's friend had his head and tail raised, poised to strike. Dipping his head and tail simultaneously, he charged a metre or two towards his foe, stopping abruptly to stare him down. Seemingly unperturbed, the invader hopped towards danger. This provocative act sent Kathy's friend into a rage and he leapt forward, landing on the other's back. There followed a scene of such frantic activity – flapping, squawking, leaping and diving – that Kathy lost track of which bird was her friend. Eventually one flew off, defeated, in the direction of the Braithwaites' next door. Although uncertain it was him left standing, proud and alone on the lawn, she declared victory for her friend, and imagined him returning triumphantly to his swooning mate.

Kathy cursed when she looked down and realized the kettle was overflowing. John was always telling her that one of these days she'd do herself some serious harm, slipping off into her daydreams like she did.

Kathy was in the bedroom, putting away the ironing. She'd left the boys to their beers and TV; they were watching the cricket, one of their few shared interests. The faint vibrations of the cricket commentary tickled her feet through the carpet, and every now and then she'd hear a congratulatory cheer or an angry shout of remonstration from the boys.

Having put the last of John's t-shirts away, Kathy turned and noticed something she'd missed earlier – she must have been somehow distracted: crumpled on the floor, at the base of the chest of drawers, was a pair of John's trousers. She picked them up, shook them straight and folded them neatly. As she draped them over the back of the chair, Kathy thought she'd better just check his pockets.

John had been a bit off with her in recent weeks. She'd put it down to the stress of managing a successful business, attracting new customers, keeping the existing ones happy, looking after all the staff and staying on top of the accounts. Numerous times over the years Kathy had offered to help out, but he always declined, saying that she was doing a grand job as it was, with the house and the boys. Said she was helping by taking a massive weight off his mind, allowing him to concentrate on the business. Bless him. God, she was proud of the twins: her greatest achievement.

But, what if John had slipped again? Given into temptation? She'd forgiven him last time. It was understandable, what he did: Kathy had been in a bit of a rut, and she wasn't much fun to be around.

She found nothing in John's pockets but a few coppers and one of his business cards. Turning to look out of the window, while absent-mindedly jangling the coins in one hand, and feeling cross with herself for another lapse in her judgement, Kathy swallowed an unformed tear.

She returned the coins to his pocket and started to do the same with the business card, when her thumb ran over a ridge. She turned the card over and let out a little gasp. On the back was a note, written in blue biro: *'Bea'* – underneath was a mobile number.

Who was Bea? John had never mentioned her. It wasn't John's scrawly handwriting. Kathy conjured an image of John standing at a bar in an expensive hotel, chatting to a busty blonde with glossy lips, high heels and butter-wouldn't-melt eyes. A woman who didn't have sagging breasts, childbirth stretch-marks, bingo wings and cellulite. *What's your name, sweetheart? Will you let me buy you a drink?* Hours later, she's stumbling into a taxi. *That was fun, darling. Perhaps we could meet again? What's your number? Here's my business card and a pen; write it on the back.* She raised the card to her nose and took a deep sniff: no hint of perfume.

Stop this nonsense, Kathy castigated herself.

It could be anything or anyone. A new business contact? Dentist? Florist? Cleaner? Perhaps John was lining up someone to help ease her burden: an anniversary surprise?

A big cheer sounded from downstairs, making Kathy jump.

She hastily stuffed the card into her bra and returned to her chores.

SIX

JAMES LOOKED DOWN, breathlessly. A bead of sweat landed on his Garmin Forerunner 620 GPS running watch. He wiped it clean against his shorts.

He ran most days: out before six, back before seven. His route was nearly always the same: out of town and into the countryside, following the single-track road lined with hawthorn hedgerows, across undulating farmland, and climbing the steep ascent up through the woods, then into the affluent village of Preston. James loved the fresh air, the peace and the solitude; it gave him the opportunity to think, mull over problems and come up with solutions.

He slowed down to nine-minute-mile pace, as the village pond honed into view. He was well on track for a half-marathon personal best in the autumn: sub eighty-five minutes. No need to overdo it and risk an injury.

In the distance, James saw the figure of a tall, slim man skulking at the water's edge. As he drew closer, he realized it was a lad: fifteen, sixteen max. The boy flicked his head towards James, but swiftly returned his gaze to the pond. His detective brain went into overdrive: *What's he up to at this hour? This isn't typical teenage behaviour.* James slowed down, eyeing him intently. The boy stood staring at the water, seemingly unaware of the attention. Deciding there was no just cause for intervention, James picked up the pace once more.

He ran beyond the pond, taking a right at the Red Lion, then along Chequers Lane. A dog walker raised her hand, and James tipped his head and uttered a breathless: 'Morning.' He stopped at the gated entrance to the dirt path which took him across farmland, into the wood. A new, handwritten notice there read: *'The alarming rise in dog mess has been noted with dismay. Please use the bins provided.'* Anger welling within him, James passed through the gate and accelerated to six-minute mile pace, for the two-hundred-or-so-metre stretch which took him into the cool shade of Wain Wood.

He dropped his pace, but felt his pulse quicken. The path split in multiple directions and, as ever, James followed the one which skirted the rim of Bunyan's Dell. John Bunyan, the seventeenth-century Baptist, was said to have preached here to his 'gathered church' which, according to the words of a local historian, printed on an information sign at the entrance to the wood, *'numbered sometimes over a thousand souls'*. James stopped and stretched his hamstrings, next to an uprooted tree trunk. Peering down into the dell, he conjured the ghosts of Bunyan's congregation praying for Lena Demyan's soul.

At his feet, James glimpsed a patch of silver, incongruous against the brown of brittle leaf litter. He kicked at it and a discarded Red Bull can revealed itself. He considered for a moment the irony of the person who had drunk it lacking the energy to carry the empty can home, or to a waste bin. The thought made his blood boil, and he reached down to pick up the can. Perhaps it was the teenager he saw earlier, been out all night with a mate, and a bottle of Bacardi stolen from a parent's sideboard? Yes, he was stereotyping, but stereotypes didn't come out of thin air.

Wait. What if the can was *his*?!

What if Perkins himself had been at this very spot, pouring an energy drink down his throat, while getting off on the memory of his vile deed? James was minded to snap on the latex gloves and put the can in an evidence bag, for forensic testing.

His mind had travelled an unjustifiably long way down that train of thought before he mentally slapped himself back to his senses. Even if it was Perkins, what was he going to do? Arrest him for bloody littering?

James picked up the can and turned to run home. He needed to clear his head.

Again.

James arrived at the Oaks Close Centre – a small shopping precinct, a mile or so from Stevenage town centre – shortly after eight. He was early – just how he liked it. He sauntered around, peering through the plate-glass windows and flashing furtive glances at the suspected brothel above the barbers. The place was a bleak concrete jungle, with litter and graffiti in plentiful supply. It was eerily calm. Inside his chest, something fluttered against his ribcage, like a moth in a lampshade. Fear? Nerves? Whatever it was, he gripped it.

He stopped at the newsagents, remembering he was clean out of mints. The shop bell triggered when he stepped inside. On a low shelf he noticed a bundle of papers tied with string: yesterday's *Herald*, ready for return, he assumed. He teased a copy from the bundle and regarded the front page. That journalist woman had been true to her word:

'REWARD FOR INFORMATION

Molly, Tindall, Chief Crime Reporter

Two years on from Lena Demyan's horrific murder, police are no nearer capturing the perpetrator. The Herald is offering a reward of £500 for any new information which leads to the arrest of the man who has been dubbed the "Dell Ripper".

Lena's body was found by a dog walker in Bunyan's Dell, at the Wain's Wood beauty spot in Preston. Her disembowelled body had been covered by leaves and foliage. Lena, 23, of no fixed address, had been sexually assaulted and strangled by a ligature made from her underwear.

Unemployed Troy Perkins, 39, a former forensic science techni-cian who lives alone in Stevenage, was arrested and charged with Lena's murder shortly after her body was discovered. The charges were subsequently dropped, after another sex worker, who claimed to have witnessed Ms. Demyan getting into Mr. Perkins's car, refused to provide a written witness statement. Subsequently, police have been unsuccessful in their attempts to locate the witness. No forensic evidence was found linking Mr. Perkins to the crime. Mr. Perkins has previously served a two-year prison sentence for offences relating to prostitution and sexual assault.'

James allowed himself a brief smile. Then sighed.

The chances of anyone reading the paper and coming forward with new information, after all this time, were small and vanishing. Still, he had to try. Somebody had to try.

'You going to pay for that paper?'

He looked up to see a dishevelled-looking man behind the counter: messy hair, moist brow, ashen complexion, inky fingers, pencil tucked behind his ear, tired eyes... James decided he was a Terry.

'What's the problem?' James said. 'You're sending them back, aren't you? No skin off your nose.'

'I'm not providing a bloody library service.'

James sighed. 'Right, if you want to play it like that…' He rummaged in his pocket for some change and made his way to the counter. 'How much?'

'Eighty-five pence.'

'Bargain,' James said dryly, placing the paper on the countertop.

'Anything else?'

He caught an unpleasant whiff: stale sweat, tobacco, an old t-shirt – not pleasant; he winced. 'Yes, as a matter of a fact…' James scanned his options. 'I'll take a couple of packs of Polos, pack of Trebors, tin of Smints and… er… a bag of Fox's Glaciers.'

Terry's lips parted, to reveal a mouth missing several teeth. 'You must like your mints?'

'That a crime?'

'Course not. Just making polite conversation.'

Terry rang up the price on the till, as James grabbed the various packets, stuffing them in his trouser and jacket pockets. He threw a tenner at the man. 'Keep the change, Terry.'

'Terry? My name's Keith.'

'Wasn't far off. 'Bye, Keith.' James turned and headed for the door.

'Not taking your paper, mate?'

'You can keep the bloody rag.'

He swept out of the shop. As the door shut behind

him, he tipped several Tic Tacs into his mouth, then checked his watch.

In his corner seat at Abby's Café, next to the window, James drained his black coffee. The place was surprisingly busy. Maybe it was the prices: four quid for a full English and a hot drink. Several groups of tradesmen were engaged in loud, animated chatter, while a handful of elderly couples ate in slow-motion silence, as if awaiting death's sweet embrace. Immediately in front of him, an old woman – late eighties? – wrapped in a headscarf and wearing a coat buttoned to her neck, despite the warmth, was staring at the wall behind James; at first, he'd thought she was looking right at him. He glanced over his shoulder, but there was nothing of any note on the wall, to justify her attention. He realized then that she wasn't looking at anything in the room. Fingers grotesquely warped, she struggled to open a small sachet of salt: arthritis, presumably. Eventually, the packet tore open and the contents spilled into her milky tea. Still staring at nothing, she stirred her drink with a plastic spoon, as if creating a vortex into which she could jump and transport herself to a happy oblivion. The scene made him think of his mother.

A shadow loomed outside, and James turned to see Luke's insufferably cheerful face beaming through the window. At least he was early; he'd be awarded points for that. Fair's fair.

'Alright, guv?' Luke said, taking the seat opposite James. His bulky frame completely obscured the arthritic woman behind him, now complaining to the waitress that her tea was disgusting.

'See what I mean about this place?' Luke said, seemingly oblivious to being within earshot of just about everyone in the café – not that anyone showed a reaction. 'Absolute shithole, isn't it?'

'You've read the case file, I assume?'

'What can I get you, love?' The waitress was now at their table: a small woman, lined face of a heavy smoker, with a stained tea towel slung over her shoulder and a pen in hand, poised to write on a tiny pad. Her weak smile didn't disguise the sadness in her eyes. Still, he couldn't fault her service; he'd be leaving a generous tip.

'Full English, ta. Extra sausage and bacon; easy on the mushrooms,' Luke said, cheerfully.

'No eggs,' James interjected.

'Sorry, guv?'

James waved a hand under his nose. 'Got this thing with smells: hyperosmia. Egg's the worst.'

Luke's brow furrowed. 'O-kay. Any particular reason why'd you choose to meet in a greasy spoon, then?'

'Hmm, good question. Guess I'm a masochist.'

The waitress coughed. 'Drink?'

'Tea, please,' Luke said, then turned to James. 'That acceptable?'

'Of course.'

'Anything else for you, love?' the waitress asked James, sweeping up his spent coffee mug.

'No, thank you.'

The waitress departed.

James had no appetite. By rights it should be the rookie feeling the nerves, not the old-timer.

'I was saying,' James said, 'have you read the case file?'

'Of course. Finished it this morning, after my run: five miles before breakfast.'

A fellow runner. James considered for a moment asking his best half-marathon time, but thought better of it, lest the answer depress him. He raised an eyebrow. 'Already had breakfast?'

Luke gave James a look which suggested he was asking a daft question.

Conversation quickly dried up. Luke thrummed his fingers on the laminate tabletop, as he stared out of the window, each strike ratcheting up James's blood pressure. At the point where James could bear it no longer, Luke turned back his head, grinning. 'Have you noticed the shop names?' he asked.

'What do you mean?'

'The puns. Look over there: the barbers.'

'"Zack the Clipper",' James noted, forcing a smile.

'And, there: the flower shop.'

'"Florist Gump".'

'It's like they're in some kind of competition. Launderette next door's called "Launderetcetera". Latin, isn't it? Wasted on the clientele around here.'

'Your breakfast's here,' James said, somewhat relieved when he spotted the waitress heading over.

Luke gobbled his food as if his life depended on it. James allowed his thoughts to drift to a distant memory, of a leisurely Sunday breakfast with Ruth. They were seated either side of the breakfast bar, Ruth in her silk kimono, loosely tied at the waist. She held a slice of toast, waving it around as she talked excitedly – about what, it didn't matter. Crumbs must have been flying about everywhere, but James couldn't remember being bothered about them back then. That was actual happiness, wasn't it? Not just his imagination.

Luke muffled a postprandial belch under a paper napkin, and James was back in the room.

'Time to go soon,' James said. 'Just hang back with me. No heroics, okay?'

Luke circled a finger above his empty plate. 'Who's paying?'

Half an hour later, the team were assembled on the external concrete staircase, James and Luke holding back behind six Special Ops officers – their leader, Sergeant Goff, mouthing instructions before initiating a fingered countdown. Two officers wielding a jammer stepped forward and rammed it hard against the white U.P.V.C. door. Four attempts and it was off its hinges. The team piled in, James and Luke in tow.

A dark, narrow hallway: threadbare carpet; bare walls, smeared and scuffed. Heavy footsteps reverberated. A foul stench of dank, stale air and body odour. James felt himself retching and held a hand to his mouth.

'Police!' Goff hollered.

The Ops Team split, with half disappearing upstairs. Luke followed.

Then came scurrying footsteps.

Banging.

Screaming.

Doors slamming.

'Police! Don't move!'

James, struggling to remain in the present, paused and steadied himself against the stair bannister. The noises around him became more distant, distorted as if his head were underwater. He heard a thudding sound to his left: an officer throwing his weight against a padlocked door. The door burst open and James peered in.

A woman – a girl – on a dirty mattress, with her head down, legs tightly tucked into her chest; long, dark red hair draped to her feet. A narrow shaft of light came through thick curtains. Should he go in?

A voice from above shouted: 'Up here!'

James shook his head as if trying to remove water from his ears. He bounded up the stairs. He was in a long corridor, with multiple doors leading off it. James forced himself to avoid peering into any of the rooms, and headed towards the huddle of officers at the far end. One was being hoisted through a hatch, into the loft space.

'What's happening?' James said, breathlessly.

'The buggers have scarpered up there. It must run the whole length of the building.'

'We can't let them get away,' James said, stating the blindingly obvious.

'Guv!' Luke's voice. He stood in a doorway. 'In here.'

James entered the room: an office, hurriedly cleared. Cables and paper were strewn over a tatty desk. A black-and-white monitor in the corner showed a view of the battered front door.

'Christ!' James said, slamming his fist onto the desk. 'I didn't see any sign of cameras.'

'Could be anywhere, guv,' Luke said. 'They can make them tiny these days.'

James grimaced. Scanning the room, he said: 'See what you can find among all this; there's got to be something here.'

Crackled conversation over police radio came from the hallway, too indistinct for James to comprehend.

Goff walked in, solemn-faced. 'Afraid we've lost them, sir. Must have slipped out through another property.' He glanced at the monitor; 'Seems they planned for this eventuality.'

'God's *sake*!'

'I've got a couple of officers speaking to the locals, to get descriptions; any intel on where they may have gone…'

Goff's words trailed off, as James moved over to Luke

and snatched a few sheets of paper from the desk, but he couldn't focus on the printed words. The air was thick and fetid, and he felt bile rising in his throat. 'Get a window open!'

'It's locked, guv,' Luke said.

'They're all locked,' Goff added.

James rushed out into the corridor, where three girls were being led cautiously down the stairs. The one at the rear looked as though her legs were about to buckle, and the officer held her tightly around the waist. James followed. In the downstairs hall, the girls were lined up against the wall.

'You're safe; we're getting you out of here,' the female officer said slowly, calmly.

The girls were terrified, understandably. James counted six. Most looked to the floor; some were holding hands; all were trembling. It was difficult to guess their ages, but he wouldn't be surprised if some were still in their teens. Children. James's thoughts turned to their mothers, and his head began to hurt like hell.

An officer came through the doorway to say that the van was ready. The girls were being taken to a place of safety.

'Wait!' James suddenly said.

He knew it was desperate – futile even – but he had to try; he owed it to her. Retrieving the photograph from his pocket, he walked along the line. 'Do you recognize this woman?'

Some stole quick glances at the picture, while others turned away. James doubted many of them understood much English. Undoubtedly, too, they'd be ravaged from the effects of drugs and alcohol. Not one showed the slightest hint of recognition. He returned the picture to his pocket and the girls filed out.

James had to get out, too, before he threw up.

He flopped onto a bench outside, convinced his heart was beating at a rate which wasn't medically possible. He clutched his chest, willing it to calm, as pain ripped through him. Was it a heart attack? It certainly felt like his heart was being torn apart. A boiling stew of emotions bubbled inside him: visceral rage, that the bastards harbouring those poor girls had escaped; anger that he hadn't prevented it; a profound and crushing outrage that situations like this could even happen in this day and age; a pitiful fear that he had failed, once again, to keep a sacred promise he had made. It took all his energy to resist throwing back his head and howling like a wolf. *I'm so sorry, sweetheart.*

In his head, he heard her soft voice respond, and he closed his eyes so that he could see hers. In an instant he felt the rise and fall of his chest quell; he saw the shape of his tortured face reflected in her liquid honey eyes. His cheek twitched when he felt the faintest wisp of her breath, and a warmth radiated to his neck and down his spine, dispersing like an electric current, to the tips of his fingers and toes. *You're doing fine, James. Just fine.*

'You okay, guv?'

James looked up and, as the image of Ruth fell away, he saw Luke's concerned face.

'Fine. Just needed some air.'

Luke held out a piece of paper.

'Found something?'

'Maybe,' Luke said, handing it to James. 'An accountant's invoice.'

James scanned it; his vision had returned to normal, thankfully. The invoice was for services rendered in the production of the final accounts, addressed to Skylark Enterprises, Ltd.; no individual's name was stated.

'It'll be a front,' James said; 'give them a veneer of legitimacy. Find out what you can about this company when you're back in the office: directors' names, share-holders, holding company, filed accounts... Follow the money.'

'Will do, sir.'

'Not exactly Amsterdam in there, was it?' James said.

Luke looked chastened. 'No, guess not. At least they're safe now, eh?'

'They're safe. But there's plenty more impressionable young women out there to take their place. I guarantee it. Nature abhors a vacuum, and all that.'

Luke puffed his cheeks, looked at his feet, then said: 'Kind of makes me feel ashamed to be a man.'

A silence followed and Luke looked about awkwardly, as if searching for a conversation topic on which to latch. Eventually, he said: 'They've missed a trick with the chippy there: Smith's Fish and Chips; I can think of a few puns they could have used.'

James raised his brow.

'"The Codfather"?'

James looked down at the invoice. 'This accountant, the address isn't far from here. Think we'll pay him a visit.'

RŪTA

'It's only a phone call,' Rūta said, giggling; 'he's not going to *see* you.'

Urtė was standing at the mirror, applying a thick layer of mascara. 'I know, dummy, but he'd be able to tell from my voice if I wasn't wearing makeup.'

Rūta knew it was futile to question her best friend's logic.

'How long now?' Urtė said.

'Five minutes.'

'This is so exciting,' Urtė squealed. 'One more day and we'll be leaving Lithuania behind!'

Rūta was the more grounded of the pair, but she couldn't help getting swept up in Urtė's enthusiasm; it was totally infectious. You could never stay down for too long with Urtė around; she brought a ray of sunshine to the darkest corner. There had been plenty of dark corners in Rūta's life, but Urtė's friendship had been a constant. Life wouldn't be worth living if Urtė wasn't in it.

Rūta had done all the work to find the agency; she could never have left that to Urtė: God-only knew what she would have found. Rūta wasn't stupid – she had a degree in business management! – though nor, to be fair, was Urtė; perhaps *naive* would be a more accurate descriptor. The internet was littered with tales of duped young girls trafficked into unimaginably awful trades – 'modern slavery' it was called, and Rūta shivered whenever she read the words. The agency she had found – Perry Johnstone International Hospitality Recruitment Agency, to be precise – was totally legit.

'Perry,' Urtė had said; 'such an English name!' Like she'd know!

The agency had a professional website with glowing reviews – Rūta had taken the trouble to email a handful of them, to check they were genuine. The man they dealt with at the agency – their *consultant* (how very grand!) – was called Jack, and although Urtė had been disappointed not to be dealing with Perry himself, she nonetheless decided that Jack looked like Hugh Grant from that film she'd seen, like, twenty times, *Notting Hill*. Rūta didn't have any grand delusions about the work he'd lined up for them; they'd be starting from the bottom: hotel reception work, cleaning dishes in the kitchen, that sort of thing. It didn't matter; as long as they worked hard, there would be no limit to where their careers could take them.

They were in Urtė's bedroom, the slightly smaller of the two in their minuscule Vilnius apartment, above the baker's shop. Urtė didn't grumble, as hers had a bigger window. 'The light's better for applying my makeup,' she said. They'd happily served notice to their miserable and miserly landlord, Jokubas, a month ago.

Urtė had been living out of her suitcase for nearly a week, having packed in a rush of excitement. The few items they had, and couldn't take with them, Rūta had taken to the charity shop. Jokubas had offered to take some items – the TV, a small kitchen table and stools – off their hands for the new tenant, but Rūta wasn't minded to give him something for nothing.

'Dialling in now,' Rūta said.

She was sitting cross-legged on the bed. Urtė sat down on the edge and the mattress squeaked. Rūta wasn't going to miss the sound of this squeaky mattress through the thin wall.

'Hello, Jack?' Rūta said. Her English was far superior to Urtė's, so she did most of the talking in their meetings. 'Rūta and Urtė here.'

Urtė waved jazz hands.

'Hello, ladies,' Jack said, his voice as smooth as honey.

Urtė held her hands to her bosom – of which Rūta was extremely envious, but tried to never let on – and mouthed the word 'ladies'. Urtė had got it into her head she was going to marry into the English aristocracy.

'Are you excited about tomorrow?' Jack asked.

Rūta covered the phone and quickly translated for Urtė's benefit.

'Yes!' Urtė exclaimed.

'All the paperwork's in place this end, so you've got nothing to worry about. All you need are your passports, work visas, air tickets and enthusiasm for hard work. Oh, and great big smiles.'

'Yes, we have everything,' Rūta said.

'Great, I can't wait to meet you both tomorrow. I'll have someone pick you up at the airport. Call me if you need anything. Have a great flight, ladies.'

After Rūta ended the call, Urtė jumped to her feet and bounced several times, clapping her hands. 'Wait there!' she said.

Not going anywhere, Rūta giggled to herself.

Moments later, Urtė had returned with a bottle of

champagne and two clear plastic cups. Well, it was sparkling wine really, but who cared? It went down the same way. She handed the cups to Rūta and, clamping the bottle between her thighs, she teased out the cork which fired across the room, leaving a mark on the wall; wine spilled to the floor.

'Up yours, Jokubas!' Urtė said, as she filled the cups to the brim.

'To our new lives,' Rūta said.

SEVEN

THE ENTRANCE WAS A SIDE DOOR, behind Ali's Kebabs. *'C.D.M. Accountancy Services'* was written in gold acrylic letters, stuck to the frosted glass – although it seemed that some wit had peeled off the letter *'o'*. The door buzzed and James pushed the door in reply, entering a small foyer containing a parched pot plant, a half-full water cooler and an out-of-order lavatory. A staircase led to the office and, as he and Luke climbed it, James pondered why so much of his work on Operation Solent seemed to be conducted above takeaways, in towns like Stevenage.

As they entered the office, James's nostrils were assaulted by a host of odours: the all-too-familiar whiff of stale sweat, barely ameliorated by cheap deodorant (Lynx Africa? He remembered the Christmas presents). But there was something else; an open window and the distant hum of the kebab shop's extractor revealed the culprit. James swallowed a gag reflex and extended his arm, as the man rose from behind his desk to greet them.

The man's hand was warm and clammy. Shaking

hands with sweaty urchins was an unavoidable occupational hazard, alas. Afterwards, James surreptitiously wiped his palm on the seat of his cloth chair.

'So, how can I help you fellas?'

James flashed his ID and introduced himself and Luke. He swore that the man's face turned white.

As a gust of wind wafted a cloud of kebab-air into the room, the vertical blinds rattled. He raised the back of a hand to his nostrils and puffed his cheeks. 'Actually, do you mind?' James said, pointing to the window. 'I've got a particularly sensitive nose, I'm afraid.'

'Oh, yeah, of course. Sorry,' the man said. 'Kind of don't notice after a while.'

As the man slouched to the window, James took the opportunity to scan the room – and pop a Polo.

If there was one word which described the ambience of the office, it would be 'yellow'. The woodchip walls, suspended ceiling tiles, plastic desk-fan… all screamed it. And not a buttercup yellow or sunshine yellow, nor certainly 'Vanilla Sundae' (Ruth's choice for the nursery – who was he to argue?). No, rather an insipid, sickly, 1970s yellow. Austin Allegro yellow. Old family photographs yellow. Nicotine-stain yellow. Jaundice.

A row of steel filing cabinets lined one wall, on top of which were a dusty yucca and bundles of string-tied papers.

Thud.

Colin closed the window, and the throb of the extractor unit became a faint hum.

James flicked his attention to the desk and took a business card from a stack, stealing a quick look at his name – Colin Montgomery. Seriously? – pocketing the card just as Colin turned around.

Colin dropped into his chair, and pushed his black-rimmed glasses up a bulbous nose beaded with sweat. James formed quick opinions of people based on appearances (he was only human), but was open-minded enough to modify them in light of subsequent evidence – which was a useful trait, given his job description.

Colin wore a cream-coloured shirt, which was probably white eons ago, and bursting at the belly. Unbuttoned collar, with a brown Paisley tie, lazily knotted. Bald head; flushed face; a smattering of freckles; sweaty brow… Restless hands, with no wedding band. Mid-thirties, James guessed.

He conjured an image of Colin's home environment: a one-bed flat in an 'eighties block; black, faux-leather recliner; remote control for an oversized TV, perched on the glass of a cheap Argos side-table – well-utilized Netflix subscription. Takeaway boxes would be piled haphazardly on the kitchen drainer. A dusty computer desk sat in a dark corner of a Star Wars-themed bedroom – box of Kleenex within easy reach.

James was seated casually, one ankle perched on a kneecap. He swept imaginary dust from his thigh, then looked to Colin and smiled. 'Guess you're wondering why we're here, Colin? Don't mind if I call you Colin, do you?'

Colin shrugged.

'Lovely name, by the way. Solid. Don't hear enough of it these days, if you ask me. Oh, where are my manners? I'm DCI James Quinn and this is D.C…' *Oh, God, what's his name?* '…Luke Porter. Now, the reason for our impromptu visit is that we've just conducted a raid in the Oaks Close Centre: a maisonette above a barbershop.'

'Jack the Clipper,' Luke offered helpfully, with a chuckle.

Colin Montgomery didn't chuckle. His mouth twitched, nervously.

'Heard of it, Colin?' James asked, innocently.

'Can't say I have.'

James regarded the accountant's smooth, pink dome and smiled. 'Don't suppose you've much need. Anyway, you'll never guess what we found.'

Colin's gaze flicked between James and Luke. He frowned. 'No idea. Sorry.'

'Well apart from six young women, held against their will and forced to perform sexual services—'

Colin jumped to his feet. 'Wait! Wait! What has this got to do with me? I know nothing about any of that.'

'Sit down, Colin, please. Here's the thing: we found an invoice there, from your good self. Nice logo, by the way. Show the man, DC Porter.'

Luke handed over the Skylark invoice. Colin regarded it for a moment, then slumped back into his chair.

'Yes, this is mine,' he said. 'But, you've got to believe me, as far as I knew Skylark was a straightforward online merchandising business: you know, men's toiletries… that kind of thing.'

'Of course: men's toiletries. Who's the managing director? The Big Cheese?'

'I can't say.'

'Can't say or won't say, Colin?'

'I'm bound by client confidentiality.'

James leant forward and slammed his fist onto the desk. 'And some of those women were bound with nylon cable ties! We need to find the people responsible and you're going to help us.'

Colin looked down at his hands; he was fiddling nervously with his fingers.

'It won't take us long to get a warrant to search your office, Colin. Who knows what little secrets may be lurking in those filing cabinets, waiting to be uncovered?'

Colin licked his lips. 'Okay, okay, his name is Marcus Pinto.'

'And, where might I find Mr. Pinto?'

'He runs a number of businesses – I only do the accounts for this one. I believe he bases himself at his club in Harpenden.'

'Club?'

'Yeah, a private drinking club.'

'Sounds good, Colin; we'll check him out. And don't be doing anything stupid, like tipping him off, will you?'

'Please don't tell him I told you.'

'Mum's the word, Colin. Don't get up; we'll see ourselves out. Oh, and if I ever feel like breaking into the men's toiletries business, I'll know where to come.'

'Wouldn't it have been easier just to look up Skylark on the Companies House website, guv? Could have probably found Pinto's details in a jiffy.'

'And where the hell's the fun in that? I pity your generation; Mister Google has sucked all the joy out of life.'

Luke smiled. 'If you say so, guv.'

They arrived back at the car park at the Oaks Close Centre. There was a battered old Citroën Saxo parked far too close to James's silver Audi A4 Quattro for his liking. 'Bloody hairdressers,' he exclaimed. 'How difficult can it be to keep that thing inside the white lines?'

'Er, that's my motor, guv.'

James raised his brow and resisted a grin. 'Right. Suppose we'll be taking mine to Harpenden, then? Squeeze in, young man, and don't chip my paintwork.'

He zapped the Audi's central locking with his fob and got inside.

Luke contorted himself into the car, picking up James's Nikon from the passenger seat as he did so. 'Hobby, guv?'

Now, should he give Luke the long or the short answer to his question? The long answer required James to explain that he'd been privately stalking Troy Perkins, ever since the murder charge was dropped. 'No realistic prospect of a conviction,' the Crown Prosecution Service had reckoned. Myopic bastards! They wouldn't have been so dismissive if they'd witnessed Perkins's slow metamorphosis from sex pest to fledging killer… If they knew the depressing details of his dysfunctional childhood: the violent father, the crack-addict mother, the lack of friends, his interest in experiments involving the family pets… If they had the full picture of the workplace harassment complaints, his inability to form lasting relationships with women, his fondness for using the services of sex workers, his history of stalking women who'd spurned his advances, his lack of empathy, his narcissism… That whole disembowelment business was straight out of the Jack-the-Ripper playbook. Troy Perkins was a sociopath; a serial killer in the making – it didn't take a degree in psychology to figure that out.

So, why was James the only one who could see it? Perhaps others *could* see it, but chose not to care? He'd heard senior officers, in unguarded moments, call women like Lena Demyan 'scrubbers', 'slappers' and 'prozzies'. Women like Lena Demyan knew the risks they were taking; they drank; they took drugs; they went out on their own at night, to have sex with strange men. Violent men. Women like Lena Demyan were never truly 'innocent'; they were fair game.

But James wasn't going to stand for it.

On balance, he decided in favour of the short answer.

'Yeah, hobby,' he said. 'Now, pop that camera on the back seat, will you?'

He put the Audi into gear. 'Buckle up, Porter. This beast is capable of breaching thirty, so I hope you've packed a clean pair of underpants!'

James had conjured an image of the Garrick, so he was disappointed to find the Kipling Club was in the basement of a nondescript, three-storey building in a Harpenden side street.

'Mr. Pinto shouldn't be too much longer,' the manager who introduced herself as Tracey said. She was an elegant looking woman: grey trouser-suit, pink blouse, light makeup and loosely bunched, black hair. There was a slight glint of mischief in her eyes. 'He's not in any trouble, is he?'

'Just routine enquiries. Mind if we take a look around while we wait?'

'Sure, no problem; I'll give you the guided tour. We're quiet at the moment, before the usual lunchtime rush.'

'What kind of customers do you get in here?' Luke asked. 'Anyone famous?'

Tracey tapped the side of her nose and gave Luke a flirtatious look. 'Now, that would be telling, wouldn't it?'

They followed Tracey out of her office, and along a wood-panelled corridor lined with artwork: fox-hunting scenes; English landscapes; dogs playing poker.

Tracey gestured to a door: 'That's Mr. Pinto's office.'

'I hear he has a number of businesses,' James said.

'Yes, he's a busy man – really successful. He's got a lovely Maserati. You into cars, Inspector?'

'No, but my colleague is; drives a V-reg Citroën Saxo. Lovely shade of go-faster purple.'

'It's all I can afford on my meagre salary,' Luke said.

'You poor thing, love.'

Tracey opened another door. 'This is the main bar. Lovely, don't you think? It's not changed much in eighty years. As you can imagine, we like our tradition here.'

James stuck his head through, catching the not-unpleasant scent of polished brass and freshly-cut flowers. He scanned the room: more artwork in gilt frames; deep carpet; thick velvet curtains at the high windows; crimson-draped, round tables; red leather booths; low lighting. There were perhaps a dozen customers scattered about the room, all middle-aged, white men.

A black-suited man stood behind the extravagantly stocked bar, proudly polishing a wine glass. James rarely frequented bars and pubs these days; he wasn't much of a drinker. He was struck by a sudden childhood memory of his mother, when she was landlady at the Royal Oak, his home up to the age of fifteen. She was in her element chatting with the punters, calling time and deftly handling those who'd had one pint too many. He vividly recalled one afternoon, before the pub had opened, when his brother David brought him downstairs and convinced him to try a shot from every optic. A couple of hours later, James was wrapped around the loo, wondering if his stomach was ever going to stop heaving. 'You've learnt a valuable lesson today, James,' his mother said, later that day: 'don't blindly do as your brother tells you.'

'Fancy a drink while you're waiting, chaps?' Tracey said, snapping James out of his trip down Memory Lane.

'No, thanks; not while we're on duty.' James looked at his watch. 'Shall we head back to your office? Perhaps you could give him a call.'

'Sure.'

Back in the corridor, Luke pointed to another door: 'What's through there?'

'Oh, that's the function room. Let me show you.' Tracey took a set of keys from her pocket and unlocked the door.

The room was spacious, but had a certain warmth and intimacy, like a theatre – perhaps because the thick carpet and heavy drapes lining the walls had the effect of dampening the acoustics. At the far end was a makeshift stage. There were neatly stacked tables and chairs pushed against the walls, covered in dust sheets, a fire exit in one corner and a curtained doorway in another.

'We use it for all sorts of events: charity galas, summer balls, cabaret nights… Great fun. We had a stand-up comic here last week.'

'Lovely,' James said, laconically. He checked his watch. 'Your office?'

They emerged from the club and made their way to the car park at the rear.

'Well, that's an hour of my life I'm never going to get back,' James grunted.

'Do you think that accountant tipped him off after all?'

'Dunno. Try calling Pinto when we're back in the office. Take a look at the businesses he's connected with; get hold of the accounts; look for money flows between companies: any large transactions or patterns. Find out the names of the directors and major shareholders; dividends paid; evidence of cash payments. How much is membership at the club? Do the numbers stack up? Income, expenditure, assets, liabilities. Wouldn't surprise me one bit if money's being laundered through the business – same goes for the barbers. Speak to the forensic accounting team. And contact Goff; see where they got with locating any of the Stevenage gang: any leads, sightings, etc. See if any of the women provided descriptions. Look into that accountant, too. Got all that?'

'Yes, guv.'

They got to the Audi as Luke asked: 'Don't see yourself frequenting joints like this then, guv? Mixing with the great and good of Hertfordshire society?'

'I'd rather gouge out my eyes with a teaspoon.'

'So, I'll put you down as a *maybe*, then?'

There was the rumble of another car arriving, and James turned around to see a familiar grey Jaguar XF. He smiled. The Jaguar parked up and the driver emerged.

'What are you doing here?' the Super asked, timidly, his eyes flicking between Luke and James.

'Following a lead from the raid; Marcus Pinto's name came up. Know him?'

'Know *of* him, obviously. How would he be linked?'

'Well, that's what we're trying to establish. The fella's gone AWOL.'

'Okay, well, keep me informed.'

'Of course, sir.' James paused, before adding: 'So, are you a member here, then?'

'Yes, I come here every now and then to catch up with colleagues past and present, over a drink in a discreet environment. You might want to try it sometime.'

'Too much work on at the moment, sir, but I'll give it some thought. Porter and I are heading back to the office now.'

'Right, well, see you later then.'

'Aren't you going to ask how the women are, sir?'

'Women? What women?'

'From the brothel raid. There were six of them. They're all safe and well now, you'll be pleased to hear.'

'That's great stuff.' Murdoch looked at his watch. 'Well, best get on.'

'Indeed. See you back at the office.'

EIGHT

MOLLY DECIDED ENOUGH WAS enough and left the office. It was approaching eight p.m. and only she and the cleaners were left in the building. And security, of course – by which she meant Bernie on the front desk, who was having forty winks, seemingly exhausted by the mental effort required to complete today's Sudoku.

She'd managed to get her article completed in time for the deadline, but was Brian happy? Was he buggery!

'This is meant to be about street fighting in Baldock,' he said, slapping the paper with the back of his hand, 'not faulty wiring and leaky U-bends. Who's going to read this crap?'

Molly was on the verge of telling him to shove the article where the sun didn't shine and handing in her notice right there and then. Oh, how she'd dreamt of making a dramatic exit. It was always done like that on the TV, wasn't it? An epic fit of pique, in the middle of a crowded office; a finger jabbed at the boss's chest; the swivel and the flouncy exit; the collective intake of breath from a gathered crowd. But life didn't imitate art; the only other person in earshot was Fat Ken from accounts, who was too busy shaking his Lion Bar free from the vending machine to notice or care. And, when she remembered that she had a mortgage to pay and a life-style to maintain, she pulled back from the brink and said, through gritted teeth: 'Okay, Brian, I'll see what I can do.'

He replied, 'Don't bother; there's no bloody time now,' and returned huffily to his office. 'Bloody amateurs,' he cursed, as he closed the door.

'Takes one to know one, prick!' Molly said, as she sat down and immediately started searching the internet for job vacancies. She couldn't care less if anyone saw her.

She made her way to the car park. Her white Range Rover Evoque – a small fortune: cheers, Mother! – was parked as usual at the far end. She figured that people who were prepared to walk farther would be more considerate when opening their doors. So far, her hypothesis held firm. As she foraged for the keys in the bag junk of her Louis Vuitton Neverfull MM (oh, the irony), she heard the sound of a car's engine starting up – it made a horrible throaty rattle, in stark contrast to the quiet purr of the Evoque. Molly looked back to see who it might be.

She couldn't quite make out the car, let alone the occu-pant, but couldn't bring herself to admit that her eyesight wasn't perfect. But it was definitely a shitty looking car – an old, red thing. One of the cleaners', perhaps? It reaffirmed her decision to park as far away as possible from the build-ing. Ah, here were her keys, hiding underneath a packet of Marlboro Lights.

As she pulled out onto the main road, the low sun streamed into the cabin and she was momentarily dazzled. She yanked down the visor and a warning bleep told her she'd drifted over the white line. *Thank God for technology,* she thought, as she corrected her position, though at this time the roads were pretty clear of traffic.

The Evoque still had that intoxicating new car smell, which Molly inhaled heartily. It seemed to have some kind of restorative effect on her mood. She switched on the radio: Abba's 'Waterloo' was playing. She turned up the volume and joined in the chorus with gusto.

Fifteen minutes or so later, she tripped the right blinker and turned into Rectory Lane; another two miles and she'd be home. Then, glancing in the rear-view mirror, she saw a red car behind her, somewhat distant. The same one from the car park? She couldn't tell.

Molly had attracted her fair share of cranks and perverts over the years, so she was cautious in situations like this – perhaps even bordering on the paranoid. She decided to slow right down and move closer to the verge, to see how he'd react – assuming, of course, that it was a *he*. There was a rape alarm in the glove box if needed, and she wouldn't hesitate to use all the weapons at her disposal: lungs, nails, teeth, a knee to the bollocks if necessary. A shrinking violet she was not.

The car – Peugeot? Definitely French – sped by. She couldn't make out the driver, but there was no indication that he was remotely interested in her.

Silly mare!

Molly slammed her foot on the accelerator, cranked up the radio and belted out Meat Loaf's 'Bat out of Hell', all the way to her cutesy, eighteenth-century Datchworth cottage.

With low beams, uneven floors, winter draughts and positively overflowing with character features, the place was tiny; 'Bijou' she called it. For the same money, she could have got a double-glazed, bland box of a house twice the size, but she found them somehow soulless. Was she looking for depth in her home, to counterbalance the shallowness of everything else?

Outside the adjoining cottage, Molly noticed that the *'Sold'* sign had come down from the weed-filled front garden, and there was a self-hire van parked out front. The cottage had been empty since Mrs. Lipton had died, months ago. She'd be turning in her grave at the state of the place now. There was a light on inside, and Molly was glad to have a neighbour again; it could get very dark and quiet out here in the sticks. She wondered who it was, and what they were like.

Inside, she dumped her bag on the floor and bolted the door, then went into the tiny sitting room and switched on the TV, without really thinking about it. She had no idea what was on, but it made her feel like she had company. Silly, really. Now, what to eat?

In the kitchen, she opened the larder cupboard and surveyed the options. She couldn't be bothered to cook; it was too late anyway and, besides, she was a lousy chef. A large bag of Honey and Dijon Kettle Chips called her name from the top shelf.

Now, where was Mr. Darcy? He'd normally be wrapped around her ankles by now, purring for his tea. Perhaps he was in the garden, doing his business in the herbs? Luckily, she didn't touch anything green and leafy; what was a cottage garden without a herb patch, though? She'd go and have her chips outside with him. Accompaniments were required first, though: fags and wine.

Moments later, Molly was seated at the bistro table in the garden – wine glass and fag in one hand, a pinch of chips in the other. The last of the evening sun had disappeared, but the night was still warm. Last summer, she'd had a man come round to install a wooden pergola *('You'll stay for a drink, won't you?')*, and the honeysuckle she was training to climb it was becoming nicely established. She'd wrapped fairy lights around the structure and, as she sat now in their low, multi-coloured glow, she felt rather pleased with herself, if slightly lonely.

'Mis-ter Dar-ceeeee,' she called, softly. His wasn't the sort of name you'd want to bellow freely.

Molly sank her wine and poured herself another glass. Beyond the back fence was the recreation ground, and she could hear distant laughter: teenagers, probably. Something caught her eye, in the freshly dug soil at the base of the fence – she hadn't yet decided what she was going to plant there. When she discovered it was a tennis ball, she threw it over the fence. Finding balls was quite a frequent occurrence, and it didn't bother her at all – although she had once inexplicably found a bra amongst her delphiniums. She knew it wasn't one of hers, dropped off of the washing line, because it was from M&S – Heaven forbid! Besides, it was a 32B and she was a 34D – and very proud of her boys she was, too.

As she was about to turn back to the pergola, she heard something knock against the fence, followed by a desperate scrabbling sound. Then came another knock. For a moment she was quite startled, then she realized what it was and let out a sigh. She unbolted the gate, opened it and the shadowy figure waddled towards her.

'Oh, Mr. Darcy, what are you like? You know you're too fat and old to be jumping fences. In you come, sweetheart.' Mr. Darcy slalomed Molly's legs, as she brought him inside for a bowl of Whiskas.

Half an hour later, Molly was back outside with another bottle of white. Mr. Darcy heaved himself through the cat flap and inelegantly jumped onto the spare chair, next to her. She tickled him under the chin and he did a 360 turn (why bother?), before settling himself down.

'So, Mr. Darcy,' Molly said, lighting a cigarette, 'tell me about your day. I could do with some good news, as quite frankly my day has been s-h-i-t.' She drew a deep drag, lifted her head to the stars and exhaled slowly, then looked back down at Mr. Darcy. 'Typical man: falls asleep the minute you want to talk deep and meaningful.'

She wagged a cigarette hand drunkenly at him. 'Well, there'll be no sex for you tonight, Mr. Darcy, and that's a promise.' She giggled at the absurdity of the conversation.

A man's voice startled her: 'Hello, there.' It came from next door's garden.

Molly swivelled clumsily and knocked the bistro table. The wine bottle fell over and the contents gurgled out, all over poor Mr. Darcy. He leapt from the chair and scurried to the cat flap. 'Shit! Bollock! Wank! Buggery!' Molly said, as she righted the bottle.

Then she looked over at the man who was standing in the shade of Mrs. Lipton's old laburnum. 'Sorry,' she said, flustered. 'Have you been there long?'

'A few moments, that's all. Sorry if I startled you. If it's not convenient–'

'No! It's fine.' Did she sound desperate? Probably. She was quite sure she was drunk now, but not so drunk as to be unaware that she was making a complete tit of herself.

God, *look* at him! Even in the dim glow of the fairy lights – or maybe *because* of it – he looked divine: the deep tan of a man who worked outdoors; slicked, impossibly black hair; a jawline you could measure right-angles with. He wore a t-shirt so tight around his pecs that she thought the fabric might rip apart at any minute. And he was so *tall!* But, so young. She was reminded of the gardener in *Desperate Housewives*. Would she? Of course she bloody would.

'I'm Tom,' he said, proffering a hand. 'I heard you, and thought I'd come and introduce myself.'

'Molly,' she said, stumbling towards him. She lightly squeezed his fingertips. For some unfathomable reason she performed a curtsey, and a little bit of wine sloshed out of her glass. She ran nervous fingers through her hair and flicked back her head, like she was in a shampoo commercial. 'Just moved in?' Stupid question, she knew, but nothing else came to mind.

'Yes, this morning, in fact. Going to be doing a bit of work over the next couple of weeks. Let me know if I make too much noise, won't you?'

Molly may have been drunk, but she noted the singular pronoun in that sentence. Once a journalist…

'Just yourself, is it?' she said, tilting her head and running a finger around the rim of her glass. Timidity got you nowhere, especially at her age.

'For now; the fiancée's staying at her Mum's until I've got the hot water working.'

Just one word: 'fiancée'. He might just as well have plunged a stiletto through her heart. *Get a bloody grip, Molly*. She quickly rallied and hoped she hadn't let any kind of vulnerability show on her face; she'd embarrassed herself enough for one evening.

Then, her imagination began to run away with her. How long might it take to get the hot water working? She imagined a scenario wherein she'd severed the gas pipe (desperate times, and all that); he'd have to come round to hers, *begging* to use her shower: dirty work fixing up an old cottage *('Oh, God, sorry; I forgot to leave you a towel. Won't be a tick. I'll close my eyes – promise!')*.

Stop it!

Had he asked her a question? She found that she was staring into nothing.

'Huh?' she said, turning to him.

'I was just saying how about you? Do you live with someone?'

'Just Mr. Darcy.'

'Oh?'

'He's twelve.'

Oh, God, the drink and the nerves were playing havoc tonight.

'My cat! You met him briefly, earlier, when I poured a bottle of wine over him.

'Look, you're probably getting a certain impression of me. It's, er, been stressful at work: deadlines; shitty boss… Hey, I'm babbling now. I think I'm going to take myself inside. Why don't you and… er… you didn't mention your fiancée's name.'

'Becky.'

Eurgh! What an awful name! She imagined a hairdresser, all fake smile and boring conversation, hooped gold Argos earrings… God, she was such a cow! 'Nice name. You should come round, the pair of you, one evening, once you're settled. We can have a chat over wine and nibbles; I can tell you what there is to do around here… which won't take long. Answer: nothing!' Molly laughed, awkwardly.

'Well, er, that might be quite difficult.'

'Oh, why?'

'Well… Becky… she's kind of seriously allergic to cats.'

The bitch!

'Oh, dear. Well, he's *terribly* clean.' She had no idea if that made the slightest difference. Or why she had just spoken like the Queen. 'Anyway, I'd best get back indoors – you know, before… erm…'

'Okay. Nice to have met you, Molly.'

Inside, she pressed herself against the back door like a

gecko, and closed her eyes. *Well, that went about as well as could be expected.*

When she opened her eyes, there sat Mr. Darcy on the cool quarry tiles, rear paw raised in a stiff salute, urgently licking his testicles clean of Gold Label sauvignon blanc.

NINE

IT WAS five minutes to eight and Kathy was nervous. She'd changed an hour ago into her black, off-the-shoulder dress, and Mark had helped with the fiddly clasp of the platinum necklace John bought her for her thirtieth. Or, rather, Kathy had bought it and John gave her the money afterward.

Dinner was cooked and ready to be served. Kathy was going to call John, to ask him how long he'd be, but she thought better of it; he hated to be mithered like that. Besides, he'd be driving home now, and it wasn't a good idea to use a phone while at the wheel.

Stop fretting, Kathy. Everything will be just fine.

Mark entered the dining room.

'Did you get hold of Ben?' she asked, wringing her hands.

'Yes, he's on his way back; Nathan's dropping him off.'

'Dropping him off? Why does he need to drive him here? The pub's only a ten-minute walk away. Oh, God, tell me he's not–'

Mark gave a half-smile, which told Kathy the answer to

her unvoiced question. She began to pace around the dining table.

Mark had helped her set the places; he'd needed to be reminded of the correct positions for the cutlery: starters on the outside; dessert at the top. The Wedgwood crockery hadn't been used since Christmas, so Kathy had given it all a rinse after taking it from the sideboard. It had been a wedding gift, and they'd broken a few pieces over the years, but there was enough remaining for each of them to have matching items.

Kathy had placed a couple of bottles of wine in the centre of the table: a cheap sauvignon blanc from Sainsbury's and John's favourite Rust en Vrede 1694 – he'd fallen in love with it on a business trip to Cape Town, years back. Three hundred pounds a crate. It was wasted on Kathy, though: to her, all red wine tasted like vinegar; the cheap white would suit her fine. In fact, she was now having second thoughts about having any alcohol out at all, what with Ben likely to be a little worse for wear…

The horrible antique tortoiseshell carriage clock – an heirloom on John's side, which stuck out like a sore thumb amongst the modern furniture – chimed eight and Kathy sighed.

'Why don't you have a glass of wine, Mum? Help calm the nerves.'

'No thanks, love. I'll wait 'til we start eating. It goes straight to my head on an empty stomach.'

She looked at Mark, a sadness welling within her. 'John will be here, won't he?' she said, aware her voice was quavering on the edge of tears. 'And, when's Ben coming back from the pub?'

Mark took a gulp of wine and smiled, unconvincingly. 'Everything's going to be fine, Mum. Relax.'

A loud banging at the front door made Kathy jump.

'I'll go,' Mark said, turning around.

'Who could it be?' Kathy said, following him. 'Ben's got his own key.'

As Kathy turned into the hall, Ben was stumbling over the threshold, and Mark grabbed his upper arm in the nick of time.

It was half-past eight, and Ben had managed to somehow pour himself a large glass of John's expensive red without spilling a drop, while Kathy sat watching in a state of powerless paralysis. Despite the mounting evidence to the contrary, she clung to the belief that the evening would be a success; John would soon come rushing through the door, apologising profusely for being late: there'll have been a holdup on the roads, no doubt. That nasty bend on the main road coming into town was an accident waiting to happen, so she'd told anyone who cared to listen. Or maybe he'd nipped somewhere, to pick her up a nice bunch of flowers? John knew lilies were her favourite. Perhaps everywhere was out of stock? *It doesn't matter, John; it will still be perfect, even without flowers. The family being together – that's the important thing.*

Kathy tried to recall the last time John had bought her flowers. Come to think of it, she wasn't sure he ever had. She'd treated herself to a bunch on the odd special occasion. She told herself that John would have bought her them, had he the time.

She looked across to Mark and saw the sauvignon blanc bottle – now sat squarely in the middle of his placemat (the special slate ones: Christmas '96) – was three-quarters empty. He was slumped in his chair, casually swiping his thumb over his phone. The youth of today were obsessed with those things!

The sound of Ben noisily wiping his mouth with the back of his hand drew Kathy's attention back to him. He was twiddling the shaft of his empty wine glass (Waterford crystal: wedding present). His blue shirt – three buttons open and curly chest hair exposed – sported a large wine-stain. As he stretched shakily from his reclined position, to grab the bottle, Kathy summoned up the courage to say: 'Don't you think you should wait for your father to get here, love?'

Ben didn't react, but Mark suddenly got up with such speed and force that his chair banged against the side-board, making the clock judder and Kathy jolt. Her side-plate wobbled on the polished walnut table and she steadied it, despite the shakiness of her hands. 'How long are we going to maintain this farce?' Mark said, angrily.

Kathy convinced herself that it was the drink talking. The poor love hadn't eaten for hours, and it was a hot day and everything…

'Have a bread roll, love,' Kathy said, holding out a chunk of French stick she'd quickly sliced with the silver bread knife (Christmas '99). 'Your dad won't be long, now.'

'I'm going to give him a call, find out where the hell he is.' Mark was heading through the open doorway, into the hall.

'No, don't do that, love. He could be driving.'

'Mum!' he yelled, gripping his hair in his hands and pacing around the hall. 'Listen to yourself!'

Kathy heard a noise, and swivelled her head to see Ben laughing to himself manically, as he filled his glass to the brim with red. There was barely any left for John. Did they have another bottle? She wasn't sure; maybe in the garage. She would go and check.

Walking into the hallway, she saw Mark, phone in his hand.

'Don't!' she shouted, with an uncharacteristic assertiveness that caused Mark to pause and look over to her. 'He'll think I've asked you to check up on him.'

Kathy noticed the twitch of his cheek and the slight shake of his head. 'I'm calling him, Mum,' he said, calmly.

She held out her hand, palm forward. 'No. I'll call him myself, okay? You just… keep an eye on your brother in there. Please.'

Mark relented and slouched past her, on his return to the dining room. Kathy heard him utter some unkind remarks as he did so, but chose to believe she'd misheard.

Now, where had she put her phone? She was all at sixes and sevens. Yes, of course, it was in her handbag on the kitchen table, next to Ben's present. Entering the kitchen, the smell of broccoli wafted over her and she realized the soup had been bubbling away on the hob for nearly an hour now. She peered into the pan, like a first-time bungee jumper looking through their fingers, into the abyss. Relieved it wasn't ruined, she gave the soup a vigorous stir and turned the hob dial down to its lowest setting.

Her eyes darted around the room, and she felt a queasiness rising in her belly. *What did I come in here for?*

The phone, you daft cow.

Kathy made her way to her handbag, and rummaged inside for the little pay-as-you-go thingy John had bought her years back, after he got rid of the landline (he told Kathy it was a waste of money). She still hadn't really got to grips with her mobile. Mark had shown her once how she could make like easier for herself by programming people's numbers into it, but she didn't have that many contacts – certainly none that she had cause to ring on a regular basis. She preferred to keep a record of people's addresses and phone numbers in the little green book she kept in the top drawer of the sideboard. It didn't really matter anyway, as she knew John's number off by heart. Falteringly, she punched it in and, after a deep breath, she went to hit the green dial button.

And… stopped.

Bea?

She'd forgotten all about her.

What if John wasn't out at golf? What if he was with *her?*

Kathy had her number; it was still in her bloody bra! She half-laughed, half-yelped. She could ring her and find out, once and for all. No. What if it all turned out to be perfectly innocent, and John got wind of her suspicions and paranoia? There'd be hell to pay.

There was an easier solution to this problem: call the bloody golf club! Kathy mentally rehearsed: *Oh, hi Shane, it's Kathy Gibbs here. Don't suppose John's still there, is he? I know I sound like one of those awful nagging wives, but his dinner's going to be ready soon. It's our anniversary dinner, you see? Expect he's lost track of time…*

Before she'd even finished, she heard the sound of car tyres on the gravel out front.

Silly mare; here he is!

Oh, God, is my hair okay? She hoped it wasn't hanging too limply in the heat. Kathy scurried into the hall and checked herself in the mirror; ran her fingers through her hair, in a futile attempt to add some volume; rearranged her breasts in the ill-fitting bra.

The bloody business card! She took it out and hastily stashed it in the console table drawer. On the table was a copy of the *Herald.* There was a front-page spread appealing for information about that poor woman murdered two years ago. A shiver went down her spine at the thought of her naked, disembowelled body lying in the woods. All alone. Whatever possessed the culprit to do such a wicked thing? And what about that other girl – the sex slave – found in that awful flat the other day, rescued by the police only to throw herself from a balcony. Kathy couldn't even begin to comprehend how the girl had got herself into that predicament. How many other women were out there, enslaved, living a hellish existence? It all put Kathy's first-world problems into perspective. Made her grateful for what she had: a lovely home, her boys. A wonderful, loving husband.

She turned to the front door just as a large, shadowy shape loomed in the frosted glass.

'Boys,' she shouted, 'your dad's here. Make yourselves presentable.'

Kathy opened the door, at the same time arranging her face into a smiling mask, behind which she could covertly look, sniff and listen for clues as to the identity of the mysterious Bea. 'Hello, love,' she said. 'I was beginning to get worried. Have you had a nice game?'

'Yeah. Got talking in the clubhouse and didn't realize the time. Are the boys here?'

'They're in the dining room. Go and get yourself seated, and I'll bring dinner through.'

'What are we having again?'

Kathy's bottom lip began to tremble, and she turned to face the kitchen before John could notice.

'It's a surprise, love,' she uttered, meekly. 'Won't be a minute.'

While Kathy poured the soup into the Jasper Conran tureen (silver wedding anniversary), she tried, without success, to decipher the low chatter coming from the dining room. If she were to hazard a guess, she'd say they were talking golf. Over the years, Kathy had picked up on some of the lingo – birdies, par, irons, wood, bunkers – but she felt nowhere near confident enough to risk an interjectory opinion. Much like with most other conversation topics, if she was being brutally honest with herself.

Dipping a home-manicured finger into the soup, she realized to her horror how tepid it had become. She thought for a moment about heating it in the microwave for a couple of minutes, but quickly dismissed the idea, reasoning that John would be too hungry to notice and, as for the boys…

Kathy carried the tureen, its porcelain lid rattling faintly and her teeth biting her tongue in concentration, into the dining room, which fell silent on her arrival. 'Excuse me, love,' she said, brushing past John and lowering the pot to a placemat. She removed the lid with the panache of a magician's assistant. 'Soup, everyone?'

Ben was first to shuffle himself upright and peer into the tureen. He puffed his cheeks and, for a heart-stopping moment, Kathy thought he was going to vomit into Delia Smith's broccoli and stilton soup. Thankfully, he merely slumped back into his chair, wafting his hand across his face.

John declined with: 'I'll wait for the mains. I had a quick bite at the clubhouse.'

Maintaining an enigmatic smile worthy of Leonardo Da Vinci, Kathy turned to Mark, who seemed sufficiently alert and sober to spot the message in her raised eyebrows. 'Oh, go on, then,' he said, holding out his bowl; 'just a little.'

As she ladled the soup, Kathy realized that John was holding the red wine upside down, with nothing more than a pathetic handful of drips falling out. 'Sorry, love,' she said, turning to him. 'Ben… erm… we… erm…'

'I can see perfectly well what's bloody happened, Kathy,' John said, sharply.

'I'll see if I can find another bottle.'

'Do you know how expensive this is?'

Kathy, sensing that it was one of John's rhetorical questions, retreated silently from the dining room, but not before noticing that Mark was pushing his spoon disinterestedly through the soup, and Ben's chin had dropped to his chest.

She sighed inwardly and went to the kitchen. Kathy was pretty sure there wasn't another bottle of Rust en Vrede in there, but she searched the half-empty shelves of the wine rack, carefully rotating each bottle to read its label, just in case. Her vision became blurred and she blinked away the watery sadness that threatened to wreck her makeup. She got to the final bottle and, even before she'd read the label, she knew it wasn't John's favourite; the shape of the bottle and the design of the label were all wrong. She had to hope there was a stash in the garage. She didn't go in there much – it was John's domain – but this evening circumstances necessitated it.

Having no windows, the garage was dark, so Kathy flicked the switch to bring the pair of strip-lights spluttering to life. Against the length of the back wall was John's workbench, above which hung the calendar still showing Miss February, sprawled topless on the bonnet of a red Ferrari. John's beer fridge was underneath the bench at the far end, and along the floor were boxes of various sizes. Kathy bent down to search among them with one hand, the other clutching the fabric of her dress to keep it clear of the dusty concrete. Inching her way along, she found an unopened case and, pretty confident it was what she was searching for, breathed a sigh of relief.

Through the wall, Kathy heard voices – and laughter,

if she wasn't very much mistaken. She wondered what they were talking about in the dining room. Not her, she hoped. No, it would be boy talk: silly jokes about sex and sport and Irishmen. Well, perhaps not sex.

After tugging the cardboard flap, to break the seal of the box, Kathy reached inside and pulled out a bottle. Unable to read the label, because she was blocking the light, Kathy spun around, only to find herself startled to be in someone's shadow.

She recognized John's legs – fat and clad as they were in overly tight golfing trousers – and went to stand up, knocking her head hard against the underside of the solid workbench. Pain flashed through her skull, but she didn't want to make a scene by crying out, so she silently bit her lip and swallowed the pain.

'What's taking you so long?' John asked, as he grabbed the bottle from Kathy's hand.

'Sorry, love,' she said. She clambered to her knee and held out a hand, but John was already on his way back to the dining room.

Kathy disguised a pang of disappointment beneath a blank expression, when she returned to the dining room to find the grapefruit-scented candle had been snuffed out. But her heart was now warming once more, at the sight of everyone enjoying the stew. Well, Ben wasn't really up to it; his just sat there on his plate getting cold, while his head lolled. But she was hopeful of requests for seconds from John and Mark. Kathy wasn't particularly hungry herself, what with all the stress of getting everything ready, so she just picked fussily around the edges of her plate.

John was first to finish; a small belch and the tidy finality of the cutlery placement (pointing between ten and four) indicated that he wouldn't be asking for more. All hopes now rested on Mark, but as Kathy turned to him, she saw that he was flagging with nearly half of his (admittedly large) portion remaining.

'Don't worry if you can't manage it, love,' she said. 'Probably this heat; it's shot my appetite to pieces.'

Mark took that as his cue to drop the knife and fork, and push his plate forward. 'Thanks, Mum. Delicious.'

Listen to those manners. Haven't we brought him up well? Kathy's heart swelled with maternal pride.

Her soft smile stiffened as she turned to see John sat in silence, elbows on the table and his splayed hands joined at the fingertips. It took a few moments for Kathy to read the situation. Christ almighty, she hadn't taken the bloody plates away!

Daft cow.

'Sorry,' she said, rising to her feet and getting herself into quite the flap as she collected the plates, scraping the leftovers into a large pile on the top.

'I'll give you a hand,' Mark said, calming Kathy in an instant.

'Thanks, love.'

Mark turned to take his brother's empty wine glass, but as soon as he touched it, Ben was suddenly galvanized from his semi-comatose state and grabbed the glass. Kathy, now holding a pile of plates, cutlery and leftovers, watched in horror as a battle of wills played out between the twins. John retained a look of unconcern, even when the glass flew from the boys' grip and shattered against the radiator.

Kathy's first thought was that there were now only three left in the set, which meant that she couldn't use them again for the next family meal, unless she could find an exact match, the next time she was in town. Her second thought, arriving moments later, was that she'd better get the dustpan and brush from under the sink, before someone did themselves an injury.

TEN

IT WAS late at HQ and the floor was sparsely occupied.

James rose from his desk and went to grab a Coke from the vending machine. He saw Luke working away at his desk. Behind Luke the sun was setting, the western sky filled with colour – red sky at night, detective's delight; something like that.

James was in an uncharacteristically cheery frame of mind. Perhaps it was because he was impressed at Luke's apparent dedication to the task. He mildly chastised himself for forming an early negative opinion. He opened his can, took a large swig and walked over to Luke.

'Time to call it a day, don't you think?'

'Okay, guv.'

'Managed to get hold of Pinto yet?'

'Not yet. Bastard's still not answering his phone. Sent uniform round to his home address earlier; wife said he's away on business.'

'Try again first thing. If still no joy, we'll escalate. Found anything interesting with the businesses?'

'I'm building up a pretty big list of names and businesses here. Don't really know which ones to start digging deeper into first.'

'Talk me through it in the morning. As my old mum used to say, Rome wasn't built in a day.' Mary Quinn was fond of inane sayings. 'Said it was slow, painstaking work, didn't I? Let me drive you back to Stevenage.'

'Thanks, guv, but if it's out of your way, it's pretty easy for me to just get the train.'

'It's no bother.' James didn't need an excuse for a trip to Stevenage. 'We'll grab a bite to eat on the way. My shout.'

'Okay, cheers guv.'

James swung his Audi into a parking space, immediately out front of Chicken Lickin', on the High Street in Stevenage old town. It was dark and the streetlights were on. Being a Wednesday, the road was quiet; a huge contrast to a Friday or Saturday, when it would be positively swarming with youngsters, staggering between the pubs and the fast-food outlets, before heading off to the clubs. James easily imagined Luke in a white Ben Sherman shirt and waxed hair, ordering another round of lagers at the bar for his posse.

James told Luke to grab a table near the window, while he waited at the counter for his order. He used takeaways far more often than he ought to. He hated cooking for himself; it didn't seem worth the effort and he never really had the time. If it wasn't for the running, he figured he'd be seriously overweight by now.

Luke tucked into his chicken and chips, hungrily. A couple of times, James caught him looking in his direction, seemingly poised to ask a question, then thinking better of it. When he did it next, James said: 'What it is you want to ask me? You didn't seem so shy earlier today.'

Luke paused for a moment, chewing on a piece of chicken, then a frown formed on his face.

'The guys in the office tell me you're tight-lipped about your private life.'

True to form, James held his lips tightly shut.

'They said you lost your wife, but wouldn't say anymore.'

James sighed inwardly. Months back, he'd got wind that a DC who James thought he could trust had told a new recruit about his wife. He bollocked her, out on the floor in front of everyone; Murdoch had later pulled James into his office to tell him that was unacceptable behaviour. Perhaps it was, but it made people think twice about being loose-tongued about his private life.

'I don't like to talk about it because it's painful. Work helps me to cope.'

'Sorry,' Luke said. Then, after a pause, he added: 'My sister died of leukaemia when she was only twelve. Our family's never been the same since.'

'Life's shit, eh?' James said. He looked down at his half-finished box of food and pushed it away.

'Mind if I finish that, guv?' Luke said, in a flash.

'Be my guest.'

James turned to face the window. On the opposite side of the road was a Lloyds Bank branch, and a queue had formed at the cash machine. Moments later, a man walked away from the machine, tucking a wad of cash into his wallet, and the queue shuffled forward. James looked at his face, instantly recognising the man.

Perkins!

What was he up to?

Only vaguely aware of Luke's voice, James watched as

Troy Perkins climbed into his parked Peugeot and reversed out of the space.

'Quick, we've got to go,' James said, springing to his feet.

Luke spoke through a mouthful of food: 'What?'

'Bring it with you. And don't bloody drop any of it on my leather seats!'

There were two cars between them and the Peugeot. Seeing Troy withdrawing what looked to have been a large amount of cash had sent James's detective brain into over-drive. Troy was now heading in a direction away from his house.

'Who is he?' Luke asked.

James had almost forgotten Luke was with him. 'Someone who doesn't deserve to be enjoying his liberty. Don't let me lose him.'

'This official police business?' Luke asked.

James remained silent.

'Guv?'

'You must have heard or read about the case: the murder at Wain Wood?'

Memories of the morning of Lena Demyan's discovery flashed through his brain, once again: her naked body amongst the dead leaves, laid out like some poor sacrificial animal. Ligature marks around the neck, blood-shot eyes, bruised limbs and broken nails. The soles of her feet were covered in sores and cuts, indicating that at some point she had been running for her life. James was beginning to feel the same nausea he experienced that morning, and he shook his head, trying to dislodge the images.

'Oh, God,' Luke said; 'the prostitute found in the dell.

Poor girl was disembowelled, wasn't she? The press called him the "Dell Ripper". Was that your case, then?'

'Yep. Perkins did it, but the damn CPS wouldn't take the case.'

'Insufficient evidence?'

'You've got it.'

'Then, how can you be so sure it was him?'

Ahead, the Peugeot took a left onto a quieter road, heading in a direction away from town.

'Where are you going, you bastard?' James muttered, pulling himself closer to the steering wheel, his eyes fixed firmly ahead. There were no cars between them now, so he held back as far as he dared.

'How do I know it was him? Because I know Perkins better than he knows himself. The moron worked in forensics, so cleaning the crime scene was easy for him. But there was plenty of circumstantial evidence and, crucially, a witness came forward. Trouble is, she disappeared afterwards.'

'Is this why you have the camera, guv? Your hobby?'

James didn't answer.

'It's not your case anymore, though, is it? It's with the Cold Case Team.'

'Those arseholes couldn't catch a cold, let alone a budding serial killer.'

'You think he's going to strike again?'

The Peugeot seemed to be pulling away from them now, and James pressed harder on the accelerator; Troy's car remained just in sight. It took a right turn.

Without warning, a car pulled out of a side street into James's path, and he slammed on the brakes. He hit the car horn and flashed his lights, then swung out to overtake.

'Easy, guv,' Luke said, concern spilling into his voice.

At the next junction, James took a right.

Troy's car was now out of sight. He cursed under his breath. 'Where does this lead?'

'Greyston Valley Park, guv.'

Thoughts swirled around his head. He took a deep breath, in an attempt to unscramble them. They approached the entrance to a narrow road.

'That's the entrance to the car park,' Luke said. 'Think I can see brake lights through the trees.'

James yanked the steering wheel and turned into the road.

When they reached the car park, they found the Peugeot parked up and in semi-darkness. There were no other cars around. James parked the Audi and grabbed his Maglite from the glove box. 'Come on,' he said, 'let's take a look.'

James shone his torch into the Peugeot; discarded cans, takeaway cartons and paper littered the seats. He hammered on the boot and shouted: 'Hello!' Best just to check. There was no response, and he judged from the hollow sound and the appearance of the car that there wasn't a significant weight, such as a body, in the boot.

James flashed the torch at a sign marking a path into the park.

'Guv, I'm not sure we should be doing this; we've got no cause.'

'So, you'll be staying here with the car then, while I go in on my own?' James said, as he started along the path. Moments later, Luke caught up with him. They continued down the path, deeper into the park, sweeping their torches in front of them in silence. Something close to rage burned in James, and he clenched his fist. *I won't let you down, sweetheart.*

Eventually, they arrived at a fork in the path.

'Is this why you have the camera, guv,' Luke repeated: 'shadowing Perkins?'

'Where does this path lead?'

'Down to the main lake. Follow the edge of it and you'll come to the boatshed – it stores the pedaloes, kayaks and stuff for the summer season. There's a café that way, too.'

'And, that one?'

'It loops around a smaller lake and a children's playground, then re-joins the main path near the boatshed.'

'We'll split, then: you go that way. Call me if you see or hear anything.'

'Guv.'

James continued, his eyes and ears attuned to the slightest movement or sound. The lake, black and silky like oil in the still, moonlit night, honed into view. Beyond it, he saw the shadowy mass of the building he figured must be the boatshed. To his left was a row of trees, rigid and evenly spaced, like the Queen's Guard. To his right, a scurrying noise in the undergrowth momentarily startled him: some kind of rodent. Where was Perkins? What was he doing? James couldn't think of an innocent reason for him to be venturing into the park.

Farther along the path, he emerged from the cover of the trees and it became brighter. James looked up at the moon: *Oh, God, a full moon!* Lena Demyan was murdered on the night of a full moon.

He stopped for a moment and surveyed his surroundings. Theories and questions jostled for attention in his mind. Was there something historically or mythologically significant about the park? What were the coordinates on the map? Was there a natural or artificial feature, oriented to the midwinter or midsummer sun? Had he arranged to meet a woman here – his next victim? James couldn't answer those questions now, so he kept walking, looking and listening.

How about Luke? Had he seen anything? James took his phone from his pocket to check: nothing. But, then again, there was no signal. *Damn.*

His pace quickened as he edged the lake. All was still and calm. He reached the boatshed; on the wall facing him, canoes were stacked and tethered neatly. Nothing of interest was revealed in the arc of his torchlight. Round the corner, he shone it through a small window: nothing that he could see. Next to the window was the door; he checked the padlock: firmly shut. James now walked along the featureless expanse of the far-side wall.

Suddenly, there was a piercing, white light, which momentarily blinded him. When his eyes adjusted to the brightness, James realized he had triggered a security light. He breathed and allowed himself a small smile, then walked to the next corner.

Luke would be here shortly. He'd wait here for him, and they could continue the search together. Lo and behold, moments later a long shadow grew across the lit ground, and James turned to greet Luke.

'See anything?' He squinted in the brightness; Luke was a silhouette against the light.

Then he smelt something familiar: cheap musk. Before he could fully process the smell, a blurry shape flashed towards him and made sharp contact with his eye socket. As a searing pain radiated through his skull, James realized it was a fist.

'What the fuck are you doing?!' The voice belonged to Troy Perkins.

Instinct kicked in and his training flew out of the window; James lobbed a punch at Troy, which landed on his cheekbone. Perkins growled and threw himself at

James, pushing him to the ground, then jumped on James and sat astride him.

Glaring into the low-life's shadowy, snarling face, rage coursed through James's bloodstream; it felt as if the veins in his temples might burst. Troy roughly grabbed the fabric of James's shirt. Troy Perkins was a large man, but James summoned an almost superhuman effort to throw him off, flipping him onto his back. James hurled his weight onto Perkins and regained the advantage.

'Why are you here?' James thundered.

Troy spat into his face, then laughed.

This action threw James into a frenzy, and he rained down a punch into Perkins's nose; he felt a sickening crunch, as Troy's nose split open and sprayed blood over the pair of them. James raised his fist once more; it was as if an external force had possessed his body and now controlled his actions.

There was a shout from behind him and he heard footsteps rapidly approaching.

'Guv!'

James released his grip of Perkins's shirt and his head dropped to the ground. James got to his feet and pulled Troy into a standing position.

Perkins raised a hand to his nose and looked at his palm. Then, turning to Luke, he smirked: 'So, this is your boss, uh?'

Luke remained silent, a look of bewilderment falling across his features.

Perkins continued: 'I'd watch your back with this one, if I were you.' Blood streamed down his face and dripped from his chin to his belly.

James stepped angrily towards Perkins, before Luke grabbed James's arm and held it in a vice-like grip.

Perkins addressed James: 'I know you've been watching

me and following me. You think I'm fucking stupid? I could get you struck off if I wanted to.'

'Why are you here?' James snarled again.

Perkins smiled. 'The last time I checked it was a free country. A man can go for a walk in the park without fear of being attacked by a bent copper, can't he?'

'I am not *bent*,' James said, pulling furiously against Luke's grip.

'We should go back now, guv,' Luke said, calmly.

James glowered at Perkins.

'Come on, guv.'

Eventually, the reasonable, logical side of James's brain regained control and his muscles relaxed. Luke released his grip. James turned to walk away.

'Hey, Quinn,' Perkins said.

James turned back. 'What?'

'You've got blood on your shirt. You might want to look at getting that professionally cleaned; blood's a bugger for staining.'

Bastard!

'I know you did it, Perkins.'

In the same beat, Perkins raised his palms to the sky and formed an innocent expression. 'Did what?'

James stormed back to the car park.

ELEVEN

Mark intercepted Kathy in the hallway, and initiated a game of tug-o'-war with the dustpan and brush. Kathy put up a valiant effort, but eventually Mark claimed inevitable victory.

As he returned to the dining room, Kathy was left staring at John's blazer on the coat rack. Her brain began to fill with a jumble of hazy memories and ill-formed theories.

She became vaguely aware of John's voice and turned her head.

'What's for pudding?' he said, in a tone which indicated it wasn't the first time of asking.

It was such a simple question, yet her brain seemed to lack the capacity to answer. Shaking her head, Kathy said: 'Sorry, love. It's, er, it's, erm…'

'Cheesecake?' Mark said. 'I saw it in the fridge.' He'd come to her rescue.

Again.

My darling.

'Yes, yes, cheesecake. I'll fetch it.'

Just as she was about to turn for the kitchen, Kathy realized she hadn't cleared the table of the soup tureen and the butter dish. But something was rooting her to the spot: a question which had percolated through her addled brain and now sat heavy on her tongue. She had to release it. Turning to John, she asked: 'Who's Bea?'

When the words came out, it felt as if time itself had stopped. For a moment, John remained totally impassive, his expression and thoughts unreadable. Then she noticed the slight twitch of his eye.

'Bea?' he said. 'What are you talking about, woman? I don't know anyone called Bea.'

'But that card, in your trousers…'

It was too late: she'd said it; she'd slipped up. Given the game away, that she'd been digging around in his business again. In front of the boys, too. Would she *ever* learn?

'Kathy,' John said, firmly, 'I'm not sure what's got into you tonight.'

'B-but,' she stammered, 'I… I…' She felt herself shaking.

'Sit yourself down, Kathy.'

She did as she was told. Pointing a trembling finger over her shoulder towards the hall console, she tried to speak, but nothing came out.

'It's all in your head,' John said, jabbing his forefinger against his temple. Two tendons had suddenly become prominent in his neck, and his brown eyes bulged.

It's all in your head.

John had said that to her many times, over the years.

But *this* couldn't be in her head, could it? Her name was there in blue ink:

'Bea.'

It was definitely Bea.

Wasn't it?

How could she have got it wrong?

She'd been wrong before, of course, and she was prone to bouts of confusion – she blamed those on lack of sleep. Kathy had suffered insomnia for as long as she could remember. Only once did she see a doctor about it, and he prescribed her some pills, which she didn't take to one little bit. The groggy morning after the night before, she discarded the remainder of the packet and took a vow never to venture onto that slippery slope again.

Kathy tried to speak again, but the words stuck in her throat. She needed water. Where was it? There was no bloody water on the table, only the wine bottles. Hold on, had she drunk *anything* today? At dawn with the blackbird, yes, but after that? Surely she'd had *something*? She couldn't remember; her head was all over the place. Oh, God, was she dehydrated? Was that why her brain was foggy? Or, worse, was she bloody *hallucinating*?

'You okay, Mum?' Mark asked. He was a blur, and it took Kathy three blinks to bring him into focus.

'Water,' she said in a hoarse whisper, pinching the skin of her throat.

'I'll get you a glass,' Mark said.

Kathy nodded her gratitude, then flicked a glance to her right, where it seemed that John and Ben were exchanging a private joke. John had his head in towards Ben, whose face wore a smirk which disappeared the moment his bloodshot eyes met Kathy's gaze.

Kathy's eyes darted around the room, trying to find a comforting object to focus on, while Mark was still in the kitchen. Finding nothing, she dropped her head to her chest and twiddled her thumbs. The clock ticked and John's fingers thrummed against the table. Then the sounds merged into a beat, which hammered against Kathy's skull:

Trrr-tick-trrr-tick-trrr-tick.

At the point where she thought she might actually explode, Mark appeared with her water and she gulped it, gratefully.

'Any chance of pudding before midnight?' John said.

The cheesecake. The bloody cheesecake! Kathy had forgotten all about it. Again.

She turned and shifted her weight to her feet, but Mark placed a hand on her shoulder. 'I'll get it, Mum,' he said.

'Don't be sil–' Kathy began to say, only to be interrupted by Ben, who now seemed miraculously rejuvenated.

"'I'll get it, Mum!"' he said, mimicking his brother in an effeminate tone. Kathy pivoted to see him affect a limp-wristed, swatting gesture.

'Ben, don't, please,' she urged, timidly.

'Shut the fuck up, you pathetic drunk!' Mark responded, grabbing a fistful of Ben's stained shirt.

'Hey, what's this all about?' John waded in.

Kathy didn't know what to do or say, and felt like she was physically shrinking.

'Tell him, Twat Face,' Ben said, with relish.

Mark released his grip from Ben's shirt but remained silent, turning his face to the table.

'Tell me!' John thundered, but Mark said nothing.

'Kathy, do *you* know something I don't?'

She shook her head, then exchanged glances with Mark and then Ben – a conspiracy of silence which John detected immediately. He slammed his fist onto the table, with a force which jolted the tureen lid free. '*Someone* is going to tell me what the fuck is going on!'

After a moment of silence, which was probably only a few seconds, yet seemed an eternity, Mark rose to his feet and declared he was going to bed.

'Sit down!' John thundered, as if addressing a disobe-
dient dog.

Kathy nodded to Mark, in a *'do-as-your-dad-says'* kind of
way, and he flopped back into his chair, immediately
folding his arms.

Ben made a noise, almost a snort, and Kathy saw that
he was smirking. 'Twat Face has got himself a new *friend*:
an *artist.*' That word – *artist* – was laced with contempt.
'Whats-ss name again?' he said, slurring his words pitifully,
and lolling his head in Mark's direction.

Mark glowered.

'I 'member now,' Ben said, trying to click his fingers:
'Maurice. Thass right: Maur*iiiicccccce*.' In another swatting
gesture, his hand dropped onto the table with a thump,
making Kathy flinch.

'This true?' John said, his eyes narrowed and boring
into Mark.

Mark flicked his eyes to Kathy, as if pleading for
support. She switched her gaze to the clock, as if the time
was now the most relevant thing. She wanted to help, she
really did, but she couldn't; couldn't take sides. Couldn't be
seen to be taking Mark's side, more accurately. She was
trapped, rendered mute and helpless by the predicament.
What kind of mother was she?

'I just want to be happy, Dad; be myself,' Mark eventually said. He spoke almost in a whisper. 'That too much to
ask?'

'Happy? Happy? Does fucking another man up his arse
make you happy?'

Kathy was momentarily taken aback by John's vehe-
mence and crudeness. It was the drink and the stress talking, she told herself; he didn't really think that.

Mark was staring through her now, his head shaking
almost imperceptibly. She tried desperately to read his

thoughts, but then there was another snort from Ben: he was laughing now. The drink again – that would be it; he'd be all embarrassed and apologetic once he sobered up. John, too.

'Or are you the submissive one: the *girl*?' John continued. 'Taking it up your ar–'

'John!' She couldn't bear it. 'Your language. It's not nice.'

'*Language*?!' Mark said. 'Is that all you're concerned about: his language?'

'I… I… I…' Kathy stammered, unable to look Mark directly in the eye. She was failing him.

John wasn't finished. 'You're a fucking disgrace!' He spat out the words.

Mark turned to Kathy, beseeching her to intervene. He desperately needed an advocate. He needed his mother right now.

The words were in her head: *It's okay, love. I support you. I love you*. She hoped her eyes conveyed what she couldn't say.

'You're no son of mine,' John said.

Pain rippled across Mark's features, as he pushed against the table and got to his feet.

Kathy's fingers curled around the butter knife.

John rose, too. 'Get out of my house, you fucking poofter!' he bellowed.

Kathy felt as though her heart had been wrenched from her chest; the pain was unbearable. But there was also something else gripping tight, deep within her stomach: blind fury. It erupted with a volcanic howl, and she hurled the knife at John. It struck him in the face, and he brought his hand to his brow.

The fury disappeared as quickly as it had arrived. Kathy held her face in her hands and began to convulse with fear. Both Mark and John were statue still; Ben was stunned. The clock ticked.

'S-s-sorry,' Kathy spluttered.

John brought his hand down and examined the knife, his brow sporting a sizeable gash. Calmly, he dabbed the wound with his white napkin. Seeing the blood, he chuckled. Had Kathy's rash action with the knife brought him back to his senses? A strange calmness began to wash over her.

Then, John dropped the napkin and moved in her direction.

He was behind her now. She could feel his great, hulking presence, as if it were a physical burden on her back. A shiver ripped through her.

Nobody was speaking. Why was nobody saying anything?

What was John going to do? Not knowing was the worst thing. It was always the worst thing.

His arm shot around her and picked up the soup ladle.

Oh no, John, no.

He slowly filled it from the tureen and she watched, mute and powerless, as he brought it towards her and above her head.

No.

Not in front of the boys.

Please.

She closed her eyes and felt the cold liquid ooze over her head, and drip down the back of her neck.

Opening her eyes again, she saw that Mark had left the room.

Ben was asleep.

John was silent.

Kathy knew she should have cleared the bloody table earlier.

. . .

After Kathy had quickly rinsed her hair and changed into something more comfortable, she found Mark packing his bag in his bedroom. For a moment she just stood there watching, nervously wringing her hands, as he furiously shoved items into his bag.

Eventually, she said: 'Your dad doesn't mean what he says. He's just a bit, you know, old fashioned.'

Mark stopped and looked at Kathy. 'Do you realize how ridiculous you sound, trying to defend him like this? There's a difference between old fashioned and a bigoted fucking twat!'

'Don't call him—' Kathy bit her tongue. 'Please stay tonight, sweetheart. For me.'

'You just left me to face that shit on my own down there. Can you imagine how it felt?'

Kathy felt her throat tighten. She coughed. 'I'm sorry, love. I didn't know what to say.'

Mark resumed his packing, shaking his head as he did so.

'Let me speak to your dad – please. Look, you can't be driving tonight; you'll be over the limit. And, what with how you must be feeling… I'd never forgive myself if you had an accident.'

Kathy looked at the bedside clock and saw that it was gone two a.m. She'd managed to snatch nothing more than a few minutes sleep here and there, since climbing into bed sometime before ten – early even by her standards. John was downstairs in the lounge, watching a film – she wasn't sure which one: there were gunfire and explosions coming through the floor, so she imagined it must be one of those war movies he liked. Kathy couldn't stand all the horror herself: the gore and the tragic waste of young life. A great-grandfather of hers – William – died at the Somme apparently, and she had a recurring dream of a man scrambling across a muddy field towards her, fear etched onto his young face, before exploding into clumps of charred flesh, which rained over her. She preferred good, old-fashioned romances; *Casablanca* was her favourite. She couldn't recall now the last time she had watched it; somehow, she never managed to find the time.

The day hadn't been the total success she had envisaged. Who was she trying to kid? It was a bloody disaster, no two ways about it. She couldn't shake the feeling that she was to blame: if she'd been a better mother, she would have grabbed the boys by the scruff of the neck and made them settle their differences years ago. If she were a better mother – no, a better *person* – they would want to spend more time in her company.

As for John… Well, he'd had to put up with all her silliness, her paranoia and her pathetic neediness; was it any wonder he'd gone looking for someone better? He had only come back to her because she begged him, and told him that she would change and be a better wife to him. It was all her fault.

Ben couldn't get out of the house fast enough, after dinner. He was in no fit state, but what could she do? God only knew where he'd gone or when he'd be back. She wouldn't be able to sleep properly until he was back, tucked up safe and sound. She'd make him drink a pint of water and swallow a couple of paracetamol. Oh, God, what if he was lying in a ditch somewhere, beaten black and blue, barely conscious and crying for his mother? She reached out, as if to stroke his hair. At least she'd managed to convince Mark to stay the night, after all. See, she wasn't *totally* hopeless.

A crashing noise downstairs jolted Kathy out of her melancholia. What was it? Ben returning? She hoped so. She should go down and see to him. *No! Leave him be. He's a grown man now, who could well do without your fussing all over him.* She'd wait until she heard him coming up the stairs, and closing the bedroom door behind him – then she could go to sleep. John would slide in beside her when he was ready for bed, and give her a gentle peck on the cheek while she slept. That would be nice.

But Ben didn't come up, so Kathy decided she'd go and have a look downstairs.

On the landing, she paused outside Mark's door, then nudged it open and peered in, to check he was okay. Sleeping like a baby, bless him. She tiptoed barefoot down the stairs, into the hall and through the double doors of the lounge.

In front of her, she saw the back of John's head on the armchair, facing the TV. Yes, it was a war movie.

She snatched her head away from the screen, then gasped in horror when she saw a pool of dark-red liquid soaked into the beige carpet.

'John!' she whimpered, through her fingers. She then noticed a wine bottle lying on its side, on the small table next to his armchair, and realized that it must be red wine, not blood. John shuffled in his sleep and grunted. *Thank God.*

The carpet would be ruined, though. Should she have a go at it now, with the 1001? At least she could tell John she'd tried.

She turned for the kitchen and felt a sharp pain underfoot: a piece of glass. She looked towards the table, and saw that Ben's anniversary bowl lay smashed to smithereens on the floor. What had happened? It must have cost him a fortune, and it was such a kind thought. She'd clear it all up and buy another one; hopefully, Ben would never find out.

A buzzing noise now came from John's side table: his phone. Who could it be at this time? Ben, perhaps? John didn't stir. Should she check?

Yes, it could be something important.

Oblivious to the presence of fragments of glass in the carpet, she walked over and picked up the phone, reading the message:

'Call me. I need you right now. B.'

It was her, wasn't it? Bea!

Kathy was winded, nauseous… She struggled to form coherent thoughts. She tried desperately to think of an innocent explanation, rather than leap to an illogical conclusion.

No, it had to be her. There was no other possible explanation.

He lied.

The whirl of emotions began to coalesce into something clearer, sharper: fear subsided and anger threatened to explode from her chest.

She carefully replaced the phone and leant over John. First, she smelled a repulsive waft of hot, boozy breath, then body odour. Was there the faintest whiff of perfume there, too? From above him, she suddenly felt powerful; she was no longer meek and subservient Kathy. A repulsion ripped through her, at the sight of his belly wobbling and that ridiculous whistling noise he made with his nose.

For the first time that she could recall, she knew precisely what she needed to do.

Kathy Gibbs crept to the kitchen.

TWELVE

MOLLY DREAMT that she was directing a soft porn movie. The man lay supine on a sheepskin rug, clamped in place by the woman's nutcracker thighs; he gripped her buttocks as she bounced astride him, like a jockey on the final furlong at the Epsom Derby. *Tone down the groaning, petal; sounds more like indigestion than ecstasy! ... Lower your head, man; camera two can't see her areola! ... Cut! We're going to have to do another take. Do you think you could manage it again, or do you need a toilet break?*

She woke to the sound of a strangely metronomic hammering noise against the dividing wall. Molly looked at the clock: six a.m.! Christ almighty, what was Tom doing at this ungodly hour? She had a good mind to go round and give him a piece of her mind. She'd have to put her face on first, of course. And brush her teeth. Squirt a smidgen of Vera Wang Princess... Slip into something silky... Wait. What was that?

Yes, there it was again: a woman's voice – and she sounded furious, as she screamed: 'Don't stop now, you bastard!' The penny dropped.

Tom must have fixed the hot water.

Molly wrapped a pillow around her ears and tried to get back to sleep, but it was hopeless. The noises next door – brutal and animalistic – grew into an urgent crescendo, ending in one final symbol clap, as the headboard smacked against the wall with such violence that it dislodged a piece of loose plaster dust, above Molly's head.

She had the familiar feeling that another great day beckoned.

Time to get up, then.

Her tongue felt like old carpet, so she headed to the bathroom to gargle Listerine. As she stood at the sink, she glimpsed herself in the mirror, which was a breach of her standard policy of avoiding her own reflection before breakfast. A shaft of low morning sunlight streamed into the room, revealing her every line and blemish. Her bed hair gave the appearance of someone who had stuck their finger in an electric socket. Molly stretched the dark shadows under her bloodshot eyes. *Look at the state of you, woman!* Still, nothing a long shower and a good slap of makeup couldn't fix. First, though, she needed a strong, black coffee.

The staircase in the cottage was old and rickety; every tread creaked. The ceiling was so low that even a short-arse like Molly felt the need to duck slightly, through fear of clonking her head on an oak beam. She found herself at the midpoint, tiptoeing gently, when she realized: why the bloody hell was she worrying about waking the neighbours? It was them who had just woken *her* with all their shenanigans – the selfish, sex-crazed bastards!

As she thudded down the remaining steps, a thought struck her: these houses weren't designed to accommodate six-foot-plus men like Tom; he'd have to be pretty much permanently stooped, walking about the place. There was only one logical explanation as to why he was living there: Becky the Bitch wore the trousers in their relationship, and he'd do anything for a quiet life. Molly pictured the scene on *Location, Location, Location*: *'I just love it,'* Becky gushes, hands held to her open mouth, eyes watering at the sight of an inglenook fireplace. The camera then turns to Tom, his neck cricked into a painful right angle. *'So, what do you think, Tom?'* Kirsty asks. *'I'm happy if Becky's happy.'* The subservient twerp. Grow a backbone, man! Molly considered herself a feminist (whatever that meant these days), but she liked her men to be *men*. She was rapidly going off Tom already.

Mr. Darcy wasn't on his chair. Probably taken himself into the garden for a bit of peace and quiet, the poor sod. She switched on the TV: breakfast news. She could only imagine what time the presenters had to rise in the morning; how did they look and sound so perky? Drugs, probably. Time for that shot of caffeine.

Another hot day beckoned, so Molly took her coffee outside to the bistro table, together with a packet of Marlboros and her mobile. Perhaps Mr. Darcy would like to join her. Now, where was the furry podgeball?

As she sat down, she looked at the garden-tool storage box against the back fence. *Not again!* It was how Mr. Darcy managed to get over it to the other side. Maybe one day the daft bugger would remember he couldn't get himself back, and quit venturing over there.

Perhaps she should restrict his calories. Weren't cats supposed to self-regulate? Trust her to get a defective one. Or was he just making up for a bad start in life? He was skin and bone when she took him in, after he was rescued from the family who neglected him. She felt an affinity with his circumstances.

Molly looked down at her stomach and patted it. Despite her own poor diet – the drink, the fags and a general lack of exercise – her figure was reasonably trim. Perhaps a pound or two on the wrong side of ideal, but nothing to worry about. By some amazing stroke of luck, she must just manage to extract something close to the right volume of calories; junk-food binges counterbalanced by the periods when she'd skip a meal, in favour of a Diet Coke and a fag. She'd read horror stories about women who gave up smoking and piled on the pounds – it was one of the reasons why she hadn't quit the habit. Or was it her genes? A fast metabolism? Her mother had been as thin as a rake her whole life. Not nice thin: scrawny and sinewy; sickly thin. Molly shook the image of her mother from her mind; she refused to let the woman sully her day.

Molly got up and opened the back gate, calling out into the deserted recreation ground to Mr. Darcy. No sign of him, but there was a crushed can of bloody Red Bull, at the base of the old horse chestnut. What was it with the people who drunk that vile stuff? Find a bloody bin! It's not difficult. She picked it up and returned to the table, leaving the gate open for Mr. Darcy.

She looked down at her phone to check the time: 6:23. *Jesus*. What to do? Head into work? No, she wasn't going to give that arsehole another pound of her flesh today. Shame that was only a metaphor (she giggled at her own little joke).

For a nanosecond, she contemplated getting into a t-shirt and some tracky bottoms, and jogging a couple of laps of the recreation ground. What *was* she thinking? Jogging was for losers with no friends. Molly felt a pang of something which she guessed was loneliness, but couldn't quite bring herself to admit it.

She slumped into her seat, lit a Marlboro, grabbed her phone and scrolled casually through her Twitter feed.

What?!

THIRTEEN

James was propped against a tree, downing a sports drink after a twenty-minute stretch of tempo running, when he heard a familiar voice looming behind him.

'Guv? That you?'

He turned to see Luke jogging effortlessly towards him, grinning broadly. Luke wore a hard-core runner's vest, accentuating his muscular physique.

'What are you doing in this patch?' James said, gruffly. Sucking in his stomach, he puffed out his chest and placed his drink back in the belt holder.

'I'm doing the Berlin marathon in October. Always looking for quality training routes.' Luke looked at his watch and pressed a button: 'Sixteen miles so far.'

James did the mental arithmetic: Luke must have been out since dawn, if not earlier. The guy looked like he'd taken a five-minute amble in the park. Bastard. 'Sixteen miles?' he said. 'That all?'

Luke grimaced when he saw James's swollen eye at close range. 'That looks nasty. You okay after… you know… last night?'

'I'll live. As you're here, why don't you give me an update on Solent? Run and talk, yeah?'

'No sweat; I'll work to your pace, guv.'

'Let's just start off with something gentle: eight-minute miles?'

'Groovy.'

They ran for another couple of miles or so, with Luke doing most of the talking. James struggled to concentrate, with his mind drifting off, reliving the events of the previous evening. His eye smarted.

They came to the edge of a small village. There was a huge oak tree and, under it, an inviting, shaded bench. 'Let's stop for a drink and some stretching,' James said, feeling moderately puffed out, but trying not to let it show.

'Sure thing,' Luke breezed.

James took out his drink bottle and dropped onto the bench. Luke remained on his feet, stretching his quads. Oh, to be young again.

'Have you heard Mel's broken up with her boyfriend?' Luke said.

'Daniel?'

'No, Declan, I think.'

'I lose track. She may have told me, but who knows; tend to switch off after the first thousand words. I'm not surprised: she seems to attract the wrong sort of fella; never learns from her mistakes, that one.'

James got to his feet and started to stretch his hamstrings.

'I'm going to make my move today,' Luke said. 'There's something about her; she's got spirit.'

James grabbed a fistful of Luke's vest. 'You hurt her and I'll wring your bloody neck! She's the best. Got it?' James released his grip and Luke smoothed down his vest.

'That's funny,' Luke said, 'because that's how she describes you, guv: the best. Says you're her role model.'

'Well, that just proves my point about her poor judgement in men.'

Luke smiled. Then, his expression changed to concern after clocking James's black eye again. 'I saw how you were with Perkins; how you lost your cool. What is it about him?'

'He's a low-life.'

'Hmm, I think there's more to it, guv. If you don't mind me asking, how much sleep did you get last night?'

'Dunno, two, maybe three hours. About normal. Why?'

'I don't think that's sustainable, guv. I think you're internalising everything – that's why you can't sleep. You've got to talk; let it all out; let others in.'

'You been reading psychology mumbo-jumbo?'

'No, I just know from my own experience, bottling stuff up never works; talking is the only way forward.'

'Bull*shit*. I can see why you're attracted to Mel. Talk's cheap, son. Talk doesn't get results. Talk won't bring my wife back.'

An awkward silence stretched out.

'What was your wife's name?' Luke eventually asked.

'Ruth.'

'Nice. Did Perkins have something to do with her death? Is that why you're obsessed with him?'

'I'm not obsessed.'

Luke laughed. 'Pull the other one.'

'You're not going to drop this, are you? Come on, let's start running again.'

'Tell me what happened to her, guv.'

James took a deep breath.

.   .   .

Numb, powerless, disbelieving, shell-shocked… James watched while the fire crew worked to cut Ruth's body from the wreckage.

At some point, he'd wake up from this nightmare.

'You must be freezing, sir,' the officer said. Her voice sounded distant. She placed her hand on his shoulder, but he shook her off.

'Why don't you go and sit in the squad car?' she suggested. 'There's a flask of tea inside.'

'No, I need to be here for her. Why are they taking so long to get her out?' He twisted around, to look at the dozens of people who'd emerged from their cars to gawp at the scene. 'THERE'S NOTHING TO SEE HERE. GO HOME!'

Fucking rubberneckers!

A few heeded his command and returned sheepishly to their cars.

Then James saw him, leaning casually against his Peugeot, his hands in his pockets, lips curled into a smirk.

'PERKINS?! WHAT THE FUCK ARE YOU DOING HERE?'

'A case of wrong place, wrong time, Inspector Quinn,' he said, cryptically.

No way was his presence a coincidence.

They glared at each other for a few moments, then Perkins said: 'Well, guess I'll be seeing you around real soon.' He opened the car door and climbed inside.

'Ignore the bastard,' the officer said; 'not worth a moment of your thoughts.'

Unfortunately, that was never going to happen.

'Shitting hell, guv, I had no idea. So sorry. Do you think he was stalking her?'

'That's what I suspect, but I'll never be able to prove it. My guess is he was following her at the time, and she caught sight of him in the rear-view mirror. It distracted her and she hit that nasty bend in the icy conditions…'

'If I ever get the chance to work with cold cases, guv–'

'You're a good lad, Porter. Now, how about some hill repeats? After a dozen of them, you'll be too knackered to talk.'

Hopefully.

James was at HQ by seven-thirty.

As he approached his desk, Murdoch intercepted him: 'James. My office, please.' He noticed the slightest twitch of reaction from the Super to his black eye.

'What happened?' Murdoch said, once he'd closed his office door behind them. 'Don't tell me, you walked into a lamp-post?'

'How did you know?' James said. He caught Murdoch's gaze shifting to his scuffed knuckles, and he put his hands in his pockets.

Murdoch dropped into his chair and pinched the bridge of his nose. James sensed there was something more pressing on the Super's mind; he looked pale, troubled, with dark circles around his eyes. He nervously shuffled some paperwork, then looked up at James. 'There's been a murder,' he said.

That'll be it then, James thought. Shame he doesn't have a Scottish burr: *Murrrderrr.* 'Murder? What? Where? Who?'

'Fifty-seven-year-old male, stabbed to death in his home, affluent area of Letchworth: John Gibbs, a wealthy businessman. His wife, Kathy Gibbs, reported it shortly after four this morning; said there'd been a break-in. SOCOs are on site. The family's been taken with the FLO, to a relative's house in Baldock.'

'Who have you appointed as SIO, sir?'

'You, James. Was going to be DI Yelland, but he's had

to deal with a family emergency; his father's at death's door, apparently.'

'What? No, I can't. What about Solent? That's consuming all my time.'

Murdoch raised his brow. 'You're going to have to let Porter take more of the slack. Think he can handle it?'

'He's good, but he's going to need some hand-holding.'

'Well, that's sorted then,' Murdoch said. 'Get yourself down to the crime scene and debrief me when you're back. Think about the team you want. Remember, we're spread thin; money's tight.'

'Sir.'

'Oh, and James, if there's anything more to that eye injury, now's the time to be telling me.'

'I've nothing to add, sir,' James said, and swiftly exited the office.

James hadn't handled a murder since the Perkins case, and he felt a twinge of apprehension, as he was checked in through the cordon at the Gibbs house in Letchworth. He dressed quickly into the disposable crime-scene suit and paraphernalia; he looked more like an asbestos-removal specialist than a detective.

He felt annoyed to have been taken from Solent, especially with it being at a critical juncture. But, part of him was pleased to have a distraction; an opportunity to put Perkins to the back of his mind for a while. Perhaps being too involved with Solent had caused him to lose perspective. Was he obsessed? Course he bloody was. What good detective wasn't an obsessive? Now was not the time to dwell; there was a murder to solve.

Behind him came a woman's voice:

'DCI Quinn, are you SIO? What can you tell me about the crime? Is it murder?'

He turned and saw it was that reporter from the *Herald*. Christ, she could be annoying. How had she got wind so quickly? He swatted her away and strode into the house, snapping on latex gloves.

'You owe me!' she bellowed.

Inside the house was a swarm of activity. The hallway alone was huge, three sets of oak double doors off of it, feeding the kitchen immediately in front of him, a dining room to the right and a living room to the left. The decor and furnishings were modern and expensive-looking, though more on the vulgar side of the taste-dividing line; *Footballers Wives* sprang to mind.

James was greeted by a SOCO, who introduced herself as Sergeant Coulthard. She ushered him into the living room. Had he encountered her before? Possibly, but if he had she clearly hadn't left much of an impression, good or bad. They stepped carefully around evidence number markers. Not one to be easily shocked, James needed a moment to steel himself and take a deep lungful of air, while he surveyed the scene.

John Gibbs's body was slumped in an armchair. The volume of blood, and the blood splatter about him, the furniture and the carpet, indicated an act of frenzied violence. His first thought was that the attack was personal, or the work of a psychopath. Possibly both.

'Estimated time of death?' he asked.

'From temperature readings, we can be reasonably confident it was between two and three.'

'Who do we know was present in the house at the time?'

'The wife, Kathy Gibbs, and their two sons, Mark and Ben.'

'And the wife reported an intruder?'

'That's right. There's a smashed pane of glass in the utility door.'

'I can't see any signs of a struggle, or self-defence marks.'

'Looks like he was caught unaware; possibly asleep. Suggests death occurred quickly.'

'Agreed. Did the wife or the sons witness the intruder?'

'No, sir. He'd fled before one of the sons found the body.'

'Do they know who it might be?'

'No, they're pretty traumatized, sir.'

'Hmm,' James said, bending to a squatting position in front of the corpse. 'There's a cut on his brow – looks pretty fresh. Do we have a weapon?'

'No.'

'Multiple stab wounds to the neck. It's a mess. Someone really didn't like this guy. I'll wait for the pathology report. Crack on.'

James stepped cautiously out of the room. He noted smashed glass in the carpet and bloody footprints leading out into the hallway, where they progressively faded towards the kitchen. He quickly moved through the house, careful not to get too much in the way of Forensics, as they documented the crime scene and swabbed for samples.

In the dining room, drawers had been pulled from a sideboard and paperwork was scattered on the table, and over the floor; a pot plant had been knocked over. In the kitchen, there was the distinct odour of bleach.

He scanned the huge garage: long workbench; a fridge; chest freezer; expensive-looking bicycles; calendar, with a naked woman draped over a red Ferrari.

Upstairs, James counted five bedrooms and three bathrooms. Three beds indicated they'd been occupied and not tidied. That, plus open wardrobe doors and chest drawers, suggested people dressing in a hurry.

James's instincts told him the intruder claim was a sham. Forensics reports would shed more light on the matter, but they wouldn't be available for a while. He needed to speak to the family individually, before they had the opportunity to get their story straight.

FOURTEEN

MAYBE THERE WAS A GOD, after all. If Molly hadn't been woken by the shenanigans next door, she wouldn't have been trawling social media in the early hours, and she wouldn't be standing here now, the sole journalist at the scene of a potentially major crime. Journalistic scoops were like gold dust in these parts, and Molly had no intention of letting it slip through her fingers. Wouldn't it be great if she could end her career at the *Herald* in a blaze of glory, and make Brian regret losing her? The icing on the cake. *Thank you, Becky.*

Trish Braithwaite – a friend of a friend of an acquaintance, whom she followed on Twitter – had posted about a swarm of police officers and an ambulance crew sweeping into their cul-de-sac, before dawn. This wasn't the sort of thing that happened in leafy Letchworth. Early bird (ha!) Twitterers – or whatever they're called – no doubt worried about the impact on the value of their houses, joined in: *'Think theres been a murder at the Gibb's place.'* Wild speculation or insider knowledge? Who cared? She even forgave them for the apostrophes; punctuation was the first thing to go out of the window in times of stress.

Cul-de-sac – French for 'dead end' (well, 'bottom of the bag' if translated literally). If she had a choice between life in a cul-de-sac or death, she'd choose the latter, no question; the very concept gave her the heebie-jeebies. She understood their superficial appeal: the safety; the community spirit; the petit-bourgeois wholesomeness; kids playing cricket on the road with the Smiths from next door; Dad buffing his Mondeo on the block-paved driveway, while Mum makes real lemonade in her John Lewis kitchen. Scratch the surface, though, and you'd soon unearth the curtain-twitching, petty jealousies, tedious gossip exchanged over fences and the remorseless pursuit of keeping up with the Joneses, which could drive you to a drink or drug habit. Or murder. She shuddered.

As if on cue, Molly spotted movement in her peripheral vision. She flicked her gaze to a first-floor window at number six, and a gap in the curtain closed. Below, in the front garden, a large, ginger tom emerged from a rhododendron bush, and she thought of Mr. Darcy back home and tucked up on his favourite chair – hopefully.

The largest house on the street was the scene of the crime. *Yeah, a crime against good taste,* Molly thought. It was a beast of a house, the incarnation of vulgarity, with its in-and-out drive and its triple garage, the size of Molly's entire cottage. It even had plastic, pastiche Georgian sashes, for Christ's sake.

A uniformed officer guarded the cordon. He looked absurdly young and wore small, round, wire-rimmed glasses; Harry Potter in a high-vis jacket. No use talking to him. Other officers in their disposable white suits formed a steady flow in and out of the front door, with their evidence bags, boxes and forensic equipment. Molly's own equipment inventory was nothing more than a pad, a pen, a nose for an interesting angle and an inquisitive mind.

She stole a look through the door, but couldn't see much of interest – certainly not a dead body lying Cluedo-style in a pool of blood, with the handle of a silver dagger between the shoulder blades. She was minded to knock on the door of the Braithwaites at number three, to get their insight, when behind her a silver Audi screeched to a halt. *Well, blow me down,* Molly thought, when DCI James Quinn stepped out. Without noticing her presence, he flashed his ID to the cordon officer and began to dress into the silly decorator's overalls.

She knew it was futile, but she shouted out anyway: 'DCI Quinn, are you SIO? What can you tell me about the crime? Is it murder?'

He flashed an irritated look at her and turned away.

Come on, you prick! Give me something to go on. I did you a favour with the Perkins reward article.

'You owe me!' she shouted, as he disappeared into the house. 'Bastard!'

Harry Potter looked at her.

'Not you.'

For some reason, the Braithwaites weren't answering the door, so Molly tried number seven, instead. A gold Mercedes soft-top was parked on the drive, and a three-tier water feature bubbled away in the centre of a manicured lawn. Tacky.

The door was opened by a tall, trim woman in a designer tracksuit, blonde hair tied loosely, sculpted eyebrows and plump lips. The word *'GUCCI'* was emblazoned across her plastic chest in gold letters, though it may just as well have read: *'TROPHY WIFE.'*

The woman leant against the doorjamb and drew on a cigarette. After exhaling a jet of smoke from the corner of her glossy mouth, she gave Molly the once over and said: 'You are hooker, yes?'

'I'm sorry?' Molly said.

'Bad luck. My husband away with business. Back tomorrow.'

The woman stepped back and placed a hand on the door, ready to close it.

'No, I'm a newspaper journalist,' Molly said. 'I'm here about next door. I'm Molly. Molly Tindall.' She proffered her hand, but the woman ignored it.

'Journalist? Which paper? You want take picture? Front page?' She puckered her lips and fingered her hair.

'I'd just like to speak to you about your neighbours, if you don't mind.'

Next door, a body bag was being stretchered out to a waiting van.

The woman stepped out, took a nonchalant glance, then turned to Molly, frowning. 'Why English men get so fat?'

She flicked her cigarette butt onto the drive and turned back into the house. 'Come. My name Yelena.'

Molly followed into the hallway.

A white-carpeted staircase swept up to a galleried landing. An enormous crystal chandelier hung from the high ceiling. As she crossed a zebra-print rug, Molly peered into the rooms on either side of her: a black-and-gold-themed dining room one side, and a living room replete with a gigantic, curved, pink leather sofa on the other. Vile. Yelena led her to the kitchen, with its black gloss cupboards and granite work surfaces. Bi-fold doors stretched along the back of the building, providing a panorama of a neat garden, dotted with statues and topiary-styled yews.

'Coffee?' Yelena said. It was more a command than a question.

'Black, please.'

Yelena flicked on a coffee machine and opened the American-sized fridge to retrieve a bottle of Evian. Molly noticed several champagne bottles.

'Nice house.'

Yelena gave an uninterested shrug. 'Is boring here; nothing happens. I prefer big city.'

'What does your husband do?'

'He owns property business: Brady Homes. You heard?'

That figured. Small world.

'Yes,' Molly said. 'Built the new estate in Baldock.'

The woman nodded.

'Nice houses,' Molly lied. 'What can you tell me about your neighbours?'

'What you want to know? Please sit.'

Molly perched herself on a stool, at one end of a ridiculously huge island unit, covered in vases of flowers. Fake, probably, like the woman's tits.

'Well, perhaps you could start by telling me who lives there.'

Yelena brought a coffee to Molly, then took a seat at the other end of the island. 'Man and woman: John and Kathy.'

'Anyone else?'

'They have two sons: twins, but don't live there anymore. One is student: very boring. The other is handsome businessman: he own gym with swimming pool. I go sometimes when am bored.'

'What was John like?'

'Fat.' She spat out the word.

'Anything else?'

Yelena shrugged. 'Likes fast cars.'

'What did he do for work?'

'He own investment company.'

'And what about her, Kathy?'

'She's… how you say...' Yelena puffed her cheeks, 'frumps.'

'Frumpy?'

'Yeah. Frumpy.'

'Do you know her well?'

'She's bitch.'

'Oh, why so?'

'I knocked on door one day, ask for milk. She say will call police if I don't get off property.'

'Can you think of any reason why someone might want to harm John?'

Yelena lit another cigarette and took a deep drag. 'Who knows? Who cares? Could have been anything. Money, probably – usually is. Or sex.'

'Did you see or hear anything last night? Arguments? Screaming? A break-in?'

'Don't care. Boring.'

Molly took a sip of coffee and concluded that she wasn't going to get any more from the Russian woman. 'Okay. If there's anything else you can think of that might be of interest, call me, please.'

She passed her business card to Yelena, who studied it for a moment. '*Hertfordshire Evening Herald*? Very boring, no? You should get proper job. Or rich husband.'

'Thanks for the advice,' Molly said, with a rictus grin. 'I'll see myself out.'

RŪTA

When Rūta stepped off the plane in England, the gravity of her decision to leave Lithuania behind struck her with unexpected force. It felt like all the blood in her body had been pulled into her stomach. Was it regret? No, there was nothing left for her in Lithuania; England was her new home. She told herself it was natural to feel like this, a whole mixture of emotions: fear, uncertainty, trepidation, hope... *Just take it one step at a time. Deep breath.*

An hour later, she was standing outside the duty-free store. She'd been waiting for a good twenty minutes now, popping back inside every so often, to encourage Urtė to hurry up. Eventually, Urtė emerged carrying two bags, her face beaming widely. Rūta found her own mood lifting at the sight of her best friend, who was clearly not burdened by any negative feelings. Oh, to be carefree like Urtė.

'What have you got there?' Rūta said. 'I hope you haven't spent all your money before we've even started our jobs!'

'Just a few things to help us celebrate the start of our new lives,' Urtė replied. She raised the bags, and the sound of bottles chinking against each other revealed their contents.

They'd flown into Robin Hood Airport, which was near a town that neither of them had heard of, called Doncaster. When Rūta had looked it up on a map, she saw with some alarm that it was hundreds of kilometres from London. Surely there was a closer airport? 'Don't worry,' Jack had soothed; 'it's the best flight we can get you. A driver will collect you and take you to London.'

'A chauffeur!' Urtė enthused.

Rūta had read about the legend of Robin Hood. 'He stole from the rich and gave to the poor,' she told Urtė.

'Urgh!' she responded. 'Sounds like a *communist*.'

Rūta grabbed one of the bags and handed Urtė back her wheelie suitcase.

They headed to the agreed pick-up location, where they found the driver waiting: a squat, fat man dressed in a short-sleeve white shirt and black tie. He folded his newspaper and tucked it under his arm.

'Rūta and Urtė?' he said, in a strange accent which seemed to cause Urtė no end of amusement. 'Welcome to England, ladies,' he said, doffing his cap. 'I'm Dave. Let me take you to the car.'

As they followed him, Urtė leaned in and whispered: 'He's all yours!'

Rūta laughed. 'I think I'll give him a miss, thank you.'

The car was a black Mercedes, which looked shiny and new. The seats were light-grey leather, and the carpet was so deep, thick and soft that Rūta felt like kicking off her pumps and sinking her bare feet into it, as if it were warm sand. It wasn't long before Urtė had fallen into a deep sleep.

Other than a handful of short and awkward exchanges with Dave – the weather, the Royal family, his family ('my wife left me last year') – the journey passed in silence. There was no way that Rūta could sleep now, even if she wanted to: she was too alert; too anxious. Once they were in London and settled into the apartment, then she'd be able to finally relax… Perhaps.

Jack had secured them a two-bedroom apartment in a new high-rise block, in a place called Battersea, where it seemed there was a famous dog's home. When they were settled, Rūta fancied the idea of a pet dog. Nothing too big – one which could look after itself for the day in the flat, and didn't need too much exercise. 'You can see the river if you squint hard enough,' Jack had said.

Rūta had felt something close to abject terror when she wired across the money, to cover the flights and the deposit on the flat. It was a small fortune ('London property is the most expensive in the world, ladies'), partly derived from the overtime she and Urtė had been working for months, but mostly it comprised what remained of Rūta's beloved Grandma's bequest. Rūta had lived with Grandma Elžbieta since the age of six months, after her parents were killed in a car accident. Apparently, little Rūta had been plucked unharmed from the mangled wreckage. To Elžbieta, Rūta was her 'Little Miracle' *('Mažas Stebuklas')*, on whom she doted – right to the point where their roles were reversed, as Elžbieta slowly succumbed to her final illness. Rūta, then seventeen – a young, naive seventeen – was utterly bereft, and it took many months (and Urtė's relentlessly cheerful support) to shake off the dark depression which had engulfed her. Grandma Elžbieta had been Rūta's last known living blood relative.

A heavy rain was now falling, and the windscreen wipers operated at full pelt. Through her window, streaked by rivulets of rain, the landscape was rendered abstract, monochrome and bleak. Rūta fought back tears, and she shifted her gaze forward.

She caught Dave looking at her in the rear-view mirror. His eyes were expressionless, and she felt a shiver run down her spine.

'Hungry?' he said.

She wasn't, but she could do with an excuse to wake Urtė. Unable to form any words in her dry mouth, Rūta simply nodded. Moments later, Dave exited the motorway and took several more turnings. Rūta tried to take in the road signs and the place names, to anchor their location, but everything was just too unfamiliar and meaningless. She figured Dave was looking for a café or restaurant; they were on a single-lane road now, with nothing but wet fields surrounding them. She took the opportunity to jab her elbow into Urtė's side.

'Wake up! We're stopping for food shortly.'

Eventually, Urtė roused and slurred: 'Where are we?'

Dave was slowing down now, and Rūta noticed a vehicle parked up ahead. As the Mercedes pulled in behind it, Rūta noted that it was a dark-grey V.W. van, with blacked-out windows. Her pulse raced.

'What's happening?' she said. Dave didn't respond.

A rear door opened in the van and a man stepped out. He was tall and wore a hoodie. Hunched against the rain, he strode towards them. Rūta grabbed Urtė's hand. The man came over to Urtė's window and peered inside. The women turned to look at each other and, for the first time that she could ever recall, Rūta saw fear in Urtė's features.

The door swung open, and the man suddenly leaned in over Urtė, unbuckled her, then yanked her out of the car.

Rūta tried to grab her, but she was overpowered by the man's brute strength. He effortlessly pulled Urtė clean from the car and kicked the door shut.

What was happening? Rūta fumbled desperately to unbuckle herself, and scrambled across the seat to open the door, but the child locks were on. Through the window she could see Urtė being dragged, kicking and screaming, to the van. She watched helplessly as she was bundled inside.

Rūta wailed a blood-curdling 'Noooooo!' as the van sped off, into the distance.

She then noticed, too late, that Dave had grabbed her arm. She felt a sharp pain and registered the syringe in his hand, just as an almighty tiredness overwhelmed her.

FIFTEEN

JAMES ARRIVED at the relative's house in Baldock and was greeted by a rather flustered family liaison officer – FLO, in cop lingo: petite; early forties, perhaps; tip of a tattoo poking from her collar; moist brow. He couldn't recall ever meeting her.

'New to the job?' he asked, stepping into a small hall.

'First week, sir,' she said; 'transferred from Bedford-shire. New role, new life, new me...' she babbled nervously. He caught her gaze lingering on his swollen eye.

'Interesting,' James said, casting glances around the house. 'Who does this place belong to?' It was a modest semi (not unlike his own), in a nondescript part of town – well lived in and somewhat shabby (very much unlike his own). He mentally added another suspect to his list of motives: jealousy.

'Mrs. Gibbs's cousin. She's taken herself off to work to give the family some space.'

'How are they? Said anything interesting?'

'How you'd imagine, sir...'

'Tell me what I'm supposed to be imagining.'

'Shaken, not saying much. One of the boys seems agitated.'

'Agitated? Now that *is* interesting. Which one?'

'Ben. They're twins, but you'd never guess.'

'Not identical, then? That's a relief,' James smiled.

The FLO frowned.

'Both at the crime scene; shared DNA and all that.'

Her face lit up as the penny dropped: 'Oh, like a *Murder She Wrote* kind of thing?'

'You've got it.'

Behind him, there was a knock at the door. He turned and opened it.

'Ah, Mel, glad you could join us. Come in.'

Mel Barraclough rolled her eyes. 'I came as soon as I got your message… guv. And what the hell's happened to your eye?'

'Rumour mill out of action today then?'

James turned back to the FLO. 'We'll speak to Mrs. Gibbs first: Katie, isn't it?'

'Kathy.'

'Yes, Kathy.'

'Have we got a suitable room to use?'

The FLO pointed to a door, slightly ajar. He pushed it open and walked in. A dining-cum-junk room, by the look of it.

He pulled out a chair from under the dining table, stacked with bundles of papers, board games and all manner of junk. He tutted. Untidy house, untidy mind – that was a phrase, wasn't it? Turning to look back into the hall, he saw Mel and the FLO woman nattering away.

'Mel?' he called out. 'In your own time. Not like there's a murder investigation to be getting on with or anything.'

She flashed him one of her looks and resumed her chat with the FLO.

He shoved some of the tabletop junk to one side and thrummed his fingers. Then, he felt something brush against his lower leg. Peering under the table, he saw that it was a cat, jet black, with big, green eyes. James smiled at it and it jumped onto his lap, then onto the table. 'Hello, gorgeous,' he said, puckering his lips and proffering his hand. The cat nudged its chin against it affectionately, purring with delight. James ran his hand down its glossy back; the cat responded by arching its spine.

'Aah, would you look at that?' Mel said, entering the room. 'Never had you down as cat man, guv.'

'I'm not,' he said, swatting the cat from the table with the back of his hand. 'Shoo.' The cat jumped off the table and disappeared into the hall.

'Too late now for the tough guy act; I saw it with my own eyes.' Mel smiled and took a seat at the table.

'Close the door will you, for God's sake?' James said.

'Do it your bloody self.'

'Ever heard of the word "insubordination", Barraclough?'

Mel gave him another of her looks. 'Is that the one next to "insufferable" in the dictionary?'

James fought hard to suppress an admiring grin. 'I'll give you that one, Barraclough. Now, you couldn't go and get me a cup of coffee, could you, treacle?'

Mel raised her middle finger.

James smiled and got up to shut the door, then returned to his chair.

'Paula's nervous as hell,' Mel said. 'Poor thing.'

'Paula?'

Mel slapped her forehead. 'Family Liaison! New to the job; trying to make a good impression. Good to see you've put those legendary people skills to good use and made her feel at ease.'

'Right, well, if it's okay with you, Mel, can we get on with the job in hand? I'll bring you up to speed, then we'll get Katie Gibbs in.'

'Are you doing it to wind me up, guv?'

'Doing what?'

Mel looked at her watch. 'Come on then, brief me; I haven't got all day.'

Grief? Shock? Guilt? Could be any; perhaps all three. Perhaps none. Kathy Gibbs sat passively in front of them, staring at a dry tissue which she passed between her hands. She'd looked up briefly while James was explaining – in the most sympathetic tone he could muster – his role as SIO, that she was free to go at any point, and his colleague would be taking notes, etc. The woman's appearance was not too far removed from the mental image he'd formed: shoulder-length hair, tousled and flecked with grey, and a world-weary face free of makeup. He saw no indication of recent tears in her pale-green eyes, but that fact told him nothing; he hadn't cried for weeks after Ruth died: not when she had breathed her last pained breath, not during the funeral service, and not even when he visited her grave alone for the first time. It wasn't as if he was trying to be the tough guy; he *wanted* to cry.

Now wasn't the time for detailed questioning; that would come later. For now, just some gentle probing; start building the hypothesis.

'I know this is hard, Mrs. Gibbs, but please talk me through what happened last night.'

Kathy reached for the glass of water the FLO had brought her, but her hand trembled so much that she put it down again. She briefly made eye contact with James, before returning her gaze to her hands. Pulling her cardigan tight around her chest, despite the warm room, Kathy drew a deep breath, as if to compose herself.

'I was asleep, but I was woken by a loud noise from downstairs – about two o'clock, I think. I… I… thought it was Ben coming back.'

'Where had Ben been?'

'Into town, to meet up with friends and have a drink.'

'Does Ben still live at home?'

'No, neither of them do now: Mark's at university in Bath, although he's on his summer holidays now, and Ben lives just outside Cambridge. He has his own business.' Kathy smiled sadly before continuing: 'They came over for a meal; it was our anniversary.' She dabbed the corner of her eye with the tissue.

'I'm sorry, Kathy. Please, tell me what happened after you heard the noise.'

'I waited to hear Ben come upstairs, but he didn't. Then I heard more noises: banging, clattering, that sort of thing. I started to panic.'

'Where was John at this point?'

'He was downstairs – probably fallen asleep in front of the TV while he was watching a film. He's a night owl, you see.' She paused, before adding: '*Was*.'

'Go on, please.' So many questions began to bubble in James's mind. But let her just talk, for now.

'I woke Mark and told him to come downstairs, to investigate with me. When we got to the bottom of the stairs, we saw him straight away. All the blood… I screamed… Mark went in to check if he was still alive…' Kathy dropped her head into her hands.

'Did you call the emergency services at that point?'

Silence.

'Kathy?'

She raised her head, then shook it. 'We were in a state

of shock, I guess, trying to work out what could have happened. Mark looked around the house. Then he came back to say there must have been an intruder, who got in through the back door.'

'Can you think of anyone who might want to harm your husband?'

Kathy shook her head.

'Did your husband have any enemies, that you're aware of?'

Again, she shook her head. 'Perhaps it was just a burglar, who got spooked when they found John.'

It was James's turn to remain silent for a few moments, after which he said: 'Was anything taken, as far as you're aware?'

'I… don't know.'

James looked at his notebook. 'You called 999 shortly after four a.m. Why such a long time after finding your husband?'

'What are you trying to suggest?'

'I'm not trying to suggest anything, Kathy. I just need to establish the timeline.'

'I suppose we were in a bit of a flap, panicking.'

'I could smell bleach in the kitchen, Kathy.'

'Well… yes… Ben came in shortly after and he was… you know… a bit worse for wear. He made a mess in the kitchen, which I had to clear up.'

'I see.'

James followed Kathy's gaze to her hands and noticed something there. 'How did you get the cut?' he asked.

'Oh, that? It's nothing: nicked myself while I was preparing dinner. Nothing serious.'

'How would you describe your marriage, Kathy?' James asked, changing the subject.

'I love him,' Kathy said. 'He's my world.' At that,

Kathy broke down and sobbed. Mel passed her a packet of tissues and placed a comforting hand on her forearm.

James felt his phone buzzing and checked it: a text message from the Tindall woman. Without even reading it, he returned the phone to his pocket.

'We'll leave it for now, Kathy. Please understand, though, we will need to speak to you again. It's important.'

The FLO – Pamela? Patsy? Pauline? – had taken Kathy to the kitchen for a strong tea, then returned to the living room to sit with Ben, while James spoke to Mark Gibbs.

'Don't mind if I ask you a few questions, do you?'

'Course not,' Mark said, smiling politely.

James noticed Mark's gaze linger on his black eye. 'Accident with a kitchen cupboard. You know how it is,' he said.

He felt a buzzing in his pocket again, but ignored it. He studied Mark's features for a moment; the guy certainly had the look of a student: cheap haircut, glasses, creased check shirt. His eyes betrayed little emotion, and he smelled mildly of stale sweat.

'Get on with your brother, do you?'

Mark's eyes narrowed into a brief look of puzzlement, then calculation and finally indifference. 'We don't see much of each other. Kind of have different interests, I suppose.'

'I see, different interests,' James said, smiling broadly as he wrote on his pad. Wouldn't hurt to unsettle him from the get-go. 'Such as?'

'Why is this relevant? You need to be out there looking for the guy that did this.'

'Of course. We're combing the house now, as I'm sure you'll understand, for any evidence – fingerprints, DNA and so on – which will help us do just that. Do you have any idea of who it might have been?'

'No.'

'Was your father the type of man to acquire enemies?'

James observed Mark's eyes darting between Mel and himself. The man's behavioural tics showed the tell-tale signs of someone who wasn't being one-hundred per cent honest. But, still, he had to retain an open mind; hone in too early on one theory and you can too quickly start looking for facts which support it, becoming blind to inconvenient facts which dispute it. In any case, who was ever one-hundred per cent honest?

'He was a successful businessman. I guess you don't get to the top without ruffling a few feathers.'

'Indeed. So, can you think of anyone who might have had their feathers ruffled by your father?'

'No.'

'Close to him, were you?'

Mark returned James's gaze, but blinked rapidly. He shrugged his shoulders and said: 'Not particularly. We kind of had…'

'Different interests?'

'Yes, I suppose.'

'Would you say that your brother and father's interests were more closely aligned?'

'I guess. Ben's always wanted to go into business, too. I'm more of an arty person.'

'Arty?'

'Books, paintings, art galleries, theatre… that kind of thing. Not a crime, is it?'

'Not at all. I'm fond of a nice picture, myself.'

At that moment, the FLO entered the room. 'Sorry, could I have a quick word, sir?'

. . .

James had cut short his discussion with Mark, when the FLO told him she couldn't contain Ben any longer; apparently the lad was keen to get home. Interesting.

'Can we get this over and done with as quickly as possible, please?' Ben then looked James in the eye and frowned; 'You been in a fight?'

Accident, kitchen cupboard, etc.

'Good night out, was it?' James said, deflecting.

Ben reeked of beer and stale sweat, and from the look of him, James guessed he was still in the same clothes as the night before. He looked like he hadn't had a wink of sleep. Apart from the height (six-two/six-three) and a familial nose (long, classical), there was not much similarity in appearance between the brothers: Ben was more muscular, his hair fairer and eyes darker; a moody kind of handsomeness which his brother lacked.

'What?'

'Your mum told me you went out after the meal.'

'What else did she tell you?'

'I'd rather hear things from your own mouth, if that's okay, Ben. Now, talk me through the events of yesterday, please.'

'Don't remember much. I had a skinful with the lads, and Mum made one of her shitty dinners. Twat Face was being his usual annoying self–'

'Twat Face?'

'That's what I call Mark. He calls me Shit Dick.'

'How quaint,' James said. 'Tell me more.'

'It's always the same – that's why we don't get together much. Mum likes to play happy families, though, so we try to make the effort for her sake. Waste of time. All I remember is Mark flouncing out of the room, 'cos of something or other. I thought, *Sod this for a game of soldiers,* so I went out.'

167

'What happened when you came home?'

'That's when I found Mum and Mark in the kitchen; they told me Dad had been stabbed to death. Couldn't get my head around it; I was still drunk.'

'An intruder?' James said.

'Suppose it had to be.'

'Any idea of who it might be?'

'No.'

James felt his phone ringing, this time cursed Molly Tindall inwardly, and took out his mobile in anger.

'Apologies,' he said to Ben, and looked to see that it was in fact the Super calling. He'd be after an update. For Christ's sake, did the man have no patience? He'd brief him when he was back in the office. He ignored the call.

James had now lost his train of thought, but in any case considered there was precious little else to be gained from speaking to the family at this point. He'd wait for the forensics reports, get initial enquiries initiated and put together the investigation team.

Turning to Ben, James said: 'Why don't you get yourself home then – sort yourself out? We'll need to speak to you again soon, I'm sure.'

With that, Ben left the house without speaking to Kathy or Mark. This family was pretty screwed up, James thought. Which was no different to any other, he supposed.

James closed the door and turned to speak to Mel, in hushed tones. 'So, what do you think?'

'Good of you to ask my opinion.'

'What's that supposed to mean?'

'Just wish you'd trust me with a bit more than note-taking. I might as well be bloody invisible.'

'Sorry,' he said. 'You're right. I'm just a bit of a control freak, that's all; you know me better than anyone. Look,

I've got to get back to HQ to brief the Super. Can you speak to the FLO—'

'Paula.'

'Yeah, Paula. Get her to tease more out of Kathy and Mark about the day: dig into the relationships between her and John, the sons and their dad, and between the boys themselves. Then, get yourself down to the crime scene; see if they've found anything interesting: the weapon, discarded clothing, anything.'

'Will do, guv.'

James paused for a moment. 'A little bird tells me you've got an admirer back at the office.'

'Just the one, guv?' Mel smiled.

'Luke Porter. I think he's smitten. Would you say yes if he asked you out?'

Mel blushed. 'I've only just split up with Declan; not sure I'm ready to have my heart broken again so soon. What do you think I should do?'

'I think you should say yes. I like him, and he's clearly got good taste in women.'

Mel palmed her chest and smiled.

'Seize the day, Mel. Life's too short to waste on wallowing in the past.'

'Thanks, guv.'

James reached for the door handle, then turned back to Mel. 'Oh, and one more thing.'

'What's that?'

'If you do say yes when he asks you out, tell the poor sod to invest in a quality pair of earplugs.'

Mel slapped him on the arm. 'You cheeky bloody git! Now, piss off back to HQ.'

· · ·

The moment James arrived back on the floor at HQ, an angry-looking Murdoch summoned him into his office.

'Sit down, James.'

'I'd rather stand.'

'Sit down!' the Super thundered, slamming the door with a force which gave James a start.

'I've been speaking to the family,' James said. 'I had every intention of briefing you as soon as–'

'This isn't about the Gibbs case, Quinn.'

Quinn? Noted.

'I don't understand, sir.'

'Troy Perkins has made a complaint: police harassment and assault; ABH, for fuck's sake, Quinn!'

'Jesus.'

'Quite. What am I supposed to do now, eh? You've put me in an impossible situation.'

James remained silent. Nothing he could say right now was going to help the situation.

Murdoch continued: 'I expect honesty and openness from my officers. Is that too much to ask? I've got so much on my plate right now, and I'm going to have to spend time I haven't got sucking up to that odious waste of space, to convince him to drop the complaint. All because of you and your ridiculous obsession with him.'

'Sir–'

'I haven't finished. This stops right now. Have you got that into your thick skull?' Murdoch jabbed a finger against his temple. 'If you so much as *think* about him, I… I won't be responsible for my actions. Now, get out.'

James rose from the chair. 'Did you want that briefing for the Gibbs case, sir?'

'I'll get it from Barraclough. Out!'

James sauntered sheepishly over to his desk. He dropped into his chair and held his head in his hands. It

honestly felt like Perkins was going to be the end of him –
and not just his career. Right now, in fact, he couldn't give
a shit about his career.

His phone buzzed and he pulled it from his pocket, to
see that the Tindall woman was calling him. 'Fuck off!' he
shouted, and hurled the phone into the bin. The phone
continued to vibrate from within the metal bucket, and he
sensed the room falling into an embarrassed silence.

Awareness grew of a presence behind him, and James
spun to look up into the rather chastened face of DC
Porter. 'What is it?' he asked, irritably.

'Was just going to give you an update on Solent, guv.
Now not a good time?'

James took a deep breath. 'Fine. Walk with me outside;
I need fresh air.'

On the way to the stairs, James noticed everyone
turning to look away as he passed. No skin off his nose;
better that than awkward exchanges of banal pleasantries.

Then, he noticed the desk of one officer – couldn't for
the life of him remember her name – covered in birthday
cards. *Shit!* He'd completely forgotten. He'd have to sort
something out after work and pay her a visit. She deserved
better than him, wrapped up in his own woes, without a
second thought for others in a far worse position than him.

Outside, they strolled through the dappled shade of the
plane trees in the park. Luke was talking but James, lost in
his own thoughts and laden with self-loathing, could barely
process the words.

They came to a pond and James's attention shifted to a
young mother, crouched at the water's edge, gripping the
reins of an excitable toddler, who threw chunks of bread
into a throng of geese and ducks. A swan glided into the

mix, and as it drew closer the child's excitement turned quickly to distress; he dropped the bread and held up his arms to his mother. She bundled him into her chest and whisked him away from danger.

Luke, as if sensing James's attention was elsewhere, motioned him to a park bench. 'Has something happened, guv?'

James's gaze remained for a few moments longer on the mother and child. He took a deep breath, turned to Luke and, against his usual instinct, decided to tell him what Perkins had done.

'I'll tell the Super I witnessed it,' Luke offered: 'he threw the first punch and you were just defending yourself. Who's going to take his word over mine?'

James smiled, and an ember in the spent fire of his belly glowed.

'You're a good man, Luke,' he said, 'but please stay out of it. You've got your whole career ahead of you. I can look after myself. Now, let me buy you a coffee.'

SIXTEEN

MOLLY'S PLAN TO arrive in the office and tell Brian she'd got a major scoop had gone tits-up: Herts Constabulary had issued an anodyne press release, to the effect that the body of businessman John Gibbs had been removed from a house in Letchworth, and the police were treating the death as suspicious. She'd gleaned precious little detail to add to this from any of the neighbours, or the officers at the scene. She was particularly annoyed that DCI Quinn hadn't been prepared to give her the time of day. That was the last time she'd be doing him any favours. Arsehole.

Hoping that he'd be busy in a meeting or a conference call, and not notice her, she strode purposefully by Brian's office. The only other route into the office was via the emergency stairwell, but that would trigger the fire alarm. Basically, the officious prick had all angles covered. She thought she'd got away with it when, half a dozen steps from her desk, she heard that reedy voice of his, which made her think of a mosquito.

'What time do you call this, Molly?'

She was in no mood for obsequiousness. Aware that

everyone in the entire office was now looking at her, Molly pivoted on her heels and said in a loud, faux apology: 'Sorry, Brian, I thought I'd told you. Been to the doctors this morning – you know, about my women's problems.'

Brian, suitably embarrassed, retreated to his office and Molly slumped into her chair. Roll on the day she could kiss the *Herald* goodbye, once and for all. While she waited for her computer to fire up, she imagined her future self at the *Daily News*: *'Molly, get yourself down to Whitechapel, pronto; another headless body's washed up in the Thames.'* Then, after work, she'd head out with her trendy London reporter friends, to a swanky cocktail bar in a gleaming skyscraper: *'Another Black Russian, Molly?' 'Don't mind if I do, thanks, Jemima.'* They'd chat about guys and politics and fashion and art and theatre and murder.

Molly's phone rang out from within her handbag, jolting her back to the reality of her life, as a middle-aged hack in a Hertfordshire backwater. She scrambled to retrieve the phone amongst the detritus. *Quinn? Please have something for me.* No, it was the woman from Especially4U.

'Lucy, hi,' Molly said, propping the phone against her shoulder, while typing her password.

'Oh, hi, Molly. It's about your date tonight with Mr. Harknett.'

Oh, God, she'd forgotten all about it. This one had shown quite some promise: a heart surgeon from St. Albans; liked rugby. Brains, brawn, money – what's not to like? 'Yes, what is it?'

'Bad news, I'm afraid: we're going to have to postpone; he's had a nasty flare-up with his eczema.'

Molly left work at five on the dot; she just couldn't hack it any longer. She'd managed to somehow put together five hundred words, which she'd fired off to Brian with an apologetic email: *'Best I can do in the circumstances.'* As she passed his office on the way out, he looked at his watch.

'Sorry, Bri, still hurting,' she mouthed, pointing downward and wearing a pained expression.

She pulled up outside the cottage and saw a woman keying the lock next door.

'Becky?' Molly called out, swinging her handbag over her shoulder.

The woman turned and shot Molly a rictus smile. She wasn't far off what Molly imagined: average height; slim; busty; brunette; unremarkable face, hidden beneath excessive makeup; immaculate attire; desperate to hold on to a better-looking husband she'd probably won over with her tits. *God, I'm such a bitch.*

'I'm Molly. Don't know if Tom mentioned me?'

'You're the one with the cat?'

'That's right. I hear you're not a fan.'

'Not really,' Becky said awkwardly, turning back to the door, apparently keen to get inside. Surely she didn't see Molly as some kind of threat? Was she that insecure?

'Hope you're enjoying life in the cottage.'

'Yes, thank you.'

'Shame the sound travels so easily through the walls, eh?'

Molly would swear Becky's cheeks turned purple – or was that just the makeup? 'Have a nice evening,' she said, as Becky closed the door behind her.

Once indoors, she picked up a pile of mail from the doormat and took it through to the kitchen. Molly then noticed that Mr. Darcy's dish of dry cat food and bowl of water were untouched. He hadn't appeared before she left for work that morning, and she'd left the garden gate open for him, so there was no reason why he couldn't get in; it was most unlike him to miss a meal. She was immediately worried and headed out to look for him, throwing the mail down on the countertop as she did so.

His territory wasn't extensive; he never went out the front, restricting himself to the garden and a small expanse of the recreation ground. She trilled his name and zig-zagged across the thick grass, checking trees and bushes. Nothing. Heading back to her garden, she glimpsed Becky at the upstairs window, who quickly turned and retreated into darkness. Did she have something to do with this? *Don't be ridiculous, Moll.*

It occurred to Molly that Mr. Darcy might have taken himself off to die somewhere. She'd read that this was an evolutionary instinct for a cat; a hangover from the time when, if they weren't feeling well, they would need to hide themselves away from predators. He'd shown no sign of being unwell, though, and surely she would have noticed some kind of change in his behaviour? She couldn't bear the thought of him passing away. He was more than just a pet to her.

Silly mare; she was probably worrying over nothing. He might have just ventured a little farther afield for once, and fallen asleep somewhere, out of sheer exhaustion? Perhaps taken an interest in an attractive young tabby, or managed to charm his way into the affections of another lonely, old spinster? Mr. Darcy being dead or seriously injured were just two out of a million possibilities and, despite maths not being her strongest suit, Molly decided the statistics were stacked heavily in her favour. So, she returned to the kitchen.

She thumbed through her mail: gas bill (she'd look at that later, to really cheer herself up), a flyer from a Mr. Tapsell advertising his Trees, Fencing & Landscaping business: *'All kinds of trees expertly felled, topped and pruned. All rubbish removed. All roots destroyed. Fruit trees expertly pruned. Conifers topped and shaped. Hedges pruned and trimmed. Turfing. Stump grinding–'*

Stump grinding? What on Earth was that? Perhaps she should invite Mr. Tapsell round for a demonstration? She conjured an image of the gardener from *Desperate Housewives*, who quickly morphed into Tom next door, toiling in the glare of the midday sun, white t-shirt removed and draped over a ripped shoulder. Perhaps Tom *was* Mr. Tapsell? Tom Tapsell? Hmm. Knowing her luck, Mr. Tapsell would turn out to be a fat bloke in his fifties, with a gammy leg and gingivitis. Not worth the risk, she concluded, ripping up the flyer and discarding it in the pedal bin. Next envelope.

Ooh, what's this? Her heart skipped a beat. A white envelope, her name and address handwritten in blue ink, the logo of the *Daily News* in the corner. Could it be? She tore it open and scanned the letter inside.

'*Dear Ms. Tindall,*

Thank you for your recent job application for the position of Crime Reporter… We would like you to come to our office for an interview…'

She held the letter against her chest and looked to the ceiling. This was it: her big chance to work at a national tabloid! The big time awaited. Her luck had changed, at last.

SEVENTEEN

THE OLD WOMAN was slumped in the high-backed chair, eyes glazed and motionless, except for a jaundiced hand, which stroked an offcut of indigo yarn between thumb and forefinger. A cardigan hung loose on hunched, bony shoulders, her legs stick thin. Mary Quinn was not yet eighty, but looked a hundred.

James lightly kissed his mother's lined cheek, but she showed not a flicker of reaction. She rarely did. 'Happy birthday, Mum.'

Mary had been in the care home for more than six years, ever since she'd become a danger to herself and others. It smelled of institutional cooking and disinfectant, and reminded James of the corridors of his old primary school: overheated; waxed parquet, with a splatter of vomit covered in sawdust by the caretaker. James tried to visit his mother at Sunny Vale whenever he could, which was never enough, and certainly not the regular routine that the nurses said was so important. She'd understand, though, James told himself; his wasn't a nine-to-five job. *Stop making excuses.*

He walked over to the bay window, and looked out onto the neat garden. He'd put Mum's old dresser in the bay; on it was a collection of framed photographs. Amongst them, he made space for the birthday card and the bunch of flowers he'd picked up from the petrol station. It was the most expensive bunch in the shop, but still cheap, nonetheless. She deserved better from her son. Still, at least he'd remembered.

When Mary wasn't in her chair, or in bed, or in the communal lounge, James would find her standing here, one hand held against the dresser for support, the other clutching a photo – always the same one. James held it now: Christmas 1982; they were at the dinner table in the kitchen, above the pub. Mum was in the middle, James to her left and David, his older brother, to her right. An enormous turkey sat on the table, and Mum and David held their Christmas crackers up to the camera, smiling broadly. James was glowering; he guessed he had probably been annoyed at having his photo taken. He'd always been a miserable sod in that regard.

James flicked his gaze back to Mary in her chair, to see that her head had dropped and she appeared to be asleep. He sighed wistfully and paced around the room. That was something he did: pace. He was never entirely sure whether he was moving from something or towards it. It was like his running: he just felt a compulsion to keep moving.

But, something in the corner of his eye made him stop: a dark, rectangular patch on the wall. He moved over to it and traced a finger around its outline. Just as it dawned on him what it was, he heard a voice behind him.

'We took the mirror down. It was frightening her.'

James turned to see Jane, one of the care assistants. Heart of gold; probably paid a pittance. 'Oh, hi.'

179

Jane stepped into the room. She held a batch of white towels against her chest. 'She was screaming at it the other night; didn't recognize the woman she saw. Probably thought she was an intruder.'

'She thinks I'm David,' James said, smiling wistfully. 'I wouldn't mind, but we haven't seen him for years.'

'That's often the way, love. You mustn't take it personally.'

'It's hard not to.'

Jane squeezed James's forearm. 'You're doing a grand job. Mary appreciates it.'

'I feel like I should be doing more for her.'

'Just be there for her. Talk to her. That's all you can do, love,' Jane said, softly. 'We'll do the rest.'

The next morning, he was outside in his running gear at first light; not a soul was around. The air was warm and humid, and angry clouds threatened rain. 'We need a thunderstorm to clear the air,' he could hear his mother saying. Maybe one would clear his head, too? Fat chance. James adjusted his watch and settled into an easy pace, which he planned on maintaining until he got to the hill.

With all the things going on at work, and Perkins's complaint, it was actually the image of the toddler feeding the ducks that he'd found impossible to dislodge from his mind, during the restless night. He knew why, of course: it was an image of a future which fate had decreed would now live only in his imagination.

Ruth would have made a wonderful mum, no question. As much as he was self-absorbed, aloof, impatient and angry, she was kind, altruistic and nurturing. Whatever did she see in him, that he couldn't see in himself? He often thought this, even when she was alive. Was he a better man then? He was happier, yes, but that's not the same thing. Oh, God, why did she have to die? Why was life so shit?

James wasn't sure if he'd given physical voice to this last thought. He picked up his pace, as if doing so would untether his bleak musings. The pace was too fast to maintain, and by the time he'd reached the base of the long climb into Preston, he needed a rest to bring his heart rate down. Drenched in sweat, he dropped onto the trunk of an uprooted sycamore. In front of him, a hedgerow was alive with birdsong, although he couldn't see any birds – perhaps because a kestrel hovered above; the circle of life. Beyond the hedgerow, a cornfield stretched like a giant carpet across the contoured farmland, to a distant line of trees, black against a gunmetal sky. He imagined running into the corn and losing himself completely.

A vivid childhood memory struck him – he couldn't have been much more than eleven or twelve: a trip to the video shop. The idea of it seemed ridiculous now, in the age of downloads and instant gratification. He'd scoured the shelves, inspected the colourful cases, read the blurb and checked the age rating. He could picture the cover of *Children of the Corn* now: a silhouette of a child wielding a scythe against a blood-red sky; an eighteen rating. No problem; he could handle it. 'It's for my parents,' he told the man behind the counter. Things were clearly more lax in the 'eighties – a bygone era. The film scared him half to death – not that he had let on to his mates. Yes, he had friends back then.

A violent clap of thunder snapped him back to the present, and he felt the first raindrops on his scalp and forearms: light and sporadic at first, then steady, before quickly developing into a downpour. James started to run up the hill, pushing himself through the pain which burned in his quads. He sucked in the air, and with it the scent of rain falling on the hot, dusty road surface. Was there a smell more intoxicating? Freshly mown grass, perhaps. Ruth emerging from a hot bath, swaddled in a soft towel, certainly.

As he ran, James tried to shift his thoughts to practical matters: deciding on the day's work allocation, priorities for the Gibbs murder, the next steps on Solent... But then Troy Perkins entered his consciousness, threatening to crowd out all other thoughts, like he always did. His black dog.

He finally reached the summit, his lungs close to bursting. Gasping for breath, he dropped his hands to his thighs. Steam rose from him like a racehorse. Time to walk for a bit now and let his pulse settle. He knew he'd overdone it; he was getting too old for that now and risked injury – or a heart attack. Right now, he didn't really care. It may actually be a blessing.

He stopped and paused at the entrance to the path leading into Wain Wood. Should he go in? As if in answer to the question, a fork of lightning flashed across the dark sky, accompanied by almost instantaneous thunder. A harbinger? James laughed at the absurdity of the thought. He didn't believe in that kind of mystical crap. Fate, on the other hand, was a different matter; determinism had a basis in orthodox science, didn't it? Not mumbo jumbo spiritualism. He found a crumb of comfort in the concept of fate: the bad stuff was just meant to be; there was nothing you could do about it, but just accept it. Trouble was, that was the downside, too.

He suddenly became aware he was standing still, drenched to the skin. A chill crept over him. He turned and headed home.

If anything, the rain was now falling even heavier. His

running shoes were waterlogged and felt like lead weights. Ahead, the road sliced through another wood and the trees formed a tunnel, offering a brief respite from the deluge. James kicked on.

Behind him, the sound of a car engine grew louder. The road was narrow: a single lane with intermittent passing points; the verges on either side were thick with undergrowth. The car engine growled impatiently and the driver tooted the horn. Well, he'd just have to wait until James reached a passing point; no way was he going to jump into the sodden undergrowth just to let him pass. The driver honked again, more aggressively this time, and James turned to show him the finger. The car's lights were on full beam in the gloom, and James drew an arm to his eyes to shield them from the blinding light.

Now, the engine screamed and the wheels began to spin. They gained a purchase on the road and the car hurtled towards him. He threw himself into the undergrowth and the car charged past.

Getting to his feet, James caught a glimpse of the car, as it disappeared into the dark tunnel.

Unmistakably, it was Troy Perkins's red Peugeot.

EIGHTEEN

Molly arrived at the office earlier than her contractual start time; she figured there was no point gratuitously riling Brian – not until she had a firm job offer in her hand, anyway. Besides, she would only have moped around the house, worrying herself sick over Mr. Darcy. Before bed last night, she'd printed a batch of 'missing cat' leaflets and popped them through the neighbourhood letterboxes – stapled a couple to telegraph poles, too. She managed to convince herself he'd be back soon, curled up on his chair, purring away with his belly full, while dreaming content-edly of his recent dalliance with the pretty new tabby across the way.

She heard the sound of animated chatter coming through the thick glass of Brian's office, and as she walked past she stole a quick look inside. Brian's back was to her at his round meeting table; opposite him was a very angry looking man. He reminded Molly of someone – someone famous. Who the devil? Richard Somebody. Madeley? No, Whiteley. Richard Whiteley – the dead one from *Countdown*: cheeky glint in his eye, flirting like mad with the brainy maths woman, Carol Vorderman. The angry Richard Whiteley lookalike glanced up and met Molly's eye; she smiled awkwardly and tottered to her desk.

She logged on to her computer and read Brian's snotty response to her draft article on the Gibbs incident. She felt crestfallen. A quick Google search found her a book titled: *Motivating Your Employees for Dummies.* She composed a covering email to Brian, and her mouse cursor now hovered over the *Send* button:

'Hi, Brian. I know it's your birthday coming up soon. I was just wondering what I could possibly get the man who already has every-thing when I saw this. Hope you like it! Molly xx.'

Perhaps best to delete the kisses, she thought; the man might not get the sarcasm.

The sound of jangling coins and the familiar mix of Old Spice and poor dental hygiene told Molly that Brian was standing behind her. Odious bastard. She so looked forward to telling him to stick the job; made her more determined not to stuff up the interview.

She flicked off her screen, fixed her face into a rictus and spun around. And, lo, there he was, hand in the pocket of his brown corduroys, blue biro poking out from the pocket of his off-white shirt – an image which screamed middle-aged geography teacher. A virginal one. Or a sex pest. She recalled the Christmas gala a few years back: black tie, round tables, low lighting and free-flowing wine. Dessert was running late, and she was chatting to Bernie on her right, when from her left she felt a hand on her thigh. She leant in towards Brian and whispered: 'Take your filthy hand off my leg or I'll rip out your testicles, smear them in chocolate and serve them as profiteroles.' As if she'd be interested in him; the man clipped his mobile to his belt, for Pete's sake! She could have made a scene, taken him to the cleaners – you'd think the man would show a bit of gratitude for her showing such restraint.

'Brian!' Molly gushed. 'How the devil…?'

'Busy?'

'As ever.'

'Do you know who I've just had in my office?'

'Well, I'm guessing it wasn't the ghost of Richard Whiteley.'

'What are you talking about?'

'Doesn't matter, Brian. Why don't you just tell me?'

'It was Rick Brady, managing director of Brady Homes. Says that after your article he's been flooded with complaints from disgruntled customers. People are kicking off big time on Bookface–'

'Do you mean Facebook, Bri?'

'Reservations are falling through the floor, Molly. This is serious.'

'And? That's a good thing, isn't it? That's what good journalism does: expose shoddy practices.'

'Well, there's a slight problem with that argument: Rick Brady is our biggest advertising account. Or *was*; he's pulled it all. Where do you think that leaves us, Molly?'

'On the moral high ground?'

'Up shit creek without a paddle, that's where. I despair.'

'You approved the article, Brian.'

'I had no bloody choice, did I? We had nothing else to fill the page with.'

He turned and stormed back to his office.

'Have a good day, Brian,' she called after him.

.   .   .

An hour or so later, Molly was filing her nails at her desk when Brian came over to her again.

'Another visit so soon? To what do I owe this pleasure?' she said, smiling broadly, but expecting another rant about how she was losing money for the paper.

'You're a cat person, aren't you?'

The smile fell from Molly's face. Cat? Why would he mention it now? What did he know about Mr. Darcy? How?

'Well, yes,' Molly frowned, 'I suppose.'

Brian sneered. 'I've just received a call. A dog walker came across a dead cat on her walk this morning.'

Oh, God. Molly clutched her chest. Her throat tightened.

'What? Where?'

'Preston,' Brian said.

Preston – that was miles away from her; it couldn't be him. Her throat muscles relaxed. 'Why are you telling me this, Brian?'

'Well, here's the thing, Molly: the animal was disembowelled.'

Oh, the poor thing, Molly thought; she brought a hand to her mouth. The owner would be devastated.

Then, a sickening feeling rose within her.

'When you say Preston…?'

He was nodding, slowly; 'Yes, Wain Wood; the cat was found in the dell, just like that woman. Looks like it's some kind of sick homage to that psychopath: a teenager, I'm guessing. The youth of today… will make a great story…'

Brian's words trailed off in Molly's head, and he became a blurred image. She flew up from her chair, grabbed her bag, barged past him and ran to the loos. She hurled her breakfast into the pan, then stumbled to the washbasins to splash water on her face. Anita from Marketing was at the next basin, applying her mascara.

'Good night, was it?' Anita asked.

The room suddenly felt small and close and hot; Molly needed air. She ran outside into the car park. It was raining buckets, but right now she didn't care – in fact, it was almost a relief. Her head was a jumble of emotions and questions. She steadied herself against a car and tried to join the dots.

Her Dell Ripper reward article – he'd read it, hadn't he? Troy Perkins. It was him. It had to be. But how?

Her eyes darted about and finally settled on something familiar and safe: her Evoque. The memory of the red car following her flashed in her mind. The discarded can behind the house. Had he been watching her? Looking for an opportunity to tell the world he was still at large? Taunt the police? Unsettle the community?

Sick bastard.

A steely anger cut through her tears. Something needed to be done about this. Perkins had to pay.

Wait. No. She was getting ahead of herself. It wasn't *definitely* Mr. Darcy, was it? There are millions of cats out there. Her imagination was getting the better of her.

She palmed her diaphragm and took deep breaths: in through the nose, out through the mouth – a technique she'd learnt years back, in yoga. That didn't last; she only stayed as long as she did because she had a crush on the teacher. What was his name? Linus? Lorcan? Luca? Whatever it was, his bridge pose had taken up permanent residence in her memory bank.

At that moment her phone rang: an unknown number. She was minded to drop the phone back into her bag. But, what if it was news?

'Hello?'

'Ms. Tindall?' A male voice.

'Yes?'

'I'm calling from Tudor House Vets. Are you the owner of a cat called…' the man coughed, then continued, 'Mr. Darcy?'

The word stuck for a moment in her throat, then finally emerged as a squeak: 'Yes.'

'I'm afraid I've got bad news–'

Molly lost her grip on the phone and it clattered to the ground. Her legs seemed suddenly incapable of bearing her weight and she slid down against the car door, slumping into a messy, wet heap.

Strangely, discovering that Mr. Darcy was definitely dead gave Molly a crumb of comfort. Thank God she'd had him tagged: at least it had brought the uncertainty to an end, and she could now think straight.

She begged the vet to let her see him, but he managed to persuade her that it wasn't a good idea. 'Did he suffer?' she asked.

'He's at peace now,' he replied, dodging the question. He explained that he would need to report the incident to the police. 'I hope they find whoever did this,' he said.

'So do I,' Molly said. She didn't feel the need to tell him that she would contact the police herself.

All being well, the vet said (strange choice of words), Molly could pick up the ashes from the pet crematorium in a couple of days. She pictured Mr. Darcy on the mantle next to *her*, and this thought sent Molly's mood once more into a tailspin.

'Molly?'

An awareness grew that she was shaking. She was freezing in her wet clothes, and the waves of cold air wafting over her from the office's air-con vent caused her to convulse.

'Molly? You okay?'

She looked up, blinking away tears, and saw Kelvin standing in front of her, wearing a look of concern. He held out a hoodie, which she gratefully took and wrapped around herself.

'Just give me a few minutes, Kelvin. I'll be as right as rain.'

He smiled sweetly and returned to his desk. Lovely guy; a junior reporter. Gay, alas.

She looked about her and saw that everyone else had their heads down. Who could blame them, really?

Her thoughts turned to the relationships she'd had over the years. Without exception, all were short-lived – some so short that she could barely call them relationships. None of them had measured up – that's what she told herself: too needy, too selfish, too sensitive, no sense of humour, mummy's boy, too stupid, too clever….the list was endless. What was it she was looking for? That was easy: her father. She could barely remember him, but in her mind he was perfect.

When will Daddy come home, Mummy?

Get back to bed, Margaret, you stupid little girl.

Had she rejected them all, before they had time to reject her? Before they had the chance to discover who she really was? And, who was she? She was a nobody: a useless, shallow, plastic shell of a woman; all surface and no depth. An empty husk. Who had she been trying to kid? Was it any wonder her best friend was a bloody cat?

Oh, Mr. Darcy, why did you leave me?

'Molly?'

She wiped her face with the sleeve of Kelvin's hoodie and spun around. 'Brian.'

'The dog walker's keen to do an interview. I said you'd get over to him this afternoon.'

Molly rose from her chair and slapped him hard across the cheek, before she had time to ask herself whether that was really the wisest move.

RŪTA

RŪTA DREAMT that she was in a pine forest, shrouded in a cold, wet fog. There was no sound, other than her breath and her beating heart. She spun on the spot, but every direction looked the same. *Where am I? Where do I go?*

She tentatively stepped forward. It felt soft beneath her feet, and she looked down to see her shoes had been swallowed by marshy ground.

Grandma? Where are you?

A sound now – distant; faint. What was it? A rook's caw? Another, this time louder; closer. Yet another, behind her. Movement in a tree? She turned quickly, but saw nothing.

A door slammed, and Rūta woke with a start.

Her head ached liked hell. Her world was fuzzy. *Where am I?*

She was lying on her back, and forced herself into a seated position, her knees held tightly to her chest. Her wrists were bruised and there was a dull ache behind one eye. She looked around, her vision blurred.

Her surroundings slowly sharpened as she adjusted to the light. She was on a single bed. The room was small, damp and cold. Behind her was a tiny window, which was boarded up from the outside. To her left was a washbasin; to the far end, a hefty door. Was she in prison? Why? What had she done? Nothing made sense. Her head was a fug, filled with glue.

She massaged her temples. *Think*. She went to stand, but her legs buckled and she collapsed back onto the bed. She tried again, lifting herself gently, and staggered to the door. Locked. She yanked the handle.

'Hey!' she tried to shout, but it came out as a croak. 'Where am I?' Louder now. No response.

Piece by piece, she recollected the events of earlier; the image of Urtė being bundled into the grey van flashed through her brain. She pounded on the door. 'Where's Urtė?' she screamed. 'Padėti!'

Oh, what had she done? God, what had she done? It was all her fault. She sank to the floor and sobbed. *I'm sorry, Grandma. So sorry.*

A torpor had engulfed Rūta once more and she lay half-asleep on the bed. Her head throbbed. She didn't know what time it was, or even if it was still the same day. Earlier, she'd quenched a terrible thirst from the basin tap. Other than the clothes she wore, all possessions had been taken from her.

The thunderclap of a slammed door startled her, and she sat bolt upright, alert now. She heard footsteps on a wooden staircase. The slit of light under the door darkened, as someone – perhaps more than one person –

approached her room. Muffled chatter. What was happening?

She gripped her knees. Her pulse quickened and bile rose in her throat.

The slit of light returned. Rūta could then make out the sound of a key in a lock, and a door opening on squeaky hinges. It then slammed shut and she jumped. Was it the room next door? She scrambled to put her ear against the dividing wall. Again, she couldn't make out the conversation, but it sounded brisk, business-like: she heard a woman and a man. The voices subsided momentarily. Then the groans and the pounding noises started.

The horrifying truth burst through the fog. Grandma's voice was in her head now, soft, sorrowful and reproachful. She could see her face; her sweet smile masked bitter disappointment. *Oh, Rūta, you silly, silly girl.*

NINETEEN

'Guv, are you listening?'

'Sorry, Mel,' James said, dragging his focus back into the meeting room. 'My head's not in the right place today. Carry on.'

'As I was saying, we've not found much yet to corroborate the intruder story.'

'As suspected, then. What can you tell me about the family?'

'Well, clearly the boys don't see eye to eye.'

'Something about different interests, I recall?'

'Think it might be more than that, guv.'

'How so?'

'Don't know; it's just a feeling I have.'

James raised an eyebrow. 'A feeling?'

'I know what you're thinking,' Mel said, flicking James an exasperated look: 'follow the evidence, not your feelings – blah, blah...'

James smiled. Intuition had its place in detective work; it was just that he preferred to think of it as instinct grounded in facts, but informed by years of experience. 'What's your *feeling* on possible motives?' he asked Mel.

'Well, clearly Mr. Gibbs was a successful businessman, so there's the prospect of inheriting the business.'

'But, one of the boys had his own business, didn't he?'

'Ben, yes.'

'Check it out – his financial situation, too. And the other one…' James clicked his fingers, in an attempt to trigger a recollection of his name.

'Mark.'

'Yes, the arty one. Doesn't strike me as someone likely to be corrupted by capitalist aspirations. What about the woman… Katie?'

'Kathy.'

'She seemed demure, passive, quiet… Any history of violence, sudden rages? What do the neighbours have to say about her? Friends? Relatives?'

'Guv, I can't do all this on my own.'

'Yes, I'm sorry. I'm onto that with the Super now; bear with. We'll need uniform support for routine enquiries. Do whatever overtime you like for now.'

His phone began to ring in his pocket, but he let it go through to voicemail. They'd leave a message if it was important.

The sound of the phone must have triggered a thought with Mel: 'We couldn't find John's mobile anywhere. Mrs. Gibbs told us he always carried one with him.'

'Interesting. Make it a priority to find it. Get hold of his records from the telecoms company, in any case. What about the murder weapon? Any joy?'

'There's a chef's knife missing from the block in the kitchen.'

The phone rang again. James checked and saw that it was that bloody journalist woman. He answered it, making no attempt to disguise his annoyance: 'I'm busy! Leave me alone unless you've got something important to tell me.'

The woman sounded hysterical, and James struggled to make her out. He swore she'd just said: 'Perkins has killed my cat!'

'What?!'

James stormed out of the room, to find somewhere more private to take the call.

'A *cat*, James?' Murdoch huffed, incredulously. 'You've just interrupted me during a murder investigation to bother me about a dead fucking cat?'

'It's him, sir: Perkins. I'm sure of it. It had its intestines ripped out.'

'And? Another animal could have done it: a fox; dog; badger? I've no idea; I hate bloody animals. That's why I'm a copper, and not a keeper at London fucking Zoo.'

'But a vet identified it as hers; it was chipped. Preston's ten miles from where she lives! She thinks he was stalking her.'

'*Thinks?*'

'The cat was missing for two days, sir. It could mean Perkins had it with him, when we saw him in Stevenage.' James didn't think it was helpful to mention the road rage incident from this morning.

'God almighty, Quinn.' A puzzled look fell across the Super's face. 'Let's just say for a second that it was him, why would he do it?'

'He's toying with us, sir; showing off; telling the world he's smarter than we are, that he's still out there.'

'No, you don't understand what I mean. Why *this* cat? Why *her*? This particular journalist?'

'I don't follow, sir.'

'I think you do, James.'

'Sir?'

'There was a piece in the *Herald*, a few days back; Mrs. M showed me it. Can't say I've really ever read the rag myself. It was an article about him, appealing for people to come forward with information. Was it her who wrote it?'

'Was there an article, sir? I wasn't aware.'

'Strange that she called you, don't you think?'

'I was the lead detective on the Perkins case, sir. She knew that.'

'And, do you think I was born yesterday?'

James looked away. An awkward silence fell.

'Can you at least just send someone round?' James said, aware there was a hint of desperation in his voice. 'Take a look in his car boot? Speak to him?'

The Super took a deep breath. 'The man's pursuing a complaint for police harassment. So, let's say I humour you and send someone round, and say they find hairs that are a match for this fucking mog? What then? Get him on an animal cruelty charge? The maximum sentence is six months. We'll be a laughing stock.'

'He might talk; let slip something incriminating about Lena Demyan's murder.'

Murdoch raised an eyebrow.

'Sir, please.'

'I've got work to do. And, more to the point, so do you.'

As James skulked out of the Super's office, Luke tried to commandeer him.

'Not now!' James barked.

Later that day, having brooded for quite some time and achieved the sum total of nothing, James sidled over to

Luke's desk to apologize – something he normally tried to avoid. 'Sorry, I shouldn't have snapped at you earlier.'

'Bad timing?'

'Something like that. What were you going to tell me?'

'Good news, guv: Goff's team have caught the two guys who escaped from the brothel. Eastern European. Tip-off from a member of the public.'

'Great. Where are they now?'

'Goff's got them in for questioning at Stevenage station.'

'I'll get over there now.'

'You'll be too late, guv; they'll be finished by the time you get there.'

James's jaw clenched. 'Why didn't you tell me–' He stopped himself; it was his own bloody fault.

Luke smiled. 'Besides, they're just the goons at the bottom of the pile. They're never going to give us anything on the big cheeses.'

'You're probably right,' James said, calming down. 'Still, at the very least we can take these guys out of circulation. You never know, they may give us something.'

'Have you had a chance to look through my reports yet, guv?' Luke asked.

'Oh, sorry, no, been up to my neck in it. I'll see what I can do today.'

'Guv.'

James detected a hint of disappointment. He didn't blame the lad; he was disappointed in himself. He returned to his desk with a resolve to review Luke's work, but it was no good; his thoughts soon snapped back to Perkins. It was like his brain was filled with iron filings and Perkins was a magnet. What to do, now that the Super seemed totally uninterested in the cat situation?

He got out his phone and found Molly Tindall's

number, pausing for a beat before dialling it. James was on the verge of hanging up, when she eventually answered. Her voice was faint.

'What is it?'

'I can't stop thinking about the cat.'

'Oh, that's kind of you,' Molly said, sniffing.

James didn't mean it in that sense, but it didn't harm the situation for her to think it, he supposed. 'I'm not sure the Super is taking it too seriously, I'm afraid. We might have to take matters into our hands – force the issue.'

'What are you suggesting?'

'Can I take a look around your place, at where he might have snatched the cat?'

'Yes, of course,' Molly said, her voice rallying.

'Where are you now?'

'I'm at home. Incident with the boss. You know how it is.'

'Oh, I see. Well, I'll knock off here about five and head over. What's the address?'

When Molly answered the door, James could tell from her swollen face that she'd been crying. He tried to think of something sympathetic to say. *My condolences.* Didn't sound right, somehow, for a cat. *How are you bearing up?* Overly dramatic? Insincere? Probably. In hindsight, he should have given it more thought on the drive over, but his mind was occupied with other stuff. Important stuff, like how was he going to bring down Perkins, once and for all. Not to mention the trifling matters of solving the Gibbs murder and bringing the Solent scum to justice. So, nothing remotely human came readily to mind.

It was Molly who spoke first: 'What happened to your eye?'

'Long story,' James said. He peered past Molly into the gloom of the cottage. It was the sort of place he detested: old, dusty, pokey, with not a straight line or right angle in sight. Whatever was the attraction?

'Come in,' Molly said.

She led him through the small lounge, narrowly avoiding a clout on the head from an oak beam, into the kitchen. He detected a familiar scent of fresh flowers, but couldn't see any. Lilies? At the base of the sink unit, he noticed two empty bowls.

'Can't bring myself to deal with them yet,' Molly said. 'Silly, I suppose. They're just bowls.'

There were things following Ruth's death he hadn't dealt with in eighteen months, James thought. 'I'm sorry,' he said, falteringly, 'about the cat.'

'That's his chair, there under the window,' Molly motioned. 'What's your tipple? I can offer you anything you like, so long as it's wine.' She opened the fridge.

'No, thank you.'

'You're off duty now, surely?' Molly asked, looking at her watch.

'It's not that. I don't really–'

'Oh, God, tell me you're not teetotal?'

'No, I just don't think there's any answers to be found at the bottom of a bottle.'

'Well, I find that by the time you get there, you've stopped asking the questions. Please yourself.'

James watched as Molly poured herself a drink, into a glass already on the countertop. He suspected it wasn't the first of the day.

'So, how do you think Perkins got hold of…'

'Mr. Darcy.'

'Mr. Darcy, right.' That figured. 'Like Bridget Jones?'

'*Pride and Prejudice*, thank you very much. Follow me.'

Molly unbolted the rear door, which James noticed had a cat flap, and led him into the garden.

'There's a big recreation ground behind me. I'm guessing he hung around there, watching me. I found an empty drink can at the base of that tree.' Molly shivered, apparently in response to the memory. She rubbed her upper arm with her free hand and wine sloshed over her glass.

'Red Bull?'

'Yes. How'd you–'

'It's always Red Bull. Show me,' James said.

At the tree, James leant against its trunk, stepped up on tiptoe and peered into the house. 'Think you're probably right,' he said. 'Don't suppose you kept the can?'

'Binned it. You get all manner of crap thrown about the place here. Teenagers. Once, I found a bloody bra–'

Molly's voice faded from his consciousness, as James inspected the tree and the surrounding area. There were no obvious sources of DNA to prove Perkins was here. If he could have it his way, he'd have Forensics over in a flash. But it wasn't his case, and there was no chance of persuading Murdoch.

'So, what's the plan?' Molly said, regaining his attention.

'Hmm…' James stroked his chin. 'It's a bit tricky, as Perkins isn't my case anymore. Might see if I can convince someone to check the cat–'

'Mr. Darcy.'

'…check Mr. Darcy's body for Perkins's DNA. I don't fancy our chances, though, what with his background in forensics. Well, you know all that, don't you?'

Molly smiled, sadly. 'Let me make you something to eat – the least I could do for you. Or, have you got to get home?'

'I… suppose not,' James said.

'Afraid I'm not much of a cook,' Molly shouted from the kitchen, amid much clanging and clattering. 'I've been known to burn water.'

'Hmm?' James uttered. He was in the lounge, examining an unmarked urn on the mantle.

'Pizza okay?' Molly said, entering the room. 'That's my mother,' she added. 'Not sure what to do with her.'

'Close, were you?'

'Couldn't stand the bitch. For some reason I can't bring myself to flush her down the toilet.'

'Human decency?'

'Something like that. Your mother still around?'

'Good question,' James mused. 'She is and she isn't.'

'Purgatory?'

'Alzheimer's.'

'Life's a bummer, eh? You've kind of got to make the most of it while you can, don't you think?'

A silence hung in the air for a few moments, which was brutally broken by noises from the neighbouring property: banging and shouting. James's detective hackles sprang up: burglary; assault?

'Give it to me now, big man!'

Oh, I see.

'Newlyweds,' Molly said. 'At it twenty-four-seven. Good thing it comes in short bursts – so to speak.'

James smiled.

'Sure I can't get you a drink?'

'Just a small one, then; I'm driving.'

. . .

All was calm next door as James – aided by a large gulp of wine – politely swallowed the final chunk of salty cardboard that Molly insisted was a Sainsbury's thin and crispy meat feast.

As Molly cleared the plates from the coffee table and took them to the kitchen, James reclined into the soft sofa and looked over at the cat's chair. A sudden feeling of emptiness struck him, as he recalled those numb days after Ruth's death.

'So, what does your missus think of you working for the police? Can't be much fun for her,' Molly said.

How does she know I'm thinking about her? Then, he looked at his hand and realized he'd been subconsciously playing with his wedding ring.

Molly returned with the wine bottle and James instinctively held a hand over his glass.

'And? Tell me about your wife.'

'I don't like to talk about her.'

'Oh, God, I've put my foot in it, haven't I? Sorry. Has she left you? Felt like there was a third person in the marriage? The Force?'

James took a deep breath. 'She died.' Only two words, but so difficult to say, even after all this time. It was as if merely uttering them closed off the possibility that her death was just in his imagination.

'Man, I'm such a bitch! Poor you.'

Molly poured the wine into his glass, and this time he didn't object. She tucked a lock of hair behind her ear – Ruth had a similar habit. James needed to change the subject, fast.

'What about you?' he asked.

'Oh, I could write a book about my love life.'

'Sounds like a bestseller.'

'Sarcasm is very unattractive in a man, don't you know?'

'I came here to talk about Perkins, not our love lives.'

Molly took a swig of wine, tucked her hair. 'Why are you so obsessed with him?'

'You've seen what he's capable of. I just want to see him where he belongs: inside, where he can't destroy any more lives.'

'Hmm,' Molly puckered her lips, 'there's more to it than that. I can see it in your eyes.'

'What exactly do you see in my eyes?'

'Well, apart from someone who needs a bloody good night's sleep, I see sadness and fear. Now, stop deflecting my questions: what is it about Perkins? It's personal, isn't it?'

James's mouth felt dry and he reached for his wine. He drank a mouthful and regretted it instantly. He felt like he was losing control.

'It's got something to do with her, hasn't it?' Molly said, motioning to his wedding band.

He remained silent, staring into space, twiddling the ring.

'Tell me if this is none of my business.'

'This is none of your business.'

She smiled. Tucked her hair again. 'You haven't even told me her name.'

'Ruth,' he said, his voice a hoarse whisper.

'Beautiful. Why don't you tell me how you met?'

'It's a long story,' James said.

'My favourite kind,' Molly said, filling his glass almost to the brim.

'Rolo?'

'No, ta, guv,' James said; 'not hungry.'

It was the dead of night and they'd been in the unmarked car for hours, watching and waiting. Sergeant James Quinn felt a curious combination of nerves, boredom and guilty excitement.

Beech House – the derelict, three-storey, Victorian building under surveillance – was cloaked in darkness. Last used as student accommodation, it was now the subject of a protracted planning application, submitted by a property developer who wanted to knock it down and erect fifty starter homes on the three-acre site. Local residents were fighting tooth and nail to stop the development proceeding; the usual litany of complaints: it'll destroy the local character, create traffic congestion, swamp the schools and the doctors' surgeries, blah, blah, blah... James had no sympathy with nimbyism; there was a national housing shortage and young people could no longer afford to buy a home in the town or village where they'd grown up – something had to be done about that.

A few weeks back, the station had started to receive reports of 'comings and goings' at the site. James had to stifle the urge to smile, when one old dear sidled up to him at the front desk, to tell him it had become 'a den of iniquity'. The trouble was the trickle of complaints soon became a flood, and they could no longer be dismissed as the paranoid grievances of those with too much time on their hands, and too little sense of proportion.

A silver Corolla rumbled to a halt in front of the building, and the driver switched off the engine. James raised his Steiner police-issue binoculars and watched as the driver stepped out. 'Oh, hello. I recognize you, matey.'

'Who is it?' Inspector Wilkins asked.

'Can't remember his name. Cautioned him for kerb-crawling a few months back. Gave me a sob story: girlfriend had left him; it was his first time; promised to never be a naughty boy again; said he worked in forensics, and I'd be destroying his career if I charged him. So on and so forth...'

'You're too soft for your own good, Quinn. I'd have thrown the charge sheet at the filthy pervert.'

'Looks like the local do-gooders could be right about it being a knocking shop, guv. Time to go in?'

'Give it a couple of minutes; let's see how he gets in. Radio Goff; check they're not in the land of nod back there.' Sergeant Goff and four constables were parked in a squad van in Duke Street, ready to be called if backup was required. James told Goff to ready his crew for Wilkins's command.

James and his boss watched in silence, as the man squeezed his way through a gap in the security fence and walked briskly up the path, casting nervous glances over his shoulder. He then walked around the side, opened a boarded-up door and disappeared into the building.

'Come on,' Wilkins said, 'let's check it out.'

They made their way through the fence and crept towards the door, as James swept his Maglite around him.

All the windows were boarded up, with many at ground level daubed in graffiti. At first-floor level, he could see cracks of light in a couple of the windows.

Wilkins tugged at the door and it opened with a rusty squeak. He turned to James and rolled his eyes; 'Bit lax on security.'

They stepped into a small, tiled lobby which smelled of damp brick-dust and urine; James wrinkled his nose. Wilkins pushed open an inner door and James followed him into a dimly lit hallway, containing a sturdy-looking wooden staircase.

'Ah, concierge,' Wilkins said, dryly.

James turned to see a grubby-looking man seated with his feet up on an old steel desk, his arms folded, chin on his chest, gently snoring. There was a prybar on the desk and Wilkins grabbed it, handing it to James. Then, Wilkins slammed his fist onto the desk. The sound echoed around the stark hallway. The man was jolted awake.

'Sorry if I woke you, young man,' Wilkins said, shoving his ID into the guy's startled face. 'Mind if we take a look around?'

The man jumped to his feet, his eyes darting over the desk's surface.

'Don't worry,' James said, 'your little play-stick is safe with me.'

The man's gaze flicked to the staircase and he hollered something unintelligible.

'They upstairs, then?' Wilkins said. 'Cuff him to these railings, Quinn, while I call in the cavalry. Let's shake things up around here.'

Moments later, Goff's van was screeching to a halt, sirens blazing.

Above the sound of the man bellowing, as James snapped shut the cuffs, there were shouts and frantic footfall from the first floor; doors slamming; screaming. James felt a surge of adrenalin. His fingers curled around the prybar and he followed the gaffer up the stairs.

They turned into a long corridor. In the distance, a man was running in their direction, then abruptly turned on his heel. Wilkins gave chase.

'Police! Nobody move!' he yelled.

James crept hesitantly along the corridor, poking his head behind a couple of doors to find dirty, unoccupied, hovel-like rooms no bigger than prison cells. The third door he came to was padlocked. He knocked. 'Anyone in there?' No answer. 'It's the police.'

A terrified voice called out from inside: 'Help me.'

James raised the bar to the padlock, then heard the door to the next room creaking open. The Corolla driver stepped out, meeting James's gaze. He raised his palms in surrender, before his expression changed from insincere contrition to a 'where-have-I-seen-you-before?' look.

'Wait right there – and don't even think about trying to leg it; we've got the place surrounded.' James padded the prybar into his palm. 'And, yes, we have met before – deviant.'

'I can explain,' the man said, smiling sheepishly.

'Yes, you damn well will be explaining – later, at the station. But, for now, put a bloody sock in it.'

It only took James a few seconds of effort with the bar to prise the lock off of the door. He took a deep breath and entered the room.

Dear God.

The woman – head down, knees held tightly to her chest, sweater pulled down to her ankles – sat shaking on the squalid single bed. James stepped slowly towards her. He crouched to his knees, gingerly placing the prybar on the hardwood floor, and placed a hand softly on her quivering knee.

'What's your name, sweetheart? You're safe now, darling. You're safe.'

She lifted her head and swiped a lock of hair, to clear her eyes. Her face was brown with dirt and streaked white from tears. 'Rūta,' she whispered.

He took his ID from his pocket and held it out to her. 'I'm James,' he said.

As her haunted but beautiful, honey-coloured eyes flicked from his hand up to his eyes, he felt them welling with tears.

James reached out unsteadily, to grab the slowly blurring wine glass from the coffee table. He raised it to his lips, only to find it empty. After blinking several times to restore visual clarity, he glanced over to Molly. A tight knot in his stomach told him he'd revealed more than he had intended.

She was standing at the window, staring out, and he watched her in silence for a few moments. Then, she spun around and smiled at him; she'd clearly been weeping. She sniffed and raised the back of her hand to her nose.

'We rescued eight women that night, including Ruth. I've lost count of how many since.'

'You're a bloody hero,' Molly said.

'We've barely scratched the surface.'

There was a momentary pause, then Molly said: 'Shall I get another bottle?'

James woke with a start in unfamiliar surroundings, and the sensation that an angry bumblebee was trapped in his head. It took him a few moments to work out where he was: Molly's living room; he lay on the sofa, covered by a floral duvet.

Oh, no. He looked under the cover and found, to his relief, that he was fully clothed. A couple of empty wine bottles sat on the coffee table.

Vague memories of the previous night filtered through the fog. What had he told her about Ruth? Everything? He'd always been so coy about the circumstances in which they'd met; he never wanted to be accused of abusing his position, or exploiting a woman in a vulnerable situation. Besides, keeping schtum about his private life came naturally to him.

Footsteps thudded above him.

He swung his legs to the floor and leapt to his feet.

'Fuck!' His head crashed into a beam with such force that he was sure his skull had split in two, like a coconut.

'Morning, James,' Molly said, as she breezed into the room.

He was seeing stars. 'What time is it?'

'Not long past seven. Ungodly hour, if you ask me. I've been awake a while, what with… well, you know.'

'Shit!'

'Coffee?'

'Haven't you got work to get to?' James said, straightening his tie and attempting to smooth out the creases in his suit.

'It's complicated. I kind of slapped my boss around the face yesterday.'

'Sometimes wish I could do the same to mine,' James said. He exhaled into cupped hands and recoiled when he sniffed his rancid breath.

He looked to Molly, standing in the open doorway. The low morning sun streamed in from the window behind her, giving her a luminescent glow. She was dressed in a silky nightgown, low cut.

'We didn't, you know…' he stammered, '…you and me, last night… at all?'

Molly laughed. 'No, love. I don't think that would have been a good idea, do you? You've got more issues than me. No offence, but that fact has kind of cheered me up.'

TWENTY

THE SIGHT of dead flowers tied to a lamppost on a busy road always gave Molly the shudders: a ghoulish shrine to some poor soul who'd met their end in a road accident. She could never quite make up her mind whether it was a good idea; a kind gesture to mark the anniversary of the victim's passing, or a token effort born of guilt? Still, without fail, whenever she encountered one, she'd ease off the accelerator and take a few moments to ponder the fragility of life, vowing not to waste whatever remained of hers. But, like new year resolutions, such vows soon fell by the wayside – such was modern life, with its absurd pressures and relentless mundanities.

Anyway, here she was at Wain Wood in the wrong footwear, with a posy of Sweet Williams plucked from the garden, scrambling down the steep, sodden bank of Bunyan's Dell. When she reached the base, she found that the ground was covered in a layer of ankle-deep leaf litter. Above her, shafts of soft, morning sun pierced the cool shade, like searchlights. Birdsong was the only sound. It was all rather beautiful, and as Molly swooshed her way towards the centre, she was overcome by a strange sense of calm and serenity.

That feeling evaporated when she saw a cloud of flies ahead of her, and a foul stench assaulted her nostrils. She steadied herself against a rusting oil drum, which was almost covered by ivy. Logic told her that some part of Mr. Darcy lay there amongst the rot; the cool, damp earth reclaiming him, just like it was doing to the oil drum.

She dropped the flowers to the ground. A lone tear followed. Then another. The tears became a trickle, then quickly an uncontrollable torrent. For whom or what was she weeping? Mr. Darcy? Her own life, its best years already behind her, with nothing to show for them? That poor woman, who'd left behind a life in Ukraine in the hope of finding a better one in England, only to fall prey first to human traffickers, then to Perkins?

It occurred to Molly now that she'd barely given much thought to Lena Demyan, the person; she was a story – a vehicle for Molly's ego and journalistic ambitions. A lack of empathy was the hallmark of a sociopath, wasn't it? Was *she* a sociopath? Was Molly no better than a deranged murderer, to whom the woman was but an instrument – a tool – to facilitate his sick fantasies? Had it taken the death of an old cat to make her realize that? Well, she was going to change, to become a better person – she meant it this time. It would be Mr. Darcy's glorious legacy. And Lena's too, of course.

James was always convinced it was Perkins, but Molly was never sure. Perhaps James had seen something in the whites of his eyes. Molly didn't need to look into the man's eyes now to know that he was evil. She was now totally convinced of his guilt. But what could she do to help James bring him to justice?

In her mind he was now James, not DCI Quinn. Last

night she'd glimpsed a different side to him; found a chink in his armour. There was a sensitivity there, a soft underbelly, deep beneath the hard shell. He intrigued her. She wanted to see more of the real him but, God, did he have issues! Probably needed professional help – though she doubted anyone would ever be able to convince him of that. Molly had sought therapy throughout much of her adulthood – a shoulder to cry on; a sympathetic ear – but she guessed it was harder for men to admit they needed help; not very masculine, she supposed. It was a shame society forced you into a binary choice: feminine or masculine. That was the root of many of today's problems, in her humble opinion.

A fly buzzed in Molly's face and she swatted it away. In the corner of her eye, something glistened. She turned to see that a ray of sunshine had caught an object amongst the leaf litter. Intrigued, she headed over to it.

'Piss off!' she screeched at a particularly irksome fly, as she bent down to inspect the object. Was it…? Yes, a ring! An imitation diamond. She could spot a fake one a mile off.

She reached down to grab it, but her hand made contact with something unexpectedly hard. She carefully cleared the area around the ring, and it took a beat for her brain to process the message her eyes were then relaying to it: the ring was attached to a dainty finger, white as snow.

With a deepening sense of foreboding, Molly brushed aside leaf litter to reveal the woman's arm, then her naked chest.

Molly stood up. Retching now, she looked about her and listened. There was nobody around.

She crouched back down and uncovered the woman's head; her long, brown hair was matted in dried mud. She had bloodshot eyes, a bruised and swollen face, blue lips and markings around her neck. Molly gently cupped the woman's face.

You poor thing.

Was it him? Perkins? It had to be.

Oh, God, that meant...

She took a deep breath and moved herself farther down the woman's body, delicately sweeping away the leaves around her stomach. A throng of flies burst angrily to life, and Molly saw the confirmation she sought.

A wave of revulsion coursed through her. She tried to steady herself.

She considered for a moment removing her cardigan and covering the woman's chest, to preserve a trace of dignity. But then it occurred to her that this was a crime scene; she shouldn't have touched anything! She should call the police. James.

TWENTY-ONE

A DISHEVELLED JAMES arrived at HQ much later than he had intended. His brain fog had barely dissipated, and he admonished himself for losing control the night before; drink was never a good idea. He vowed never to let himself get in that situation again.

Being a Saturday, HQ was thinly populated, and it was a perfect opportunity to catch up on both the Gibbs investigation and Solent, hopefully without interruption. Luke was off duty this weekend, and Mel was on the ground in Letchworth, along with two other DCs James had managed to secure for the case. As for Murdoch, Lord only knew what he was up to: playing golf or being henpecked were his best guesses. Things had gone quiet on the Perkins complaint, and James wasn't going to push or provoke Murdoch any further on that front. In fact, he was going to try and push all thought of Perkins and the bloody cat out of his mind today.

Right, what to start with? The Gibbs case – more urgent; Solent was a long game. James opened the database and saw that various reports had been added: neighbour interviews, crime scene report, initial statements from the three family members present at the scene... no pathology report yet. Lazy bastards! Didn't they know it was a murder case? No, tell a lie: there it was. Technology wasn't really James's thing; he preferred the old-school paper and file approach to policing. He supposed he was an analogue detective in a digital age. Mind you, there was still plenty of paper around. Wasn't the world supposed to have gone paperless years ago? He opened up the report and honed in on the important stuff.

Seventeen wounds to the neck and upper back, inflicted by a blade, estimated length twenty centimetres. Seventeen wounds! Frenzied, indeed. The spinal cord had been severed; that explained the apparent lack of any reaction from John Gibbs: instant paralysis and death, most probably. Neat way to go: no pain; no awareness.

This fact could support the theory of the wound being inflicted by someone with knowledge: a professional. But, then, why the other sixteen? Why risk making such a mess? To disguise the professional nature of the job, perhaps; make it look like a savage, domestic attack? Or was it just fortuitous (or not, depending on your point of view) that the spinal cord was severed? He pondered this thought, while he opened the crime scene report.

His phone rang from his pocket. He sighed and checked who it was. *Please, not Molly.*

Phew.

'Mel. What have you got for me?'

'Good morning, guv. How are you?'

'Yep, that too.'

'We found a butter knife.'

'Well, I'm so glad to hear it. Now you can enjoy your toast.'

'Good one, guv; tell me when I should stop laughing.

No, we found it in the dining room, underneath the sideboard; somehow it got missed on the first sweep. It has blood on it.'

'You're not suggesting his spinal cord was severed by a bloody butter knife, are you?'

'Of course not. The knife's gone to the lab, but we're pretty sure it's going to be the victim's blood.'

'Oh, how so? Tell me more.'

'Remember the wound above his eye?'

'Ah, yes, I see. So, who did it? Let me guess: the angry fella, Mark.'

'Ben.'

'Yes, that's who I meant.'

'No, it was Kathy.'

'Oh, Kathy.'

'Yes, Kathy. I told her we were sending the knife to the lab, but she could save me the trouble now and spill the beans. Turns out there was an incident during the evening meal–'

'An incident?'

'Will you just let me finish, guv?'

'Fair point, Mel. Continue.'

'Thank you. Well, it seems that John Gibbs had… now, how can I put this… old-fashioned views. You see, Mark was in a homosexual relationship that he'd been keeping secret from his father. Ben let it slip over dinner and John flew into a rage with Mark. Kathy said she was initially frozen by a conflict of loyalty, but then she just flipped; wanted to bring an end to the confrontation between John and Mark. The butter knife was to hand and she just hurled it in his direction, not anticipating actually hitting him.'

James paused and let this information sink in for a moment.

'Good work, Mel. So, the way I see it, all three of them have plausible motives, but Kathy's admitted to a sudden act of violence. I think we should speak to her in a more formal session. Bring her in for questioning at Stevenage; I'll be there in an hour.'

'Will do, guv.'

James's brain fog was clearing at last, aided by a strong, black coffee, paracetamol and a comforting feeling that the Gibbs investigation was moving along nicely.

He was just going to have a quick look at the remaining reports, before driving up to Stevenage, when his phone rang again. He picked it up, expecting it to be Mel, when he saw instead that it was Molly.

What now?

He was minded to ignore her call, but she would only persist until he finally bit. Also, a small part of him was actually warming to the woman – the teeniest part.

'Can't really talk right now; kind of urgent stuff on at work.'

'James…' Her voice was breathless. Panicked.

'Whatever is it?'

'There's another body.'

He struggled to process the comment. 'What? How? Where?'

'I'm at Bunyan's Dell. I just found it.'

'Another bloody cat, you mean? What are you doing there? I don't understand.'

'I was laying flowers for Mr. Darcy – but that's not important right now. It's a *woman*, James, lying there with her guts…' Her voice cracked.

'Oh, Jesus Christ,' James slumped in his chair.

'James? You there?'

What to do? *Think.* The room started to spin. He closed his eyes.

'James?'

'You shouldn't be contacting me about this,' he eventually said. 'I can't touch the case; got to keep clear of Perkins. Call 999 and report it to them – *now*. I've got to go.'

James killed the call and sank the rest of the coffee.

He had to get outside.

TWENTY-TWO

'HAVE you been working all night, guv?' Mel asked, regarding James's crumpled clothes with a pitiful expression.

He straightened his tie and smoothed down his shirt. 'Where is she?'

'Interview room three. She didn't want a solicitor. I've told her it's still informal.'

'Let's see if she's ready to talk.'

James strode towards the interview room.

'Guv?'

'Mel?'

'Let me at least ask *some* questions, won't you?'

'I'd never deprive you of an opportunity to talk.'

James took a deep breath, tried to shake all thoughts of Perkins and the body from his head, turned off his mobile and walked into the room.

Kathy's appearance was a contrast to the previous time James spoke to her: her hair was scraped into a tidy bun, her face was lightly made up and she wore a smart twin set. She kept her hands hidden from view on her lap and, behind the makeup, her countenance was inscrutable.

'Mind if I call you Katie?' James said, sitting down. Mel took the seat next to him.

'Well… I suppose not,' she said, confused. 'But you know it's Kathy, right?'

James winced at his own unprofessionalism. His head was all over the place; not that that was an acceptable excuse. He imagined Mel rolling her eyes. 'Sorry, Kathy, I'm hopeless with names,' he chuckled unconvincingly. 'I should reiterate that you are here voluntarily, and are free to go at any point. Understood?'

Kathy nodded.

'Good. Now, DS Barraclough has informed me about the incident with the butter knife. Is there a reason why you didn't tell us about it?'

Kathy paused, chewing her bottom lip before speaking. 'I suppose it was difficult to explain. It was nothing, really – just one of those silly things you do in the heat of the moment.'

'I see. And, have you done anything similarly silly before, in the heat of the moment?'

She shook her head.

'I understand your son's in a relationship with another man. That right?'

'Yes, Mark. His partner's called Maurice, but I've never met him.'

'And, how do you feel about your son being gay, Kathy?'

A puzzled look fell across her face. 'It doesn't bother me. I just want him to be happy.'

'But John didn't feel that way, did he?'

'No, he was just a bit old fashioned like that. He would

have come round to the idea, eventually. You know, deep down he was quite… loving.'

'How would you describe your marriage?'

Kathy looked down at her hands, then at James. 'Like any normal marriage, I suppose: we had our ups and downs, but it lasted. I've never loved anyone else…'

Kathy began to sob, and brought a tissue out from up her sleeve. James's mother always used to have a Kleenex in the same place. *'You never know when you might need one,'* he could hear her saying.

James allowed a moment for Kathy to compose herself, then he said: 'Did John ever love anyone else?'

A pained expression shot across Kathy's face, as she dabbed her eyes. She took a deep breath, but then failed to speak.

'I've seen the calendar in the garage, Kathy,' Mel said: 'the one with the topless women.'

Nice move, Mel, James thought.

Kathy lifted her chin, a hint of steel flashing in her eyes. 'Well, there was a time, a few years back: I discovered John was having an affair.'

'How did you discover it?' Mel said.

'I saw a message on his phone: it was from Tanya. She was supposed to be a friend.'

'It must have hurt?' Mel asked.

'Yes, I suppose. It was my fault, though.'

'Why so?' Mel said.

'Well, I wasn't supplying him what he wanted in the bedroom department. There's more to life than sex, isn't there?'

'What happened in the end – with the affair?' James asked.

'He brought it to an end, I forgave him, and I promised

to be more attentive in the future… to his needs.' Kathy dropped her head.

The man sounded like a neanderthal. James felt a surge of pity forming for the woman in front of him. A murder investigation was no time for sentimentality, however. 'Has anything happened recently, to cause you to believe that he may have been having another affair?'

Kathy kept her head down and shook it.

James allowed a few moments of silence. Sometimes suspects felt the need to fill it, but not Kathy, it seemed. He changed tack. 'You know, Kathy, I'm not buying this whole intruder idea; nothing in the forensics reports show the presence of a third party. None of you have given me the faintest hint as to who it might have been, or why they would want to harm your husband. The way I see it, the three of you each have a motive. Eventually, the evidence will lead us to the culprit; it's in your interests to tell us anything you've been holding back.'

Kathy gradually lifted her head and her gaze met that of James. He detected sadness, but nothing else. Again, he allowed the room to fall quiet.

The silence was broken by a loud hammering at the door.

Seething silently, James strode out to the corridor, closing the door behind him. An officer held a clear evidence bag containing a mobile phone.

'We found it in a copse, a few hundred metres from the property, sir,' the officer said. 'We've got the knife, too.'

James thanked him and returned to the interview room, placing the bag in front of Kathy. 'Is this John's phone, Kathy?'

She studied it for a moment. 'It could be,' she said.

'It won't take us long to confirm. Why don't you save us all a bit of time by telling us why you disposed of it?'

Kathy took a deep breath. 'I think I ought to speak to a solicitor.'

'Of course,' James said. 'Take your time and speak to us again when you're ready. I'll leave it to DS Barraclough to make the arrangements.'

He left the room.

Outside in the corridor, James found a seat.

He needed to find out what was happening, after Molly's discovery of the body. She would have dialled emergency services and they, in turn, would have informed Murdoch. Who would he assign the case to? God, he wished it could be himself; it would be such a pleasure to bring Perkins to justice, once and for all.

James looked up at the sound of the door opening, to see Mel and Kathy emerging from the interview room. He watched as they walked in tandem towards the exit. The Gibbs case brought him no satisfaction at all; in fact, it was all rather depressing – there would be no happy ending there. Justice could be an odd concept to get your head around, sometimes.

James took out his phone and switched it on: no texts or voicemails. Surely Murdoch would inform him, out of courtesy? There was no point hanging around here. He got to his feet and walked towards the exit.

As he drew closer, the double doors swung open and two figures appeared. First, he clocked the familiar sight of that fat oaf, DI Yelland. What was he doing here? It was then that James saw who Yelland was accompanying.

Perkins.

A broad smile broke across Perkins's face when his gaze landed on James. His nose was plastered and there was a yellowing bruise around his eye. He also had three parallel gashes on his cheek… scratch wounds?

James strode past purposefully, without saying a word.

As he swung open the doors, Perkins shouted out: 'You're on borrowed time, Quinn.'

James allowed himself a tiny grin.

He sat in his car sipping a Coke, while he waited for Yelland and Perkins to emerge from the station. He supposed it was a good sign that Perkins had been brought in for questioning so swiftly: at the least, it was an indication he was in the frame as prime suspect. Did they have something concrete to pin on him already? That was extremely doubtful.

James was surprised the Super had assigned the case to Steve Yelland. In fact, it felt like a kick in the teeth. The man should have been quietly retired off years ago. He was everything that James wasn't: fat, lazy and in it for what he could get. A clever man like Perkins would run rings around him. That thought brought James little comfort.

Nor did the fact that his unheeded warnings, that Perkins was bound to strike again, had been proven correct. James was the only one in the Force who saw the hallmarks of a fledgeling killer. Sure, it was big news at the time, and there was wild speculation in the press, but the interest was in the killer, not the victim – and even that soon faded. The victim was a sex worker, illegally trafficked; vermin, as far as most were concerned, including his colleagues in the Force. But to him she was a person – he'd never allow himself to forget that. Every human life was precious, and no one had the right to snuff out another. He felt gripped by a sudden sense of powerlessness.

His thoughts turned to the latest victim. What was her name? Where was she from? What had been her dreams? Everyone had dreams, didn't they? He pondered for a moment whether there was a mother, a father or a boyfriend out there, at their wit's end, unable to sleep and desperately awaiting news. The sad reality was that it was unlikely.

As he always did, he then thought of Ruth. He closed his eyes and transported himself to a happier world.

Moments later, a distant noise alerted James to the station entrance. He sank low in his seat and watched Yelland traipse to his Focus, then Perkins walked breezily past him and out to the pavement.

As soon as Perkins had disappeared from view, James leapt from the Audi and jumped in front of Yelland, blocking his exit from the car park. He stepped around to the passenger door and got in. His nose twitched, and he saw that the car was littered with discarded cans and food wrappers.

'For Christ's sake, James,' Yelland said. He took a bite from a Snicker's bar and spoke through a full mouth: 'You're going to give me a bloody heart attack.'

'Have you got anything on him?'

'Who? Perkins?'

'No, Lord Lucan. Of course Perkins.'

'You know we're not supposed to talk about this, James.'

'Since when did you care about protocols? Well, have you got anything?'

'No, nothing. Gave me the usual bollocks; said he was being framed, blah, blah…'

'What about the victim? Any idea who she was?'

'Early days. We're checking against missing persons – you know the drill. Forensics are up at the wood now.' Yelland looked at his watch. 'I need to get back to Sky Sports; I've missed enough golf today, as it is.'

'Get his car checked out; CCTV; get the team to talk to the sex workers–'

'Woah, hold it there, tiger! This is my case now, and I don't take orders from you. Now, please, haven't you got anything better to do with your Saturday?'

'Don't let him slip through the net, Steve,' James said, opening the door.

'Enjoy your weekend.'

James slammed the door and watched Yelland merge into the traffic, then disappear. The man seemed to have not a care in the world. Perhaps he had it right.

A sudden thought occurred to James: he'd send a text to Molly; give her Yelland's number; tell her that he'd be ever so keen to talk to her today, about the case. Half a smile formed.

James returned to HQ, thinking that by throwing himself back into Solent work, he'd be able to take his mind off of Perkins. There wasn't much he could do on the Gibbs case, while waiting for her to engage with a solicitor. On Solent, he'd pretty much left Luke to his own devices over the last few days, and felt a pang of guilt as a result. He was a good lad, and James owed him his attention, at least. On the database was an impressive array of output from Luke's investigations – if he could maintain his enthusiasm and work ethic, he had a promising future ahead of him.

The sound of muffled chatter came from Murdoch's office, and James popped his head around the door to see the Super at his desk, finishing a call on his mobile. Murdoch glanced at James and returned his attention to his computer. 'James.'

'Alright, sir. Not like you to be in at the weekend.'

'I'm assuming you've heard the news?'

'The body at Wain Wood? Yes, bumped into DI Yelland at Stevenage station.'

'So, you've not spoken to the journalist?'

'Which one?'

Murdoch cast him a disdainful look. 'Anything else, James? I'm sure you can appreciate I'm rather busy. The chief constable's going to come down on me like a ton of bricks. Not to mention the press.'

The Super seemed uncharacteristically flustered. He normally took this kind of pressure in his stride – a quality of which James was hugely envious.

'I'm hopeful we'll have a breakthrough soon on the Gibbs murder, sir.'

'That's great,' Murdoch said, without breaking his attention from his screen.

'Think Yelland's up to it, sir?'

'Whyever not?'

'No reason, sir. If you need any help, let me know, won't you?'

Murdoch didn't respond.

Just as James closed the door, Murdoch lifted his gaze. 'Oh, I forgot to tell you: I sent a DC to Perkins's house, on the guise of smoothing him over regarding his complaint.'

'And?'

'Looks like he's had his car valeted. I think we should put that cat business to bed; we've got bigger fish to fry.'

'Shit,' James said, slapping the doorjamb.

Murdoch fell back into his own distracted world and James returned to his desk. Despite his best efforts to engage, he was no longer in the right frame of mind to go through the Solent reports. Instead, he printed them off and headed home. He'd go for a run, then settle down in the home office, to study them in peace.

TWENTY-THREE

IT WAS Sunday and James was back at Stevenage station, having received a call from Mel that morning, to say that Kathy was ready to make a statement. He had expected her to wait until Monday. Still, it would be great if he could get the case sewn up before the working week had even started.

On the drive over, James had castigated himself for not spending enough time studying the Solent papers the previous evening; he'd been too distracted by the media attention on the Wain Wood murder. Murdoch had fronted a televised address appealing for witnesses to come forward – the Super was good at that kind of thing: speaking with authority and conveying a sense of compassion for the victim. Yelland was there, too, but Murdoch did most of the talking. Would the Super have asked James to lead the presser, had he been SIO? As much as James wished he was in Yelland's place, the thought of performing live on camera made his stomach turn.

Murdoch said the victim's identity was as yet unknown, and that her murder bore a striking resemblance to Lena

Demyan's. Several journos tried to get Murdoch to speculate as to whether the cat killing and the murder were linked, but all he said was that was a consideration for the investigation. Asked if they had Troy Perkins in custody, all Murdoch would say was that a man was helping with their enquiries.

Kathy's solicitor looked bored. Middle-class, middle-aged, double-barrelled name: Charles Bogging-Smyth or something – James wasn't really listening. He exuded the look of someone who'd rather be tucking into roast game and sipping claret, a napkin tucked under his fat chin. James caught Mel casting a disobliging eye over the man, too.

Having got the preliminaries over with, James asked Kathy to talk through the events the day of the murder, starting with the evening meal. Kathy appeared calm and composed as she began to speak. Was she resigned to her fate? She explained how she'd spent the day preparing the anniversary meal, her disappointment that John had chosen to spend the day at the golf course, that the boys were arguing and Ben had got himself drunk, seemingly because he was going through a sticky patch in his relationship with his girlfriend. After the meal and the confrontation between Mark and John, she had to convince Mark to stay. Ben disappeared into town with friends and John retired to the living room, to drink alone and watch TV, while Kathy cleared the dining room. She took herself to bed early, as did Mark, but she slept fitfully.

While Kathy took a sip of water, her solicitor looked at his watch with barely concealed boredom. James wondered what the man earned: a multiple of his police salary, he'd wager.

Kathy continued: 'I heard a crashing noise downstairs and waited for a while, thinking it might be Ben coming home. But the house went quiet, so I decided to investigate. I checked in on Mark, but he was fast asleep. Downstairs, I found John in the armchair. I saw red liquid on the carpet, and thought for a minute he'd been hit, but it was just red wine. Then I saw the bowl – Ben and Carla's anniversary present – was smashed; John must have knocked it off the table. I don't know whether he'd done it deliberately or not; I guess we'll never know.' Her voice trailed off.

'Go on, Kathy, tell us what happened next.'

'John's phone started buzzing, but he was fast asleep. I hesitated for a moment, then thought I would have a look – you know, that's how I discovered the affair last time…'

'Go on, Kathy.'

'I picked up the phone and saw there was a message from a woman, who wanted to see him, desperately – at two in the morning, for goodness sake!' She paused, then continued: 'Well, all the memories from John's affair with Tanya came flooding back; I couldn't bear the thought of it happening all over again. It… it just came over me: the need to put a stop to it all. I thought, if I can't have John, then nobody can. So, I went to the kitchen and got a knife, came back to the lounge… I stood over him for a minute or two. It felt like I'd left my own body – that I was floating up to the ceiling, watching someone else.'

'What happened, Kathy?'

Even the solicitor seemed to show an interest now. Kathy leant into him, and he whispered in her ear.

'Tell us, Kathy,' James said, gently.

'I stabbed him in the neck. Just once. He slumped down. Then, I heard a creaking noise upstairs: it was Mark getting out of bed.'

'Was Ben around at this point?'

'No.'

'Carry on, Kathy. We know there were more wounds to John's neck and back.'

'I guess it all just came out: the anger I'd been bottling up for years. I stabbed him over and over and over. I'm so sorry.' She started to cry and pulled a tissue from her sleeve.

'Thank you for telling us, Kathy. You've done the right thing. If you can, please tell me what happened next.'

'Well, Mark came down. He grabbed me, took the knife out of my hands. I looked into his eyes and... well, there was just disbelief; shock, I suppose. We both kind of just stood there. Then I heard Ben at the front door, fumbling at the lock. Mark let him in. He was so drunk.'

'What time was this, Kathy?'

'I'm not sure; sometime after two. Two-thirty, possibly.'

'Why didn't you tell the truth straight away?'

'It was my idea; don't blame the boys. Mark's prints were on the knife; his footprints in John's blood; blood was all over his clothes... I thought he might get blamed; I didn't want to take the risk. He has his whole life ahead of him...'

'Are you sure you're not covering for one of your boys, Kathy?'

'I'm sure. They were just trying to help their mum; to protect me. They're good lads. Will they be in trouble after this?'

'That decision is above my pay grade, Kathy; obstructing the course of justice is a very serious offence. But you've done the right thing today; that will be taken into account, I'm sure.'

'What will happen to me?'

'Your solicitor will explain all the details to you. But, assuming you plead guilty, you won't have to face a trial. It's a mandatory custodial sentence, of course, and after prison you'll be on licence for life. You might be offered bail pending your hearing, but you'll need to face up to the possibility that it will be denied: murder is a very serious charge, you understand?'

Kathy gave the slightest nod.

'Thank you for being cooperative, Kathy. You've done the right thing.'

James emerged into the hot air outside Stevenage station, feeling oddly deflated. Kathy's confession had brought the case to a conclusion far quicker than he'd expected. By rights, he should have felt an enormous sense of satisfaction. Perhaps he should have offered to take Mel to the pub, to celebrate and thank her for her hard work.

But, something nagged at him.

He glanced back at the station. Mel was inside, dealing with Kathy and the solicitor, and all the paperwork. Should he wait?

He got into his Audi and turned on the radio. On the passenger seat lay a folder containing a batch of Solent papers. He thumbed through them, almost absent-mindedly. There was a gardening programme of some description on the radio, where the presenters were enthusiastically spouting Latin names. It all seemed unfathomable to James, so he switched it off.

Silence. Much better.

In the folder, he paused at a print-out of business names and addresses. The name of one – Mornington Recruitment Services – meant nothing, but its address piqued James's interest. It was just around the corner from the secondary school he attended, in Peterborough. He hadn't been back to his home town for years; there'd never been much need since he brought his mother down to be closer to him, in Hertfordshire. James remembered the address as being a popular place at lunchtime. He recalled fondly Mr. Singh's newsagents and the chippy next door, and was pleased to see them both still there when he pulled up Google Street View on his phone (handy, that thing – though, he wouldn't be mentioning that to Porter). There was a narrow, gravel pathway to the side of the newsagents, which James guessed must lead to the recruitment business.

Nice and discreet.

He looked through the paperwork. What was the director's name again? Jack Tomkin. He held multiple directorships, for a diverse range of businesses. Why did that name ring a bell?

Ruth and her friend Urtė had been duped by a guy pretending to be a recruitment consultant. Was *his* name Jack? God, he couldn't remember.

Ruth remembered everything, which was useful because she'd had no paperwork; her abductors had taken all her possessions. He recalled those desperate months when he'd tried to help her locate Urtė. He recalled how Ruth wept when her attempts at finding the recruitment agency and their so-called consultant on the internet failed; all trace had seemingly been removed. Sources at the constabulary told James that it took someone with expert I.T. knowledge to remove an electronic footprint like that; the gang were clearly no amateurs. But, still, Ruth beat herself up constantly; blamed herself: it was all her fault that Urtė was missing. She never gave up hope of finding her best friend until the day she died. Then James picked up the baton, even though, in his heart of hearts, he knew that Urtė too must also be dead.

He searched through the clutter of his memory: Jack. Was it? Yes. No. Possibly. Don't know. He was hopeless with names. Could just as well have been a Jake or a Jim. Or, Norman, for all he knew. And, if it was Jack, was it the *same* Jack? Or just a coincidence?

Suspicion of coincidences was written into his detective DNA.

TWENTY-FOUR

Molly slipped into the office unceremoniously late on Monday morning, to find a lovely freesia and rose bouquet from Waitrose on her desk. She inhaled their gorgeous scent, then noticed that the price tag was still left on – which told her they were from a man. Still, better than nothing. She opened a small yellow envelope and took out a *'Thinking of You'* card. Inside, it read: *'So sorry about Mr. Darcy. From Brian and all the team at the Herald.'* A tear began to form and she patted it away with her sleeve, lest she ruin her eye makeup.

Sensing a presence behind her, she turned to see Brian, hands in pockets and wearing a subdued expression.

'Friends?' he said, removing his hands from his pockets, as if to offer a hug.

'Friends,' Molly replied, her body language telling him, however, that a hug was out of the question.

A few awkward seconds of silence followed; Brian pocketed his hands and lifted himself up onto the balls of his feet, then back down. He withdrew a hand to look at his watch.

'Don't tell me, Brian: there's lots to write about before tonight's edition?'

'Well… er…'

'Already onto it.'

With that, Brian turned on his heel and retreated to his office.

Business as usual had returned.

At the photocopier, Kelvin flashed Molly a warm grin and blew a kiss. Molly caught it and mouthed the words *'thank you'*.

A warm flush of sentimentality fizzed through her veins, and for the first time in years, Molly wondered whether she did want to leave after all. Should she cancel the interview? She'd sleep on that one.

In all her years at the *Herald*, she'd never faced the dilemma of two concurrent murder stories – well, three if you counted Mr. Darcy; was that strictly murder? *It bloody well should be*, Molly thought. Unbelievably, Kathy Gibbs's confession would actually now be relegated from the front page.

Stop faffing, Moll; you've got words to write and deadlines to meet.

She owed it to Mr. Darcy to get this right. And James. What could she do to help him bring that psycho to justice? There must be people out there who know something? Perhaps they were too scared to come forward. Maybe they need an incentive. Five-hundred pounds didn't cut the mustard last time, and she told Brian that. Could she persuade him to up the offer; exploit his current contrite state? The trouble was, he was as tight as a duck's arse, and she knew what he would say: readership's falling; advertising revenue's going down; everyone's getting their news online now… There was no harm in asking, though, was there.

TWENTY-FIVE

JAMES STOOD IMPATIENTLY OUTSIDE the Super's office, waiting for him to finish a call.

He'd worked through the night on the Solent files, absorbing every detail. The evidence Luke had uncovered, with the help of the fraud team, pointed to a widespread network of corrupt businesses and individuals, involved either directly in human trafficking or the laundering of money associated with it – perhaps both. James was convinced the evidence was overwhelming.

Despite the complete lack of sleep, he didn't feel remotely tired when he'd arrived at HQ before seven. A crash at some point was inevitable, but right now adrenalin coursed through his veins. He'd been surprised to find that Luke was already in, and had gone over and given him a pat on the back; told him what a great job he'd done. James didn't know what had come over him.

The Super ended his telephone call and beckoned James into his office.

'James,' Murdoch said, grinning broadly.

'Sir?'

'You're not going to believe this. That was Yelland: Forensics have only gone and found a tiny trace of DNA under the woman's fingernail. Can you bloody believe it?'

James grabbed the back of a chair to steel himself. His legs suddenly felt weak. 'Have you got a match?'

'We most certainly have.'

'And?'

'It's him: Perkins! We've finally got him, James. He's messed it up this time. Hubris was always going to be his downfall.'

James could barely process the words. Could this actually be it? The end? After all this time, and all those hours of toil?

He stopped himself from getting carried away; it wasn't over until a jury delivered a guilty verdict. 'Til the fat lady sang. When she did, he'd be joining her in the chorus.

'That's great, sir. Do we know her identity yet?'

'No, we're not getting any hits against missing persons reports. We're having to cast our net wider: internationally.'

'What about Perkins? Where's he now?'

'Steve's bringing him in. Wish I could be there to see that smug grin fall from his face.'

For a brief moment, James felt annoyance that Yelland, of all people, would get the credit he didn't deserve. He pushed that feeling aside; it didn't matter right now.

'There's something else interesting, James,' Murdoch said: 'Forensics are having difficulty determining the date of death.'

'Why so?'

'Her body was frozen at some point.'

'Bloody hell,' James said. 'That suggests Perkins was playing a long game; waiting for the right moment to dump the body.'

'That's what it looks like,' Murdoch said. 'Was there something else you wanted to speak to me about?'

'Yes, I think we're ready to make a move on Solent, sir. I've put together a list of names and businesses here, summarized the evidence and the justification. We need a coordinated strike across Hertfordshire and Cambridgeshire.' James handed Murdoch a stack of paperwork. 'We should move fast. I need your approval for the warrant application, sir.'

Murdoch took the paperwork.

'Great work, James. I'll deal with this as a matter of priority and come back to you. You confident it'll be water-tight this time?'

'It's an extensive network, sir. I'm confident we've got the main players, here.'

'Sounds like we may have grounds for celebration soon, eh?' Murdoch said, a glint in his eye. 'You should come around to our place for one of Mrs. M's suppers; we won't take no for an answer this time. Bring a lady friend.'

James disguised a grimace. 'Okay,' he said, hopeful that something would come up, to give him an excuse to get out of it.

Later, James was reviewing the Gibbs file; Mel had done a fine job getting all the paperwork in place. Tiredness was creeping up on him, despite the Coke and the black coffees he'd knocked back.

Murdoch appeared from his office and gave a thumbs up. 'All good to go. Get it done; report back when it's over.'

That was the shot of adrenalin he required, and James leapt into action. He grabbed Luke and instructed him to contact the relevant operations teams across the Hertford-shire and Cambridgeshire forces, to coordinate the raids in the morning. Once he'd got the warrant approved from the court, he'd go for a run.

Things were looking up, at last.

It was early morning in Sunny Vale, and James was waiting in the communal lounge, while Jane washed and dressed Mary. He'd decided not to interfere with the Solent raids this time, and thought that the best thing to do to distract himself was visit his mother.

He picked up a copy of the previous evening's *Herald* and read Molly's front-page article:

'DELL RIPPER STRIKES AGAIN?'

Police were called to Wain Wood in Preston, at 10.30 a.m. on Saturday, by a Hertfordshire resident who discovered the body of a woman in Bunyan's Dell. Her body was subsequently removed and taken for forensic investigation sometime afterwards. The death of the woman, who has not yet been identified, is being treated as suspicious by Hertfordshire Constabulary.

The woman has been described as white, slim build, 5ft 2in and in her early twenties.

The discovery comes just days after a dog walker found the body of a disembowelled cat in the same location. The circumstances of the cat's slaughter bore the grim hallmarks of the individual who has become known as the 'Dell Ripper'. Police have refused to comment when asked if the unknown woman's death was being linked to either Lena Demyan's or the cat's killing. They also refuse to confirm whether any particular individuals have been arrested or taken in for questioning.

Please contact us if you have any information which may

assist the police. The Herald now offers a reward of £750, should a reader provide information that leads directly to the perpetrator's arrest.

In other news, Kathy Gibbs, 51, of Brookfold Way, Letchworth, has been remanded in custody, after confessing to the killing of her husband, John Gibbs, in a fit of jealous rage. Her sentencing hearing is expected to take place in the coming months. Turn to page 3 for the full story.'

James folded the paper and returned it neatly to the coffee table, where it joined worn copies of *Woman's Weekly* and *The People's Friend*.

He wondered if Molly had spoken to Yelland. If she had, he must have remained uncharacteristically tight-lipped. He guessed that Murdoch had laid down the law that Troy Perkins being held in custody, following the discovery of the DNA, was to remain out of the public realm for a while longer. These things had a habit of leaking before long, but Murdoch would want to create a sense of urgency among the public, to prompt people to come forward, who may have seen or heard anything suspicious; the more corroborating evidence they could obtain, the better.

Beside himself, the lounge was empty, but from the vantage point of his high-backed chair, he could see through an open door into the adjoining dining room, where a handful of residents sat hunched at round tables as, slowly and silently, they were spoon-fed their breakfasts by patient staff in plastic aprons.

Jane appeared at his side and said: 'She's all ready for you now, Mr. Quinn.'

'Thanks, Jane.'

There was no reaction from Mary when James walked

into her room. She was seated, as ever, in her chair, eyes glazed, hands resting in her lap. He sat restlessly for a few moments next to her, unable to think of anything to say, then walked over to the window.

On the dresser, he noticed that the photo of him and Ruth wasn't in its usual place; it had been moved to the front. Had she been looking at it? He picked it up and returned to sit next to Mary. He turned to face his mother, but she was just staring impassively into empty space.

They sat in stony silence for a few minutes. He resisted the urge to get up and pace the room. Jane's words came to mind: '*Just talk to her.*' That's what everyone kept saying to him: just talk. But, what to say? Ruth would have been so much better at this than him.

He returned his gaze to the photograph. It was taken at their friends' wedding: Josh and Lydia; June 2009, if he remembered correctly. It was a clear but breezy day, and James was squinting into the sun, smiling awkwardly. He hated having his picture taken. Ruth must have given the camera to someone, but he couldn't remember who. Ruth was a picture of health and serenity, her perfectly white teeth a glorious contrast to the bright-red lipstick; gorgeous, flawless skin. She held onto her hat, and strands of hair had fallen down over her face. James closed his eyes and imagined running his fingers through her hair, tucking the wayward strands behind her ear. He recalled the nervousness he had felt on that day: he was Josh's best man, and the prospect of delivering a speech had sat uncomfortably in his stomach. Ruth had stowed a hip flask of brandy in her handbag, and made him swig from it, 'to take the edge off.' In the end, the speech went as well as could be expected, and when he sat down after the applause, Ruth squeezed his hand and whispered in his ear: 'Well done, darling.'

Josh and Lydia moved to Canada not long after. The last time they'd corresponded (a Christmas card, two or three years ago), Josh told him he was a superintendent in the British Columbia Sheriff Service, and Lydia was on maternity leave with their second child – a girl, he thought, but couldn't be certain. He couldn't recall the name of the first, either – a boy. Him and names! He smiled, inwardly.

He ran his thumb tenderly across Ruth's face. 'I miss her so much it hurts, Mum,' he said, his voice cracking. 'What am I going to do?' A tear rolled down his cheek. Normally, he wouldn't allow anyone to see him like this, but he may just as well be on his own; she was somewhere else. In the past? Who knew? For him, it felt like he was staring into a terrifying future.

He felt a faint tickle on his forearm, as Mary placed a bony hand on him. He looked at her and saw that she was smiling; a spark of life glistened in her eyes.

'Hold out your hand,' she said, her voice barely a whisper. She reached for something on the table, to the side of her chair.

James held out his palm and she dropped a small object into it: a brown, plastic button.

'Go and get yourself some penny sweets, David,' she said, 'before your father gets home.' Mary gently closed James's fingers around the button and brought a shaky finger to her lips.

Before James could think of any words, Mary's eyes glazed over and she turned her head, sinking back into her silent world.

TWENTY-SIX

Mary had a little lamb,
Its fleece was as white as snow,
And everywhere that Mary went
The lamb was sure to go.

KATHY GIBBS CLOSED her eyes and transported herself to an imagined future. She was rocking in a chair, next to a roaring fire, cradling her perfect new granddaughter: Bethany, she called her. Beautiful. The air was warm and the light was soft. Bethany blew a contented raspberry, and Kathy gently cleared the drool with the tip of her little finger. She took a long intake of breath and savoured the glorious baby smells: milk, warm biscuits and talcum powder. But, for some reason, she couldn't get past the first verse of the nursery rhyme; kept repeating it in a low whisper, over and over.

She opened her eyes and immediately the spell was broken. The cold reality of her new life hit her in all its brutal starkness.

How was she ever going to survive?

It was dark and stuffy and silent in her new home: a cell no bigger than one of the bathrooms back home. Her bottom lip began to quiver at the thought of home. It was where she belonged – with the boys; with John, the love of her life.

Her mind snapped back to that moment after her wicked deed, when she looked down at the knife as it fell from her bloodied hands. She felt the question growing in her head like a balloon – always the same question:

Why did I do it?

She clenched her fist and brought her hand to her temple; hit it. Slowly at first, then faster. Harder. Pounding now, trying to burst the balloon.

Why, why, why?!

There was no answer. No justification. She deserved her punishment. Suicide had crossed her mind, but that was the coward's way out. How could she leave the boys without a mother, as well as their father?

A noise jolted her: distant keening. A pang of maternal concern gripped her stomach and blew away her self-pity. She was powerless to help. Surely an officer would tend to the situation? Another wail of haunted grief echoed from beyond the cell door.

'Shut the fuck up!' someone screamed.

Someone else banged on their wall, then another; the noises sound metallic and hollow. Before long, it seemed the entire landing had joined in the chorus.

Hurried footfall outside. Chants, shouts and wails.

Kathy turned on the hard, narrow bed to face the wall; she wrapped the thin pillow tight around her ears. As the sounds dulled, the voice of her mother grew louder and clearer.

'I always said you'd amount to nothing, Kathleen.'

She brought her knees tight to her chest and opened her mouth wide, to make way for a silent scream.

TWENTY-SEVEN

Molly had a reasonable night's sleep, for the first time since Mr. Darcy's passing – perhaps because it felt like he was back home, where he belonged; his ashes were in a little cardboard box on the mantlepiece. At the weekend she'd take a trip to the shops and find a nice urn for him. She'd moved Mother to a new home in the kitchen: a high cupboard, behind the tinned tomatoes.

Her mobile buzzed and she saw that it was the switchboard from work. Well, switchboard-slash-reception-slash-security.

'Bernie? Whatever is it at this time?'

'Morning, Molly. Got someone on the line who wants to speak to you: says her name's Bea. Calling in response to your article.'

'Ooh, fancy that. Put her through, cheers, Bernie.'

'Doing it now, Molly.'

'Hello, Bea?'

'Sorry, Molly, still me; can't seem to work this bloody phone.'

'Did you press the hash button, Bernie?'

'Oh, no. Let me try again.'

'Thanks, Bernie.'

'Bea?'

'Hello. Yes.'

'Molly Tindall here. You're calling about the article?'

'Yes. I know who the girl was.'

'That's fantastic, Bea. Let me just get a notebook and pen.'

'No, I don't want to do this on the phone.'

'Okay. Do you want to meet somewhere?'

'Do you know Mario's Café in Stevenage?'

'No, but I can find it.'

The humid air of the cafe reeked of frying bacon and chip fat. It was the sort of place – all-day full English breakfasts; laminated menus; a loo to be used only by the truly desperate – where a generous tip meant tossing a twenty-pence coin into the tip jar next to the till.

Bea was tiny. Skeletal. Her jet-black hair was scraped into a bun so tight that it looked like the thin skin on her forehead might rip. She pushed up the sleeves of her charcoal sweater, taking her watch halfway up her forearm in the process. Molly found herself staring at her self-harm scars, and Bea must have noticed, as she quickly pulled the sleeves down once more, clasping them tight with bony fingers yellowed by nicotine.

The gum-chewing waitress arrived to take food orders.

'Who's paying?' Bea asked.

'It's on me,' Molly said, placing her hand on the back of Bea's.

'Full English for me, ta. Extra sausage, two fried eggs, extra bacon, no tomatoes; can't stand the squishy, red fuckers. And I'll have a pint of full-fat Coke.'

Molly's mouth dropped.

'What?'

Ten minutes later, Bea scraped the last remnants from her plate with a square of white bread, forced out a burp and patted her lips with a serviette. *Must be the first time she's had a hot meal in weeks. Either that or she has the metabolism of a hummingbird,* Molly thought.

'So, I guess you want to hear what I have to say?' Bea said, leaning back in her chair, hands planted on her now distended belly.

'You don't mind if I record this chat, do you, Bea?' Molly asked, placing her mobile in the centre of the table, propped against the serviette dispenser.

'Do what you like, love, but I ain't going to be giving you me name and address, if that's what you're expecting.'

'Okay. Just take it from the start for me. Slowly.'

'This reward in the paper – how do I know it ain't just a con?'

'You have my word. If the information you tell me helps the police find the man responsible, you'll get the money. You've just got to trust me.'

'Am I going to have to speak to the Old Bill?'

'You will have to, yes; they'll need to take a statement. You may even have to go to court.'

'Court? Wait, I'm not sure the money's worth it.'

'You want to see this man behind bars, don't you? Where he can't hurt any more women?'

Bea took a deep breath.

'I ain't ashamed: a girl's gotta earn a living somehow, and it's hard when you're not born with a silver spoon in your mouth.'

'I'm not going to judge you.'

'Like I said to you earlier, I knew the girl who was killed.'

'Who was she, Bea?'

'She called herself Daniela – who's to say whether that was real, though? Most of us have street names.'

'How well did you know her?'

'We weren't best buddies or nothing; just a bit of chatter, here and there. We both worked the same patch. She was no trouble. Said she came here from Hungary… Bulgaria…? Don't know, they're all the same to me. Said she wanted to be an actress in the West End.' Bea smiled, sadly. 'We all had our dreams. I always wanted to be a nurse.'

'You still could be. Never give up on your dreams.'

Bea snorted, derisively.

Molly allowed a few beats of silence, before bringing the conversation back. 'How can you be so sure it's Daniela?'

'Well, I saw her getting into the fella's car. Never saw her since.'

'And, did you know who the man was?'

'Yes.'

'Who? Tell me.'

'He had a shitty red Peugeot. Tall bloke; large build; greasy hair. Bit of a weirdo, if you ask me.'

'Troy Perkins?'

Bea shrugged; 'If you say so. He never told me his name. That's not how it works.'

'But you knew him?'

'Sure. Been with him a couple of times.'

'God! Did he ever say or do anything to make you think he was capable of killing someone? Were you afraid of him?'

'Nah, he was nothing out of the ordinary. Perhaps I wasn't really his type. Daniela, she was young and pretty; look at me.'

Molly put a comforting hand on Bea's arm, but she shook it off.

'Were you aware he was arrested for a similar murder two years ago? Lena Demyan?'

'Yeah, I heard about her. But I've only been up this way for the past year or so. Used to work in London.'

'Do you think you will be able to speak to the police about what you know and saw? You may be asked to help reconstruct a picture of him, or pick him out of an identity parade. It's vital you cooperate.'

'I dunno; me and the Old Bill don't exactly see eye to eye, you know.'

'They won't be interested in any past history – I'm sure of it.'

Bea raised an incredulous eyebrow.

'I need that money.'

'Speak to them, please. Think of all the women like Daniela you'll be helping if you do.'

'I'm going to have to think about it,' Bea said, getting to her feet. Her seat screeched across the floor and other customers looked in their direction.

'Do the right thing,' Molly said, scribbling onto a paper napkin. 'Here's the number of the detective leading the case.'

With that, Bea snatched the napkin and hurried out of the café.

Molly smiled, then picked up her phone to send a text message:

'Hi James. Want to hear some good news? M. xx.'

His reply was almost instantaneous:

'Just tell me.'

TWENTY-EIGHT

JACK TOMKIN SAT CASUALLY opposite James and Luke in the interview room. His arms were folded against his chest and he wore an expression of defiant indifference. Tomkin looked significantly younger than his fifty-three years: blond hair; smooth, tanned skin; blue, piercing eyes; James saw a man seemingly unburdened by anxiety or stress. He had been arrested at his home, in an affluent village to the west of Peterborough, earlier that morning, on suspicion of committing offences relating to modern slavery and money laundering. James was of the opinion that, although they had sufficient evidence to charge him now, there was benefit to questioning Tomkin further, in the hope that he might provide more information to locate the owners of the passports recovered in the raid of his premises. Unusually, Tomkin had voluntarily presented himself for interview under caution, and had waived his right to have a solicitor present. This usually indicated either naivety or arrogance; despite the absence of previous convictions, Tomkin's demeanour suggested the latter. James intuited that Tomkin was a key player in the trafficking network.

Luke had finished the preliminaries and it was now over to James to start the interrogation.

'When Cambridgeshire Constabulary raided your premises, they found twenty-seven passports. Can you explain how they had come into your possession?'

'We're a recruitment agency; we need to validate people's identity, to confirm their eligibility to work in the country.' He smiled superciliously, then feigned a contrite expression. 'I would *hate* to be an unwitting party to fraud.'

'I see,' James said, as he opened up a folder. He removed a sheaf of A4 paper, then turned over the top sheet and placed it on the table in front of Tomkin. He repeated this with perhaps ten more sheets: photocopied identification pages of the recovered passports. 'Can you see a pattern here, Jack?' James asked.

Tomkin leant forward and glanced cursorily at a few pages, before sinking back into a casual position. 'Sorry, I don't have my glasses on me. My eyesight's not what it used to be.'

'Of course,' James said, his sarcasm barely concealed. 'Then, let me help you.' He dropped his finger onto a sheet of paper: 'Daria Kowalchuk, age seventeen. Last week she committed suicide by jumping off the eighth floor of a council flat tower block – probably couldn't bear the shame of having been kept as a sex slave. All our attempts to identify her failed, until we found her passport at your office. What do you have to say about that, Jack?'

Jack Tomlin shrugged.

James continued, jabbing his finger onto successive photographs. 'And, here: Miljana Lewitzki, twenty-two... Vida Mrozinski, nineteen... Olga Zema, twenty-five... Zivka Bozovic, nineteen... Shall I go on?'

Tomkin laughed. 'Perhaps you should work a bit more on your pronunciation. It's terrible.'

'Where are they now, Jack?'

Tomkin shrugged. 'Who knows? Looking for their passports, probably, now you fellas have nicked them.'

'Well, here's the interesting thing,' James picked up one of the sheets of paper from the table: 'Miss Miljana Lewitzki, here – do excuse my poor pronunciation – we actually know where she is right now: safe and well, you'll be pleased to hear, Jack. You see, last week we rescued her from a brothel. She was scared out of her wits, locked up in a room and forced to have sex with strangers, day in and day out. What can you tell me about how she came to be there, Jack?'

Tomkin showed barely a flicker of a reaction. 'I don't keep tabs on everyone who comes through the agency. How can I? There are hundreds of them each year. We specialize in the sectors that attract young, overseas candidates: fruit picking, manual labour, hospitality… Perhaps this one–'

'Miss Lewitzki,' James interjected, angrily.

'Alright, keep your hair on, mate,' Tomkin said, grinning broadly. 'Perhaps she was one who never passed the initial interview; I'd have to check my records. Oh, I can't, can I, because you've taken them. I'm afraid, then, I can't help you; my hands are tied. Sorry, fellas.'

Under the table, James's foot was tapping uncontrollably. Rage was building and he was fast losing patience.

'This is how I think your business works, Jack – tell me if I've got any of this wrong: you have a recruitment agency that specialises, just like you say, in those industries that attract people from eastern Europe, the kind of work our natives turn their noses up at; too much like hard graft for their liking. Demand for work is high and the supply is almost limitless. Margins are low, but run an efficient and seemingly professional operation, and the opportunity to make decent, reliable, if unspectacular profits is all yours. But that's not enough for you, is it? You're greedy. The fast cars, the designer suits – they don't come cheap.'

Tomkin looked at his watch and yawned. 'Have you finished yet?'

'I've barely even started. There's another side to your business, isn't there? Off the books, lucrative, tax-free returns? An arrangement where you supply young women to the sex trade? You have the ideal set-up to sift through your applicants for the perfect kind of candidate. How much do you make per woman, Jack? A grand? Two-grand? What's a destroyed life worth to you? And those passports; I imagine they have quite a value on the black market. What were you doing there? Building up a stock-pile before selling them on? What was it: buy two, get one free?'

Tomkin laughed and looked at Luke. 'Your boss sounds a bit mental to me. What's it like working for him?'

James slammed his fist down on the table. Tomkin didn't flinch.

James continued: 'I think you've been in this game for years, Jack. You think you're untouchable.'

He took a copy of Urtė's photograph from his pocket and threw it towards Tomkin. 'Do you recognize her?' He sensed Luke shifting uncomfortably next to him.

Tomkin frowned and regarded the photo for a few moments, before throwing it back towards James. 'Who's that, then? Another poor, helpless whore you rescued?'

'She's been missing for over ten years. Her name is Urtė Cuda. She flew into Robin Hood Airport from Vilnius, Lithuania, believing she was starting a new job and a new life in London the next day. Not long after she'd landed in this country, she was seized by a criminal gang and she hasn't been seen or heard of since.'

'Robin Hood Airport, you say? Didn't she know where London was, the daft cow? That was just asking for trouble.'

'What happened to her, Jack?'

'Guv,' Luke interjected, 'do you think we should take a break now?'

James glowered at Luke, then turned his attention back to Tomkin, who looked at his watch.

'Tell you what, let's make it a long break, shall we?' Tomkin said. 'I think I'd like you to contact my solicitor, after all. I'm sure he'd be *very* interested to hear your justification for going down this line of questioning.'

James rose from his seat, scraping it across the tiled floor, and stormed out of the room.

'What happened just then, guv?'

Luke had found James in the kitchen area. He was downing a large glass of tap water.

Begrudgingly, James beckoned Luke to a quiet table and explained Urtė's disappearance. Lithuanian authorities had long lost interest in her case; Urtė had no family there pushing for answers, or for justice. Similarly, the attitude in the UK had been one of cold indifference to her plight, and her case had been quietly closed.

'I don't think you had cause to ask him, guv. We've no evidence suggesting Tomkin had any involvement in trafficking before he established his recruitment agency.'

Luke was right, of course. But the burden of trying rested entirely on James's shoulders. He was her only living advocate.

'Do you think you can handle the rest of the interview on your own?'

'Yes, no sweat, guv.'

'Thank you. He's not going to admit to anything, but we have enough to charge him. Have another go at getting him to name names; dangle the possibility of leniency if he coughs up anything useful. He won't bite, I'm sure of that, but we have to be seen to try.'

Try.

As that pathetic word tumbled from his mouth, the thought occurred to James that *trying* was all he'd been doing for years. 'When you're done with Tomkin, check with Interpol whether they've found any matches against missing persons records.'

Luke nodded and left the room.

James hurled his glass into the kitchen sink, smashing it into tiny pieces.

TWENTY-NINE

ALL THINGS CONSIDERED, the week ended satisfactorily.

First came the charging of Jack Tomkin, Marcus Pinto and three others on modern slavery offences, for their involvement in an organized crime syndicate.

Then came the icing on the cake: Perkins being arrested and charged with murder.

They finally got an identification on the dell body, too, when Interpol matched her dental records against a missing person report in Romania: Daniela Sirota, twenty-three years old, believed to have travelled to the UK voluntarily, three years ago. No records were recovered of where she'd lived or worked in all that time.

James didn't know what had come over him. For some reason, when he called Molly to tell her the good news, that the eyewitness had successfully identified Perkins in a line-up, he let it slip to her how keen the Super was for a celebratory dinner. Perkins's arrest must have made him come over all gooey and sentimental. 'Oh, let's do it!' she said, excitedly. 'It could be *such* fun.'

So, here they were, in a leafy Letchworth enclave, on a

warm summer's evening. The Murdochs' house was similar to the mental image James had formed, only larger: art-deco detached, double-fronted, in an expensive part of town. Immaculate front lawn with well-stocked borders, black front door with a stained-glass window; a *'Neighbourhood Watch'* sticker in the corner. The house was well beyond James's means, and he contemplated for a moment how Murdoch could have afforded it. Mrs M. had never worked, as far as James was aware, and the salary of a superintendent wasn't exactly enormous. Perhaps there was family money? Or maybe they'd just struck lucky, years back, when property prices weren't as ridiculous.

James, clutching cheap garage carnations and the half-price tin of toffees in one arm, pressed the doorbell, and the chimes of Big Ben reverberated deep inside. He turned to see Molly on the drive, disdainfully taking in the surroundings.

'Pssst,' he said, 'don't leave me on my own here.'

He turned back as a shadowy shape appeared in the glass. The door opened.

'Mrs. Murdoch?'

The woman was no taller than five feet. Twinset and pearls; thin, grey hair lacquered into a rigid nest which could withstand a force-nine gale.

'Please, call me Estelle. And you must be the elusive Detective Chief Inspector Quinn? Ian's told me all about you.'

Her gaze shifted to the gifts James held and her smile dropped. James thrust the flowers and toffees to her. 'Oh, how kind. You really shouldn't have gone to such bother.'

Molly sidled up.

'And, this must be the lovely Mrs. Quinn?'

'No, I'm Molly. Molly Tindall.'

A puzzled expression formed on Estelle Murdoch's face. 'Molly Tindall? Why do I recognize that name?'

Molly flashed her business card. 'Chief Crime Reporter for the *Herald*. Perhaps you've read one of my front-page spreads?'

Estelle Murdoch regarded the card for a moment, then said: 'No, I'm thinking of Molly Tapley, treasurer at the bowls club. Molly's such a common name these days.'

'Oh?' Molly said.

'Between you and I,' Estelle said, her voice now a conspiratorial whisper, 'it seems that she's *quite* the trollop.'

She stepped back. 'Well, don't just stand there. Come in.'

James entered a capacious hallway which smelt of beeswax and lavender. Molly followed, but they were impeded from advancing any farther by Estelle. She placed the flowers and toffees onto a polished walnut side-table and motioned to a couple of sheets of newspaper on the carpet: the *Herald*, James noted with a wry smile.

'If you wouldn't mind removing your shoes, please. Unfortunately, we had a guest, easter 2007 – turned out he'd stepped in some… *dog's mess*. Traipsed it all over our Berber twist in the blink of an eye; took me three washes with the HydroWave to remove all trace. We've had to *insist* on a no-shoes policy ever since, I'm afraid.'

James dropped to a knee to untie his laces. Next to him, Molly stooped to push off her heels, flashing James a bemused expression as she did so.

Tomato odours entered the hallway, and James stood up and saw the slippered figure of the Super entering from the kitchen, clutching a dark bottle. 'Been waiting for an excuse to try this beauty for months,' he said.

'You go steady with that, Ian,' Estelle said, sternly.

'Gout,' she said, turning to James and Molly, a hint of pride in her tone.

'Kopke port, 1980,' Murdoch said. 'And you must be Molly? Thank you so much for coming. We've been trying to get this one over for years.' Murdoch flashed a wry grin at James.

'My pleasure,' Molly said.

My hell, James thought.

'Well, come in,' Estelle said; 'we don't stand on cere-monies here. Ian, perhaps you could take our guests into the dining room while I finalize the first course?'

The dining table had been set formally. James was immediately reminded of a TV programme Ruth had made him watch with her, about preparations for a state banquet at Windsor Castle; some poor sod dressed like a snooker referee had to measure every place setting. James wondered whether Estelle had sent the Super in with a yardstick while she prepped dinner.

'Feels like the denouement of an Agatha Christie,' Molly said.

Murdoch carefully placed the port bottle on the side-board and sat down. 'Well, I think we already know our culprit, eh?' he chuckled.

James went to sit, but Murdoch stopped him; 'She'll want you in that seat, there. Molly, this one.'

'Does it matter?' James asked.

'I find it's easier when you don't question. So, are you two an *item* then?'

Molly laughed. 'No! How would you describe us, James? Friends?'

Good question; what *were* they? Before he could answer, Estelle swept into the room, a tiny ball of nervous energy, clutching a basket of assorted breads.

'Oh, Ian,' she said, in a tone which combined disapproval and disappointment, 'you've got it wrong. How many times must I tell you? It's boy, girl, boy, girl.' She gestured to Molly and James. 'I'm sorry. Now, up you get.'

Even though Estelle was tiny and the Super was a large man, it was he who seemed the diminished figure.

'Musical chairs,' Molly muttered. 'My favourite.'

'I'm sorry, dear?'

'I said that's a lovely picture.'

'Oh, yes,' Estelle said, proudly looking at the large frame above the fireplace. 'The Ducal Palace, Canaletto. Isn't it *magnificent?* Not an original, I hasten to add. Have you been to Venice, dear?' Without pausing for Molly to give an answer, she continued: 'We haven't been since the 'eighties, alas.'

She turned to look at James. 'We have a holiday home in Madeira now. I expect Ian's told you all about it, Detective Chief Inspector? We go there as much as we can. It has a *wonderful* year-round climate. Where do you go, *en vacance*, James?'

'I'm not really a holiday person.'

'He's a workaholic,' the Super added, as he attempted to surreptitiously pluck a bread roll from the basket. Estelle whisked the basket away before he could grab a roll, and set it down at the far end of the table.

'I do *so* admire that. There's nothing worse than idleness in a man, is there, Molly? It's best to keep them busy, otherwise you soon find they're up to no good.'

Molly let out a small giggle and James flashed a look at the Super, recalling all the long lunches he'd taken over the years.

'Wine, anyone?' the Super asked, brandishing a bottle of white.

'Oh, yes, please,' Molly said, eagerly.

'Remember your gout, Ian,' Estelle said. 'I'll fetch the soup.'

James caught Estelle flashing the Super a castigating look when he tipped his bowl and noisily slurped the last remains of the tomato soup. He didn't seem to notice and, after dabbing his mouth with a napkin, he leant back in his chair and laced his fingers over a fat stomach, no doubt turning his mind to the main course.

In the absence of chatter, the sounds of the mantel-piece clock, distant traffic and clinking soup spoons seemed exaggerated.

'I'm guessing, then, your kids have flown the nest?' Molly said.

'No, Ian and I never had children.' Smiling wistfully, Estelle dropped her spoon into her half-full bowl and turned to face the window. James thought he detected a faint tremble in her lip. She brought a hand to her fore-head and winced, as if she had a migraine. She took a sip of water. James suspected she was teetotal.

'I'm sorry,' Molly said. 'I just figured, with the size of the house and everything…'

'It just wasn't mean to be, I suppose,' Murdoch said, reaching for the wine bottle and filling his glass, before changing the subject.

'We should raise a toast to James and all his hard work on Solent.'

'Hear, hear!' Molly said, lifting her glass, which she then quickly drained.

'Who would have thought we were living in such a hotbed of criminality?' Estelle said. 'One just never really knows what goes on behind closed doors.'

'More wine, Molly?' Murdoch asked.

'Don't mind if I do, thank you.'

Estelle, wearing a disapproving expression, said: 'So, Ms. Tapley–'

'Tindall.'

'Oh, do forgive me.' Estelle's gaze dropped for a moment to Molly's low-cut blouse. 'You must be having a field day at the *Herald*?'

'Well, yes, it does make a change from the normal nonsense we see: littering, garden boundary disputes, that sort of thing.'

Estelle winced, and James supposed that she didn't consider either of those examples to be trifling matters.

Murdoch interjected: 'It was Molly's cat that...' the Super made a hand gesture, as he searched in vain for the right words, '...well, you know ...'

'Goodness, you poor thing! How *awful*, dear,' Estelle said, placing a hand on Molly's arm, her face contorted into a look of exaggerated sympathy. 'Mind you, I can't say I'm a feline fanatic. Don't you find they make such a terrible mess of your furniture?'

'Not anymore, Estelle,' Molly said, tersely. 'Not anymore.'

A sinking feeling washed over James that this was going to be a long night. He thrust his glass at the Super: 'Couldn't top me up, could you, sir?'

The main course – lamb cutlets in gravy *('It's red wine jus, Ian')* – passed slowly but without incident. They were soon tucking into a Black Forest gateau. James had to suppress a smile at the small portion Estelle had allocated her husband. He had flashed her a disgusted look, but she effected not to notice.

Estelle looked up to James for a moment, narrowed her eyes then turned to Molly: 'Your beau is quite the enigma, Molly.'

'We're not…' Molly started to correct her, but Estelle turned her attention back to James.

'You've been so taciturn this evening,' she said, sucking a tiny morsel of gateau from her spoon. 'Tell me, why do you think that monster removed those poor women's… *innards?*'

'Don't you think we should wait 'til we're finished eating, love?' the Super said, through a mouthful of dessert.

'Nonsense, Ian; stop being so squeamish. Go on, James, I'd like to hear your opinion.'

James cleared his throat. 'Well, I don't give all that stuff too much attention. It's too easy to attribute some higher meaning to these things, and we end up talking him up into this psychopathic monster. The media loves all that stuff, don't they?' Molly frowned.

James continued: 'We all do; everyone's fascinated by the Dennis Nilsens, the Fred Wests, Harold Shipmans and Jack the Rippers of this world. The thing is that's what they want; they crave the attention and the notoriety. That's all Perkins wants. And, what do we do? We hand it to him on a plate. I prefer to think of him as what he is.'

'And what's that, James?' Estelle said, apparently spellbound.

'A pathetic loser; nothing more, nothing less. A man incapable of forming meaningful relationships in the normal world. One who invents an alternative reality in which he is dominant; king of all he surveys; in control. He wants to leave his mark on the world: a fame seeker. The best service we could do his victims is to deprive him of the oxygen of publicity; smother it in a cloak of indifference and honour the victims, instead. We always remember the killers, don't we? Never the victims. Let's celebrate *their* lives; keep *their* spirits and dreams alive.'

Molly tilted her head and smiled slightly, as if a penny had just dropped.

'Hear, hear,' Murdoch said. 'Well, hopefully we'll have him behind bars soon, and we can all forget about him.'

He scraped the last remnants of his gateau and reached over to the sideboard. 'Now, who's for a glass of this delicious port?'

THIRTY

THE GOLDEN SUMMER had collapsed into a grey, stormy autumn. Westerly winds blew remorselessly into December, before the weather pattern abruptly changed and a bitter continental chill gripped the country. The news had been full of stories of grounded flights, paralysed transport networks and pensioners dying because they couldn't afford to heat their homes; 'The Big Freeze' the tabloids called it, with a fair dose of hyperbole.

James put down his book and sloped over to the window. He felt like a caged animal. How much longer must he wait? It had been three days already, sequestered in a room at the Crown Court, waiting to give evidence. Outside, a light snow was falling from a bleached sky, onto a road covered in a film of filthy slush. A bus pulled out from a stop and a car behind blew its horn and skidded, somehow managing to avoid a collision.

Beyond the road was the park, and amongst the bare trees schoolkids – silhouettes against a white canvas – spent the last minutes of their lunch hour hurling snowballs at each other and unsuspecting passers-by; it looked like a scene from a Christmas card. James had used to like Christmas, before Ruth died. Now, he would spend that protracted period from October to December – when the shops steadily filled with overpriced festive tat, and there was no escape from Slade and Wizzard and Cliff Bloody Richard playing at max volume, on a continuous loop from dawn 'til dusk – longing for the new year and a clean slate.

Life in these four walls felt to James like incarceration. He had little to occupy his days other than books and magazines, but couldn't really concentrate on either. He was forbidden from watching TV, accessing the internet or reading the newspapers.

Feelings of boredom and frustration competed with a nagging fear of taking the witness stand; the courtroom would be packed to the rafters and all eyes would be on him. An utter nightmare.

Perkins's defence team had persisted with the ludicrous notion that James had framed their man. How they'd got this far without a shred of evidence to prove it was beyond James. He almost relished the prospect of crushing the barrister's arguments. What could they say? The truth was on James's side and, despite everything, he had faith in the British justice system; the jury would see straight through Perkins's lies.

Wouldn't they?

He turned his attention back to the Curry's store in front of him. As if in defiance of the court's strictures, the TV sets in the tinsel-adorned window were showing the news, and he could make out the figure of a reporter, dressed in full winter garb, standing on high, windy ground outside what he guessed to be Luton Airport – he didn't need the sound to know what was being said. Seeing the reporter made him think of Molly Tindall. She'd be in her element, in court, watching all the drama unfold during the day, filing her reports in the evening. Months back, she told James that she had turned down an interview for a job at the *Daily News* in London; said there was more than enough excitement in Hertfordshire for her at the moment. A little bit of James was pleased with her decision – not that he told her, of course.

There was a knock at the door and he jumped. The court clerk entered the room.

'Ready?' she said.

'As I'm ever going to be,' he replied, feigning coolness.

The clerk smiled warmly, and James wondered how many times she'd heard witnesses utter those words.

James followed the clerk into the courtroom and took his place on the witness stand. Fear squeezed his heart. He took a few moments to scan the room, breathing deeply and slowly, in an attempt to calm the nerves. Ease the tight knot in his stomach. Bring down his heart rate. He deliberately avoided looking in the direction of the dock. He peered through the row of barristers and court officials and beyond, to the public gallery, hopeful of finding a familiar face to quell a rising sickness, which threatened to fell him before he'd even uttered a word. On the back row, he spotted the Luke and Mel, then Murdoch. The Super had decided a few weeks back to take early retirement. The news had come as a shock to James; he always thought the gaffer had a couple more promotions left in him. Guess you never truly know about people's motivations, priorities and ambitions.

Anyway, he was pleased they were here to lend him their support and show solidarity. A tingle of gratitude calmed him slightly. He studied their features, for any hints at how the case was progressing, but their blank expressions gave nothing away. Farther along, a couple of rows closer to the front, he found Molly, notebook on her lap; she flashed him an inscrutable smile.

His attention was snapped back to the court clerk, who now asked him to swear the oath on the Bible.

Once the preliminaries were over, a barrister stood up, whom James presumed was the lead defence counsel. The room fell deathly silent. Underneath the ridiculous wig, the woman wore a stern expression. He guessed she was mid to late forties. Experienced. Queen's Counsel, no doubt. He recalled the advice he'd received from the prosecuting counsel: answer the questions directly; don't try to pre-empt; think before you speak; don't set yourself up for error.

After asking James to introduce himself to the court, the barrister passed him a piece of paper, via the clerk. A copy was also despatched to the jury.

James studied the paper and his heart sank.

'Detective Chief Inspector Quinn, could you tell the court what this is?'

'It's an article from a news—'

'Louder, please.'

James cleared his throat. 'It's an article from a newspaper.'

'Which newspaper?'

'The *Hertfordshire Evening Herald*.'

'Can I ask you to read the headline, Detective Chief Inspector?'

'"*Two years on: the man who got away with Lena Demyan's murder*".'

'"The man who got away with murder",' the barrister repeated the words slowly, and turned theatrically to the jury.

'For the benefit of the court, could I please ask you to explain your involvement with Ms. Demyan's case?'

James allowed himself a brief glance at the jury. Twelve sets of eyes bore into him, like daggers. Turning back, he addressed the barrister: 'I was the senior investigating officer on her murder case, which means I had day-to-day responsibility for leading the investigation.'

'And, what was the outcome of the investigation?'

'We arrested and charged Troy Perkins – the defendant – with the murder.'

'And, what happened after that?'

James felt his mouth drying and licked his lips. 'The Crown Prosecution Service refused to take the case.'

'And, why was that?'

The words stuck in James's throat. He took a shaky sip of water. His shirt was drenched with sweat. 'Insufficient evidence,' he said, barely more than a whisper.

'Louder please, for the benefit of the court.'

'The CPS said there was insufficient evidence for a prosecution.'

'Could you tell the court, Detective Chief Inspector, whether, subsequent to the CPS's refusal to take the case, you identified any further evidence pointing to the defendant's guilt for that crime?'

'No.'

'Is it correct that the case is now being handled by the Cold Case Review Team at Hertfordshire Constabulary?'

'Yes. Correct.'

'And, so, would I be right in stating that your involvement ceased when the case was transferred?'

Shit.

'Detective Chief Inspector? It's a simple question.'

'No.'

'Oh? Please, do expand.'

'I continued to covertly watch Perkins – sorry, the

273

defendant. I feared that he was likely to commit a further offence.'

'And, was this covert surveillance sanctioned by a senior officer?'

'No, I did it in my own time.'

'Oh? That is interesting, Detective Chief Inspector. Would it be fair to say that you developed quite an obsession with the defendant?'

'I believed he was guilty and I wanted justice to prevail.' James flashed a look at Perkins in the dock – he couldn't help himself. Perkins wore a smart suit and a neat haircut; he was clean-shaven – a picture of respectability.

'*Believed*, Detective Chief Inspector? Is *belief* the standard of proof the police seek to charge a man with murder?'

'No, of course not.' James knew he had made a mistake the moment he uttered the word.

'Are you aware of a complaint Mr. Perkins raised to Superintendent Ian Murdoch, your superior officer?'

James flicked his gaze to the Super, who was looking down to his lap. 'Yes.'

'What was the nature of that complaint?'

'Police harassment and assault occasioning actual bodily harm. He subsequently dropped it.'

'But Mr. Perkins did incur an injury – a broken nose – did he not?'

'Yes, that's my understanding.'

'And, are you aware of how that injury was incurred?'

'I followed Mr. Perkins to a country park in Stevenage. It was dark and he surprised me; I punched him, and I regretted my actions immediately.'

'I put it to you that your *obsession* with Mr. Perkins was totally out of hand by this point, and your ability to carry out your job objectively and professionally was totally compromised. Correct?'

'If you're trying to suggest–'

'I'm not trying to suggest anything, DCI Quinn; I'm trying to establish the facts – a concept I believe you should be familiar with.'

The barrister paused and consulted with her colleague for a few moments. Then, she resumed her questioning.

'What has been your involvement in the investigation of Daniela Sirota's death?'

'I've had no involvement whatsoever.'

'I see. Can I ask you to look again at the article from the *Hertfordshire Evening Herald*?'

James picked up the article. His hands were shaking and he could barely focus on the printed words.

'Could you tell the court, please, the name of the reporter who wrote the article?'

Where was this line of questioning going? James dabbed his brow.

'Molly Tindall, Chief Crime Reporter.'

'And, how would you describe your relationship with Ms. Tindall?'

'It's a professional relationship. I've spoken to her from time to time about cases I've investigated. It can be a useful way of appealing to the public for information.'

'Of course. But, can I ask where you were on the night of July thirteenth, Detective Chief Inspector?'

Shit.

James sought out Molly in the public gallery. *'Sorry,'* she mouthed.

'I was at her house.'

'You were at her house?' The barrister arched her brow. 'And, the next morning was when Miss Sirota's body was discovered? Correct?'

'Yes.'

'For how long did you stay at Ms. Tindall's home?'

'Objection, your honour!' The prosecuting barrister rose. 'I don't see the relevance of this line of questioning.'

'Objection overruled,' the judge said. 'Answer the question, Detective Chief Inspector.'

'I believe it was until about seven the next morning,' James said, crestfallen. 'There was nothing untoward happening; I slept on the sofa.' He knew he sounded desperate now.

'I'm not interested in your sleeping arrangements,' the barrister said. James could swear she was smirking. She pivoted to address the jury: 'I'm now going to play a short recording to the court.'

James recognized immediately that it was a recording of a 999 call: Molly's call reporting the body. He glanced over at her, but she looked down at her notes. He shifted his attention to Murdoch, who puckered his lips and shifted in his seat.

'Do you recognize the voice of the woman reporting the discovery of the body?'

'Yes, it's Ms. Tindall.'

'After you left Ms. Tindall's home that morning, did you have any further contact with her?'

James looked over at Molly again. Her head was in her hands.

'It's a simple question, Detective Chief Inspector.'

'Yes.'

'And, what was the nature of the contact?'

'She called me to say that she'd found a body. She'd gone to lay flowers… for her cat.'

A murmur of laughter rippled around the room. James looked to Perkins, who was struggling to conceal his glee.

The barrister waited for the laughter to abate. 'Oh, I

see,' she said, arranging her face into a look of mock puzzlement. 'And, what did you tell her?'

'I told her to report it to the emergency services.'

'You are a police officer, are you not? A member of the emergency services?'

'Yes.'

'Then, why did you feel the need to tell her that?'

'I didn't think it appropriate for her to report it to me.'

'And, did you tell your superior officer about this conversation?'

'No.'

'Is there a reason why Ms. Tindall might have contacted you first?'

'Objection! Speculation.'

'Objection sustained.'

The defence barrister moved on to her next question: 'In your investigation, you obtained DNA samples from Mr. Perkins, is that correct?'

'Yes, it's routine to obtain it from suspects.'

'Of course, Detective Chief Inspector. No further questions.'

The barrister resumed her seat, and James watched as she whispered into the ear of a colleague, who he swore just grinned.

How could her questioning be over? He had no further chance to explain. The jury surely wouldn't believe her insinuation that he'd got Molly to plant the DNA, would they? The very idea was absurd. Preposterous! He looked to the jury, trying to gauge their reaction, but couldn't read it.

The prosecuting barrister rose. Perhaps now he'd get the opportunity to set the record straight?

'Detective Chief Inspector Quinn, can you please tell the court how many years you have worked for the police?'

'Nearly twenty-three years.'

'And, in those twenty-three years, have you ever been subject to any disciplinary proceedings or internal investigations?'

'No; on the contrary, I've received numerous commendations.'

'No further questions, your honour.'

What?!

'I need to explain some things,' James pleaded.

The prosecuting barrister mouthed the word: *'No.'*

The judge spoke: 'You are dismissed, Detective Chief Inspector. Thank you.'

James turned and left the stand, his head bowed and his stomach in knots.

THIRTY-ONE

JAMES NEEDED TO GET OUTSIDE. Fast.

The frigid air hit him like a sucker punch; he'd spent too much time in the fusty warmth of the courthouse.

He was consumed by a deep sense of foreboding. Was Perkins about to walk free again? All because James had stuffed up on the stand? Allowed himself to be beaten up by the defence barrister? The thought was almost too awful to bear. If the jury believed the ridiculous story that James had framed Perkins, did that mean he himself would face a trial? Quite frankly, such thoughts were secondary to the sickening feeling that he'd let down so many people: Lena Demyan; Daniela Sirota; Ruth; the Super; even that sodding cat with the ridiculous name, which escaped him right now.

Consumed by the maelstrom in his head, it was minutes later when he registered that it was snowing heavily. James turned up his coat collar and set off in the direction of the park. Perhaps a walk in the bitter conditions could bring him some clarity of thought. Hunched against the bitter wind, he stepped into the road. A horn screamed angrily and a car swooshed past just feet from him, sending a wave of dirty slush halfway up his trousers. Right now, he didn't care.

Dusk was falling, and the streetlamps which lined the path through the park rendered the falling snow a sickly yellow. Under a thick layer of snow, the path was barely distinguishable from the grass. The evidence of the kids playing here hours earlier was gone.

Evidence.

What had happened in the preceding days, while he had been sequestered? Had the forensic evidence been discredited? Did the eyewitness show up? Had Perkins testified? Did he hoodwink the jury? Did the defence call witnesses to testify to Perkins's good character? Did Molly stand? Was that how the barrister knew that James had spent the night at her house? He hadn't told anyone, so it could only be her. How could he have been so stupid? Questions swirled like the snow.

He should have waited at the court; spoken to someone who could bring him up to speed. He should head back; proceedings would be concluding for the day. No, he couldn't face all of them right now. He'd call Molly, instead; she'd give him the unvarnished truth.

Despite red-raw hands, James managed to switch on his phone, which had been off since lunchtime. Two voice-mails flashed up: they were both from Jane – that wasn't a good sign. The feeling of foreboding seeped through him again, as he played the messages.

'James, it's Jane from Sunny Vale. Call me as soon as you get this message. Mary's had a fall. We're on our way to Lister now.'

Then, the second message:

'James, where are you?' There was a hint of distress in

Jane's rushed words now. 'You need to get to the hospital, fast. She's not going to last much longer.'

Oh, God. The last message was two hours ago.

His phone started to buzz, and he looked down to see that it was Murdoch. He killed the call and dashed to his car.

The snow had eased slightly, and James snaked his way towards the hospital, which was about three miles away. Tapping impatiently on the steering wheel, he hoped he wouldn't be too late; he couldn't bear the thought of not being there for Mary at the end. The grieving process had started years ago, and he'd often thought – though never voicing it – that it would be better for everyone, not least her, if Mary could just quietly and painlessly slip away; her old, lucid self would have hated the thought of what was to come. Yet still, now that moment appeared to be close, James felt no sense of impending relief.

He came to a halt: ahead of him, a line of stationary traffic stretched ahead, as far as he could see, exhaust fumes rising and dissipating in the cold air. It was approaching rush-hour and the conditions wouldn't be helping the situation one jot.

He looked at his phone: no further calls from Jane, thankfully; a couple more from the Super and one from Molly. They could wait; they weren't important now. He switched on the radio, to see if he could catch a traffic report.

The traffic was stop-start for the next twenty minutes. Nothing came on the radio to tell him what the situation was ahead, nor did his satnav indicate any issues, as James inched toward a junction. The road to his left offered an alternative cross-country route; it was longer and the surfaces wouldn't have been treated as well, but the Audi was four-wheel drive, so driving through deeper snow shouldn't cause any problems. He inched forward. And again. Time to decide.

Cross-country it was.

As he suspected, the narrow road was untreated, but empty of traffic, too. The Audi gripped the snow well, and James was able to maintain a steady speed. He looked at the clock and calculated that he could be there in less than fifteen minutes. *Hang on, Mum.* He tentatively feathered the accelerator; no heroics.

In the rear-view mirror, the amber ribbon which was the main road shrank into insignificance. In front, beyond the rhythmic swipes of the wipers, the full-beam headlights pierced the snowy blackness with a cone of white light. The journey continued in the same vein for several minutes, until two small, red lights appeared in the distance. The lights grew larger and brighter, and James realized that it was a stationary car. As he neared, he saw that there was another car in front of it, which was evidently in trouble, because it was being hoisted onto the back of a rescue truck.

For a moment, he considered turning back to the main road, but that would require a deft manoeuvre, on a narrow road in terrible conditions. Besides, the route ahead would surely be clear in just a few minutes. He flicked his gaze to the clock, then back to the stricken car.

The memory of that fatal night, almost two years ago, slid to the surface…

The row had been brewing since the first snowfall, three days before. James had thought the matter was settled; they were going to keep the sex of the baby a surprise. 'That's why we painted the nursery yellow, no?'

'But I've changed my mind, James,' Ruth said. He was always 'James' when Ruth was cross with him, not 'Jay'.

'Let's sleep on it, hun,' James said, trying to mollify the situation.

'No, I need to know. The appointment's booked.' Ruth could be headstrong at times.

She was in the hall, putting on her thick winter coat, which she struggled to stretch around her bump. 'I'm going to the clinic. Are you coming or not?'

'I've got work to do, hun. Can't it wait 'til Monday?'

James had his head buried in the case file, and only looked up when the front door slammed. By the time he had darted outside and shouted 'Wait!', it was too late: Ruth was wheel-spinning into the icy road.

James was shaken out of his memory by the sound of a car horn behind him. He looked in the rear-view mirror to see flashing headlights, then flicked his gaze forward and realized that the road ahead was now clear.

The remainder of the route to the hospital passed without incident.

In the car park, he swung the Audi untidily into the first space he could find. He raced through the automatic entry doors and was immediately embraced by the sterile warmth.

He waited impatiently, while a kind but inefficient receptionist tapped away on her computer. He checked his phone: nothing. Eventually, the woman brought out a paper map and pencil, and traced the elaborate route to Mary's ward. James snatched the map and hurtled towards a set of double doors. Smashing through them, he entered a labyrinthine world of bright corridors, covered passageways and human obstacles.

He dodged trolleys and wheelchairs, and weaved his

way through white-haired patients in their hospital gowns and comfortable slippers, who shuffled glacially towards their destinations, wherever they may be – zombies with mobile drip stands. Something vile assaulted his nostrils: diarrhoea?

James pushed through a door and popped a Polo, as he climbed four flights of stairs, clearing three steps at a time. He emerged through a door at the summit, to find himself at the end of an eerily silent corridor, which stretched almost endlessly into the distance. He paused for a moment to catch his breath and check the map. Nearly there. He kicked into the last dash and, as he ran, the squeaks from his shoes echoed around the stark, sterile tunnel…

James had been running for over a mile when he ripped off his jacket and threw it into the verge. The forecasters had said it wouldn't get over zero degrees all day, yet he'd run so fast that he was overheating.

He knew something wasn't right; Ruth had been gone too long. He rang the private clinic, and they told him she'd left nearly an hour ago. Even in snowy conditions it was no more than a fifteen-minute drive, and she was coming straight home – he knew that.

He'd sent her a grovelling apology the minute she'd left the house: 'Sorry, hun. You're right. We should find out. Love you. Jay x.'

Ruth replied from the clinic: 'I'm sorry too. I hate it when we fight. Going in now. Wish you were here. R xxx.'

He tuned in to the radio, to check if there were any reports of traffic snarl-ups; he heard nothing that gave him cause for concern. Then he tried the traffic police frequency. His heart lurched when he heard emergency services were tending to a serious QC just outside Great Wymondley; Ruth's route would take her through the village. She hated the bypass; 'People drive like maniacs,' she always said.

James came to the back of a line of stationary vehicles. Several people stood on the road next to their cars, craning their necks, trying to work out what the hold-up was, as James weaved his way through. In the distance, blue lights pulsed and, as he got closer, grotesque mechanical groans swelled louder and louder. Somehow, he just knew it was her.

'Sir, you can't go through there!' the officer shouted, as James barged through the cordon, the woman's words dissipating into the December sky.

Then he saw it.

The car lay upside down, crushed and twisted and warped. A paramedic lay on her belly at the driver's window. On the other side, a fire crew was cutting into the car.

'Sir, get out!' someone hollered.

'She's my wife, for God's sake!' James shouted back, his words ricocheting off the car. He threw himself onto the ground, next to the paramedic.

Then, he saw Ruth, her bloodied head crushed into a hideous angle against the car roof, which was now the floor. She looked tiny and lost amongst the metal, broken glass and semi-deflated airbags. The paramedic held an oxygen mask over her mouth.

'Is she all right?'

The woman said nothing.

Ruth must have heard James and she slowly opened her eyes. She brought a hand to the mask and pulled it aside. 'James,' she wheezed.

'You're going to be fine, hun. Don't try to talk. They'll have you out in a minute.' He took hold of her icy hand.

She took a few more slow, raspy breaths. Smiled weakly.

'It's a girl.' Her voice was a whisper, but somehow all other sounds had faded to distant white noise.

'That's beautiful, sweetheart.'

'She needs oxygen,' the paramedic said, but Ruth resisted her attempts to reposition the mask.

Ruth's eyes closed and her face contorted into a grimace. She took two or three more laboured breaths.

Her eyes opened once more. They bore into James's.

'Find Urtė,' she whispered. 'Promise.'

'I promise, sweetheart.'

Then the light went from Ruth's eyes, and James's world was plunged into darkness.

Finally, James found the ward.

He scanned the room breathlessly, but couldn't see Mary. Had he been given the wrong information? Was she somewhere else? He'd ask a nurse. Where were they when you needed them?

He dropped his hands to his thighs while he recovered his breath. When he looked up, he noticed the bed in the far corner was curtained off. *Oh, God.*

A small dagger of fear stabbed his chest, as he started towards the cubicle. Each step felt laboured and unnatural, like he was wading through treacle. Like he was dreaming. Childhood memories flashed in ephemeral images, as if a cinematic reel was spooling in his head: learning to ride a bike; his first day at primary school; bursting through the finish tape in the hundred-metre sprint. His mother was present in every image, her face beaming with maternal pride.

Jane emerged from behind the curtains and the illusion snapped. She dabbed her eyes with a tissue. When she noticed James, she gave him a watery smile and shook her head. He slipped wordlessly past her, into the cubicle.

And there Mary lay, lifeless. Her bony frame barely made an impression under the white sheet; her stick arms were held in a tidy V-shape, her mouth was agape and her eyes half-closed.

James lightly took Mary's skeletal hand in his and planted a soft kiss on her forehead, which felt cool and dry to the touch. He brought his hand tenderly down over her eyes, to close the lids. 'I'm so, so sorry, Mum. I love you. Sleep tight.'

He felt a hand on his shoulder, and he turned to see Jane, her eyes red and teary.

'She'd been asleep for the last hour or so, and wouldn't have known you weren't here. It was very peaceful. Don't beat yourself up, love.'

He tried to say the words *'thank you,'* but they caught in his throat. Jane pulled him into a tight embrace. As she patted his back and whispered to him, 'It's okay, it's okay,' he began to weep like a baby.

THIRTY-TWO

AFTER A RESTLESS NIGHT, Molly was in court early to claim her seat, just like every morning of the trial. James had been the last witness to take the stand, and all that was left now were closing arguments.

At the start of the trial, Molly had been totally convinced it was an open and shut case: his DNA on her body and eyewitness testimony placing the defendant with the victim before she went missing. DNA plus witness: that was the gold standard, wasn't it? But now she didn't feel so confident.

Poor Bea had been put through the wringer. Molly had felt a desperate pang of pity when that snooty defence barrister – Ms. Cordelia Knatchbull QC, for goodness sake – mercilessly attacked her credibility. Bea put up a good fight, bless her, stuck to her guns, but she was shaking like a leaf. And, when the poor woman was asked if she'd received a reward from a newspaper… well, if looks could kill! Troy Perkins had bellowed at her that she was a lying bitch. That had sent a ripple of indignation around the courtroom, like a Mexican wave; the judge told him to put a sock in it. Quite right, too.

As for the insinuation that Molly had somehow planted Perkins's DNA under the victim's fingernail, what the hell was that all about? Please! Was she supposed to have just happened upon a dead body? Kept a stash of Perkins's DNA on her person to cover that eventuality? Ludicrous! She could only assume that it was a desperate move from the defence to undermine the case against their client; to sow a seed of doubt in the jury's mind. Surely Molly would have been called as a witness, if they were remotely serious about the theory? Part of her wished they had done; she would have relished her moment in the spotlight, and given them both barrels – unlike James.

Oh, her heart ached. She could tell that the man had hated every minute of it. And, when Cordelia bloody Knatchbull had got him to admit he'd spent the night at her place…! Molly desperately wanted to explain how that information had found its way to the defence: she blamed that lazy idiot Yelland. He wasn't a patch on James.

And where was James? She'd tried to call him to explain, but of course he wasn't picking up. She imagined he was brooding somewhere. She smiled, wistfully.

Molly became aware of increased chatter around her. The courtroom was filling up, the jury taking their places. Molly had spent a great deal of time over the last three days studying the jury; she'd even given a few of them nicknames. Flibbertigibet for one: a middle-aged woman, tall and stick-thin; glasses tied to a chain. Couldn't sit still for a moment, shuffling and fidgeting as if she'd been covered in itching powder – too much nervous energy, Molly guessed. In total contrast to Flibbertigibet was Three Chin Glyn, a great walrus of a man; bald as a coot, comically tiny face marooned like a tiny desert island in a great ocean. During the quiet moments you could hear him unwrapping his toffees; Molly lost count of the times she'd seen him surreptitiously pop one into his mouth like a ravenous pufferfish – that was as animated as he ever got. But her favourite had to be Attentive Nel: late sixties, she guessed, pearl necklace, bookish. The Neighbourhood Watch type; never stopped taking notes for a second. Her records were probably more comprehensive than the bloody court stenographers.

'All rise!' the court usher hollered.

As she got to her feet, Molly looked over at the dock, where Troy Perkins stood, soldier-straight, in his smart suit and crisp, white shirt, his face a picture of inscrutability.

Despite being a non-believer, she found herself looking to the ceiling and praying that this would finally be the day that justice was served.

THIRTY-THREE

For the first time in months, James had slept through the entire night. He figured his body and mind must have just shut down. Yet, despite the long sleep, he didn't feel particularly well-rested.

After seeing to the various matters at the hospital yesterday evening, James had gone home to ring the handful of friends and relatives he could think of, who needed to be informed. His brother David was the first person he called, of course. David took it in his stride, as he always did. Couldn't promise he'd be able to make it to the funeral, though: 'Last minute flight prices can be astronomical.' That was as good as a 'no', then.

Years ago, not long after Mary was given the diagnosis – when she still possessed a reasonable amount of lucidity and self-awareness – her first response was to tell James in great detail what she wanted for her funeral. She never once showed the slightest degree of self-pity over the course of her long illness – that was typical of her. James was comforted by the thought of his mother finally being at peace, but this feeling competed with a host of other emotions, bubbling in the cauldron of his heart: regret that he'd always prioritized work over her; guilt for packing her off to a home, when the going got too tough; anger at David, for leaving him to shoulder the burden of responsibilities alone.

His thoughts shifted to the court case. Murdoch had left him a message last night, to tell him it was closing arguments this morning, after which the jury would retire to consider their verdict; told James he was confident the jury would see through Perkins's lies. There was something in the Super's tone, however, which belied that apparent confidence.

James had pondered for a moment whether he should drive back to the court to sit through proceedings, but decided he'd rather not listen to the closing arguments; he had no desire to endure another public humiliation, as the QC distorted the facts and ridiculed his testimony. Nor was the prospect of hanging around the court, making polite conversation while the jury deliberated, remotely appealing.

As the trial date had approached, the Super insisted James take a couple of weeks' annual leave. His workload had been much more manageable over the preceding months – a few more arrests on Solent, the rescue of a dozen more women from more brothel busts – but Murdoch had correctly judged that the prospect of testifying and facing an accusation of framing Perkins would weigh heavily on his mind, impacting his ability to carry out his duties. The trouble was, other than making arrangements for the funeral and sorting out Mary's effects at the home, James wasn't entirely sure what he would do to occupy the time and keep his restless thoughts at bay.

He'd been trudging mindlessly through the house for much of the morning, wiping a dusty surface here, arranging and rearranging the furniture there. He was in the back bedroom now, at the window.

He looked out across the white rooftops to the snow-covered Chilterns, which glistened under a liquid-blue sky. The hills were calling him. Yes, he'd run to Preston and back. Perhaps then he'd be ready to slip back into the courtroom for the verdict.

THIRTY-FOUR

MOLLY STOOD OUTSIDE THE COURT, hopping from one foot to the other while she puffed a cigarette. She felt the low winter sun on her cheek, but it did little to relieve the bitter cold.

Closing arguments had finished more than two hours ago, and the jury was deliberating. It was anyone's guess how much longer they'd take, and Molly had learnt from her own experience of jury service, many moons ago, that all kinds of factors can influence the process. That was a straightforward case: a serial shoplifter – open and shut, no question; caught red-handed trousering a set of miniature screwdrivers in B&Q. Should have been a case of bish-bash-bosh, guilty, move on, but – oh, no – some bright spark happened to suggest that if they could just drag matters out for another two hours, they could claim sixty quid lost earnings from the government instead of thirty. So, there everyone must have been – the accused, the judge, the barristers, the court officials and the public – all stuck in limbo while twelve proles (well, eleven plus Molly) chatted celebrity gossip and sucked hard-boiled sweets 'til the clock struck one.

Molly wasn't feeling at all confident now about the verdict. She hated the woman, but she had to admit that the defence's argument had been pretty slick: 'Can you really be *sure* that Mr. Perkins killed Daniela Sirota?' She was also troubled by the fact that smart-suited, serious-looking Troy didn't look or sound like the maniacal psychopath built up in the press. Would his argument that the police, desperate to get closure, had pursued a personal vendetta against him hold any sway with the jury? Had his barrister convinced them that James had orchestrated the planting of DNA evidence – via her! – to frame him? How reliable was the witness testimony of a prostitute known to have had a drug problem? And, poor James; one little slip-up, which that woman had exploited to the max: 'A suspicion, a hunch, a *belief* is not sufficient to convict a man,' she said to the jury, hamming it right up. 'If you cannot be *sure* he is guilty, there is only one verdict you can return: not guilty.'

Suddenly, Molly was in shadow and she turned, raising a hand to her brow to shield her eyes from the sun's glare. It was DI Yelland, lighting a cigarette. He was dressed in a crumpled suit, his tie hanging stained and untidy over his fat stomach. Despite the lack of an overcoat, he didn't seem remotely perturbed by the cold. He pulled out his phone and inspected the screen.

'Anything from James?' Molly asked.

'Not a dicky-bird.'

'I hope he's okay.'

Yelland blew out a jet of smoke and smiled. 'I'm sure he'll be fine.'

'So, what do you reckon the verdict's going to be? I'm nervous.'

Yelland shrugged: 'Anyone's guess. That posh bird put in a good turn, didn't she? I'd want her defending me, if I was on a murder charge.'

Molly took one more drag from her cigarette and stubbed it out; she had no desire to be hanging out here with this idiot any longer. Time to get back in the warmth of the courtroom.

Twenty minutes later, Molly was in her seat, reading back over her notes; there was plenty of material here to sustain a few more editions of the *Herald*, whatever the verdict. Her mind drifted to thoughts of what could have been, if she hadn't turned down the interview at the *Daily News*. Had she made the right choice? Had she burnt her bridges?

Molly became aware of excited chatter around her, and looked up to see that the room was filling, fast. She turned to the woman next to her: 'Is it the verdict?'

'Looks like it.'

Behind her, Murdoch and Yelland took their seats. Murdoch met Molly's gaze and flashed her a nervous smile. Still no sign of James.

Now the jury filed in, bookended by a stern-looking Attentive Nel at the front and Three Chin Glyn – busy probing an upper molar for a morsel of lunch – at the back. If Nel wasn't the foreman (too old-school to be a fore*person*) then Molly would eat her hat. The jurors took their seats.

Molly looked over at Perkins, who sat in the dock, scanning the jurors, presumably trying to divine the verdict from their behaviour and body language. What was the rule: if the jurors didn't look at the defendant it meant a guilty verdict was on its way? That was a load of old bollocks. Molly recalled studying the shoplifter's face intently as the guilty verdict was read out. She was hoping for a hint of contrition, regret or humility, but saw only arrogance and contempt. Mind you, that fella only got six months – probably out after three with good behaviour; no kind of justice at all. Molly caught Glyn flashing a furtive look at Perkins, before stifling a belch; Flibbertigibbet's eyes were darting all over the place, so there was no deeper meaning to be discerned there; another woman examined her fingernails; Attentive Nel put her glasses on and looked down at her lap, puffing her cheeks – was her big moment coming?

'All rise!'

The sound of loud chatter dissipated to a hushed whisper, as the judge took his seat. The room was packed; standing room only in the public gallery.

Those who could sat down and the judge addressed the jury, asking them who'd been appointed foreman. Attentive Nel rose and Molly performed a small fist pump. The woman next to her flashed her a castigating frown.

'Sorry,' Molly whispered; 'inappropriate.'

'Members of the jury, have you reached a verdict on which you all agree?'

Nel cleared her throat. The room fell to complete silence. 'Yes,' she said, her voice clear and nerveless.

Molly looked across to Perkins. The noise of him drumming his fingers could be heard against the backdrop of near silence.

The court clerk approached Nel and they exchanged papers.

'On the count of murder,' the clerk asked Nel, 'how do you find the defendant: guilty or not guilty?'

Nel looked out to the court for a moment. Milking it?

Perkins was still, expectant. You could hear a pin drop.

Molly had to stifle a sudden urge to break wind.

'Guilty.'

Molly brought a hand to her mouth and, for a moment, the court remained silent, as if it were taking a collective intake of breath. Then, excited chatter broke out. Perkins called out from the dock: 'You've got it wrong!'

He switched his attention to Murdoch and Yelland: 'I've been fucking framed! This is an outrage.' Two security guys moved in to restrain him.

The judge appealed for calm, before addressing Perkins: 'Mr. Perkins, you have been found guilty of murder…'

The judge's words faded from Molly's consciousness, as her thoughts turned to James. He should have been here in court to hear it. Where the hell was he?

She glanced over her shoulder. Murdoch was looking to the ceiling, puffing his cheeks in relief. The tall, good-looking one was back again, having taken Yelland's place; he must have joined them at some point since she'd last looked around, and was attentively listening to the judge's words, a satisfied smile on his face. Could Yelland not even be arsed to sit through the verdict?

Molly grabbed her belongings and headed out to the lobby. She'd ring James; tell him the good news. Perhaps he'd resigned himself to a not-guilty verdict? Ever the pessimist.

The dial tone rang for an age before clicking through to voicemail, so she hung up and sent a text: *'Where r u? We won!! Guilty! Champagne? Molly xx.'*

She waited for several minutes, but received no response. *Sod him,* she thought. There was plenty of work to do; she'd drive to the office and get the story written up.

Outside, the cold hit her with a force, almost taking her breath away. She tied her coat tightly around her waist, and briskly made her way to the car. The Evoque was covered in a layer of snow, so she opened the boot to get the scraper.

As she cleared the windscreen, Molly saw the tall policeman heading in her direction. For a moment she felt a flutter of attraction, but quickly admonished herself; she was old enough to be his mother, for God's sake. He stopped near an old, purple Citroën and took out his phone from his pocket.

'Any word from James?' she called out. 'Sorry, I mean DCI Quinn.'

He looked up. 'And, you are?'

'Molly. Molly Tindall. I work for the *Herald.*'

'Oh, yes, I think he may have mentioned you. I'm DC Porter. Luke.'

A warm tingle ran down her spine. 'Oh, he mentioned me?'

Luke was distracted by his phone. He bit his lip, then turned back to Molly. 'Nobody seems to be able to get hold of him. I know he's private, and all that, and he's meant to be on leave, but something doesn't add up; he's been working toward this day for years.'

Molly thought for a moment. 'Do you know where he lives?'

'No, but I can soon find out with a phone call.'

'Let's head over, tell him the good news in person. The poor bugger's probably flaked out on the sofa; he's been working himself to the bone.'

Molly pointed at Luke's Citroën. 'I'll follow you, if you think that old jalopy can make it.'

After a frustratingly slow journey, Molly pulled up behind Luke's tiny Citroën, in a street lined with identical-looking 1930s semis. Was this where James lived? Surely not. She couldn't imagine him in a place like this; she'd pictured him in some remote, stone farm building, surrounded by nothing but windswept fields.

Luke came over and opened her door.

'How kind, young man.'

'His place is number thirty-eight, there.'

Molly checked her phone for messages or calls: nothing. They headed over to the house. James's Audi was parked on the drive, covered in a thick layer of snow; clearly he hadn't driven it for a while. Recent footprints to and from the front door suggested he was at home.

Molly felt a familiar sensation of curtains twitching and a shudder rippled through her. She rang the doorbell, then stepped back to regard the house and those of the neighbours; James's place looked tidy and well maintained, while the adjoining semi was rather rougher. She noticed a collection of garden gnomes on the front lawn, poking out from the snow. Hideous.

'Where are you, you little bugger?' Molly said, ringing the doorbell again.

'I'll check out the back,' Luke said, his breaths creating little puffy clouds in the frigid air.

Molly moved over to the window and pressed her head against the glass. Inside it looked spartan, the furniture arranged neatly at right angles. There were no pictures or ornaments, or anything that would make a house a home. God, she could never live in a place like this.

Where are you, man? She hammered on the glass. No sign of movement. Molly tried the front door, but it was locked.

She got out her phone and dialled James's number. Seconds later, a muffled ringtone sounded from deep within the house. She lifted the letterbox flap and stole a look into the hall.

'James?'

There was no response and nothing to see – nor could

she discern the location of the phone. The ringing stopped.

'Luke!' she shouted. 'Something's not right. We need to get in.'

But, how? Her eyes darted around. All windows were firmly shut, of course. Then, she remembered the gnomes next door. She quickly retrieved one and, without a moment's hesitation, hurled it through the front window – the hole it created was big enough for her to put her hand through and release the catch. She swung open the window and climbed into the living room. Inside it was warm, and Molly held her hand to a radiator to find that it was hot.

'James!' she shouted. 'Are you here?'

She heard a commotion in the next room and made her way into the hall. Luke walked in from the kitchen.

'How did you get in?' she said.

'The back door was open.'

'Shit,' Molly said, 'didn't think of that.'

Luke brushed past her and poked his head into the living room. 'He's not in there,' she said, before clambering up the stairs. She turned onto the landing, then stopped in her tracks.

'James!' she screamed.

He lay prone on the carpet, perfectly still and white as a sheet. He was dressed in running gear, a beanie pulled down over his ears, the timer still running on his watch: over four hours. She touched his cheek with the back of her hand: his skin was dry and cool.

Luke arrived beside her in seconds. He rolled James onto his back and Molly let out a yelp when she saw that his lips were blue. She dropped to her knees and frantically slapped his lifeless cheeks. 'James! James! No!'

'He's not breathing!' Luke said.

Molly lifted a closed eyelid and James's eyeball rolled back into his head.

'Get back!' Luke shouted. 'I can feel a weak pulse.'

She slumped against a wall and watched helplessly, as Luke pumped James's chest.

'Call an ambulance,' he shouted, breathlessly. '*Now!*'

THIRTY-FIVE

'THE DAILY CHRONICLE

COERCIVE CONTROL AND DOMESTIC ABUSE: THE TRAGIC STORY OF HANNAH GROUSE AND HER CHILDREN

By Molly Tindall, Investigative Reporter.

The warning signs of coercive control might not be physical but can lead to fatal outcomes for victims of family violence, despite new legislation.

"Coercive control" encompasses a series of non-physical behaviours – including threats, humiliation, monitoring and isolation from friends and family – which can often cause severe depression and post-traumatic stress disorder for victims.

Rebecca Grouse asks herself every day whether her daughter and grandchildren might still be alive had they better understood the offence, and sought police help before their situation escalated into homicidal violence.

"I never thought of it as abuse, as he never hit me." These are words which haunt Rebecca Grouse. Her daughter, Hannah Grouse, who was burnt to death last week, along with her three children, told her mother that she had questioned herself "for years" about whether she was in a domestic violence situation.

The devastated mother told the Daily Chronicle her daughter's story, of the control and manipulation that preceded her ultimate fear for her physical wellbeing. When they were together, Hannah's former partner, Peter Hicks, controlled minuscule details of her life and constantly undermined her confidence. He told her what to wear. He punished her with silence. He monitored her phone. He isolated her from her family. He mocked her in public. He dictated her weekly budget. Hannah's family said the control presented itself in small ways, like the fact that he wouldn't allow Hannah to wear short dresses or anything revealing. "Little things like that," Rebecca said in the beginning. "We just thought, 'He's a prude.' In hindsight, we know now there was more to it."

Yet, Hannah knew she was in danger after leaving her partner in July. She and her children moved in with her mother, three miles away from her previous home. Over the following months, Hannah and Peter fought an increasingly bitter custody battle. Events came to a tragic head when Peter jumped into Hannah's car while she was strapping in the children, prior to the school run. He doused the car in petrol and set it ablaze, then fled the scene. Hannah escaped the inferno. A witness said they will never forget the sight of her writhing in agony and screaming for help, as her body burned and her skin fell away from her body.

Peter Hicks later stabbed himself in the chest with a kitchen knife, but survived the apparent suicide attempt. Hannah Grouse died the next day in hospital. Her three children – Topaz, 6, Lily, 4 and Violet, 3 – all perished in the car.

"This is such a tragic event," said Rebecca. "We want to be able to help people in a similar situation to that Hannah was in,

and raise awareness of early signs of domestic abuse that are not easy to see. Not all domestic abuse is physical."

'BASTARD!' James exclaimed, and hurled the newspaper onto the passenger seat.

He checked his watch. He'd been here now for over two hours, waiting for a clear shot. Earlier, they'd appeared together briefly at a first-floor window, but by the time he removed his gloves and grabbed the Nikon, they'd retreated back into the dark bowels of the house.

Come on, it's brass monkeys.

Even inside the car he could see his own breath; wrapped in winter clobber, a beanie pulled down tight around his ears, James couldn't risk turning over the engine and putting the heater on. It was supposed to be bloody spring, for god's sake. The street, though packed nose to tail with parked cars, was stony silent and an idling engine would just draw attention to his presence.

The woman's gaudy Mercedes was parked several spaces up, but it barely stood out among the Astons and Maseratis in this very ostentatious part of Kensington. James pondered for a moment how much laundered money there might be tied up in these rows of white stuccoed houses, with their five storeys, polished doors and architectural topiary. That was someone else's problem now; his brief was to get proof of the woman's adultery.

Easy.

He sighed. Was this his new future: chasing trophy wives around the country?

Movement in his peripheral vision snapped James's gaze back to the big, black door of number 27, across the street. He pulled off his gloves and grabbed the camera, heavy and cumbersome with its long telephoto lens. The door opened and they stepped out, arm in arm. She – much taller and younger than the man – wore a ridiculous fur hat and animal-print coat. James raised the camera to his eye and pressed the shutter, firing off a rapid succession of shots. At the end of the path, they chatted for a few moments, then she leant in for a long kiss.

Bingo!

The man turned up his collar and walked off. She headed in the opposite direction to her Mercedes.

James brought the camera down to his lap and cycled through the images, content that he now had the evidence his client sought; time to warm up and get back home. He turned over the engine. Some distance ahead, he could make out the figure of a traffic warden, worming his away along the road, inspecting windscreens. Lucky James had got what he'd come for, as he had no more loose change for the meter: four quid an hour, for god's sake. Daylight robbery.

Just as he was about to put the Audi in gear, his phone buzzed. He looked down to see that it was Molly Tindall and sighed. Presumably she was calling to gloat about her article, and her new-found fame as an investigative journalist in London?

The phone continued to buzz, and the traffic warden was nearly upon him. *Let it ring through to voicemail. She'll leave a message if it's important.*

Since Molly had moved down to London, their calls and text conversations had become less frequent; it was always she who initiated them, of course. He supposed that, when he was being completely honest with himself – which was seldom – a small part of him missed her. He looked down at his phone, at her name, recalled all those times that he'd cursed her or, worse, simply ignored her;

she was just doing her job. Everyone had to earn a living somehow.

A pang of guilt jabbed at him. He accepted the call.

'What is it?' he said abruptly. Force of habit; old dogs and new tricks, etcetera.

Before he could correct his impoliteness, Molly voice rang out through the Audi's speakers. 'James – are you sitting down? I've got some news you're not going to want to hear.'

The traffic warden appeared next to the Audi and inspected the meter, which had long since expired. James wound down the window and said to the guy: 'I'm going now!'

'No, wait, hear me out.' Molly said.

'No, I'm talking to a bloody traffic warden. Give me a moment; I'm just pulling out. Now, what's this about news?'

'I'll keep this brief if you're driving, James. Look, I don't know if you've read my article–'

'No, sorry,' he lied. 'What's it about?'

'Not important right now. Remember Kathy Gibbs?'

'Stabbed her husband. Went down for life? Of course I remember Kathy Bloody Gibbs. I had a heart attack, not a bloody lobotomy!'

'Well, one of her boys has contacted me– he's probably read my work, knows how influential I am–'

'Which boy?'

'Would it actually help if I told you his name?'

'Probably not. What did he say?'

'Don't quite know how to tell you this…'

Behind him a car horn sounded, and James looked in the rear-view mirror to see the driver gesturing to him to speed up. 'Piss off!'

'Assume that wasn't directed at me, James?'

'Sorry, Molly. Go on.'

James realized he was barely going at a snail's pace. On his left, ahead of him he saw a free parking space and pulled into it.

'He's saying Kathy shouldn't be in prison. Looks like he's been holding something back.'

'Eh?! What is it? Surely it wasn't *him*? She confessed. The forensic evidence corroborated the confession?'

'He didn't say. I've not gone back to him yet; thought I'd better speak to you first.'

James's head swirled. Had he missed something during the investigation? Been too distracted by Perkins? The thought that Kathy Gibbs might be in prison because of his incompetence was almost too much to bear.

'James? You there?'

'Yes. We'll have to speak to him.'

'We'll do this together, okay? I don't want you carrying the burden on your shoulders alone, you know, after … now you're not working …'

Molly's words trailed off. James didn't feel the need to tell her he was doing a bit of freelance work. The doctor had told him he had to take it easy. Rest up. His heart was permanently weakened. But he'd had a bellyful of resting; boredom – *that* was what was going to kill him.

The memory of waking up in hospital and seeing Molly and Luke at his bedside flashed in his mind.

'Look,' Molly continued, 'let me get hold of him and see if I can make an appointment. When's good for you?'

'Doesn't matter. Any time.' James felt his focus was drifting away from the conversation.

'Leave it with me, Jimbo. I'll be in touch. Take care.'

'Bye.'

He switched off the phone and dropped his head onto

the steering wheel. The past had caught up with him. Again.

He became aware of a shadowy shape in front of him, and he looked up to see the traffic warden grinning smugly, as he slapped a ticket on his windscreen.

THIRTY-SIX

MASKING his repulsion at Rick Brady's hot breath and musky cologne, James removed the A4-sized black-and-white photograph from the folder. He supposed he could have just emailed a copy to him, but where was the drama in that? Besides, James was hopeless with technology.

Brady regarded the picture for a few silent moments as the faint flicker of hope in his eyes dissolved into reluctant acceptance, before morphing into blind range. He leapt from the sofa, screwed up the photograph, then hurled it to the floor.

'I'll fucking kill her!' he screamed. He turned and stormed out of the room into the hallway. James followed, and watched him as he flung open the front door and stormed down the drive to his Lexus.

'I'll pop the invoice in the post then, shall I?' James called out after him.

Brady got into his car and drove off.

Then James turned to see Molly farther down the road standing next to her white Evoque, grin on her face, taking a last drag from a cigarette. She hurled the butt into the gutter and walked over to James.

'You're early,' he said, gruffly.

'And very nice to see you too, James,' Molly said. 'How the devil are you?'

'Oh, yeah, I'm fine. Sorry.'

'Who was the angry fella?' Molly said. 'Looked kind of familiar. Or was he just another angry white man? I've had it up to here with them.'

'Just found out his wife's been cheating on him.'

'Eh?'

'Got a phonecall out of the blue a few weeks back. Asked if I would help get him the proof.'

'Thought you were supposed to be convalescing?'

'I am! Sitting in a car and taking a few snaps isn't exactly strenuous.'

'Bit of a comedown from catching serial killers, eh?'

'Perkins wasn't a serial killer: have to be at least three victims to qualify.'

'There *were* three.'

'Mr Percy doesn't count as a victim.'

Molly rolled her eyes. 'Mr Dar–'

'I'm kidding! I remember his name. You know I never forget them.'

Molly looked over James's shoulder, into the house. 'Not being funny, Jimbo,' she said, 'but it's bloody freezing out here. Aren't you going to invite me in?'

'Oh, yes, sure. Come in.'

Molly dumped her handbag on the bottom stair, shucked off her coat and draped it over the bannister. 'You looking after yourself, Jimbo? Taking your medication?'

'Who are you? My mother?'

'A concerned friend,' Molly said, casting her eyes around the hall. James sensed a degree of disdain for the decor. She turned back to him. 'So, made many plans for retirement, you lucky thing?'

James had reluctantly accepted ill health retirement from the force. They'd offered him a dead-end desk job but his pride couldn't take it. 'Don't push it,' he said.

'You going to offer me a drink?' she said. 'I'm gasping.'

'Yes, of course, sorry. Only got instant coffee, I'm afraid. None of those Americanos and cappuccinos you're probably used to now in the Big Smoke. How do you take it?'

'Like my men: strong and black,' she chuckled, then did that thing with her hair, tucking it behind her ear. James caught himself looking at her for perhaps a beat too long. Molly smiled, then gestured to the living room. 'Shall I take a seat?'

'Yep. Be right with you.'

He brought drinks into the living room, and found Molly seated on the sofa, looking at the photograph she'd picked up from the floor and straightened out.

'I knew it,' she said. 'It's that Russian woman from Letchworth, isn't it? More plastic in her than Hamley's.'

'I can't really say,' James said: 'client confidentiality.'

'And him: Richard Whiteley with a temper; he's that housebuilder, Brady. It's all coming back to me now. Glad he didn't notice me; it was my article about shoddy quality building which opened the floodgates to all those complaints. His company never did recover; went under – not before he'd made his millions, alas. I'm surprised at you for helping him. Thought you were ethical?'

'Like I say, client confidentiality.'

Molly wrapped her fingers around the coffee mug, took a sip and grimaced. James noticed she'd left a lipstick imprint on the rim. He breathed in the combined aromas of Nescafé, cigarette smoke and her sweet perfume, and a warm, nostalgic feeling washed over him. His gaze shifted from her plump lips to her green eyes, which were now looking over to the framed photograph on the front window cill.

'So, that's Ruth then?' she said. 'She's a stunner all right.'

'No, that's Urtė, Ruth's best friend.' The Ruth pictures were up in their bedroom. He'd put Urtė's in the front window as a constant reminder of that sacred promise he'd made but never fulfilled.

Molly took a sip from her mug and smiled. 'You're a dark horse, Jimbo.'

'Oh, no, it's not like that. God, how do I explain...'

'Long story?'

James took a seat on the armchair, took a deep breath, then began...

...'So, anyway, shortly after we rescued Ruth, she returned to Lithuania, but there was nothing there for her any more: no home, no family, no friends. No Urtė. She couldn't settle, so she returned to England to continue the search for her best friend. She got nowhere, of course. Then, she turned up one day at the station where I worked at the time. I was just uniform back then. It was that rescue that spurred me to make the move to detective work. That was the making of me ... god, where was I ... yes ... Ruth begged me to help her. How could I say no? Well, here I am today, still looking for Urtė.'

'Bloody hell, James. Why didn't you tell me this before? I could have done something to help you find her – I still could. I've got a national platform now.'

'Thanks,' he said, after taking a large mouthful of coffee, 'but I guess I've been trying to do it my own way. It was always a hopeless task. Work got in the way. Maybe now, with more time on my hands … part of me clings to the belief that she somehow managed to escape, find her way back to Lithuania, or maybe another country, and start a new life under a different name. But the other part tells me, well, that's she's got to be …' His voice trailed off.

Molly came over and crouched next to his chair, putting her hand on his. 'You need to let others help. People care, you know.'

James pulled his hand away and looked at his watch. 'God, look. It's time for our appointment with the Gibbs boys.'

THIRTY-SEVEN

Barrington Hawke Investments occupied the second floor of a smart, modern office block, not far from Letchworth town centre.

As they sat waiting on a black, leather sofa, in the capacious and fresh-flower-scented reception, Molly consulted her phone while James thumbed through a glossy magazine, crammed with pictures of prosperous-looking people – driving flash cars, dining in posh restaurants, enjoying a cruise – interspersed with graphs and figures charting the performance of various investment funds. They all sounded alien to James: *'Special Situations'*, *'Global Index Trackers'*, *'Biotechnology Investment Trusts'*… He was solvent – comfortable even, with the police pension he received, now he'd retired on ill-health grounds – but he could never imagine throwing caution to the wind and entrusting his life savings to a pinstriped spiv with gelled hair, a gold fountain pen and the promise of inflation-busting annual returns. Perhaps it was his frugal Scottish blood. Or the cynical old detective?

He looked over at the receptionist, who appeared to be

masking her boredom behind a smart suit and designer specs. As she stared at her computer screen, occasionally clicking the mouse or tapping a key, James regarded the company name emblazoned on the wall behind her. There was something familiar about it, but for the life of him he couldn't recall what.

A translucent glass door slid noiselessly open, like a scene from a sci-fi film. Only, it wasn't Captain Kirk who entered the room; it was that tall, familiar Gibbs fella, extending his arm. Ben? Mark? Which was the arty one?

'Mark,' Molly gushed, palming his hand, 'so glad to meet you. You remember James, don't you?'

'Of course,' he said.

James shook Mark's hand. The hand of a repentant killer?

'Come through, won't you?' Mark said. 'Samantha – you couldn't bring drinks through, could you? Coffee okay?'

'Oh, I'd love an Americano, please, Samantha,' Molly said, 'if that's not too much trouble.'

'Sure.'

'I'll just have it however it comes,' James said.

Mark brought them into his large office and they were seated at a rectangular table, at the other end of the room to his desk. There were several paintings – modern, abstract rubbish – hanging from the walls, which James suspected were Mark's handiwork. 'I wouldn't expect to find you working here,' James said. 'Thought you were more of a creative type?'

'Well, unless you're Damien Hurst or Grayson Perry, art doesn't really pay the bills.'

James flicked his gaze to a garish painting, which looked like it could have been created by a chimpanzee with a blank canvas and a tin of orange paint. 'So it seems.'

He turned back to Mark: 'Where's your brother now? Ben, isn't it?'

'Well remembered,' Mark said, with a wry smile. 'He's here, too – with a client at the moment; he'll join us as soon as he's finished. Perhaps I should explain a bit about the two of us before he gets here.'

'Please do,' James said.

'You may recall that we didn't really see eye to eye at the time of the… you know… incident?'

'Different interests, I recall,' James added.

'Indeed. Well, following Dad's death and Mum going to prison–'

'How is your Mum doing, Mark?' Molly asked.

Good question, James thought. *Must remember those conversational niceties.*

Mark let out a long sigh. 'It's difficult to say, really. She puts on a show when we visit, makes out she's all fine and that she's being treated well; mustn't grumble, and all that. She doesn't want us to worry, you see. Typical Mum. But underneath you can tell she's withdrawn – frightened, almost. As weird as it sounds, she's kind of lost without Dad, too.'

James allowed a short silence, before bringing the conversation back on track: 'You were saying, about you and Ben?'

'Yes. After Dad died, we kind of realized life was too short for petty feuds, so we buried the hatchet–'

'Interesting choice of metaphor,' Molly said.

Mark let out a short, embarrassed laugh. 'It was for Mum, too. The thought of her whole family disintegrating was worse than prison, in her eyes. Anyway, Dad hadn't made a will, which surprised me, as I always thought he'd want everything to go to Ben, so by default his estate went equally to us both; you know, Mum couldn't benefit from her crime and all that. So here we are, running the place jointly. No major bust-ups so far. Who'd have thought it?'

'Ben owned another business, if I remember rightly,' James said.

'Yes, but not anymore; that's in the hands of ex-wife now: Carla. The divorce was quite messy.'

'Shame,' Molly said.

Mark looked up at the door; 'This must be drinks.' He gestured to Samantha and she entered the room, carrying a tray of coffees.

As Samantha was carefully transferring the drinks to the table, Ben strolled in with the confident, casual swagger that James recalled from the previous summer. He caught Molly casting a coquettish glance at him and doing that thing she did with her hair. Ben sat down opposite her and she extended her hand; James felt a tingle of something he suspected was jealousy.

'Hi, I'm Molly,' she said. Ben eyeballed Molly for a moment.

Samantha left the room and closed the door.

'I'm a major journalist,' Molly said, running her fingers through her hair, 'in London. Did your brother not mention it?'

'Yeah, Twat Face – sorry, Mark – told me. Not really into newspapers: full of gossip and lies, if you ask me.'

'Oh,' Molly said, failing to mask her disappointment. She turned to Mark: 'You told me Kathy shouldn't be in prison. Explain why.'

Mark's gaze flitted between Molly, James and Mark, before finally settling on Molly. 'Where to begin? Your articles about coercive control… I recognized some of your examples in Mum and Dad's relationship. Things like… he would never let her go to work, even though she wanted to once we were at school. He'd restrict her access to family and friends. Control the money. He gave her a weekly allowance for the shopping, but it was never enough; she'd always have to beg him for more. If we did ever go out with friends or family, and it looked like she was enjoying herself, he'd make sarcastic comments, humiliate her and tell her to stop embarrassing herself in public.'

'Was there ever any physical abuse?' James asked.

'It doesn't have to be physical, James,' Molly added, giving him a reproachful look.

Ben and Mark exchanged looks, then Mark spoke: 'Not really – not that we knew about, anyway. Does pouring soup over her head count?'

'Bastard,' Molly said.

'He did that at the end of the meal that night. Guess we should have told you.'

'Didn't see that it helped us,' Ben added.

James leant forward, but Molly held out a hand, signalling that he shouldn't speak. 'Carry on, Mark.'

'The thing is, Mum idolized Dad. She'd do anything he asked.'

'She was a fucking doormat,' Ben said.

'She just wanted everything to be perfect,' Mark said, 'but really she was a prisoner in her own home. Kind of ironic, I suppose.'

'Okay,' James said, 'I can see how the case might be made that she was the victim of coercive control; that's a specific offence on the statute book now. But, those women Molly has written about–'

'Thought you said you hadn't read my articles, James?' Molly said.

He grinned, awkwardly. 'None of those women murdered their partners. It's not like a case could be made for provocation, or loss of control, as we now call it: John was asleep; Kathy went to the kitchen to fetch a knife. I can't see how any of these revelations will help her now.'

'But, don't you see, James?' Molly said. This was beginning to feel to James like a private discussion between him and her. 'What if she was suffering from a mental condition, brought on by years of emotional abuse—'

'Diminished responsibility?' James said, interrupting her. 'That was considered, but there was no evidence it applied to Kathy.'

'That was before coercive control was a crime in itself. No one considered its relevance in Kathy's case.'

'It never occurred to us, either,' Mark said. 'What do you think we should do? *Is* there anything we can do for her?'

'Do you think she'll speak to me?' Molly asked.

'I don't know about that. She still defends Dad. I doubt she'll even open up to you.'

'Let me at least try. I know the best lawyer there is who can help her.'

'Prisons don't like inmates talking to journalists,' James said. 'They'll make you jump over every procedural hurdle they can to prevent it.'

'Let them try,' Molly said, defiantly. 'The first step is for Kathy to write to the governor: tell them she wants to speak to a journalist about a potential miscarriage of justice in her case. Do you think she'll do that? I can help with the letter, of course.'

'I can only ask,' Mark said.

'You're good lads,' Molly said. 'This can't be easy for you.'

'We should have been more honest at the time we were interviewed,' Mark said, turning to James. 'Thank you for not charging us with perverting the course of justice.'

'You were just protecting your mother,' James said. 'I would have done the same for mine.'

'I wouldn't have,' Molly said; 'mine was a bitch.'

Everyone laughed, and James felt the tension in the room dissipate.

'Are you okay showing them out, Ben?' Mark asked his brother.

'Sure,' he said.

'I'll speak to the lawyer,' Molly said. 'Please work on Kathy; convince her to speak to me.'

As Ben escorted them to the exit, Molly said to him: 'You were pretty quiet in there. I get the feeling you're not one-hundred per cent on board with all this.'

'Well, Mark was always the mummy's boy; I tended to side with Dad. I was angry at her for what she did; we didn't speak for months. I suppose it's taken me longer to come round to the idea that he wasn't the man I thought he was.'

'I understand,' Molly said.

Abruptly, Ben stopped in his tracks. 'There's something else about him you should probably know.'

'What's that?'

'Not here,' Ben looked over his shoulder; 'Mark doesn't know. Come to my office and I'll tell you.'

'Whatever is it?' Molly asked, after Ben had closed the door behind them.

If anything, the room was larger than his brother's. There was no artwork on display here, but the window provided a panoramic view over Letchworth.

'This was Dad's office,' Ben said; 'we tossed a coin and I won.'

He took a deep breath. 'Well, I was clearing out his stuff – twenty years of accumulated rubbish – when I came across an envelope in his desk drawer. Couldn't believe my eyes.'

'Whatever was in it?' Molly asked.

A pained expression shot across Ben's face, and he briefly turned to look out of the window. 'Let me show you.'

He retrieved a white, A4-sized envelope from the desk and pulled out the contents, handing them to James. They were photographs, perhaps a dozen or so.

James flicked through them. They were pictures taken from a party: men in tuxedoes and women in various costumes, some leaving little to the imagination; all were wearing eye masks. Molly sidled next to him.

'What's this?' she said. 'Some kind of masquerade ball? Looks fun.'

'Keep going,' Ben said.

James flicked past another couple of pictures, then stopped. 'Shit!'

'Come on, woman, think of your dignity!' Molly added.

The photo was of two men and a woman, smiling at the camera. She wore a sequinned dress and had a feather boa around her neck. One man had a hand clamped to her breast, while the other was gripping her inner thigh, her dress hitched up to the waist.

'I take it that's your dad, on the left?' James said.

'Yup.'

'And, that chap on the right,' Molly pointed, 'you know who that is, don't you, Jimbo?'

James strained to see, but wasn't totally sure, because of the eye mask. He was drawn to an out-of-focus woman in the background, her face white from the camera flash; young, blonde hair, black corset. She looked startled.

'Richard bloody Whiteley,' she offered.

'No, it's R—' Ben started.

'Rick Brady,' Molly said, completing his sentence, 'I know. The spitting image of Richard Whiteley, though, don't you think?'

Ben frowned and ignored the question. 'He was our neighbour.'

'I know,' Molly said; 'I met his wife. Lovely lady.'

James was confused. 'What?'

'The morning after the murder,' Molly said, 'I met her. Russian woman… Ghastly…'

Molly's words disappeared into the ether. There was something else troubling James about the pictures. The venue looked vaguely familiar. 'Any idea where this party was held?' he asked Ben.

'I'm not completely sure, but a letter came through shortly after he died, from a club in Harpenden: something about the annual membership fee increasing. Guess it could have been there. One of those private drinking clubs.'

'The Kipling Club,' James and Ben then said, in unison.

'James,' Molly said, turning to him, puzzled, 'how would you know? Didn't have you down as that type.'

'Long story.' He turned to Ben: 'I presume Kathy had no knowledge of this?'

Ben shook his head. 'She'd have had kittens. I've kept it to myself; no point upsetting her even more, is there?'

'Mind if I take this photograph?'

'Be my guest; take the whole envelope, if you like. Don't really know why I've bothered keeping them, to be honest.'

'Cheers. We'll be heading off now, then.'

'I'll be back in touch about your mum,' Molly added.

. . .

'Well I never,' Molly said, the moment they were out in the car park. 'You never know what's going on behind closed doors, do you?'

She turned to James: 'What's going on in that brain of yours? I can hear the cogs turning.'

'Just wondering who was taking the photographs.'

'What?'

'Fancy a trip to see an old friend?'

THIRTY-EIGHT

'JAMES! MOLLY!' Ian Murdoch said, when he finally answered the door. 'What an unexpected pleasure.'

It had been a few months since James had last seen him – they'd merely exchanged a few brief text messages – but Murdoch had aged by years. He'd lost a considerable amount of weight and the layer of fat under his chin had disappeared leaving behind leathery drapes of skin. His broad smile didn't disguise sadness in his dark-rimmed eyes. There was a note of whisky on his breath. Christ, James thought, if this is what retirement does to a man …

'May we come in, sir?' James said.

'Of course. Suppose I'm not "sir" anymore, though. Call me Ian.'

James held the envelope and noticed Murdoch's gaze flick to it, but he wasn't inclined to mention it.

Inside, James was struck by the stale, musty smell. There was a hint of something acrid, too. Mothballs? Time for a mint. The heating was on full blast and James felt like his eyeballs were drying out. The hallway was unkempt, and a pile of mail sat unopened on a side table.

'Shoes?' Molly said. She removed her coat and threw it on a stand. James followed suit.

Murdoch smiled. 'No need,' he said. 'Come through to the kitchen and I'll make you a drink. Tea? Coffee?'

'Coffee please, Ian,' Molly said: 'black, no sugar; I'm sweet enough as it is.'

'Same for me,' James added; 'I want to stay bitter.'

In the kitchen, Murdoch flicked on the kettle, which sat almost hidden amongst the clutter. 'Excuse the mess, won't you?' he said, but didn't elaborate.

The state of the place, and of Murdoch, told James that Estelle was clearly no longer around. He wondered why. Divorce? Death? James didn't feel it was his place to ask.

Right on cue, Molly said: 'So, where's Estelle?'

Murdoch was rummaging for something in a high cupboard. 'She's a little under the weather.' It didn't ring true, James thought, as Murdoch pulled out a jar of Gold Blend.

'Take a seat, please; make yourself at home,' Murdoch said, pointing to the circular breakfast table.

James and Molly sat down. There was a bowl of half-eaten cornflakes in front of James, and he pushed it away from him to make room for the envelope. Molly's face contorted in disgust.

'So,' Murdoch said, as he brought over three mugs of coffee and joined them at the table, 'how are things going with the cheating wife case, James?'

'Er, how did you know that?'

Murdoch smiled and took a sip from his mug. 'Well, I pointed him in your direction, when he told me about his… problem; said I knew just the man to get the job done quickly and professionally for him.'

'You know Rick Brady, then?' Molly asked. 'Friend of yours?'

'I wouldn't say friends; more of an acquaintance. We play golf at the same club.'

'Interesting,' Molly said.

'Interesting?'

'You know I'm not one to beat about the bush, sir – sorry, Ian,' James said, 'so I'm just going to come straight out with it: why did you never mention the fact that you knew John Gibbs?'

Murdoch puffed his cheeks and scratched his nape. He frowned for a moment. 'John Gibbs?'

'Come on, you know full well: stabbed to death by his wife, Kathy.'

Murdoch's pallid cheeks flushed red. He took a deep breath. 'How have you found this out? Why now?' he said.

'I've been doing a lot of work on coercive control, recently,' Molly said; 'you may have read it. Anyway, turns out John Gibbs had been abusing Kathy for years – we think that's what drove her to kill him. It wasn't just jealous rage; she was driven to it after years and years of his abuse.'

'Coercive control? Abuse? I knew nothing about any of that,' Murdoch protested. 'I would have been the first person to call that out if I had.'

'So, you're not denying you knew him?' James said.

There was a flash of panic in Murdoch's eyes. before he composed himself. 'Yes, you're right: I knew him. Just a casual acquaintance at the golf club; exchanged a few pleasantries here and there, nothing more. Why would I mention it to anyone? It had no bearing on the case.'

'The golf club, too? Okay,' James said, blankly. 'Never seen the fascination with golf, personally.'

Then, he opened the envelope and pulled out the picture of John, Rick and the boa girl. 'Recognize this?'

Murdoch took the picture from James and regarded it for a few moments, before placing it down on the table in front of him.

'You'll recognize the venue, I'm sure. And your two *casual* acquaintances.'

'I'm not sure I'm following.'

'Come on, Ian,' James said, raising his voice. 'I wasn't born yesterday.'

Murdoch scratched his temple with his middle finger, as he looked again at the photograph.

'Who took the picture, Ian?'

'W-what? I don't understand. You're not suggesting…'

'That you, John Gibbs and Rick Brady are best chums? That's exactly what I'm suggesting. You see, I called Luke Porter on our way over here; I asked him if he still had the membership list for the Kipling Club – you'll remember we seized it before the club was shut down after Pinto's arrest. Lo and behold, who turned out to be on it? That's right: the three bloody stooges–'

'Oh, my god,' Molly said, with a suddenness that gave James a start.

'Whatever is it?'

'I've just remembered something about Brady–'

'Well, can it wait?'

'No. That morning, after the murder, I was the first journalist at the scene – you might remember, James; you ignored me. Well, I spoke to the neighbour: the Russian woman married to Brady – the one you've just caught on candid camera.'

'Small world, eh?' Murdoch chuckled, awkwardly.

'Well, no, not really, is it?' Molly replied. 'You'll know as well as anyone, Ian, that hideous cul-de-sac is the most exclusive address in Letchworth. It's where all the money is.'

'Where are you going with this?' James said.

'The first thing she asked me, when she opened the door, do you know what it was? "Are you a hooker?" At the time, I thought she was just making some kind of wise-crack about the way I dressed – typical bloody rude Russian, I said to myself. She said her husband was away on business. Now, when I think about it, I reckon she knew he liked to dabble with prostitutes; perhaps he was totally open about it. She clearly couldn't care less; she had the nice clothes, the house, all the money–'

'I still don't get the relevance, Moll,' James said. He flicked his gaze to Murdoch, who fiddled nervously with his coffee mug.

'Hear me out. As you know, I was in the public gallery the whole time, during Perkins's trial. You were there a great deal, too, I seem to recall, Ian. *How nice of you,* I thought, *to be supporting your man.* Perkins's accusation that the DNA was planted – we all thought it was such a ludicrous thing to say, didn't we? *"I was framed, m'lud"* – that's what every guilty man says, don't they? Desperate stuff. The thing is, I watched him in the dock: if it wasn't for the fact that he was accusing me and James of planting the DNA under the poor woman's bloody fingernail, you know what? I might have believed him. If he ever gets out of jail, there's a glittering career awaiting him in the West End.'

'I… I… don't follow,' Murdoch spluttered.

'Oh, I think you do,' Molly said.

James remained quiet for a moment. The jigsaw pieces were beginning to coalesce in his head. Molly looked at him, and she must have sensed that from his expression. 'Want to take it from here, James?' she said.

He nodded, paused for a moment, then turned to

Murdoch. 'Where were you on the night of Daniela Sirota's murder, Ian?'

'I, er, I don't know what you're—'

'Spare me, Ian.'

'Oh, God,' Murdoch said. He dropped his head into his hands for a few moments, then looked up.

'Just give me one moment, will you? Then I'll tell you everything, I swear.'

Ian Murdoch returned to the kitchen with a bottle of Glenfiddich and a tumbler. He sat down at the table and poured a large glass. 'Want one?' he gestured to James half-heartedly, and James shook his head. James caught Molly raise a finger and he shot her a castigating look.

'I've carried this burden for five long years; it almost feels like a relief to talk about it at last. What I'm about to tell you, please understand... everything I did – *everything* – was driven by a desire to help others. Including you, James.'

'Don't you dare try to put any blame on me—' James began.

Molly put her hand on his arm to stop him. She flicked her eyes to Murdoch. 'Let him speak,' she said.

'So, Molly,' Murdoch said, 'you're right: Mr. Brady did have a fondness for prostitutes. He liked them young and pretty. Naive. Game for experimentation. He was willing to pay good money, and there was a plentiful supply of girls prepared to do the things he requested – young Daniela was one of them. His wife, Yelena, was away quite often – and you're right, Molly: she was well aware of her husband's fondness for prostitutes. Theirs was a marriage of convenience: she liked his money and he liked having an attractive young wife on his arm.'

'But it turns out he couldn't stand the thought of her having her own life?' Molly said.

'It seems not,' Murdoch said. 'I suppose he must demand loyalty of others, but not of himself.'

'Probably dented his male pride,' Molly added. 'Prick.' James didn't disagree with that sentiment.

'Well, anyway, Rick Brady was into rough sex: sado-masochism. Each to their own, I suppose. Have you heard of sexual asphyxia at all?'

'Of course,' Molly said, matter-of-factly: 'where you restrict the airflow during sex. Makes orgasm more intense.' James flashed Molly a look.

'Apparently,' she added.

'Turns out John Gibbs was in to it, too. All too willing to slip round to Rick's house, while Kathy was tucked up in bed. They put a ligature around the poor girl's neck and she passed out. Of course, you can guess what happened next.' Murdoch smiled ruefully. 'She didn't come round. So, there they both are, panicking. First time anything like this has happened. Eventually, John comes up with the idea of storing the body in his garage freezer, until they can think of a way to permanently dispose of her.'

'Jesus,' James said. 'I always wondered where Perkins had found a freezer to store the body; there was nothing big enough at his house. I assumed he must have rented some facility somewhere, under a false name. The answer was staring me in the face all along – at the damned Gibbs crime scene.

'You seem to know a lot of the details. What was your involvement, then?'

'I had nothing to do with the sex or the killing. I was never into all that…' Murdoch grimaced, trying to find the right words. '…the *active participation*.'

'Go on, get to the point.'

'Remember that day you saw me at the club?'

'Of course.'

'Well, John had called me the night before, to suggest meeting up there, for a lunchtime drink and chat. Nothing out of the ordinary, although it was a bit of a surprise to see you in the car park. Anyway, not long after you left he found me in the club, dressed in his golfing clobber; he told me to come back out to the car park. Said he had something he needed to tell me in total confidence.'

Murdoch took a gulp of whisky before continuing: 'So, I climbed into the front seat of his Range Rover, and he starts talking about this spot of bother he's in, and he needs my help. Then, from the back seats, Rick Brady's voice suddenly pipes up and makes me jump; he was also in his golfing gear.' Murdoch sighed. 'That's when John told me about the episode with the prostitute and the body in the freezer.

'I told him, obviously, that they needed to report it, explain it to the police. Then John kicked off big time: how was he ever going to explain away a dead body in his freezer? Besides, nobody had reported the poor girl missing. It seemed nobody knew or cared about her; why risk getting done for murder? I went to get out of the car, but John grabbed my arm. "You don't understand," he said; "we need your help *now*!" That's when Rick got out of the car and opened the boot.'

'Don't tell me they had the bloody body in it?'

Murdoch nodded and drank more whisky. 'John said he couldn't keep hold of the corpse any longer; Kathy had a habit of sniffing around and he couldn't risk her finding it. They needed the body cleaned, to make sure that if she was ever discovered nothing could be traced back to them. I'm ashamed to admit that's when I agreed to help them.'

'Why the hell did you go along with it?' James said.

'Risk your career? Your freedom? Everything. It makes no sense at all.'

'Well, they could embarrass me about these parties, couldn't they?'

James sighed. 'Don't tell me: the women who came to the party – they were paid for their services, weren't they?'

'They were willing participants, James.'

'Next you're going to tell me they were trafficked.'

Murdoch's gaze flitted to the photograph, then to his glass. He stared at it in apparent embarrassment.

'Jesus Christ!' James exclaimed, his eyes boring into Murdoch's bowed head. 'But even so, was that *really* a good enough reason to risk *everything*?'

'I ask myself that same question every day, James. Once I'd crossed the Rubicon, there was no turning back…'

James sighed and glanced down at Murdoch's nearly empty glass. He was tempted to grab it and drain the rest himself. 'What happened next, then?' He spat out the words with derision.

Murdoch addressed his glass, speaking slowly, his voice quiet. 'Before I knew it, Rick and John were bundling the poor woman into my boot. I couldn't exactly kick up a fuss; there were other people around at the club – cameras, too. Anyway, we agreed a rendezvous for that night, two a.m. After that, I went straight to work and the pair of them went back for a game of bloody golf, not a care in the world. I was having kittens.' At that, Murdoch looked at Molly. 'Sorry.'

James dragged his hands down his face. This had to be a dream, surely? He'd wake up soon: *It's okay, Toto, we're back in Kansas.* He composed himself, swallowed a desire to shout. 'Are you seriously saying that, for the rest of the day, your car was parked up in HQ with a sodding dead body in the boot?'

'Afraid so. It was difficult to concentrate, I can tell you.' Murdoch filled his glass with more Scotch. 'Anyway, I got home that evening, and thankfully Estelle was out, on one of her fundraising dinners in Baldock; it gave me a two-hour window to clean the body. I took her into the garage and unwrapped her – God, she looked so young… so tiny. No more than a child, really.' His lip trembled and he took a sip of Scotch, then wiped his mouth with the back of his hand. 'As you can imagine, we had every cleaning product under the sun in the house. When I finished, I wrapped her up in fresh bin liners and got her back in the boot, together with some garden tools: a shovel, spade, what have you. The girl was as light as a feather.'

Murdoch looked up at James. 'I realize how absurd all of this sounds.'

'*Absurd* doesn't even begin to cover it,' James said, barely concealing his rage. 'Come on, tell us how this girl ended up in that fucking dell, with Perkins's DNA under her fingernail.'

'That night, I snuck out of the house, shortly after midnight. Mrs. M took pills to help her sleep – nothing out of the ordinary; the woman's a terrible sleeper. Besides, we'd been sleeping in separate rooms for God knows how long.' Murdoch smiled, wistfully. 'Said she couldn't bear my snoring.'

His eyes moistened and he switched his gaze to the window for a few seconds, blinking away the tears. He turned back and continued: 'I drove out to the rendezvous: a derelict farm building in the middle of the Suffolk countryside. I arrived shortly before two. Rick Brady was already there, pacing about. We waited and waited for John, but there was no sign. Eventually, Rick sent John a text, asking him to call; we didn't want to risk alerting Kathy – little did we know, at that very moment, she was standing over him like Norman bloody Bates with a kitchen knife! I've always wondered whether John ever did intend to join us. He'd already washed his hands of the body, so what was the downside for him?'

'What if your text was the straw that broke the camel's back with Kathy, Ian?' Molly said. 'How do you feel about that?'

'No worse than I already do. The whole thing, from start to finish, is a bloody mess.'

'Come on. You're at the farm building in Suffolk,' James said. 'What then?'

'We decided we couldn't wait for John. Rick got into my car. I was fuming with him for dragging me into it; John, too. We drove around the country lanes, looking for somewhere we could dispose of the body. Then, a lake flashed up on my satnav, and we agreed to take her there. We'd dressed into forensics suits by this point. Twenty or so minutes later we got to the lake… and I suppose that's when fate intervened.'

'John's murder?' James said.

'Yes. My phone buzzed and I assumed it was John, of course. Never thought for a moment it would be *about* him. Well, that threw a spanner in the works, as you can well imagine. My mind was somersaulting, trying to work out why he may have been killed; whether there was any connection to the girl's death. Rick was agitated, trying to hurry me along, to get the deed over and done with, but I told him I couldn't. I suppose I had one of those moments of realization: I was a superintendent, for Christ's sake! I was supposed to be solving homicides, not covering them up. I told Rick we were aborting the plan, and that I'd think about how we could extricate ourselves from the situation. I took him back to his car, then got myself home, put the girl in the garage, washed and changed my clothes, and got down to HQ.'

James allowed a silence to fill the room for a few moments, to allow some time for the revelations to sink in and catch his breath. His lip curled as he regarded Murdoch, in front of him. He looked like a pathetic old man. Weak. Drunk.

'So, how long did it take you to come up with the dell plan? After Molly's cat was found?' James eventually asked.

Murdoch shifted his gaze briefly to Molly, then to James.

'I did it for you, James. Failing to bring justice to Perkins was eating you alive – I could see that. We all knew he was guilty of that first murder... and the bloody cat. That assault complaint was hanging over you and wasn't going to go away. He could have wrecked your career.'

'No. No. No.' James jabbed his finger at Murdoch. 'The only person you were thinking of was yourself. You're a pathetic, selfish bastard! I'm ashamed to have ever worked for you! So, I'll hear no more of that *"did it for you"* nonsense.

'Tell me, how did you get the DNA on her body? Perkins's defence looked into that with a fine-tooth comb; they found nothing untoward in the records. That's why they just left it as a general inference, hoping the jury would fall for it. That whole framing accusation hung around my neck like an albatross, for months. Gave me sleepless nights and probably contributed to my heart attack. *That's* what snatched my career away from me. My job was the only good thing left in my life; I loved it. All the time it was *you!*'

Molly squeezed his hand, but he jerked it away from her grip.

Murdoch fingered the Scotch bottle, but before he could pour himself more, James snatched it from him. Murdoch didn't protest.

'You did… *that thing*,' Molly said, her face contorted into a look of horror, 'with her intestines?'

Murdoch didn't respond; he just peered into his glass.

'And, what about Bea?' Molly continued. 'She witnessed Daniela getting in Perkins's car.'

Murdoch sighed. 'I'm afraid there's more to Bea than meets the eye. She wasn't exactly an innocent bystander.'

'Oh, this just gets better,' James said, his fury tempered by a sense of macabre incredulity.

'Bea was Daniela's madam. To her, the girl was her prized asset: young, beautiful, naive. So, losing her in these circumstances was quite a financial blow to her.'

'My heart bleeds!' Molly said. 'I can't believe I was taken in. I thought I was such a good judge of character. Poor Daniela was just a commodity to her.'

'I'm guessing that Bea needed to be compensated for her loss?' James said. 'And I'm sure Brady was only too happy to oblige?'

'Indeed. It was his idea for her to speak to you, Molly; he saw your article and the reward. Quite fortuitous that, don't you think? Of course, seven-hundred and fifty was just small change – that was never going to do the trick; add a couple more zeros, and you're getting closer to the kind of money Brady put up for her to step forward.'

'And the DNA?' James asked. 'Where did that come into the equation?'

'Well, as you know, Perkins has a fondness himself for street girls; he was well known among the community – and to Bea, of course. You must understand that I have no connection with her; this information comes from Brady. Bea always suspected it was Perkins who killed Lena

Demyan, but Lena wasn't one of her girls and business was business. She told him, though, if he ever hurt a hair on one of her girl's heads, she'd personally rip off his genitalia. Apparently, he was her client in the distant past, before she was... promoted. Despite her size, she knew how to handle herself, it seems. It also turned out that she had a fondness for cats: when she heard about the disembowelled cat at the dell–'

Molly let out a distressed welp.

'Sorry,' Murdoch said. 'When she heard, she went round to give him a piece of her mind and Perkins laughed at her, which sent her into a rage. Before he knew what was happening, she'd lashed out at him like a wild animal, scratched his face – obviously that yielded a fresh source of DNA.'

Murdoch stood up and took himself over to the sink and poured himself a glass of water, which he drank thirstily. 'Of course, getting the body down in the dell was easy. Rick and I took her in the dead of night. No houses in the vicinity, no CCTV; perfect place, really.

'So, now you know,' he said, pocketing his hands.

The room fell into a deathly silence. There were no words, really.

Something in the photograph then seemed to catch Murdoch's eye, before he quickly looked away, a reaction flashing across his face.

James noticed; 'What is it, Ian?'

'What?'

'I just saw the way you looked at the photo: like you'd just seen a ghost.'

James grabbed the picture and studied it. 'Is it the girl in the background? Was she underage, or something? She looks it.' He peered closer, before a horrible thought crossed his mind. 'When exactly was this party, Ian?'

'Oh… gosh… I wouldn't be sure. They tended to hold these parties in the summer. I didn't attend many.'

James turned the photograph over and saw a date printed on the back.

Dear God!

It was the night of Lena Demyan's murder.

'That's her, isn't it? That's Lena fucking Demyan!'

There was a fatal pause, before Ian Murdoch gestured innocence.

James slumped into his chair and ran his hands through his hair. 'Tell me you didn't frame Perkins for this one, too?'

Molly brought her hands to her face. She seemed speechless, for perhaps the first time in her life.

'Ian!' James said, smashing his fist on the table. 'Tell me I've not been pursuing an innocent man for murder all this time!'

Murdoch licked his lips and fixed his gaze on James. 'No! That man did it! You know it and I know it. We've got CCTV of his car that night, placing him in the vicinity, and we know he was showing the classic signs: obsession, escalating violence…'

'And the eyewitness who disappeared?'

'I don't know what happened there, I swear; I had no involvement.'

'So, how did Lena go from being at this party to getting into Perkins's clutches? He wasn't at the party, too, was he?'

'Good God, no.'

'Then, what happened?'

Murdoch sighed. 'Not long after that picture was taken, the room fell into blackness. We think it was Lena who tripped the electrics, and used the opportunity to escape.'

'So, not all the girls were there willingly?'

'I think it was her first time at one of these parties. Probably got cold feet.'

Disgust and bewilderment rippled through James. There were a few beats of silence, then Murdoch said: 'What are you going to do, James?'

'What am *I* going to do? How *dare* you?! Don't put this on me. *You* need to confess everything to the police. You know that's the only option.'

Murdoch nodded, sadly.

'You've got until tomorrow to do it. If not, I'll report you myself. Do you understand?'

Murdoch's face contorted into a pained expression. 'I wonder if you'd be so kind to give me a little while longer?'

'And, why on Earth would I do that?'

'Come with me. I'll show you.'

Murdoch ushered them into the dining room.

'Oh, my god,' Molly whelped.

'Jesus,' James said.

'The doctors say it's the size of a tangerine,' Murdoch said: 'glioblastoma, the most aggressive kind of brain tumour there is.'

Murdoch took Estelle's hand gently in his. 'She's been in a coma since yesterday. It's just a matter of days now.'

James regarded poor Estelle Murdoch for a few moments, and the image of his mother in the hospital flashed briefly in his mind. It was hard to reconcile the cadaverous figure he saw before him – motionless, except for the shallowest movement of her chest – with the memory of the spritely woman with strong opinions and barely contained nervous energy. She was seated almost upright in bed, her head propped against an enormous pillow.

Murdoch dropped into a seat next to her. Behind him, the sideboard was covered with various boxes and bottles of medication. The dining table was pushed against the window – on it were numerous bunches of flowers, some wilting, others clearly dead.

'I'm so sorry,' Molly said.

'She's refused all treatment,' Murdoch said, as he mopped his wife's forehead with a flannel. 'The doctors told her it was incurable, but an operation and radio-therapy would buy her a few more months. She told them she wanted to die with dignity, at home, with no fuss. The Macmillan nurses have been wonderful.' Murdoch was fighting back tears. 'She's so much braver than me.' His shoulders began to convulse.

'She looks peaceful, Ian,' Molly said. 'You need to look after yourself, for her sake. She needs you to be strong for her right now. Come on, James.'

Molly closed the door quietly behind them, as they stepped into the hall.

As Molly put on her coat, James's eyes wandered to the pile of unopened envelopes on the hall table. He casually looked through them, stopping when he saw a familiar company logo: *'Barrington Hawke Investments.'* The letter was addressed to *'Mrs. E. Murdoch.'*

'Well, are we going?' Molly said.

'Hmm?' James said, barely registering her.

'You've no business looking at their mail,' she said.

'It's a letter from the Gibbs' investment company. I think this might help explain his actions; I need him to admit that he was in Gibbs and Brady's pocket.' He turned, poised to confront Murdoch.

'Leave it!' The sternness of Molly's tone stopped him dead in his tracks.

'I need to find out,' he pleaded, 'if Brady, Gibbs or Murdoch were part of the Solent network.'

'Not now, James. Grab your coat; we're leaving.'

THIRTY-NINE

'WELL,' Molly said, when they were back in the Audi, 'who would have thunk the day would turn out like this?'

James knew she was trying to make light of the situation, but he was raging. His anger towards Murdoch was mixed with annoyance, that he'd somehow allowed himself to be duped and betrayed by his former boss. He didn't speak.

But, clearly Molly wasn't one to tolerate silence for very long.

'So, what are you going to do?' she said.

He turned over the engine and pulled the car onto the road, pressing the accelerator so hard that, after an initial wheelspin, the tyres gripped the road and Molly was pushed back in her seat. He eased off the pedal and settled into a pace marginally above the speed limit.

Molly reached for the grab bar. 'You do realize that shopping Murdoch will mean that Perkins will be a free man? Is that what you want?'

'You seriously think I hadn't thought of that?' James

said. 'But I can't just overlook what Murdoch's done. What Brady's done. I've been taken for a fool.'

'We all have, James. Slow down, for Christ's sake!' There was panic in Molly's voice. 'You saw Estelle: she needs him right now. What difference will a few more days make?'

James drew within inches of the rear bumper of a red Fiesta. 'Come on!' He dropped a gear, swung out and floored the accelerator. An oncoming car mounted the pavement to avoid a collision.

'James!' Molly screeched.

The lights at a pelican crossing, metres ahead, were about to turn red when he sped through, just as a woman had stepped into the road. He then took a sharp left, the wheels squealing as he did so.

'Where are we going?' Molly hollered.

He ignored her.

'James!'

'Do you still have that Bea woman's number? Phone her.'

'You're scaring me now. Slow down! We can talk about this when you're in a calmer frame of mind.'

He floored the accelerator.

'James! You're going to kill us both.'

Suddenly, Molly grabbed the wheel and yanked it towards her. James slammed on the brakes and the car came to a messy halt.

'What are you doing, woman?!' He turned to her. She looked angry.

Then, her expression changed into something which looked like pity. 'Let's get you home before you blow a gasket,' she said.

'No, I need to speak to him. Now.'

'Who, James?'

'Brady, of course. I want to look him in the eye; get him to tell us the truth. How the hell do we know it was an accident?'

'You're not in the police anymore, James; this isn't your job. Leave it. Think of your health.'

'You're welcome to get out. I can deal with this on my own.'

'That's your problem, James: I don't think you can.'

They pulled into the Letchworth cul-de-sac, and James leapt out of the car. Molly followed him to the front door. He rang the doorbell and rapped the knocker. No response. Nor was there when James tried Brady's mobile. He had to be here; Brady had told him that morning that he was working from his home office, working on plans for a new business venture, apparently.

'He could be anywhere,' Molly said: 'clearing the air with his wife at a restaurant, or a pub perhaps? Or, he might be at the golf club, taking out his anger with a nine iron? Leave it be.'

James hammered on the door once more.

'This all seems familiar,' Molly said, a hint of resignation in her voice.

'Hmm?' James said. He tried the handle and the door opened. Without giving much thought to the rights or wrongs, he stepped into the cavernous hall.

'Brady!' His voice echoed around the vast space.

Next to the door was the control panel for the house alarm, which he noted had not been activated. 'Something's not right,' he said. Molly responded with some kind of protest, but he didn't register her words.

James made his way through the ground-floor rooms. Everywhere looked as neat as a pin. In the kitchen, a fruity fragrance filled the air; two huge blooms of orange roses sat at opposite ends of the enormous island unit. The only sign of human activity was a spent mug on the kitchen drainer. He noticed a faint ticking noise: a clock, presumably, though he couldn't see one in the kitchen. He followed the sound to an internal door off the kitchen: a utility room, or maybe a larder. He opened the door and stepped into a dark room.

It took him a moment or two to find the light switch. He turned it on and instantly someone screamed. A woman. It made James jump. It took him several beats to realize it was Molly. 'What the hell are you doing?' he said. 'You're going to give me another bloody heart attack!'

'*Me*, give *you* one?' She held a palm to her chest. 'I was trying to find the bloody switch.'

They were in a windowless room. The walls were wood-panelled and there was a hefty-looking desk, behind which was a leather chair. A door was open on the far wall, and James realized that there must be another entrance from the living room. Molly stood next to the desk. 'Don't touch anything,' James said.

On the desk there was a stack of paperwork and, reading upside down, he noted a solicitor's letter, threatening legal action if a debt of more than two-hundred thousand was not repaid in twenty-eight days. Was he in financial trouble, or was this Brady's normal way of doing business? Something in his water told James that he wasn't going to receive payment for his detective services for quite some time, if at all.

'You know what?' he said. 'I reckon both John Gibbs and Ian Murdoch were in Brady's pocket. Explains why Gibbs would readily help Brady take the body off his hands, and why Murdoch would allow himself to get involved.'

'You're probably right, Jimbo.'

'Let's check upstairs,' he said.

On the landing there was a scent of sickly-sweet perfume. James poked his head through multiple doors: a couple of bedrooms, a bathroom and another room, which was probably designed as a bedroom, but had been given over to an enormous dressing room. The wardrobe doors were open and there were large gaps on the rails, indicating clothes had been removed in a hurry.

Curiouser and curiouser.

There was another door in the dressing room, which he assumed would lead through to the master bedroom. James walked through it and was immediately assaulted by a thick, metallic stench. He knew what it was before he saw the body of Rick Brady, slumped against the four-poster bed.

'Shit!' Molly cried out when she entered. 'Is he dead?'

'Well, if he's not, he's doing a damn good impersonation of a corpse,' James said. He snapped on his latex gloves and checked for a pulse: nothing. There was a huge wound on Brady's forehead, and his entire face and upper body were caked in blood. James examined the wound and his fingertip disappeared into a hole. 'Looks like he's been struck by a heavy object.'

'Like a dumbbell, for instance?' Molly said.

'Huh?'

'There.'

James followed Molly's gesture to a rack of dumbbells underneath the window. He crouched down to inspect it: there was one missing.

'Found it,' Molly said. James turned to see her on all fours, peering under the bed. Molly got to her feet.

'So, what do you reckon, then? He came home to

confront her over the affair, found her in here, things got heated and she walloped him one, then scarpered?'

'That's how it looks,' James smiled, wryly, 'but looks can be deceptive. Best leave it to the professionals.' He took out his phone and dialled 999.

FORTY

K<small>ATHY'S</small> <small>EYE</small> had swollen so much that it was now completely closed. Walking around the yard half-blind felt strangely disorientating, almost as if she might topple over at any minute.

Her mind wandered to a distant memory; she couldn't have been more than six or seven years old. It was a hot, summer day and she was on the lawn. One of her brothers – Billy, no doubt – had passed her the old broom handle, told her to poke one end in the grass and hold on to the other, then run around in fast circles. Round and round and round she went, screaming her head off. When she let go, she went careering across the lawn, through Dad's vegetable patch; she barrelled into the fence and toppled over it, straight into the horrible green water of the Masseys' fishpond. Billy was too bent over with laughter to help get her out.

Kathy sat down on the bench, in the little patch of garden she and a bunch of other prisoners had helped build in the autumn. It was nothing special – a rockery and a smattering of shrubs and spring bulbs – but it was her little sanctuary.

There was a stiff, cold breeze and Kathy wrapped her thick, woollen cardigan tight around her, sinking her hands into the deep pockets. Her eye throbbed and she withdrew a hand to gingerly prod the puffy skin. She winced. It was her own daft fault, really: just because *she* liked to listen to Radio Four at five in the morning didn't mean that others did. She had the volume on low and thought that Suzie was fast asleep, undisturbed. But who could blame Suzie for throwing the radio against the wall and lashing out at Kathy in frustration? The poor woman had had a hard life, bless her. She soon calmed down and apologized for her behaviour; said she'd forgotten to take her medication. 'No need to apologize, love,' Kathy had said; 'I understand.'

A faint squeak from the cotoneaster bush punctured her consciousness. She strained her ear… another squeak. Kathy stepped over to the bush and dropped to her knees, scanning the foliage, which was dotted with red berries. She brought her hand to her chest when she found the source of the sound: a stricken hatchling. Kathy looked up and around her, but there were no trees; no obvious location for a nest. The poor little creature's mouth was agape, gasping for help. Where was its mother? What to do?

About her, other prisoners trudged in an anti-clockwise circuit around the yard, like normal – some alone, lost in thought, others in groups, engaged in animated chatter; all blissfully unaware of the bird's plight. Should Kathy ask for help? She couldn't be sure they'd care. She returned her attention to the bird. It was a strange-looking thing: big, closed eyes, long neck, pink, fleshy beak. It had no feathers, just a patchy mess of yellow down. How was it ever going to survive in the cold, without its mother?

Oh, what to do?

'Gibbs? That you? What you doing down there on your knees? Praying's not going to do you any good.'

Kathy recognized the voice of prison officer Miss Green. She glanced over her shoulder. 'Just admiring the berries, miss,' Kathy said: 'beautiful, don't you think?'

Miss Green looked at her watch. 'Time for you to be getting back inside.'

'Miss.'

Kathy looked back to the bird and surreptitiously wrapped her fingers around its little body. She could feel the fast beat of its heart. As she stood up and turned to face Miss Green, she placed her hands in her cardigan pockets and smiled.

'On your way, Gibbs.'

Under Miss Green's gaze, Kathy walked briskly back to the prison building. She wondered what on Earth she was going to do with the bird. It surely had no chance of survival, but she could at least make sure it left this cruel world knowing that it was loved.

As she drew close to the building, she heard flapping above her: a pigeon was perched on a ridge, above a third-floor window. Kathy would swear that the sad eyes of a bereft mother were looking down on her.

Kathy sat at the tiny desk in the cell and opened the battered, old biscuit tin.

The click of the boiled kettle made her jump. She composed herself and poured a mug of water. After that, she stirred in several sachets of sugar with a plastic spoon.

She returned her attention to the biscuit tin. Removed the photographs and placed them carefully in a new safe place: inside the cover of a Delia Smith cookbook. Fat load of good that book was on the inside, now. Every now and then, she'd thumb through the pages and conjure memories of happy family meals; she'd skip over the broccoli and stilton soup recipe, of course.

Kathy needed to hurry: Suzie would soon be back from lunch, and Kathy had a busy afternoon ahead of her, with the new teaching job. Unbelievably, some of the girls inside couldn't read or write. Prison was a real eye-opener for Kathy, and it had made her realize how fortunate she'd been, relatively speaking. She was only too happy to take the opportunity to help out those less privileged than her.

She lined the tin with the warmest, softest material she could find: a pair of thick, thermal socks Mark had brought in for her, a few visits back. He wouldn't mind her using them in this way; he had a heart of gold. Kathy's heart ached for her favourite boy.

She reached into her pocket and brought out the little hatchling. Breathing a sigh of relief to find its little chest still pounding, she laid him gently in the tin – something told her the bird was a boy. She dipped a finger into the mug and found the sugar water had cooled sufficiently, then, with a shaky hand, she took a spoonful of it and brought it over the bird's mouth, which instantaneously gaped open, reminding Kathy of a beautiful orchid. As gently as she could, Kathy tilted the spoon and liquid dribbled down into the bird's throat. He gobbled and squeaked and spluttered, and for an awful moment she wondered if the poor thing was choking to death. It opened its mouth again, and she took this as a sign it was safe to continue the feed. After four or five more spoonfuls, she decided that was probably enough.

Nearly time to head off for work. She grabbed her nail scissors and forcefully punched and twisted several holes in the tin lid. 'Stay safe, sweetheart,' she said to the bird, blowing him a kiss before sealing him inside.

'Who you talking to, Kathy?'

Kathy looked up, startled; Suzie's bulky frame leaned against the doorjamb. She wiped a smudge of food from her top lip.

'Oh, no one,' Kathy said, forcing a smile; 'just myself. You know what I'm like.'

Kathy gingerly placed the tin on a shelf. 'Right, off to work. See you later, Suzie.'

Kathy sucked in her stomach and squeezed her way past Suzie, onto the landing.

Then, the bird squeaked.

Kathy turned to see Suzie looking for the source of the sound.

'Have you got a pet, Kathy?' Suzie said, her face breaking into a broad beam as she reached for the tin. 'Didn't think you had it in you to break the rules.'

'It's not what you thi—'

Suzie opened the tin and her face contorted in disgust. 'What the *fuck* is that?'

'I think it might be a baby pigeon, fallen from its nest. Don't hurt it, Suzie. Please.'

Suzie brought a hand to her enormous bosom. 'What do you take me for?' She looked at Kathy's eye wound. 'Thought we'd cleared the air after, you know, our little *misunderstanding* this morning? No, you toddle off to your class, Kathy; I'll look after this young fella 'til you're back.'

'Promise, Suzie?'

Suzie gesticulated. 'Cross my heart and hope to die, treacle.'

The English lesson ended and Kathy hurried back to the cell. As she approached, she saw Suzie standing out on the landing, hands on her hips.

'What's happening?' Kathy said.

'Screws are doing an inspection.'

Kathy's heart began to race as she peered inside. Miss Green and Mrs. Patel were standing in the centre of the cell. Kathy immediately saw her photographs on the floor; pictures of John and the boys carelessly strewn and covered in boot prints. Her lips quivered. She looked up and met Mrs. Patel's gaze, just as Miss Green said: 'Take a look in that, will you, Deepa?' Miss Patel took hold of the biscuit tin.

'No!' Kathy called out. 'Please be careful.'

Mrs. Patel tilted her head and arched her brow. 'Oh? Why's that then, Gibbs?' She opened the lid and peered inside. 'Well, well, well,' she said.

Kathy brought her hands to her mouth and stepped forward.

'Stop right there, Gibbs,' Miss Green barked.

Suzie moved to stand at Kathy's side.

Mrs. Patel's hand disappeared into the tin. It emerged clutching a batch of clear plastic bags, each containing white powder.

'I-I don't understand,' Kathy said.

'Kathy Gibbs,' Suzie said, raising her hand to stifle a giggle, 'you naughty, naughty girl.'

It was gone ten and Kathy lay on the bottom bunk, teary-eyed and unable to sleep. Above her, the upper bunk sagged under Suzie's bulk; her awful snoring reverberated like a drill around the bare walls.

Suzie had sworn blind they were being framed by the screws, but what was Kathy to believe? All she knew was that she was worried sick about the punishment for drug smuggling. She didn't much care that her possessions had been taken away, but what if they stopped the boys from visiting her? That thought was too much to bear.

And, what had happened to the bird?

She found the answer later, when she crept to the loo to empty her bladder. She took a piece of toilet paper and wiped the rim; as she was about to drop the paper into the pan, she saw a film of yellow down on the surface of the water.

Kathy took another sheet of toilet paper, dropped onto the loo seat and silently dabbed her eyes, while she contemplated the thought of another twenty-two years trapped in a living hell.

FORTY-ONE

JAMES WAITED in the cold of the churchyard, out of sight. He watched as the pallbearers carried the small coffin of Estelle Murdoch into the church, then waited patiently as the mourners filed in behind. The steam from their breath swirled and dissipated above their heads. Ian Murdoch was immediately behind the coffin, his head bowed, his gait unsteady.

Several minutes later, the church organ started and James took the opportunity to slip inside and take a place on an empty pew, against the back wall. He'd decided to go to the funeral out of respect for Estelle Murdoch. He didn't want to cause a scene or any unnecessary distress to Ian Murdoch, so he kept his distance – of course, he also hadn't wanted to get trapped in an awkward situation, forced to engage in painful small talk.

An old man with a shaky hand and a respectful smile shuffled over to James, with a copy of the funeral order of service. On the front was a picture of Estelle Murdoch, and her date of birth and death: she was sixty-one. No age, really. Still, a good deal older than Ruth.

He scanned the pews in front of him and noticed several former colleagues – of course, he couldn't remember all of their names. Halfway down he could make out Mel Barraclough and, next to her, the tall, broad figure of Luke Porter. On the second row, an elderly lady sniffed and dabbed an eye with a tissue pulled from a handbag. In front of her, alone on the front pew, Ian Murdoch sat motionless, staring beyond the coffin, into a dark corner. The abyss? Despite his secret double life and his deceitful actions over Daniela Sirota's body, James had formed the impression that Murdoch's love for his wife and his grief were the genuine article.

Today was a much larger turnout than the last time James had come to Our Lady's Church: Ruth's funeral. He tried to recall her service, but his memory of everything was hazy, except for the hollow, numb feeling in the pit of his stomach.

The music stopped and the place fell stony silent. The priest stepped forward to the lectern. He was perhaps a sentence or two into his solemn reading, when James felt he couldn't bear to be in the church any longer. He dipped his head respectfully towards Estelle's coffin, then slipped back out into the cold.

There was a bench in the churchyard, from which James could just about make out the words on Ruth's gravestone: *'Rūta Karolina Quinn. Until we meet again.'* He didn't need to read the words, though; they were engraved on his broken heart. In life, she insisted on the Anglicized version of her name – it had something to do with wanting to fit in, to feel at home in England. But, James had thought it appropriate to use her correct name for the inscription; death was too formal for sobriquets.

The bench was covered in a layer of frost, and the cold quickly seeped through the thin layer of his trousers; he felt its tentacles creep around his body. James hardly ever came to Ruth's grave; it made him think of her as crumbling bones in the damp earth. He closed his eyes, in an attempt to banish that inhuman image.

'You alright, guv?'

The deep voice jolted James awake. He raised a hand to his brow, and it took a few moments for his eyes to readjust to the crisp, winter light: it was Luke and Mel; he saw that they were holding hands.

'It was getting a bit stuffy in there,' Mel said. 'I needed some fresh air.'

James noticed an engagement ring on Mel's hand. 'You two didn't hang about! Congratulations.'

'Cheers, guv,' Mel said, then, after a pause, 'MCU isn't the same without you. Mind if I sit down?'

'Of course. Sorry,' James said. He shuffled along the bench and gestured to the warm patch he'd vacated. Mel dropped down onto the bench and Luke remained standing, hopping from foot to foot to stay warm.

'That your wife's grave?' Luke asked.

James nodded.

'Sorry,' Luke said.

Mel turned to James: 'Mind if I ask a question?'

'When have I ever stopped you?'

'I can think of a few times,' she laughed. 'What do you think Ruth would say to you now, seeing you here like this?'

He paused for a moment, then said: 'Stop moping about. Sort yourself out.'

'I didn't know her, obviously, but it sounds to me like she'd want you to be happy. I reckon she'd tell you to let go of the past; embrace the future.'

'The future's a scary place, Mel.'

Mel's hand hovered over James's leg for a second, then she clearly decided better of it and pulled back. 'There's only one way to overcome your fears,' she said. 'Confront them.'

James remained silent.

'We'd better get back in, guv. You going to the reception at Murdoch's house, after the service?'

'It's not really my scene.'

'Well, then you take care.'

Luke extended a hand to Mel, which she grabbed, and pulled her to her feet.

'Any news on Brady's wife?' James said, apropos of nothing.

'Yelena?' Luke said. 'Completely disappeared. We suspect she's fled to Russia, but of course the authorities there aren't playing ball. Expect she'll never be brought to justice.'

'Shame,' James said.

Luke smiled placidly, then turned as Mel threaded her arm into his. James watched as the happy couple slowly made their way back to the church.

'Wait!' he shouted.

They stopped and glanced over their shoulders.

'I've never thanked you, Luke.'

'For what?'

'Saving my life.'

Luke smiled. 'Just doing my job, guv. Catch you later.'

FORTY-TWO

MOLLY HAD a mental image of life in a women's prison, which she would happily admit had been forged by gritty, post-watershed ITV dramas: hardened offenders roaming the landings in orange jumpsuits; trivial arguments escalating rapidly into canteen-destroying riots; dangerous characters with time on their hands and axes to grind, lurking in dark corners; power-crazed guards inflicting petty torments in the dead of night. A shiver rippled down Molly's spine, when she imagined herself sharing a dirty bunk with a schizophrenic lesbian psycho serving life for murder. How would she ever cope? She wouldn't. She couldn't. The only way out would be suicide. Or escape. She closed her eyes; pictured herself slithering like a salamander through effluent and discarded sanitary products, along an almost endless sewage pipe, emerging breathless and thirsty into a moonlit night on a dirty shingle beach.

She opened her eyes and found herself back in the visitors' room. Two tables away from her there was now a couple sitting opposite each other – a mismatched pairing if ever she'd seen one. He – the visitor – was a weasel of a man: bald head, buck teeth, monobrow, lips as thin as cotton thread, beaky nose… When God handed out good looks this poor fella had clearly been at the back of the queue. Behind his ear there was a badly drawn tattoo: a dragonfly? He took off his black, leather jacket and draped it over the hard plastic chair. Under it he wore a Black Sabbath t-shirt and his scrawny, pasty forearm sported another tattoo: an amateurish heart and arrow with *'M + S'* inked underneath. Molly chuckled inwardly; she doubted it was a homage to Marks and Spencer. Martin and Susan? Miles and Sadie? Marvin and Sandy? Yes, that was it, she decided.

Sandy was a great brute of a woman. Her thunderous thighs, too fat to fit under the table, were splayed at an unnatural angle. Great rolls of blubber cascaded from her torso, threatening to burst free from her clothing at any moment. She leaned in towards Marvin and her stomach shoved the table forwards. She clamped her huge hands around his ears and, as if she were lifting the F.A. cup, pulled his face to her plump, moist lips. It was less the romantic gesture of a lovesick jailbird and more the desperate act of a ravenous human cannibal; Molly was reminded of the nature programme she'd watched a while back, about sexual cannibalism – transfixed, she was. Surprisingly common in a number of spiders, scorpions and mantids, it turns out. Take the female praying mantid, for example: devours its mate in thirty per cent of sexual encounters; starts with the head and works her way down, but leaves the chap's reproductive bits intact, to allow him to keep on copulating. Brings a whole new meaning to the phrase 'mindless sex'. It all had a kind of macabre logic to it, Molly supposed. She wondered whether some of the guys she'd encountered over the years would have tried it on with her, if they'd been faced with a thirty per cent chance of being eaten alive. Probably. Apparently, those mantids were more likely to eat the males if they were hungry and skinny at the time. The males here seemed to have cottoned on to this fact, and were more attracted to the chunkier ladies. Perhaps Marvin was just playing it safe, after all?

A distant metallic slam jolted Molly; a grumpy-looking prison guard was escorting Kathy Gibbs to her. The cacophony of prison noises – ubiquitous chatter, hollered reprimands, jangled keys, scraped chairs – jabbed like a headache. Molly had wanted a private room, but apparently that would have involved more bureaucratic hurdles. She had to treat this as a personal visit, which meant that no recording equipment was permitted and their conversation had to remain confidential. Right now, she was just grateful for the opportunity to persuade Kathy that she had grounds for appeal.

After Kathy had sat down and they'd exchanged awkward greetings, Molly suddenly found herself uncharacteristically tongue-tied. She thought of enquiring how Kathy was finding prison life, but the answer was already there in Kathy's haunted eyes, her pallid skin, her bitten nails. Was there the faint outline of a black eye, too? Kathy looked like a dowdy, world-weary old aunt, and not a crazed killer. Molly felt a pang of guilt for all the sensationalist crap she'd written about her.

'You're the one who called me the "bunny boiler", aren't you?' Kathy said, as if reading Molly's mind.

Molly felt her cheeks flush. 'Yes, I'm sorry about that. Please forgive me. Those lurid headline days are behind me; I'm a serious investigative journalist now. I'm here because I want to help you.'

'Well,' Kathy said, 'it's the first time I've ever been compared to Glenn Close.' She broke into a smile.

'Besides, the rabbit stew was done in the slow cooker; I'd hardly call it boiling.'

'Point taken,' Molly said. 'I assume Mark explained why I wanted to see you?'

'Yes, he mentioned something about "coercive control"? I'm not sure how it helps me, though; surely it doesn't mean that women like me are free to murder their husbands?'

Kathy's lower lip began to wobble and she bit it. 'No, that's not how it works. It wasn't a specific offence when you pleaded guilty, but now it's on the statute book. If we can prove your mental functions were diminished by years and years of John's coercive control, your conviction may be reduced to manslaughter. It's worth a shot, don't you think?'

'There's nothing wrong with my mental functions; I knew what I was doing when I fetched that knife: I intended to kill him, and I've had to live with the burden of that decision every day since. How could there have possibly have been an injustice? I deserve to be here.'

Kathy's eyes welled with tears and Molly squeezed her hand. She recognized self-loathing when she saw it; it had plagued Molly for much of her adult life. 'John wasn't the only victim, Kathy; you were, too. The boys told me how John treated you.'

'I loved him; he was my world. I still love him.'

'I know, and that makes you a good person. I've had dozens of women write to me, some of them in not dissimilar situations to you, Kathy. I understand why you did what you did to John. And, hey, let's not allow ourselves to paint all women as the victims; there are plenty of men who've suffered at the hands of controlling women. Take my bloody mother, for instance – dead now, thankfully: she drove my father out of my life with her domineering, controlling behaviour; I last saw him when I was seven. Don't let this drive you away from your boys, Kathy. They love you – they told me so… Well, not in so many words; you know what men are like when it comes to expressing their emotions.'

The prison guard sauntered past their table, giving Molly a judgemental look. Molly flashed a mirthless smile in reply.

Over at Marvin and Sandy's table, the conversation appeared to be getting a little heated. Sandy grabbed the fabric of Marvin's t-shirt and pulled him towards her. A guard pounced and gave Sandy a warning. She let go of Marvin and he recoiled into his chair.

Kathy sighed: 'My mother hated me, too. I was the only girl; she showered all her love on my brothers. I have four. They were either academic or sporty – some of them both; all of them are in successful careers now. She said I'd amount to nothing, that no man would ever desire me. I wanted to prove her wrong by being a good wife… a good mother.'

'And you are a good mother,' Molly said; 'your boys are a credit to you, Kathy. If you really were a heartless, cold-blooded murderer, do you think Mark would have bothered contacting me, begging me to help you? We need to get you out of here to be with them, for their sake as much as yours. That's got to be worth fighting for, hasn't it?'

Molly became aware of a commotion at Marvin and Sandy's table: 'And that gives you the right to screw my fucking sister?!' Sandy sprang to her feet, sending her chair clattering across the floor. Two guards ('*screws*' – that was the lingo, wasn't it?) ran over and heaved her, screaming like a banshee, back into the bowels of the prison. Marvin skulked out with his tail between his legs. At least he would live to see another day.

The room soon settled back into hushed chatter.

'So, what would I have to do?' Kathy said.

'First thing's first: I should put you in touch with a lawyer I know, Theresa Bartlett. She's the best in the business. She'll be able to arrange a confidential meeting with you, in a more convenient and private environment. Then, I'd imagine, she'll have you referred to a psychologist; they'll make an evaluation of the state of your mental health at the time of the incident. Hopefully, then, she will build the case for an appeal. How does that sound?'

'How long will it take?'

'I don't know; the wheels of justice turn slowly. That's why you want someone like Theresa on your side: if anyone can make things happen, she can.'

Kathy cast a look around her. 'I suppose I've nothing to lose.'

'That's the spirit. I'll be with you every step of the way.'

A guard hollered that visiting time was coming to an end.

'Do you think one day you'd be able to talk to me, about some of your experiences living with John?' Molly asked Kathy. 'If we can get your story out there, it may encourage others to seek help.'

'I don't think I'm ready for that yet,' Kathy replied. She shuffled to her feet.

'Well, whenever you're ready, I'll be there with a sympathetic ear. I promise.'

FORTY-THREE

JAMES'S DILEMMA was something akin to physical torture. He'd brooded about the situation ever since Murdoch revealed the truth, nearly two weeks earlier. Murdoch had put him in a position whereby, whichever decision he made, he was complicit in an injustice. James's insomnia had roared back to life, and this time he was insufficiently busy with work to distract himself from the torment. Molly had returned to London, immersed in her own work and, besides, he hadn't felt it appropriate to converse with her about it on the phone.

Brady was dead and Murdoch, it seemed, was a man broken by grief and guilt. Was that justice? Perhaps not in the legal sense, but maybe it was a form of natural justice? Was that a purer kind? As for Perkins, he was serving life for a crime he hadn't committed. All appeal attempts had failed, as there were no grounds on which the jury's verdict might be considered unsafe.

But Perkins's innocence of the particular crime he'd been convicted of was a mere technicality, wasn't it? He *was* guilty, just of a different murder. A hideous, depraved murder.

Wasn't he?

James's rock-solid conviction that Perkins was guilty had now taken a battering. A seed of doubt had been sown.

What to do now? Supposing he shopped Murdoch for the cover-up, what then? Perkins would walk free, for sure, and he'd have just cause to sue the Force. The scandal would hit the national press, and public confidence in the police would surely plummet. And, what about Perkins? After receiving a huge sum in compensation, would he just slip away, live the quiet life of a Trappist monk?

Fat chance!

He'd be emboldened. The police wouldn't dare go anywhere near him. For all intents and purposes, he'd be above the law. What if he was the murderer? Free to commit another depraved and monstrous act on an inno-cent woman? If he did, James wouldn't be able to live with himself.

So, that was that; his decision was made: justice had been served. Imperfect, but justice nonetheless. He'd go and tell Murdoch his decision. If the man still wanted to confess, that was up to him.

James pulled up on Murdoch's drive after dark.

His was the only car there, so James assumed the funeral reception had finished. Had it not, he would have turned straight back.

There were no lights on at the front of the house. James guessed that Murdoch was either in the kitchen, nursing a glass of Scotch, or had perhaps taken himself to bed for an early night. That's precisely what he had done after the tortuous reception he felt obliged to hold after Ruth's funeral. He shuddered at the memory.

James was poised to ring the doorbell when he noticed a low grumble. An idle engine? He looked back to the road, but there were no cars about. He followed the noise around the side of the house, and along a short stretch of gravel to Murdoch's garage. Fumes, tinged red, seeped through the gaps around the twin timber doors. It took James only seconds to register what was happening.

He pulled at the doors, but they were locked. He quickly looked around the perimeter of the garage for alternative forms of entry, but there were no other doors or windows. James pounded his fist against the doors. 'Murdoch!' he yelled. He wondered momentarily whether he should try to get in the house and look for a garage key, but figured time was not on his side, so he rushed back to the Audi and grabbed the prybar from the boot. He hacked furiously at the lock.

Suddenly, from inside, a continuous car horn sounded.

'Selfish bastard!' James muttered, as he continued to hack and pound and lever with the prybar. Eventually, the lock gave out and he swung open the doors.

The interior of the garage was initially a dense fog of exhaust fumes and only the rear lights penetrated it. Then, as the fumes began to disperse into the open air, James saw the hosepipe and yanked it out of the Jaguar's exhaust. Lifting his coat collar to the bridge of his nose and holding his breath, he fought his way to the driver's door. Murdoch's head was slumped against the steering wheel.

James opened the door, reached in to turn off the engine, then grabbed the fabric of Murdoch's jumper in both hands and desperately tried to yank him out. As his head flopped away from the steering wheel, the deafening car horn ceased. Although the Super had clearly lost a significant amount of bulk, it took all of James's strength to heave the dead weight free of the car, and drag him out of the building.

As soon as they were outside, James allowed himself to breathe. Despite the freezing air invading his lungs, his chest felt like it was on fire. He dropped to his knees and gulped in more and more air; tried to steady his breathing. He was damned if he would allow Murdoch to be the cause of another heart attack!

Suddenly, Murdoch began to cough and splutter. His eyes opened and registered James's presence. 'You should have left me,' he wheezed.

James felt incapable of speaking. He rolled onto his back and clutched his chest, willing its rise and fall to calm. Above him, the huge, black sky was speckled with stars; he felt small and insignificant – a speck of dust.

He turned to face Murdoch. 'Time for the truth, Ian,' he panted: 'you knew Gibbs and Brady were part of the Solent network all along, didn't you? You took their dirty money and helped them cover their tracks in return. All that misery, the ruined lives, the deaths... for what? A holiday home in a subtropical climate and a fancy painting above the fireplace? Well, I hope it was all worth it.'

Murdoch took a long breath, then said: 'I'm so sorry.' James watched a tear roll down Murdoch's cheek and drop onto the gravel.

Seconds later, he heard rushed footfall and voices behind him.

'Whatever's happened?'

'Oh, my god.'

'Ian?'

'Someone call an ambulance, for Christ's sake!'

James turned back to face the sky, seeking solace in the infinite cosmos.

The next morning, James was out on a long run: a gentle, steady pace, on a flat route through open farmland. There was a keen breeze and a light drizzle, and the doctor's orders (*"Don't overdo it!"*) ringing in his ears.

He'd done more than ten miles when he felt a buzzing in his pocket. He pulled out his phone to see that it was Murdoch. James felt strangely calm, all things considered. He stepped onto the verge to take the call.

'Ian. You still in hospital?'

'Just been released; no harm done. They put me on oxygen and kept me under observation overnight. Told me I was never at any risk of killing myself: catalytic converter, you see? I can't even get that right.'

'You're not going to try anything else stupid, are you?'

'No, James. Not unless you count confessing everything to the police as stupid.'

A white van zoomed past, spraying James with dirty rainwater and buffeting him with its downdraft.

'James?'

'There's not much I can say, is there?'

'Guess not. You know this means Perkins will be released, don't you?'

'Really? It hadn't occurred to me,' he said, dryly.

Murdoch gave a wry laugh. 'Don't go near him with a barge pole; let the Cold Case boys handle it.'

'Of course, 'cos they did such a sterling job last time! Look, I have no intention of getting involved; I've moved on with my life. You sure you're ready for prison? They're bound to throw the book at you, and it won't exactly be a bed of roses inside for a bent senior copper.'

'It's no more than I deserve. Time to face up to the consequences.'

James became aware that he was shivering. He should get moving again, get a sweat on.

'Well,' Murdoch said, 'goodbye, James.'

'Goodbye, sir.'

James ended the call, put his phone back in his pocket and started running. In no time at all he was breaking seven-minute-mile pace.

FORTY-FOUR

It was a Saturday, and Molly was feeling overjoyed to be back in Datchworth. She turned the key and stepped inside the cottage.

The temperature inside was the same as out: bloody freezing. She rushed straight through to the kitchen, to fire up the boiler.

It was only then that she realized how grubby and unloved the place looked: the walls were marked and discoloured, the light switches were surrounded by dirty fingerprints and the carpet was covered in various stains – she shuddered to think what they might be. The place smelled of cooking oil and cheap air freshener. Of other people. It felt like the cottage's soul had been ripped out. It was no longer a home – merely a house. It had only been tenanted for a few months, but it looked as if it had been years.

Molly sighed sadly and wandered back into the living room. She made a mental list of the things she'd need to do, before arranging for her furniture to be brought back out of storage: top of the list was contacting the bloody rental agents to get the place professionally cleaned, at the tenants' expense.

Molly looked towards the front window. Underneath it was a pile of newspapers and junk mail, stacked lazily in the exact spot where Mr Darcy's chair had stood.

Her little munchkin.

Despite the radiators clanking into life, the room suddenly felt much colder. Smaller, too. Her head began to fill with feelings of self-doubt and regret, about giving up her London lifestyle and returning to the sticks. She felt a desperate need to get outside, into the garden for a cigarette.

As Molly opened the back door, she saw that the tenants had sealed the cat flap with duct tape. Perhaps she should get rid of the cat flap entirely; what was the point in keeping it now? She stepped outside and her heart sank: her beautiful cottage garden was a matted mess of over-grown plants and dormant winter weeds. She looked to the back fence and felt a chill shudder down her spine, remembering that day he was taken from her.

It had been three days since Troy Perkins's release. The thought had crossed her mind that he might come and pay her a visit, but apparently he was starting a new life in Scotland. Molly wasn't sure whether she believed that. She reached up to the deadbolt, to check that it was securely fastened.

She lit a cigarette and took a deep drag, then turned to survey the messy garden again. The nicotine had an instant calming effect, and Molly was able to see the situation from a more positive perspective; the house and garden were only small; she would have them restored to their former glory in no time.

A speck of silver caught her eye, in what used to be the herb patch. She cautiously pushed her way through a thicket of brambles to see what it was: a can of Fanta. Nice change from Red Bull, she supposed. She smiled to herself and thought of James Quinn. She wondered what he was doing right now. He hadn't responded to her email about the article. Typical James. Had he even read it? There was no telling, with him.

For some godforsaken reason she missed the miserable old bugger. Perhaps she could get him to come round to help tidy the place? It would give her an excuse to talk with him about the situation with the Gibbs appeal, and the fallout from Ian Murdoch's revelation. She took out her phone and sent him a text.

Molly was surprised to get a near-instant response, but she wasn't particularly surprised that it was a terse *'no'*; busy at work, apparently. She wasn't so sure about that.

'Okay,' she texted back, *'maybe another day then? Take care x.'*

He sent another text thanking her for the article, and she figured he must have felt a pang of guilt at being short with her. Progress, for him. She took another long drag on her cigarette.

'Molly?'

The voice came from next door. Tom. He stood against the dividing fence. Despite the cold, his grey hoodie was unzipped, exposing a tight-fitting, black t-shirt; Molly guessed he'd recently been to the gym. 'Tom. Hi.'

'Are you moving back, then?' he said. She would swear there was a hint of hope in his question.

'Yes,' she said, 'got tired of living in a soulless flat in London; missed this place. How's Becky?'

Tom's smile dropped. 'She moved out a while back. Things turned a bit nasty.'

'Oh, shame,' Molly said. She wondered why Becky was the one moving out and not Tom. Perhaps she'd done the dirty on him. The cheating bitch. Molly never did warm to the woman.

Tom looked out across Molly's garden. 'Let me know if you need any help settling back in.'

'Well… actually,' Molly said, never one to look a gift horse in the mouth, 'that would be a ma*hoosive* help, if you could.'

FORTY-FIVE

IT HAD BEEN YET another night of fitful sleep.

James stood staring aimlessly out of the living room window, coffee mug in hand. What to do today? The prospect of another endless day moping around the house with thoughts of Perkins' release swirling around his head was too much to bear. He needed to *feel* busy, even if he wasn't.

He took a sip of coffee and winced. It was now stone cold so he set it down on the window sill, next to the photograph. He stared at Urtė's pretty, innocent face for so long that it became a blur. Then he shifted his gaze to the walls, the ceiling, the carpet. Perhaps he could redecorate? He decided then that would be his project for the next few weeks: to redecorate the house. Perhaps he could pop out now to one of the DIY stores and choose the colour scheme? That was never his forte. He was always happy for Ruth to make those kinds of decisions.

James looked at his watch, even though time had precious little meaning now; he had oodles of it. It occurred to him that he hadn't checked his emails since

Thursday. Perhaps there was a juicy new request for help waiting for him in his inbox? He trudged upstairs and settled himself at the desk in the box room he'd converted to a home office. The room that would have been the nursery. The room that was still painted vanilla sundae.

His computer loaded up and he opened his email programme. There was just the one, from Molly, written yesterday.

'Hi James. You okay? Hope you don't mind but I've penned an article about Urtė and it's on our website. Click on the link below. I managed to convince my editor that I could use her story as a case study in a broader piece about modern slavery and human trafficking. We get over 5 million people reading our site each day (slightly bigger reach than the Hertfordshire Evening Herald, huh?). Fingers crossed. You never know, it might spark a memory or generate a new lead. Can't do any harm? Take care now, M.'

James smiled at Molly's tenacity and thoughtfulness – and the small hint of an ego trip. He clicked the link, sank into his chair and read through the article. He had to admit to himself, she could certainly write well; her talents were wasted at the *Herald*. Thank god she turned down the job at the tabloid and went for the opportunity at the *Chronicle* instead. As he neared the end, his phone pinged and he saw that it was a text from Molly. Was she telepathic?

'Have you seen my email? I'm back in Datchworth at the cottage. Turfed out the awful tenants. Got the keys this morning. Place is a right state! Fancy coming over to help clear up the mess? There's a pub lunch in it for you. Won't inflict my cooking on you again! M. x'

. . .

He felt a warm flutter in his stomach. Should he? Something held him back: his own stubbornness, for one, not wanting to be seen to dance to her tune. But there was something else too: a feeling that he was somehow being disloyal to Ruth. He sent a reply: *'Sorry. Busy at the moment.'*

Her response was almost instant. *'Okay, maybe another day then? Take care x'*

James felt a pang of guilt for giving such a terse response, after she'd gone to the effort of writing the article. He tapped another message: *'Thanks for doing the article by the way. Appreciate your help.'* He paused for a moment, contemplating whether to add a kiss, but thought better of it and hit send.

He got up and slouched around the first-floor rooms, making rough calculations of how many tins of emulsion he might need for the walls, but kept losing count as his thoughts drifted to Molly, to Perkins, to Ruth, to Urtė.

The rattle of the letterbox from downstairs startled him.

He went down and found a postcard lying on the mat. A scene of Edinburgh castle at sunset. Who could it be from? No one sent postcards these days. Perhaps it was junk mail, a marketing ploy? He turned it over.

'Hi James. Guess you heard about my release? I know what you're thinking but I'm not bitter about being sent down for something I didn't do. Had a lot of time to think inside. Found God, would you believe it? I just want to live the rest of my life in peace, start a new life up here in Scotland. Please don't come looking for me. For what it's worth, I'm sorry about your wife. I didn't mean her any harm. That's the honest truth. Take care and god bless. Troy.'

. . .

James slumped onto the bottom stair. What to make of that? He was sceptical about the God thing. About the apparent contrition. Wouldn't trust Perkins as far as he could throw him. But he had no intention of going after him; he'd paid too heavy a price for that obsession and nothing was going to bring Ruth back. He had no choice but to leave it in the hands of the Cold Case team. Thankfully, he'd learned Luke Porter was now part of the team. If anyone could find something to hang Lena Demyan's murder on Perkins, Luke was the man to do it.

James headed to the kitchen bin and ripped the postcard in to tiny pieces.

Later that day, he was driving back home with a bootful of paint and decorating equipment; he'd finally accepted there was sod all else to keep him busy. There had been a special offer on a shade of matt emulsion called *'Pearl Grey'*. He imagined Molly's reaction to his colour choice: *Boring as hell.*

Thinking of her now made him realize how selfish and pig-headed he'd been. All she'd asked for was a bit of help tidying her house and what was his response: to tell her he was too busy, when he wasn't. *Knobhead.* That's what Mel Barraclough would have called him. She'd have grabbed him by the lapels, shook him, told him to kick his stupid male ego out of the window and get his sorry arse over to Datchworth. Pronto.

He turned on the radio, which was still on the station Molly had tuned it to a couple of weeks' back; some hideously cheerful Spice Girls track was playing. James turned up the volume and, before long, he found himself almost involuntarily tapping the steering wheel and mouthing the catchy chorus. He smiled inwardly and imagined the words would be stuck in his head for weeks to come.

As he approached the edge of town, a brightly painted sign at the side of the road caught his eye. Should he?

He turned in.

What the hell, you only live once.

He stood at Molly's doorstep, holding the box and praying for her to answer, so that he could get out of the freezing cold. Her Evoque was parked on the road, so he was sure she was in. He rang the bell again. Moments later, there was the sound of hurried footsteps from inside. The door opened.

'Oh, James, I wasn't expecting you.' Molly cast a nervous look over her shoulder, before turning back to James. She regarded the box for a second, with a puzzled expression. He noticed the top button of her blouse was undone; maybe he'd disturbed a midday snooze?

'Sorry, have I caught you at a bad time?'

'No, no, I was just… cleaning the mess in the kitchen; right state. What's in the box?'

'Oh, it's just a little something… to welcome you back. Sorry, I realized what a twat I'd been earlier. I really appreciate you writing that article about Urtė. You didn't have to, you know. Hey, it's brass monkeys out here; any chance I can come in?'

As Molly went to speak, James heard footsteps from within the house. Moments later, the figure of a tall man loomed behind her, his head slouched to avoid clouting a beam. Molly tucked a stray lock of hair behind her head and gave an embarrassed smile. The man smiled at James.

'Sorry,' James said, trying to disguise any emotion in his voice, 'I've disturbed you. Maybe another time?'

Molly looked down at the box. 'That for me?'

A flush of embarrassment radiated across his cheeks. 'Er, no… My mistake. Stupid, really. Better be heading back, I suppose. Leave you two to it.'

He turned and walked towards the Audi. He should have known it was a bad idea to go against his instincts. He felt stupid, foolish. There was a higher calling to attend to: his mission to find Urtė, to fulfil Ruth's dying wish; this was no time for frivolity.

'James, wait,' Molly shouted. 'It's not what it looks like.'

He didn't glance back; he couldn't have her reading his emotions. He tucked the box under one arm and fumbled in his trouser pocket for the key fob.

He heard the erratic click-clack of heels, as she tottered down the garden path in his direction. He rolled his eyes and allowed himself a brief smile. Rearranging his face into inscrutability, he turned to Molly. Behind her, the tall man was stepping over the dividing fence, into the front garden next door.

'Yes?' he said, brusquely.

'Sorry,' Molly said, as she closed the front door behind James. 'That was Tom, my neighbour; offered to help me get the place straight. I didn't think you were going to come.' She gestured to the living room.

'See what you mean about the place,' James said, surveying the scene. 'I've seen more attractive crack dens.'

'That meant to make me feel better?'

'Sorry,' James said, 'still working on that small-talk thing.'

Inside, the radiators were blasting out heat and the

place felt horribly claustrophobic and stuffy. He carefully placed the box on the floor, then took off his jacket and draped it over the arm of the sofa.

'Aren't you going to tell me what's in that bloody box, then?' Molly said.

James's stomach had begun to growl, and he used the opportunity of Molly's momentary distraction to pop a surreptitious mint into his mouth. 'Oh yes, sorry; open it, please. Be careful, though!'

Molly waggled her fingers, excitedly. 'Ooh, intriguing,' she said. Her eyes narrowed and she turned to James: 'And stop bloody saying sorry; can't stand apologizers.'

'You said it your sodding self, a minute ago,' he said. But Molly wasn't listening; she was on her knees, crouched over the box, tentatively pulling back the cardboard flaps.

'Oh, my god!' she gushed, bringing her hands to her mouth.

'I can take it back if it's inappropriate. Don't know what came over me, really.'

Molly turned to him and spoke in a deep voice: 'Don't you dare!' She plunged her hands into the box and they emerged holding the mewing kitten. She snuggled its grey fur against her cheek.

'Like it, then?'

'I bloody love him.' She tickled the cat under its chin. 'Assume it's a boy?' She turned it upside down and smiled; 'Yep!'

Molly set the cat down on the carpet and watched him tentatively exploring his new environment for a moment. Then she came over to James and put her arms around his shoulders, pulling him down so his head was at her level, their faces inches apart.

'Thank you,' she said, beaming. 'I don't think anyone's ever been so thoughtful to me.'

Their gazes met. He closed his eyes for a moment and breathed in the scent of perfume and cigarette smoke. He opened them again to see her lashes flutter, almost imperceptibly. Neither spoke; James swallowed his mint. It must only have been seconds, but they felt like minutes, as their lips drew closer. She dropped her arm from his shoulder, and he felt her hand lightly squeeze his. He felt the faintest brush of her lips.

Almost involuntarily, he snapped his head to the side, and Molly planted a peck on his cheek.

'Right,' she said, flicking a stray lock behind her ear. 'Er… hungry? We can't have you working on an empty stomach.' She made her way to the kitchen. 'I picked up a few packets of sarnies in Sainsbury's, on the way over; special offer: egg, I think.'

'Egg?'

Molly rummaged in a bag on the countertop. 'Yep, egg. That a problem? Not allergic, are you?'

'Got this condition: extreme sensitivity to smells. Had it since… well… since Ruth died. Thanks for the offer, though. Don't worry, I'm not really hungry, in any case.'

'Oh, so that's what the mint thing's all about? Grief does funny things, I suppose. Cup of tea, then?'

'Sure.'

James sank into the sofa and thrummed his fingers on his knee, while Molly boiled the kettle. The action had the effect of drawing the kitten's attention, and it bounded over to him, disarmed him with the cutest look, then sank its claws into his shin. 'Ah, bugger off!' he cried, kicking out desperately. The cat remained steadfast.

'Whatever is it?' Molly called out.

'Bloody mog's clamped itself to my leg. Got claws like sodding razor blades! Look at it!'

Molly giggled at the spectacle. 'It's a sign of affection. Didn't you know?'

'Really?' James said, as he finally prised off the cat and threw it in the direction of the cardboard box.

Molly came over with a couple of mugs and handed one to James, then seated herself next to him.

'Seems to like it there, in Mr. Darcy's spot,' she said, nodding towards the window, where the kitten was bouncing merrily in and out of the box. 'What do you think I should call the little fella?'

'How about Freddy Krueger?'

'Not sure about that. Think I'll sleep on it.'

She took a sip of tea and her expression changed to concern. 'Hey, you don't think Perkins is going to cause us any more bother, do you?'

'Funny you should say that,' James said: 'he sent me an email.'

Horror flashed across Molly's face.

'Don't worry, I doubt he'll be bothering us anytime soon. He'll want to keep his head down, pursue his compensation claim. His message was, basically, stay out of my business and I'll stay out of yours.'

'And, will you…' she said, 'stay out of his business?'

'Whose business?' James smiled and raised his palms. 'See? I've forgotten him already.'

Molly arched her brow, then prodded his chest. 'Just remember to look after your heart; your wellbeing is the most important thing, now. Leave all that business to the police.'

'This is getting a little too touchy-feely for my liking,' James said, looking to the window.

Thankfully, Molly seemed to take that as a cue to change topic. 'I ought to give the little chap something to eat. Don't suppose you bought any cat food?'

'Er… no. Sorry.'

'Men!' Molly tutted. 'Who'd have 'em?' She got to her feet. 'Don't think I've got anything suitable in… unless he likes an egg sarnie?'

'Aren't they supposed to be carnivores?'

'Joke, James. Joke.'

She went over to the box and looked inside, then back at James. 'Where's the rascal disappeared to?'

He shrugged. 'Hiding, to pounce on his next victim?'

Molly puckered her lips and made a cat-beckoning sound. She looked about the room, then headed to the kitchen. 'Puddycat! Here, puddycat!'

James winced.

A few moments later, Molly called out: 'Oh, God.'

'What is it?' James said, getting to his feet.

'I've been taking the duct tape off of Mr. Darcy's old cat flap. You don't think he could have got outside, do you?' She palmed her chest. 'He'll catch his bloody death out there.'

James rolled his eyes. 'I think he'd somehow cope, with all that fur.'

'I'll go and take a look,' Molly said, wrapping a coat around her shoulders; 'it'll be dark soon. Why don't you make yourself useful: check if he's gone upstairs?'

'You serious?' James said.

The rear door slammed shut, so he guessed the answer to that question was 'yes'. He sighed and trudged towards the stairs, cautiously stepping through the doorway into the hall, lest the sharp-clawed beast lay in wait on the other side.

All clear.

He climbed the rickety old staircase, cocking his head at an unnatural angle to avoid concussion. Ridiculous. At the top was a tiny square landing and three doors, all slightly ajar. He trained his ear for any sound of the kitten. Nothing. Was the little bugger poised to pounce?

James slammed his foot on the floorboards, then burst into the rear-facing room; the door bounced off a wall.

It was a small bedroom, bare except for a few boxes dumped in the centre of the floor. He flicked a look inside them to find no cat, just hordes of Molly's clothing: blouses, vests, bras, a silky negligee. He paused for perhaps a beat too long, before closing the flap of the last box, then made his way over to the window.

In the garden, Molly was bent over, sweeping her way through the overgrown plants. She held a cigarette in her hand and he watched, momentarily transfixed, as the bright red of the lit end moved haphazardly in the fading light.

James made his way back to the landing and did his stomping trick, before opening the middle door. The smell of wet socks and rotting wood informed him that it was a poorly ventilated bathroom. He needed a mint, fast. The room was in semi-darkness and he fumbled inside for the light switch, soon locating the cord. The light revealed a pink and gold suite: a toilet, washbasin and bath, with a mouldy shower curtain pulled across it. He stepped over to the bath and grabbed the curtain.

There was a faint scratching noise from within the bath. 'Gotcha, you little bugger!' He yanked back the curtain.

And immediately recoiled.

'Jesus Christ!' he hollered.

FORTY-SIX

Molly had scoured the garden, but couldn't find him anywhere. She hoped to God he was still inside. No doubt James would call out to her at any minute.

She was at the back fence, standing before the gate. The memory of the day of Mr. Darcy's abduction struck her. History wasn't repeating itself, was it? Surely not. She smiled at the ridiculousness of that thought.

Her eyes scanned the fence. Was a little kitten even capable of clambering over a barrier taller than she was? Molly took a deep drag on her cigarette, then looked down at her feet. There was a small gap under the gate – could he have squeezed through it? That question had never arisen with Mr. D, the bloody great sack of blubber that he was. Best check.

She unbolted the gate, squeezed open the latch and walked through it, into the bleak and empty expanse of the recreation ground. Not a soul in sight. A gust of wind sent a chill through her, and she turned up her collar.

After taking a last draw on her cigarette, she flicked the butt towards the huge trunk of the bare chestnut, immediately chastising herself for littering. Force of habit. *Bad Molly. Must try harder*. She waltzed over to the tree and reached down to pick up the butt.

As she did so, she heard a contented mewing from behind the tree. A warm smile broke out across her face and Molly sprung upright, ready to scoop the pesky little thing into her arms.

It was then that Troy Perkins emerged from behind the tree, holding the kitten and stroking its back with his gloved hand, like a Home Counties Ernst Blofeld.

Perkins's thin, ruby lips parted to reveal small, white teeth. 'Hello, Molly – long time no see. I have a big knife in my pocket, so I suggest you don't scream, there's a good girl.'

FORTY-SEVEN

JAMES GLARED AT THE RAT, mesmerized and repulsed in equal measure: a dirty, great beast of a thing, sniffing and shuffling around in the bathtub, which was peppered with brown, jellybean droppings. He figured the rodent must have been there for some time. But why? And how the hell had it got inside the house in the first place? There was an adage, wasn't there: no one's ever more than six feet away from a rat? He'd always believed that to be a load of old bollocks – not anymore. Perhaps the rest of its family were also in the house somewhere, lurking in dark corners? A shiver ran down his spine.

He thought for a moment of opening the back window and hollering out to Molly. No, she'd be appalled by the presence of the verminous creature in her cottage. He needed to grow some balls, fast: trap it and surreptitiously release it outside, then clean up the mess. She'd be none the wiser.

He made his way to the kitchen, and a search under the sink quickly yielded a dustpan and a bucket. He clambered back up to the bathroom and carefully placed the bucket on its side, in the centre of the bathtub. Then, he attempted to nudge the rat into the plastic trap with the dustpan. For some bizarre reason, the critter didn't want to play ball, and instead ran frantic circuits of the tub. Eventually, James lost his patience and walloped it one, as it came down the home straight. Suitably stunned – or dead – it scraped compliantly into the bucket. Bingo. Now to dispose of it, without Molly seeing.

Before heading outside, James stole a look from the back bedroom window. The gate at the garden fence was open, and he scanned the recreation ground beyond. No sign of life. How far away could the kitten have scarpered in that time? He needed to join Molly in the search.

When he flung open the kitchen door and stepped into the garden, the cold air struck him, almost taking his breath away. Clutching the bucket, he made his way across the garden and into the recreation ground. He took a quick look around. In the gloomy light, the far side of the rec was barely visible. 'Molly?' he hollered. No response.

He bent down and upended the bucket. The rat slid down the edge and plopped to the ground.

A rustling noise nearby startled him, and he looked up to see the kitten emerge from a bush. It ran over to jab playfully at the rat when, almost as if someone had waved smelling salts under the rat's nose, the creature burst back into life and lunged at the kitten, which let out a distressed mew, jumping perhaps a metre into the air. Sensing its escape opportunity, the rat scurried into the bushes. James scooped the kitten into his arms.

A pang of concern now gripped James. 'Molly?' he shouted, into the gloom. Where the hell was she? He reached for the phone in his jacket pocket, but realized he wore only a thin shirt; his coat was back in the house. He stepped towards the horse chestnut, scratching his head, and noticed her smouldering cigarette butt.

A faint whiff of something familiar caused his nose to twitch.

Oh, God!

No.

Cheap cologne.

Perkins.

There was no doubt about it.

Holding the kitten tightly under his arm, he spun on the spot, shouting: 'Molly! Perkins!'

His eyes flitted about, trying to locate the route Perkins would have taken into and out of the rec. He saw a narrow gap between two cottage rows, and when he ran to it, he discovered a pathway which led back out to the road.

Ahead of him, perhaps a hundred metres away, was his Audi. He sprinted to it, scrambling for the key fob in his trouser pocket. As he approached the car, he zapped it open and threw the cat into the back seat – it let out a squawk of protest.

James started the engine and floored the accelerator. There was no time to lose.

FORTY-EIGHT

Molly swallowed the sour tang of bile, took a deep yoga breath and soberly assessed her prospects. It didn't take her long to reach the conclusion that they were bleak. She yanked her cuffed wrist one more impotent time, away from the door handle to which she was tethered; the slack cuffs became instantly taut, and pain rippled up her arm.

'Relax, Molly,' Troy Perkins said, his voice a sinister whisper. 'Perhaps some classical music would help?'

He reached over to turn on the radio, and odours of rotten egg and cheap musk washed over her. She went to stifle the gag reflex, but when she saw that her hand was trembling, she quickly hid it under her thigh. Buggered if she was going to expose her fear to a madman with halitosis and a dreadful taste in aftershave.

Perkins momentarily released his grip from the steering wheel, to finger a tune on an invisible piano. '"Clair De Lune." Do you like Debussy, Molly?'

'Too depressing. I'm more of a 'seventies pop kind of girl.'

Perkins smiled and placed his hands back on the steering wheel. 'It's a shame things have to end like this,' he said, a wistful tone in his voice. 'I would never have gone anywhere near you if you hadn't got yourself entwined in Quinn's obsession.'

Molly sensed his eyes running up and down the length of her torso. 'You see, I like lamb,' he sniffed and wiped his nose with the back of his hand, 'not mutton.'

'Cat, too?' Molly said assertively, not wanting to register the hurt.

Perkins threw back his head and laughed. Molly felt tears welling and she closed her eyes.

When the tears abated, she opened her eyes to find herself in near darkness. Ahead of them, the Peugeot's headlights illuminated a narrow country road, devoid of any other traffic. She flicked her gaze to the wing mirror, and saw the streetlights which marked the perimeter of the village disappearing from view. Her home. Her sanctuary. She knew she'd never see it again. She clung to the sight, until the last ember dissolved into blackness.

Troy Perkins pressed hard on the accelerator, pushing Molly into her seat. 'I'm sure you can guess where we're heading?' he said. 'A bright girl like you?'

Molly's mind flicked to Bunyan's Dell. Black-and-white images flashed through her brain: the grisly tableaus of Lena Demyan, Daniela Sirota, Mr. Darcy. Fear squeezed her heart.

She looked in the mirror once more, and found herself praying to see the headlights of a silver Audi, speeding to the rescue. There was nothing. Was James even aware she was gone?

The thought that Perkins was snatching a happy future from her, at the very moment it was finally within her grasp, ignited a spark of anger in her belly. She turned to

Perkins: 'If you hurt me, James will hunt you down and tear your limbs off one by one, you sick fucker!' Flecks of spittle sprayed over him.

Keeping his eyes on the road, he ran his hand down his cheek. He looked at his finger and broke into a broad smile. 'I didn't realize you two were an item; thought he had better taste in women. But, hey, I guess grief does funny things to a man.'

Molly turned to look out of her window, trying to will herself to another place.

Perkins continued: 'Do you know how it feels to be locked up in prison for a crime you didn't commit, Molly?'

She briefly looked at him, arching her brow.

'Endless days trapped in a tiny cell, with these thoughts swirling round in your head.' He jabbed a finger into his chest. 'It eats away at you from the inside, I'm not going to lie. Leaves you with an overwhelming need for... now, what's the word... justice.

'When I got out I decided to move up to Scotland, start a new life, turn the page – that's the gods' honest truth. But, after a couple of days, I decided I didn't much care for the scenery up there; overrated, in my opinion, so I came back home. Found out about Quinny Boy's retirement; shame about the heart attack, eh? The poor thing! Anyway, I started watching him. Oblivious to my presence, he was – fucking amateur. Well, when I followed him to your place, that was a turn up for the books. And, when that *disgusting little beast* crawled out from under the gate, well, I thought all my Christmases had come at once...'

Molly couldn't contain her rage any longer. 'You bastard!' she shouted, and flung her fist at his chest. As quick as a flash, he grabbed her wrist in the firm grip of his left hand, and forced it back onto her lap.

'Relax,' he said; 'contain your excitement. We'll be there soon. Promise.'

He turned up the radio volume.

FORTY-NINE

THE TOYOTA in front of James slowed, as the traffic lights switched from green to amber. Without a moment's hesitation, he swung the Audi into the right-hand lane and floored the accelerator, crossing the junction just as the lights went red. A light sleet had begun to fall, and he flicked on the wipers.

A minute or so later he was out of the village, heading cross country on dark, narrow roads, in the direction of Wain Wood. He figured that must be where Perkins had taken her: the symbolism would be too much for him to resist.

Surely?

If he was wrong, she was as good as dead already. He should have alerted the police to cover other possibilities, but his bloody mobile phone was back in Molly's cottage; he couldn't risk losing any more time retrieving it, or otherwise seeking help. How much of a head start did Perkins have? All that time he was pissing around with the rat! Five minutes? Ten?

How and when had Perkins come to be stalking Molly

again? Had he followed James? Was James his intended target? Both of them? He pushed the questions to the back of his mind; there was nothing to be gained by asking them now. His only option was to dedicate all his energy to getting to the dell, as quickly as was humanly possible. He held no advantage over Perkins in terms of local route knowledge, but he had the much more capable car – time to put it to good use.

James flicked the headlights to full beam, gripped the steering wheel and channelled his inner Colin McRae.

FIFTY

THEY TURNED a bend and the headlights lit up a tractor, which was pulling out of a side road. Perkins slammed the horn and sped past. Molly looked in the wing mirror, to see the tractor driver flashing his lights in fury.

'Almost there, sweetheart,' Perkins said. 'Just this one last hill.'

The dark mass of Wain Wood loomed above them; Molly's heart pummelled against her chest. 'Don't call me sweetheart, you sad piece of shit!' Her voice cracked in her dry throat and she swallowed hard. She flicked her gaze to the rear-view mirror and he met her eyes. In that brief moment, she hoped he couldn't see through them, to the dark crater of bubbling fear which lay behind.

'As you wish,' he said, the quiet of his voice belying the evil in his soul.

The engine groaned as the incline steepened. Perkins shifted into a lower gear and his hand brushed against her thigh. A jolt of revulsion radiated through her, like electricity; she shifted position and turned away from him, to peer through the window, into the inky blackness.

Molly wished her heart would stop pounding; she feared Perkins might hear it, above the whining engine and squeaky beat of the wipers, battling against the heavy sleet.

The car accelerated as they emerged from the final bend. It wasn't visible, but Molly knew that on her side was a steep, grassy slope which led down to dense woodland. A flash of green in her peripheral vision snapped Molly's attention to the digital clock on the dashboard: another minute had ticked by. How many more minutes belonged to her future? Whatever the answer, she was gripped by a resolve that death was going to be on her terms, not his.

The headlights revealed a small gap in the hedgerow, metres in front of them. If she didn't act soon, her chance would be gone.

It was now or never.

'What's that?!' Molly hollered, as loud as her broken voice would allow.

Perkins flinched, and she took the opportunity of his brief confusion to grab the steering wheel and yank it hard, towards her. Perkins pushed her away and tried to regain control, but it was too late: the car mounted the verge and careered through the gap in the hedge.

Molly felt the sensation of the car leaving the ground. It could only have been for the briefest moment, but it was as if time had slowed to a dreamy crawl; an eerie silence stretched out around them. Two white cones pierced the sleety sky.

Then, a sickening metallic crunch snapped the illusion of floating, as Molly's head smashed against the roof. There was an awful snapping sound, which she couldn't be sure wasn't her neck; she felt no pain.

The car hurtled down the hill; its headlights revealed the faint outline of trees in the distance. Perkins gripped the wheel and desperately pumped at the brake, but gravity had taken charge.

'You fucking bitch!' he roared, above the whine of the engine, the juddering plastic, the crunching metal and the overworked suspension.

Molly shielded her face with her free arm, closed her eyes and braced her neck, as the car barrelled down the hill, bouncing and lurching over uneven ground, sliding on wet grass, all the while gathering more pace; it shook with such violence that Molly was sure it would disintegrate into its component pieces at any moment.

As if on cue, the windscreen popped and shattered. Cold, wet air blew in like a gale; Molly could barely breathe in the face of its ferocity. She dared to lower her arm and open her eyes, just in time to see a thick, gnarled tree trunk in the glare of the headlights.

And then... nothing.

FIFTY-ONE

JAMES TOOK the racing line around the final bend. Anyone coming in the opposite direction wouldn't stand a chance, but the odds of that were tiny; the roads were deserted.

The probability of Molly already being dead was infinitely greater.

As the Audi's tyres squealed through the apex, he glimpsed two red lights, high off the road in the near distance. He slammed the brakes. A tractor? Yes. Climbing the hill at a snail's pace.

Damn. The road was too narrow for him to pass.

He palmed the car horn and flashed his lights. 'Out of the fucking way!'

The tractor driver continued his leisurely ascent, unconcerned by James's plight. He sounded the horn again, pushed into the vehicle's slipstream. The tractor's left blinker came on and it mounted the verge. James did the same on the opposite side and powered past, his wing mirror clipping the huge rear tyre. The tractor driver hammered his horn, but James didn't care.

There were numerous routes through to the dell; he

had no idea which one Perkins preferred. James screeched to a halt outside the first he came to. A sole lamppost stood guard, casting down a cone of amber light, and he leapt out into the cold air.

As he went to slam the door, he heard a pained cry from within. The kitten jumped up onto the centre console, a petrified look in its eyes.

'Sorry, fella, I forgot all about you. Look after the car, won't you?'

He shut the door and went round to the boot, retrieving the Maglite and prybar. Then, he set off down the path.

It quickly became pitch dark and he switched on the torch. The sleet had turned to wet snow; the ground was thick with mud and riddled with puddles. He ran faster and faster, heavy footfall soaking his lower legs in freezing water, as he passed familiar shapes and features: the information sign; the fork in the path. Deeper into the trees, which provided more shelter from the wind, but not from the cold. Darker here, too.

There was rustling to his left. Too alert to be startled, he swung the torch in the direction of the sound. Two dots reflected back at him: a fox? Badger? No concern. It scurried off into the darkness. His heart knocked hard.

Deeper now, he passed the upended trunk, approaching the dell. He slowed to a brisk walk and caught his breath. Torch aimed low into the dell, he scrambled down the bank, treacherous with wet leaves and slick mud. Struggling to stay upright, he slid the last few metres to the bottom.

Get up.

He swept the torch about him: an oil drum, litter, the remains of a bonfire. With knees bent, prybar raised, he crept forward to the centre. He spun around. Stopped. Listened. Sniffed.

Nothing.

'PERKINS!? MOLLY!?'

No response.

Shit.

They're not here.

Where the fuck has he taken her?

FIFTY-TWO

MOLLY WOKE with a pained gasp into blinding light. She snapped shut her eyes, opening them again slowly into a squint, as they became accustomed.

The sound of distant ticking grew louder. A clock? No, this was slow, metallic, with an uneven beat. She couldn't work out what or where. Something else, too: hissing. Like steam escaping from a boiling kettle.

Where am I?

What's happened?

Suddenly aware of a dull ache in her temple, she raised her index finger and pressed it into a deep gash, warm and slick. *Not good.*

Convulsing with cold, her breath formed steam. She tried to draw her arms across her chest. There was a jangling sound and her left wrist snagged. She tugged, trying to overpower the resistance, but it was futile – and painful. She looked down, saw the cuff, the blood, and it all came back to her in a flash.

Molly was seeing everything at once: the missing windscreen, the tree trunk, the headlights beaming into the ghoulish woods…

Perkins!

She twisted her sore neck to face the driver's side, and there he was, his head slumped against the steering wheel, motionless. Lifeless? *Please, God, be dead!* How could she be sure? *Test his pulse.*

She released her seatbelt, then hesitantly prodded him, to see if he'd react. Nothing. Good sign. *Breathe, Molly.* She brought her index and middle finger together and pushed them under the collar of his jacket. A wave of revulsion passed through her when she made contact with the cold skin of his neck. Where was she supposed to check for a pulse? How hard to press? She was clueless. She tried various places and different pressures, then held her hand under his mouth. She felt nothing. But, then, she was almost numb with cold.

She couldn't trust that he was dead. She gave him another prod to his shoulder – harder, more assertive this time. Still no reaction.

She heard the hissing noise again. The ticking, too. Both sounds came from outside the car. Images from an American TV drama flashed through her brain: a car crushed under a truck; fuel leaking from the tank; *drip, drip, drip.* A distressed damsel plucked from a smashed window and dragged to safety, the mangled wreckage exploding into a giant fireball in the background. Chunks of hot metal raining down.

Oh, dear Jesus! It's a ticking timebomb! Get out!

But, how? She was cuffed.

The keys? Where are the fucking keys?!

Think. Stay calm.

His pockets.

Molly ran her hand over Perkins's puffer jacket. She

found an external pocket, zipped, and fumbled with her numb fingers to open it, cautiously sliding her hand inside. She felt something smooth and slimy, and pulled it out: a latex glove. She shuddered and discarded it, then plunged her hand back inside. Aside from the other glove, there was nothing.

To get to the opposite pocket, she had to push her hand under his slumped torso, twist her arm at an unnatural angle. Fortuitously, this pocket was partially unzipped. She probed inside. Nothing.

'Fuck!' she screamed, and punched his head, again and again. '*You fucking fucker!*'

His head fell away from her, dropping into the gap between the steering wheel and the driver's door; Molly jumped and held her breath. He was motionless.

She saw that his jacket had ridden up his torso, revealing his belt. Clipped to it was a pouch.

The cuff holder!

She lifted a velcro-fastened flap; the key had to be inside. *Please.*

Yes!

She had it.

Don't drop it, Moll, for Christ's sake!

Her heart knocked hard enough to shake her arms. The hole in the cuffs was tiny and it took several attempts to engage the key. She turned it, waggled it and *click*: she was free!

No time to rejoice. *Get out!* She pulled the door release, but it wouldn't open. Then, again: no response. *No!*

The windscreen – her only option for escape.

She couldn't feel her toes, her feet, her legs. Was she paralysed? Were her bones broken? No time to dwell. A primal instinct for survival and a surge of adrenalin took over. Feeling returned to her body. She manoeuvred herself into a squatting position on the seat – thank God she was small – then scrambled over the dash, through the shattered remains of the windscreen. She kicked out against the seat, landing on the crumpled bonnet, still warm to the touch. She heard the tick of cooling metal and snow falling. Struggling to gain purchase, writhing like a lizard, she willed herself forward: *Get away from the car! Fast!*

It was then that Molly felt his cold fingers curl around her ankle.

She let out a half-laugh, half-cry, and twisted her neck to look back into the car. His blood-soaked face was contorted into manic rage. His free hand was inching towards her other ankle. She kicked back hard, felt the heel of her shoe snap as it made contact with his face. He howled in pain, but didn't release his grip. She kicked again and again and again, until he finally let go.

She heaved herself forward, over to the edge of the bonnet, and dropped to the cold, wet ground. She got to her feet and kicked off her heels – no utility now.

Then, she ran.

Follow the light, into the trees, as deep as you can. Get away; just get away from him.

She ran through sodden ferns, over boggy ground, dodging logs and boulders. She brushed against gorse, barely registering pain. *Don't look back. Don't waste time.*

Darker now, the trees denser; out of the snow and out of the wind. She could hear only the sound of her own breathing. *Don't stop. Onwards, onwards, onwards.*

Her foot caught on something: a tree root? There was a ghastly snap: wood? Bone? There was no pain, but she buckled and fell flat on her face. *Get up! Get up!*

But she couldn't: her foot was trapped. She turned to

look at her ankle, then back towards the car. She shielded her eyes from the light.

Where is he?!

His silhouette appeared in front of the car.

Was he moving? If not, why not? Too injured to move? No, he was out of the car, standing. What was he holding?

A dot of white light appeared, stationary at first, then it started to move in a haphazard pattern, morphing into new shapes, contracting back to a dot.

A torch! Shit, he's coming for me! Move!

Molly wrapped both hands around her ankle and pulled at it, twisting it. She flicked her eyes to Perkins and back again. *Come on, you bastard!* She yanked again at her foot and it finally came free, sending her onto her back. She righted herself and got to her feet. The left foot immediately gave way and she shifted her weight to the right.

Half hopping, half running, she went farther into the trees, glancing over her shoulder. The white dot was bigger now, his silhouette more distinct. She turned to face forward again…

And crashed straight into a wire fence.

Dazed for only a moment, she recovered her composure. She assessed the fence: a barrier for deer, she guessed. *Get over it, now!* She grabbed the wire above her head then lifted her good foot, getting purchase on the fence; the cold wire cut into the skin of her bare foot. She lifted up her other leg. She was shaking, the weight of her body pressing down onto the thin wire.

Stuck fast.

As she whimpered, she heard Perkins approach from behind her, his footsteps a steady trudge on rough ground. She willed herself to move, but she couldn't.

She felt a sharp pain in her back and fell to the ground, winded.

She heard the snapping of latex gloves, and felt him grip the back of her coat. Then another hand on her shoulder. He twisted her over, onto her back.

A bright light shone into her eyes and she looked away, her gaze settling on his hand, which held a silvery object dripping with black liquid; Molly's remote brain instantly made the connection between the weapon and the pain in her back. She looked at his other hand and saw a leather doctor's bag.

Perkins dropped to his knees, placing the bag on the ground. It was bathed in white light, and Molly traced the source of the light to his head-torch.

Molly's legs scrabbled for purchase on the wet ground, as Perkins cocked his head towards her, blinding her in light. Seconds later, she felt the searing pain of his fist splitting open her nose. She flopped to the ground, feeling her nose and throat fill with blood, and her vision faded to blackness…

She heard the sound of him opening the bag and rummaging inside…

She felt his hot breath on her cheek, as he whispered into her ear: 'Now, sweetheart, if you keep on fighting, this is just going to take longer than it needs to.'

FIFTY-THREE

JAMES BURST through the double doors of the Red Lion and shoved his way past an elderly gent, who was gingerly collecting two fresh pints of bitter from the bar.

'I need a phone,' James barked at the startled barman.

'You can't just barge in here causing havoc—' the man spluttered.

'I need it now!' James screamed. 'A woman's been abducted. Do you want another dell slaughter on your conscience?'

A look of acceptance fell across the barman's face and he handed over his phone.

James called 999 and impatiently explained the situation, gave a description of Molly and Perkins, and relayed the registration number of the Peugeot – there was nothing more he could usefully provide. He then threw the phone back to the man, ran out of the pub and jumped into the Audi.

What now? He had no plan. No clue. *Just drive.*

He slammed the car into gear and wheelspun away from the pub, out of the village, back into the dark countryside. Perhaps he should go back to Datchworth and retrieve his phone: call Porter or Barraclough, anyone at MCU; get them on the case. He didn't trust uniform to act fast enough. It was probably too late, anyway.

Damn! How could he have been so naive to think Perkins would have let things be?

His headlights revealed a distant vehicle, its hazard lights blinking. As he drew closer, he realized it was the tractor, parked on the verge, in the same place he'd over-taken it earlier. Had it broken down? The driver jumped out into the road, waving his hands over his head. James slammed the brakes and leapt out.

'Are you police?' the man said.

'No. Yes, kind of,' James said, confused. 'Why?'

The man looked over the verge, into the darkness. 'A car's gone over,' he said. 'Hell of an incline. You can see it down there,' he gestured. 'I don't fancy their chances one bit.'

'Jesus!' James cried.

Perhaps two- or three-hundred metres away, he could make out the outline of a vehicle smashed into a tree, its headlights on, facing the dark mass of dense woodland. He turned back to the man: 'Did you see it happen?'

'No, but I'm pretty sure it must be the same car that overtook me further down the road. In a right hurry, it was.'

'Was it a red Peugeot?'

'Yes. Do you know them?'

Without answering, James shot back to the Audi. He reached in through the driver's side, and grabbed the Maglite and prybar from the passenger seat, slamming the door.

'You've called emergency services, yes?' James said, as he made toward the gap in the hedge.

'They're on the way. Wait! You're not thinking of going down th–'

The man's words trailed off, as James jumped down into the wet grass. He scrambled down the bank, slid and stumbled, struggling to keep his torch trained on the terrain. Occasionally, he glanced up for any sign of life.

And then he saw it: a faint dot of white light beyond the car, amongst the trees – motionless for a while, then it moved. Torchlight? It had to be Perkins. James switched off the Maglite, gripped the prybar tighter and hurtled towards the light.

He came to the crashed Peugeot and stopped. The driver's door was wide open, as was the boot lid. He swept his Maglite around the interior: no occupants. He noticed the handcuffs attached to the passenger side and shuddered.

He switched off his torch again and looked ahead, into the trees, following the line of the headlights.

His eyes settled on a distant shape: a rock? A bush? A person? Where was Perkins? There was now no sign of torchlight. He kept his eyes trained on the distant object. Crouched low, he inched towards it.

The indistinct object was the last thing he saw before the car's lights flickered out.

Shit. His weak heart hammered. Pitch dark.

Should I use the torch? Perkins had the advantage: his eyes would be better adjusted to the dark. *Maybe he's already gone; spooked.*

Head to the object, now. It might be Molly. If she's not already dead, she needs me.

Listen. Smell. Keep low. Move.

James crept forward, sweeping the prybar before him, feeling for obstacles. His foot clattered into something. He cursed inwardly and knelt down to feel a round object, hard and artificial: a hubcap, he deduced. He paused for a moment, to listen for any hint of a reaction. There was a faint rustle, almost imperceptible, ahead of him: probably the wind. *Keep going*.

He moved slowly and quietly. He had some vision now; there was a blurred shape ahead. *Nearly there.*

What was that sound?

Stop.

Whistling. Was it breathing. Was it his?

No, it came from the ground; someone was fighting for breath. *Molly!*

Get down to her. Help her. Quick!

He needed torchlight, so he flicked on his Maglite. He first swept it around him: no sign of Perkins. He set the prybar on the ground, then flashed his light over her.

Dear God.

Her face was a bloody pulp, red bubbles forming from her lips. Wire – a coat hanger? – was twisted around her neck; Molly's clawed fingers were clamped to it. James held the torch in the grip of his teeth and untwisted the wire, his frozen fingers slowing him down.

Molly's breathing grew fainter, shorter, intermittent.

He leant down to her. 'Molly, it's James. I'm here; you're safe. Hang in there, sweetheart.'

He could smell Perkins's cheap musk in her matted hair and a sickening thought grabbed him: had he…? *Please, no.* He parted Molly's coat and tenderly lifted her blouse to inspect her abdomen: it was white and cold to the touch, but there was no sign that Perkins had defiled her. Thank God. Now, where was the bastard?

There was the sound of a twig snapping behind him. James spun around.

'Hello, Quinn. Good of you to make it.'

In the blinding light of Perkins's head-torch, James

flinched and the Maglite fell from his mouth. He fumbled for the prybar but, before he could grab it, Perkins swung something hard into his temple and he fell back, his head snapping against the ground. Stars exploded in his vision.

He sensed Perkins towering over him, and twisted round to look up, raising his hand to his brow, to shield against the painful light which scythed through his brain like a migraine.

Distant sirens sounded, and Perkins flicked his gaze back up to the road. In his dulled vision, James saw that the man held a knife in one hand and a club-sized branch in the other. Perkins turned back. 'So, you've called your mates?' he said. 'Looks like I'm going to have to make this quick, then. Shame, I was hoping for a cosy chat over old times.'

James knew that the prybar lay inches from his arm. He fixed his gaze on Perkins while he moved his hand towards it. But Perkins saw the movement, and slammed his boot into James's groin. Pain ripped through his stomach and he curled into a foetal ball.

Perkins discarded the branch and picked up the prybar. 'Much better,' he said. 'Now, which would you prefer, the knife or the bar? I'm easy.'

'Go to Hell!' James said, through gritted teeth.

Perkins laughed. 'Eeny, meeny, miny, mo,' he said, leaning over James. 'Okay, the knife it is. Ready, James?'

James closed his eyes and turned away, reconciled to his fate. *So sorry, Molly.*

Suddenly, Perkins yowled in agony.

James opened his eyes to see Perkins arched in pain and screaming into the sky. *What?!*

There was no time to analyze. He grabbed the knife from Perkins's slack hand and, in one swift move, plunged it into his femoral artery.

Perkins staggered backward, his legs buckling. He dropped the prybar and clutched at the knife buried in his thigh, falling to the ground.

James, pushing through the pain, got himself unsteadily up onto his feet and picked up the prybar. He raised it above his head, then brought it down with all the strength he could muster, into Perkins's compliant skull.

James then dropped to his knees.

As he watched Perkins draw his last spluttered breath, a little grey kitten, the picture of innocence, bounded towards him.

FIFTY-FOUR

JAMES TOOK a sip of tepid coffee, winced and returned the mug to rest on a sheet of paper – one of dozens scattered across the desk. He rubbed his sore eyes and pinched the bridge of his nose.

He'd been at it since four a.m. Tired, but glad to have a new assignment to sink his teeth into, he reached for a new document to interrogate.

A vague shadow flashed in the corner of his eye and, before he knew it, the damn mog had spring-boarded off James's lap onto the desk, and knocked over his bloody half-drunk Nescafé.

'Freddy!'

James leapt to his feet, righted the coffee cup and rescued his phone, before the burgeoning brown puddle could cause too much damage.

At that moment, his mobile pinged. It was all go this morning! A text from Luke Porter: *'Hey guv, wanted to let you know. Mel's pregnant! So happy.'*

James's lips curled into a small smile while he thumbed his reply: *'Congratulations both. Great news.'*

An almost instant response pinged back: *'Mel says if it's a boy she'll call him James. I'm not so sure. LOL.'*

Something alien buzzed deep in his stomach: a warm, fuzzy feeling. That kid'll have a bright future, with those two for parents. He composed a reply: *'I'm with you on that one.'* He contemplated augmenting the message with an *'LOL'* or a smiley face, but soon thought better of it and sent the text.

James looked up from his phone to see the kitten on the desk, engaged in a game of chase with a Chinese worry ball. Bloody thing had left a haphazard trail of tiny, coffee-coloured paw prints all over his paperwork. 'Hey!' James barked. 'Stop that, right now.'

Much to his surprise, little Freddy obeyed his command, dropped to his haunches and observed the worry ball as it rolled off the desk, landing with a dull thud on the carpet. The cat turned to regard James. Disarmed by a tilt of its head, a twinkle in its eye and a soft mew, James relaxed. Big mistake: in the next second the beast launched itself at him, legs stretched and claws unsheathed. Landing on his chest, it scrabbled to gain purchase on the thin fabric of his shirt, before cramponning its way up to James's shoulder; the pain of a million pin-pricks exploded.

He grabbed the kitten by the scruff of its neck and it mewled in protest. 'Right, you, back downstairs.'

James carried the cat down into the dining room – correction: the room formerly known as the dining room, for it was now the luxury play-suite of a pampered kitten. He dropped Freddy to the floor. 'Off you go. Play with your toys.'

After flashing James a backward scowl, little Freddy took a cursory sniff at a felt mouse, then settled down to a seemingly enjoyable session of groin cleansing.

Above the unpleasant sound of moist lapping, James heard ticking and looked at the clock. *Shit. Visiting time!*

He dashed to the kitchen and retrieved a pouch of Felix, bringing it back to Freddy's room. Turning his head from the smell, he squeezed the contents into the luxury 2-in-1 feeder bowl with automatic water dispenser. Freddy switched attention from his groin to the food, scurrying over to tuck in hungrily to the salmon-in-gravy luncheon.

'Now, are you listening?' James said. The kitten turned its head to him, licking its lips. 'Good. If you need to scratch your claws, use that,' he gestured to the multi-level tree tower activity centre, 'not my bloody oak dining table, capiche? Nor do I want to see any more near misses at your tray. It ain't difficult.'

James crept from the room back into the hall. As he pulled the door quietly towards him, he stuck his head into the room and stole another peek. Freddy looked up at him with beseeching eyes, and James felt his heart melting.

'Daddy won't be long. Promise.'

The cat blinked.

'And if you tell anyone I've just referred to myself as your daddy, I'll wring your bloody neck. Okay?'

Back in the hall, James grabbed his coat and car keys, and opened the front door.

'Bloody hell,' he said, when he saw a lanky, startled lad standing in front of him. 'What are you doing there?'

'Package, mate.'

James followed his gaze to a box that the lad was holding. Ah, yes, his latest order from Pets at Home: a four-way play tunnel. Couldn't resist. He tutted and looked to the sky; 'The wife's been at it again, splashing out on that stupid mog. Spoiling it rotten. Ridiculous!'

The lad smiled awkwardly, handed James the box and slouched back to his van.

James threw the play tunnel into the hall, locked up and hurried to the Audi. He needed to get to the hospital.

When he arrived Molly was asleep. Or was she sedated? Worse – had she lapsed into a coma?

Hospitals always did bring out the paranoia in James – for good reason. He sought the advice of a nurse, who was standing at the next bed with a clipboard, pen and a studious expression. 'Is she okay?'

The woman looked up from the clipboard and flashed James a toothy smile. 'She's absolutely fine, love. Doctors say she's out of the woods now; just needs to rest. A couple of nights, I reckon, and you'll have her back home.'

'Oh, she's not–' James swallowed the correction he was about to make, as the nurse returned her attention to the clipboard.

On Molly's overbed table there was an unopened sand-wich packet, a plastic water jug and beaker, and a folded newspaper. James made space for the pink carnations and bag of seedless grapes he'd picked up from the petrol station, and seated himself on the wipe-clean visitor's chair.

Molly looked awful: wan skin, limp hair, lips drained of colour. Mercifully, though, the bruises and gashes were fading and the swelling had gone. Her nose was twisted from the break and she looked shrunken and vulnerable. But she was alive. To think that only last week the doctors had put her chances of survival at less than ten per cent, and even if she did survive, they said there was the very real risk of permanent brain damage. That's what wrap-ping a coat hanger wire around a woman's neck for kicks does. *Bastard!* Rotting in Hell now, hopefully.

He plucked a grape from the bag and popped it on his

tongue, rolling it around in his mouth. He thrummed his fingers on the arm of his chair, scanned the newspaper headline, puffed his cheeks, folded his arms, unfolded them, stretched out his legs under the bed... What was he supposed to do?

He recalled Jane's advice, at Sunny Vale: 'Just talk to her.' But, what to say? He stole a quick look about the ward, to check that no one was in earshot, then turned back to Molly. After a few moments of cogitation, he sat forward and said to her: 'Weather's shit.'

Good one, James.

He slumped back into the chair and watched the shallow rise and fall of her chest under the white sheets, for perhaps a minute or two. Almost hypnotic. It made his eyelids go heavy. And his heart glow warm.

He felt the words form in his chest, push up through the resistance of his tight throat and fall off his tongue, in a hoarse whisper: 'Love you, Moll.'

There, he'd said it. That wasn't so bad, was it?

Behind him, there was the sound of squeaky wheels and asthmatic breathing. James twisted his neck to see a sturdy woman in bulging overalls and plastic apron, huffing and puffing her way across the ward with a food trolley. When he turned back, Molly's eyes were open and she wore a weak smile.

'Hello, Jimbo,' she croaked.

'Thought you were asleep.'

'Nice to see you, too. I was just resting my eyes.'

James felt his cheeks flushing. 'Oh, erm, you didn't... er... hear what I said earlier, did you?'

Her eyes narrowed. 'And what was that?'

'Nothing important.'

'Small talk?'

'Something like that.'

Molly grimaced and shuffled in the bed. 'Help me sit up, will you?' She raised her bare arms painfully and, after moving the overbed table to one side, James obliged with a clumsy hoisting manoeuvre, which left Molly upright but groaning.

'Sorry,' he said.

Molly waved a dismissive hand. 'Thanks for the flowers. You've not left the price tag on, have you?'

'Shit,' James said, never one to waste his words.

Molly giggled, then winced. 'Don't make me laugh,' she said; 'it's bloody agony.'

There were a few moments of silence, then Molly said: 'So, how's my little hero?'

'I can't really grumble, in the circumstances.'

'Not you, doofus. The cat!'

'Oh, Freddy? He's fine, I suppose. Wrecking my furniture and costing me a small fortune in cat food, stopping me working, climbing the curtains, shitting all over the carpet...'

'Don't worry, Jimbo, I'll be taking him off your hands in a couple of days, fingers crossed.'

'Fingers crossed,' James echoed, lying.

'The pair of you not bonded, then?'

'Only in the literal sense.' James undid a couple of shirt buttons and parted the material, to show his claw wounds.

Molly wrinkled her nose. 'Aww, bless.'

'He's a bloody menace.'

'Well, if it wasn't for those claws we'd both be pushing up the daisies, eh?'

'Suppose.'

'So, what have you been up to?'

'Got a new gig: insurance fraud. Keeping me out of mischief.'

'That's good. You thinking of making a proper go of this PI thing then?'

'Perhaps. Haven't decided yet.'

'Can't wait to be back at the office, myself.' Molly flicked a look at the newspaper. '*Chronicle*'s gone downhill in my absence,' she chuckled, then winced in pain. 'Any news on Urtė?'

'Not a dicky-bird.'

'You need me out of here, so I can help put rocket boosters under the search. If she's still out there, we'll find her. You and me together: invincible.'

James smiled. 'Do you think?'

Molly's eyes darted to one side and she shuffled position. 'How do I look, Jimbo?'

'Like death warmed up. Why do you ask?'

'Cheers, mate; knew I could rely you on for a morale booster. Don't look, but Doctor Coppola's starting his rounds.' She tucked a lock of hair behind her ear and puckered her lips. 'Bloody gorgeous.'

'Oh?'

'Married, obvs, but it doesn't hurt to dream.'

James had started to dream again. 'Molly?' he said.

She switched her gaze back to him.

'I... I...'

'Spit it out, Jimbo.'

Behind him, James heard the woman with the squeaky trolley come to a halt. 'Something to eat, Molly?' the woman wheezed.

'No ta, Bella; not hungry. Still got this sandwich from yesterday.'

The woman made the expression of someone who'd never declined an offer of food in her life. 'Suit yourself, love,' she tutted, then trundled off to her next customer.

'Pass the sarnie, will you?' Molly said.

He picked up the packet and peeled back the little plastic window, clocking too late that it was egg mayonnaise. He readied himself for the stench.

Yet, oddly, he smelt nothing untoward. Quite pleasant, in fact. *Strange*.

'You going to pass me that thing, or am I going to die of hunger waiting, Jimbo?'

'Yeah, sorry.'

He passed her the packet and Molly took out the sandwich, taking a pained nibble. She dropped the packet to her lap, then said: 'You were going to say something? Before Bella came over?'

James looked at his watch and sprung to his feet. 'Got to get back to work. Deadline.' He hesitated, then gave Molly a peck on her forehead.

'Same time tomorrow, Jimbo?'

'Maybe,' he said, 'if I can squeeze you into my busy schedule.'

Molly blew him a kiss and closed her eyes, seemingly exhausted.

He waited until she was fast asleep, then swept out of the room.

EPILOGUE

SIX YEARS LATER

THEY WALKED arm-in-arm along the overgrown footpath: wildflowers, bluebells, blackthorn, hawthorn and apple blossom. Kathy raised her face to the warm sun, closed her eyes and inhaled the scent of spring. The scent of freedom.

'You okay?' Mark said.

'Yes, love,' she said, tears streaming down her cheeks. 'It's just so beautiful.'

'Well, we love it here. The country air, it feeds the soul.'

'You sure you don't mind having me? I hate imposing like this.'

'Don't be daft, Mum; you can stay as long as you like. Sorry the accommodation's not the five-star luxury you've been used to over the last six years.'

Kathy laughed. 'I'd happily live in a cardboard box, as long as I can be near my boys.'

Something flashed in the corner of her eye. 'Look!' She pointed to a beech tree beyond the hedgerow. 'A blackbird. He's taking food to the nest.' They watched the scene in silence, until the bird had flown away.

Then, Kathy said: 'Do you believe in reincarnation?'

'Of course not!'

'I sometimes imagine your dad as a bird, flying free, tending to his brood, instead of lying there all alone in the ground. Silly, hey?'

'Well, if he was a bird, he'd be a cuckoo or a vulture. Or a great, fat turkey.'

Kathy slapped the back of her hand against Mark's forearm. 'Don't be so mean, love.'

The bells of the distant village church started to toll.

'We should be heading back,' Mark said. 'Dinner will be ready soon.'

'Wish you'd let me help out Maurice with the cooking.'

'You're best off out of the kitchen; Maurice thinks he's Gordon Ramsay. Besides, he wants to surprise you with his signature dish.'

'It's not rabbit bloody stew, is it?'

'Ha! Of course not; we're vegans now, don't you know?'

'Vegan? And gay? Your dad would be so proud!' Kathy burst into a fit of giggles. It was the first time she'd properly laughed since… well, she couldn't remember.

Mark proffered his elbow. 'Come on. Ben and Sally will be at the house now. You know how she hates lateness.'

Kathy smiled at the thought of the five of them being together – at last. It felt like a lifetime had passed. Her smile dropped when she thought of John, gone forever. She still loved him with all of her heart, in spite of everything. Silly mare.

Overhead, there was the sudden sound of flapping: the blackbird again. He landed on a crooked fence post, metres in front of them. Kathy squeezed Mark's arm and made him stop. The bird held a snatch of grubs in his beautiful yellow beak. He turned to look in their direction, tilting his head; Kathy found herself mirroring his gesture.

Then, the bird looked away and launched himself into the air, headed back to his family.

Kathy looked up into Mark's kind eyes. 'Everything's going to be okay now, isn't it?'

'Yes, Mum. We're going to be just fine.'

She nestled into Mark's shoulder, and felt his warmth radiate through the thin fabric of his shirt. 'Love you, son.'

'Love you too, Mum.'

READERS CLUB
FREE DOWNLOAD

I hope you enjoyed this book and are keen to follow James Quinn's next adventure.

I also hope you will forgive me for leaving Urtė's fate dangling. I had originally intended to write only one James Quinn novel, but I quickly realized Urtė's story needs a whole book to do her justice.

Join my Readers Club to be the among the first to hear about the release of the next book in the series and also to receive a free copy of my novel: *Lies That Kill*.

Lies That Kill tells the story of teenage insomniac, Kevin Hughes, who finds himself drawn into a terrifying mystery involving his oddball neighbour.

On an infrequent basis, I send an email telling readers when a new book is launched, or when I have something else that I think you will want to hear about.

It's completely free to sign up to the Readers Club and you will never be spammed by me, and you can opt out easily at any time.

To join the Readers Club, visit my website at dpjohnsonauthor.com.

PLEASE LEAVE A REVIEW

Please do tell others what you thought about *Stolen Lives*. I hugely appreciate each new review and read every one of them. If you wouldn't mind sharing your thoughts on any e-store, your own blog or anywhere else, that would be also hugely appreciated.

Thank you!

ALSO BY D.P. JOHNSON

Lies That Kill

A teenage insomniac yearning for adventure. An oddball neighbour accused of murder. Secrets waiting to be unearthed.

No friends, depressed mum, absent dad, dead brother. Fifteen-year-old **Kevin Hughes** isn't one to grumble but he knows his life could be better. No wonder he craves escape and adventure. So when Kevin witnesses his creepy neighbour, "Crazy Ray", digging in his garden in the dead of night, he feels compelled to discover why.

Kevin learns that Crazy Ray stood trial for the brutal killing of his wife a decade ago. When the case collapsed, everyone in the community believed he got away with murder. But Kevin Hughes isn't so certain. He might not yet have a GCSE to his name but he's read the books, watched the movies. Innocent until proven guilty, right?

Kevin's undercover investigation gets underway, and he's soon unearthing long-buried secrets. But as he inches closer to the horrifying truth, the killer is closing in on Kevin.

Lies that Kill is a standalone young adult / crossover psychological thriller set in the London's East End. If you like gritty adventure filled with twists and turns, then you'll love Kevin's story.

The book is currently available as a FREE download when you join my Readers Club. For more information go to www. dpjohnsonauthor.com.

Printed in Great Britain
by Amazon